THE MASTERPIECE

ÉMILE ZOLA was born in Paris in 1840, the son of a
Venetian engineer and his French wife. He grew up in
Aix-en-Provence where he made friends with Paul Cézanne. After an undistinguished school career and a brief
period of dire poverty in Paris, Zola joined the newly
founded publishing firm of Hachette which he left in
1866 to live by his pen. He had already published a novel
and his first collection of short stories. Other novels and
stories followed until in 1871 Zola published the first
volume of his Rougon-Macquart series with the sub-title
*Histoire naturelle et sociale d'une famille sous le Second
Empire*, in which he sets out to illustrate the influence
of heredity and environment on a wide range of characters and milieux. However, it was not until 1877 that his
novel *L'Assommoir*, a study of alcoholism in the working
classes, brought him wealth and fame. The last of the
Rougon-Macquart series appeared in 1893 and his subsequent writing was far less successful, although he
achieved fame of a different sort in his vigorous and
influential intervention in the Dreyfus case. His marriage
in 1870 had remained childless but his extremely happy
liaison in later life with Jeanne Rozerot, initially one of
his domestic servants, gave him a son and a daughter.
He died in 1902.

ROGER PEARSON is Fellow and Praelector in French at
The Queen's College, Oxford, and the author of *Stend-
hal's Violin: A Novelist and his Reader* (Clarendon Press,
1988). He has also translated and edited Voltaire, *Candide
and Other Stories* (1990) for World's Classics.

93-2115

DATE DUE

THE WORLD'S CLASSICS

ÉMILE ZOLA

The Masterpiece

Translated by
THOMAS WALTON

Translation revised and introduced by
ROGER PEARSON

Oxford   New York
OXFORD UNIVERSITY PRESS
1993

FIC
ZOL

93·2115

Oxford University Press, Walton Street, Oxford OX2 6DP

Oxford New York Toronto
Delhi Bombay Calcutta Madras Karachi
Petaling Jaya Singapore Hong Kong Tokyo
Nairobi Dar es Salaam Cape Town
Melbourne Auckland

and associated companies in
Berlin Ibadan

Oxford is a trade mark of Oxford University Press

British Library Cataloguing in Publication Data
Data available

Library of Congress Cataloging in Publication Data
Zola, Émile, 1840-1920.
[Oeuvre. English]
The masterpiece / Émile Zola: translated by Thomas Walton;
translation revised and introduced by Roger Pearson.
p. cm. — (The World's classics)
Translation of: L'Oeuvre.
Includes bibliographical references.
I. Pearson, Roger. II. Title. III. Series.
PQ2511.04'5 1993 843.8–dc20 92–5293
ISBN 0–19–282906–8

Typeset by Pure Tech Corporation, Pondicherry, India
Printed in Great Britain by
BPCC Hazells Ltd.
Aylesbury, Bucks

CONTENTS

INTRODUCTION

WRITING in November 1879 Henry James commented that 'Zola's naturalism is ugly and dirty, but he seems to me to be *doing something*'—which, in James's view, was more than could be said for most, if not all, other novelists of the day. The prospective reader of *The Masterpiece* may be heartened to learn that in this particular novel Zola's Naturalism is not especially ugly or dirty but that its author is indeed most definitely 'doing something'.

Quite what he is 'doing', however, has been the subject of some debate. Many early readers, inevitably more vulnerable to the impact of topicality, were aghast. Paul Cézanne (1839–1906), Zola's childhood friend of over thirty years' standing, wrote briefly to thank him for his complimentary copy and never spoke to him again. Claude Monet (1840–1926), too, politely acknowledged his gift but professed himself 'troubled and uneasy', fearing that those opposed to the new school of painting would exploit the novel to portray Edouard Manet (1832–83) and the Impressionists as no less of a failure than Zola's doomed hero, Claude Lantier. These being what have been dubbed 'the Banquet Years', Monet further organized a 'dinner of protest' to which the likes of Camille Pissarro (1830–1903) and Stéphane Mallarmé (1842–98) came to share their chagrin on a filling stomach. The landscape painter Antoine Guillemet (1843–1918), who had kindly supplied Zola with technical information and asked to have this now famous writer's latest work dedicated to him, thought he could see himself in the meretricious figure of Fagerolles. All thoughts of a flattering dedication gone, he complained bitterly to the author—who promptly spread the word that actually it was the successful artist Henri Gervex (1852–1929) whom he had had in mind. Gervex himself, on the other hand, seems to have been rather flattered by this and blithely bade his friends call him Fagerolles. Equally flattered was Zola's wife Alexandrine, who clearly saw herself in the amiable figure of Henriette and ever after preferred *The Masterpiece* above the rest of her husband's literary creations.

Now that over a century has passed since the first of eighty serialized instalments of the novel appeared in *Le Gil Blas* on 23 December 1885, it is possible to take a more distanced view of these matters. Is *The Masterpiece* simply an attack on Impressionism, or does Zola have wider aims in mind? When he first started to plan the Rougon-Macquart series of novels in his late twenties, he envisaged some ten volumes, the ninth of which would be devoted to the realm of art. In his preliminary notes for the series as a whole he declared his intention

to study the ambitions and appetites of a family launched upon the modern world, making superhuman efforts but always failing because of its own nature and the influences upon it, almost getting there only then to fall back again, and ending up by producing veritable moral monsters, the priest, the murderer, the artist. The times are in turmoil, and it is this turmoil of the moment which I shall depict.

The artist in question would exemplify a 'singular effect of heredity' whereby his 'genius' would be inherited from illiterate working-class parents (eventually Gervaise and Lantier in *L'Assommoir* (1877)). Where other offspring of the illegitimate Macquart branch of the family would suffer for the intemperance and insanity of their forebears through being ruled by insatiable physical appetites and the need for alcohol, this one would have unbridled 'intellectual' appetites of such a violent kind that ultimately they render him powerless to create. Thus he would constitute a focal point in the novel's depiction of the contemporary passion for art, of 'what is called decadence [this in 1868] and which is but the result of wild mental activity'. In short, the work would present a 'poignant study of the artistic temperament in a contemporary context' and 'the terrible drama of a mind devouring itself'.

In time the Rougon-Macquart series evolved into a collection of twenty novels tracing the 'natural and social
history of a family under the Second Empire', and several
other areas of 'activity' were added to the original list,
notably mining (*Germinal* (1885)) and the land (*Earth*
(1887)). But Zola never wavered in his determination to
devote one novel to art, nor did his original conception of
the central character essentially change. He introduces
Claude Lantier in *The Belly of Paris* (1873) as an art student
who chances on many a paintable scene as he wanders
through the markets of Les Halles (the Covent Garden of
Paris); and in the family-tree of the Rougon-Macquart
published with the preface to *A Page of Love* in 1878 he
describes him as 'born in 1842—a mixture, a fusion', taking
mostly after his mother Gervaise both physically and mentally and serving as the living example of 'an inherited
neurosis turning into genius'.

When in 1885 Zola began to write *The Masterpiece*, now
the fourteenth novel in the series, the emphasis on heredity
had faded, and the work was intended principally to depict
the pain and suffering involved in creative endeavour. 'In
Claude Lantier', Zola observed in his preparatory notes, 'I
want to depict the artist's struggle with reality, the sheer
effort of creation which goes into every work of art, the
blood and tears involved in giving of one's flesh, in trying
to make something that lives: the endless battle to achieve
truth, and the endless defeats, the struggle with the angel.'
No longer is this simply the condition of a flawed genius,
for now it is the lot of every artist, not least Zola himself.
'In a word, I shall tell the intimate story of my own efforts
to produce, this endless, painful process of giving birth.'
And childbirth figures repeatedly in the many titles which
Zola envisaged for this novel before he finally settled for
the less specific *L'Œuvre*, meaning literally 'The Work'.

In the first instance, therefore, far from being specifically
an attack on Manet, Cézanne, or the Impressionists, *The
Masterpiece* is a confessional work and by far the most
autobiographically based of the Rougon-Macquart novels.

The childhood paradise of Plassans shared by Pierre Sandoz, Claude Lantier, and Louis Dubuche corresponds to the happy times enjoyed by Zola, Cézanne, and Baptistin Baille in Aix-en-Provence as they, too, roamed the hills and read Hugo and Musset to each other. The regular forgatherings of young hopefuls intent on conquering the world of Parisian art and their swaggering progress along Baron Haussmann's new and spacious boulevards recall similar meetings of Zola, Cézanne, Pissarro, the sculptor Philippe Solari (1840–1906), and others. More importantly, in the characters of Lantier the failed genius and Sandoz the successful novelist, the champion of supposedly objective Naturalism is evidently portraying two sides of his own personality.

In Sandoz we have the thinly disguised self-portrait of Zola the impecunious journalist struggling to make his way, the budding novelist with an ambitious masterplan and the belief that literature must learn from the natural sciences, the dutiful son of an ailing mother, the husband of a path-smoothing wife, the host of Thursday dinner-parties for his old (artistic) chums, and the man who finally makes it, largely perhaps by virtue of dogged persistence and pedestrian self-discipline. In Lantier, on the other hand, we have the man ahead of his time, who has the originality to see the direction in which his art should best develop (as, to a lesser extent, Sandoz also has) but who lacks the patience and technical accomplishment to put his own ideas successfully into practice, the man who is looked up to as the leader of a school but who is gradually deserted or betrayed by his followers, as Zola felt he had been by Joris Huysmans (1848–1907) and Guy de Maupassant (1850–93). On the one hand, then, the new type of writer, the nine-to-five professional with a 'scientific' approach to literature and, on the other, the traditional Romantic seeker after an impossible ideal.

Nevertheless one should not exaggerate this confessional aspect of the novel. It was central to Zola's aesthetic of Naturalism that literature should convey 'the truth', describe how things really are and not how things are conventionally

perceived or traditionally idealized. As Sandoz puts it: 'All
... exactly as it is, not all ups and not all downs, not too
dirty and not too clean, but just as it is....' (p. 43). It
would have been surprising, therefore, if in a novel about
artistic endeavour Zola had not drawn upon his own experience of the labour of art. Given the conscientious zeal with
which he gathered documentary evidence for his novels,
visiting mines, interviewing the staff in a department store,
drinking with farmers, or lurking in the Gare Saint-Lazare,
it must have been something of a welcome convenience
merely to look in the mirror and consult his memory. For
Jory the young art critic he had only to remember his own
articles on the 1866 Salon and the scandal that ensued—
though for the womanizing he had (being as yet the faithful
husband) to refer to the model of his close friend Paul
Alexis. For Bongrand, the acknowledged master overtaken
by a new generation and finding it more difficult to live up
to his reputation than to have acquired it in the first place,
he had only to reflect on the rise of Symbolism and his own
misgivings in following the great successes of *L'Assommoir*,
Nana (1880), and *Germinal*. What those other old masters
Gustave Flaubert (1821–80) and Gustave Courbet (1819–77)
had suffered, so now perhaps would he.

The determination to base his fiction on the solid foundation of observed fact explains why Zola drew so heavily
on his knowledge of contemporary painters for much of the
novel. As Monet acknowledged, he made sure that no single
character exactly resembled 'any person living or dead', but
essentially he was ready to risk giving offence in the interests
of authenticity. Thus Claude Lantier is largely an amalgam
of Cézanne, Manet, and—as the Christian name suggests—
Monet (though Claude also figures as the eponymous hero
of Zola's first published novel, the partly autobiographical
Claude's Confession (1865)). As well as being the model for
Lantier's Provençal childhood, Cézanne also provides his
physical appearance, his obstinate and volatile temperament,
his timidity with women, his vaulting and obsessive artistic
ambition, his murderous self-doubt (and tendency to put a

fist through his canvases), his growing isolation from his fellow painters and a reputation for being a 'madman', his failure to have a painting accepted for the Salon except once (in 1882) as an act of 'charity' on the part of a lesser, derivative artist (here Antoine Guillemet is indeed the model for Fagerolles), and—in common with Manet and the Impressionists—his enduring lack of public recognition as an original and talented artist.

While Cézanne is now considered a key pioneer in the development of modern art, he was not so considered in 1885, least of all by Zola. Perhaps the odds against one's best friend at school turning out to be an original and influential genius are so heavily stacked that he may be forgiven for rejecting the notion on the grounds of probability alone. But even if a complete stranger had painted like Cézanne, Zola's taste in art was simply not sophisticated or knowledgeable enough for him to have seen his friend as the potential founder of a school of painting. For this aspect of the portrait of Claude Lantier he drew on the model of Edouard Manet.

In 1863 the complaints lodged against the members of the Selection Committee for that year's Salon were so numerous and so vociferous that the Emperor Napoleon III intervened in the row and decreed that the rejected works should be exhibited in an adjacent gallery. This exhibition was soon dubbed the Salon des Refusés, and all Paris flocked to laugh and be outraged. The picture which caused the most hilarity was Manet's *Déjeuner sur l'herbe*, and onlookers vied with one another in ribald explanation of quite what this naked lady was up to with two fully, if casually, dressed young men. Originally entitled *Le Bain* ('Bathing') this picture was at once a *tour de force* of colour harmony and a provocative debunking of the conventions of the École des Beaux-Arts (the French Academy's School of Fine Art). The painting which Claude Lantier exhibits at the Salon des Refusés bears a considerable resemblance to it, and its reception is no less cruel. In the early days of the so-called École des Batignolles (after the name of the Paris district) when young painters, most of them future Impressionists, congregated in the Café Guerbois, Manet was looked upon as leader just as Lantier in the earlier part of the novel is the principal figure at the Café Baudequin. Compulsive strolling around the streets of Paris and a desire to decorate the Hôtel de Ville are among several other features of Claude's existence which Zola has borrowed from the life of the artist who died in 1883, two years before *The Masterpiece* was begun.

One of the most important aspects of Claude's art is his role as a pioneer of 'Open Air' painting. '. . . that's what we need now', he tells Sandoz, 'sunlight, open air, something bright and fresh, people and things as seen in real daylight' (p. 43). In this he represents the revolution in painting brought about by the Impressionists, notably Monet, who forsook the even daylight of the traditional north-facing studio and sought to capture the play of sunlight in the open with ever more subtly juxtaposed dabs of colour. The term 'Impressionism' was first given currency in an article written by the artist and dramatist Louis Leroy (1812–85) in *Le Charivari* on 25 April about the first independent exhibition of paintings by the new school in 1874: it derives from Monet's painting *Impression. Soleil levant* (*Impression. Sun rising*) which was one of the exhibits. As a label (intended pejoratively by Leroy) it stuck successfully because it conveyed well what was the central ambition of the new generation of painters, namely to capture on canvas how a person or object actually (and fleetingly) strikes the eye and not how we think it ought to look or 'really' is. If, in a certain light, grass appears blue, then blue it shall be.

Writing later in the *European Herald* in July 1879 Zola shows how well he understands the painters' purpose:

The Impressionists have introduced open-air painting, the study of shifting effects in nature depending on the innumerable variations of weather and the time of day. They consider that Courbet's technique, superb as it is, leads only to magnificent studio paintings. They themselves take the analysis of nature further, breaking light down into its constituent parts, studying the effects of air movement, the shading of colour, the random variations of light and shadow, all the optical phenomena which make a vista so changing and so difficult to render.

Obviously this ambition is directly comparable with Sandoz's expression of the Naturalist aesthetic ('not too dirty and not too clean, but just as it is'). The term 'Naturalist' (one who studies nature) had been used by Zola as early as 1866 to define the proper function of the literary or art critic as being to uncover the true workings of human society from beneath the aesthetic surface under observation. In adopting this term Zola was following on from the famous essay on Honoré de Balzac (1799–1850) by Hippolyte Taine (1828–93), first published in the *Journal des Débats* in 1858, and his preface to the second edition of his *Essais de critique et d'histoire* in 1866. In the first of these essays, Taine, who succeeded Eugène Viollet-le-Duc (1814–79) as professor of aesthetics and the history of art at the École des Beaux-Arts in 1864, compares Balzac's methods as a novelist with those of a naturalist and notes how the author of *La Comédie humaine* observes the human species within a natural world governed by determinism. In the preface he develops a parallel between the naturalist and the historian, the essential task of both being to examine man as but one member of the animal kingdom and just as subject as its other members to the shaping influences of heredity and environment.

The importance of heredity apart, Balzac himself had said much the same thing in his Foreword to *La Comédie humaine* in 1842; but Taine was developing the analogy under the influence of Auguste Comte (1798–1857) and his Positivism, in which scientific method is brought to bear in the analysis of human society to the exclusion of all theological or metaphysical concerns. In his Introduction to his *History of English Literature* (1863), Taine asserts the interdependence of the physical and the psychological and stresses the importance of these factors in the study of cultural and social development. In particular he elaborates on the need to examine the relative roles of *race*, *milieu*, and *moment* (i.e.

racial and familial inheritance, environment, and historical
circumstances) as determining forces in the emergence and
particular manifestations of any social or cultural phenomenon. His notorious statement that 'vice and virtue are
products like vitriol and sugar' was used by Zola as the
epigraph for the second edition of *Thérèse Raquin* (1868).

Not for nothing had Zola ended up as head of publicity
at Hachette. The man who was later to use sandwich-men
to advertise his novels soon began to bandy the words
'Naturalist' and 'Naturalism' with a frequency which his job
as a journalist greatly facilitated, hammering the nail into
the public consciousness (as he later expressed it to a
disapproving Flaubert) centimetre by centimetre. With one
particular blow of his promotional hammer he ceased referring to the future Impressionists as Realists (in 1866) and
started calling them Naturalists (from 1868). Needless to
say, the publicist was somewhat put out six years later when
the term 'Impressionism' began to catch on. 'Realist' had
been a term of abuse recently levelled at the work of Courbet
and then, like 'Impressionism' itself, proudly taken over as
a compliment (just as Théophile Gautier (1811–72) had
become the champion of 'Art for Art's Sake'). In literature
the novelist and art historian Champfleury (1821–89) sought
to found a school of Realism (with a manifesto in 1857),
and was seconded by another novelist Edmond Duranty
(1833–80), who started a short-lived journal called *Realism*.
Dedicated to the scrupulous and unsensational reproduction
of the details of everyday life, these particular Realists
produced little more than unreadable accounts of the squalid
and the mundane.

The young and ambitious Zola wanted to distance himself
from their second-rate productions and to make a name for
himself: hence the importance of his new tag 'Naturalism'.
At the same time he believed that the new generation of
painters, including Manet and Pissarro (who were ten years
older than Zola, Monet, Auguste Renoir (1841–1919), and
the other Impressionists), were heading in the same direction as he: they, too, therefore were 'Naturalists'. Just as

Claude Lantier is contemptuous of the classical style of Dominique Ingres (1780–1867) and feels that the Romantic Eugène Delacroix (1798–1863) and the Realist Courbet are both played out, so Zola (like Sandoz) rejects the tradition of the 'psychological novel' and strives to break out of the shadow of Romantic Victor Hugo (1802–85) and Balzac, the forerunner of the Realists. The Lantier of 'Open Air' wants to capture nature 'as it is': the subject does not matter as long as the artist is sincere in his portrayal of it. Hence his notorious claim that 'a bunch of carrots, studied directly and painted simply, personally, as you see it yourself, [is] as good as any of the run-of-the-mill, made-to-measure École des Beaux-Arts stuff' (p. 41). Similarly Sandoz (like Zola) wants to 'devote [his] whole life to one work and put everything into it, men, animals, everything under the sun!' (p. 43). Painter and novelist both rise to the challenge of exploiting the aesthetic potential inherent in the banal and the ugly (thus seeking out what Charles Baudelaire (1821–67) called the 'Flowers of Evil'), and both see themselves as servants of 'the truth' as they aspire to complete honesty and accuracy of observation.

In the 1860s Zola had warmed to the originality of Manet and the future Impressionists as they sought to free themselves from the dead hand of the École des Beaux-Arts. Eager to make his name by associating himself with the scandalous avant-garde, but also genuinely in tune with the desire to jettison tired convention and to pass beyond the inflated posturing of second-rate Romanticism, he became their courageous champion in print. The outcry was such that no French newspaper editor would agree to publish his art criticism between 1868 and 1880. In 1875, however, thanks to the intervention of Ivan Turgenev (1818–83), he found an outlet in the St Petersburg monthly magazine the *Vestnik Evropy* (*European Herald*) to which he was to contribute some sixty-four 'Letters from Paris' over the following years. In some of these he reported fully and forthrightly on the world of Parisian art, particularly the Salons of 1875 and 1876, the second Impressionist exhibition in 1876, and the Exposition Universelle in 1879.

From these articles one can see that during the 1870s Zola remained a loyal admirer of Manet, whom he continued to praise as 'a realist, a positivist', 'a naturalist, an analyst'. Gradually, however, his attitude towards the Impressionists became more critical. He lost touch with many of the exponents of the new school, never frequenting their new meeting-place, the Café de la Nouvelle-Athènes, as he had the Café Guerbois; and in his article on the second Impressionist exhibition, he is prepared to find fault with several of the artists, such as Gustave Caillebotte (1848–94) (too photographic) and Edgar Degas (1834–1917) (good at sketches but likely to spoil everything 'when he adds the finishing touch'). He bestows praise on the paintings of Monet, Berthe Morisot (1841–95), Pissarro, Renoir, and Alfred Sisley (1839–99), hailing them as innovators and as the saviours of French art; but he ends by exhorting them to keep searching 'for one or more painters sufficiently talented to bolster the new artistic formula with masterpieces'. By implication, therefore, they had yet to produce either a master or a masterpiece. And in his article of July 1879 even Manet begins to come in for criticism, as Zola comments that 'his hand is not comparable with his eye . . . If the technical side of the business equalled the accuracy of his impressions, he would be the great painter of the second half of the nineteenth century'.

The story of Claude Lantier thus represents Zola's view of the development of French painting between 1860 and 1885. The bold originality which is mocked at the Salon des Refusés and the invigorating removal of the painter's easel from the studio to the riverbank are followed by an endless process of experimentation which somehow fails to produce the desired masterpiece that would clinch the final victory over the École des Beaux-Arts. In the case of Monet and others Zola felt that there was undue facility and sloppiness of execution, that they never tried hard enough (or, like Manet, were simply unable) to 'finish' a picture satisfactorily.

(For them, of course, such 'finishedness' would have been detrimental to the truth of an 'impression'.) Worst of all, he felt that they gave insufficiently of themselves: they were merely pioneers, and not accomplished masters, because they failed to give expression to their innermost selves.

Claude Lantier at least tries to do this: 'What was Art, after all, if not simply giving out what you have inside you?' (p. 41). But there seems to be a congenital flaw in his eyesight which means that, as with Manet, vision and technique are never successfully in accord. Lantier's sketch for his final, great painting of the Île de la Cité is masterly, and he paints in the barge-unloading scene with accomplishment; but the more he continues to strive after special effects of light and shadow, the more of a mess his painting becomes. Finally, like French art itself (in Zola's view), he falls victim to Symbolism, which is but another, yet more bizarre manifestation of the old canker of Romanticism.

When Sandoz objects to the presence of the dominant figure of the nude in the centre of Claude's final painting, he represents the voice of Naturalism speaking out against the new trend represented in the works of Gustave Moreau (1826–98), Odilon Redon (1840–1916), and others. For Sandoz women simply do not swim or stand up naked on a boat in the middle of the Seine, whatever the season: for Lantier his great, obsessing nude figure is the symbol of Paris, a physical manifestation of the soul of the city which he has sought to evoke in his depiction of the Île de la Cité itself. By the end of the novel she has become 'like an idol belonging to some unknown religion . . . made . . . of marble and gold and precious stones . . . the mystic rose of her sex blooming between the precious columns that were her thighs, beneath the sacred canopy that was her belly' (p. 406). Nature 'as it is' has become a Decadent emblem of unassuageable sexual desire; and the wholesome, girlish body of Christine Hallegrain at the beginning of the novel has been replaced by an evil goddess demanding the sacrifice of human flesh. The sculptor Mahoudeau survives the violent embrace of his disintegrating statue, but Lantier finally pays with his life. He, and not the picture, finally hangs.

In this way Lantier's final hours are symbolic of what Zola believes to have happened to his contemporaries, and what Sandoz describes at Lantier's funeral:

The century has been a failure. Hearts are tortured with pessimism and brains clouded with mysticism for, try as we may to put imagination to flight with the cold light of science, we have the supernatural once more in arms against us and the whole world of legend in revolt, bent on enslaving us again in our moment of fatigue and uncertainty. (p. 422)

It is no wonder, therefore, that Monet found *The Masterpiece* 'troubling' and that Cézanne refused to have anything more to do with his friend. In the novel Impressionism succeeds only in the derivative hands of second-rate panderers to bourgeois taste, and any real originality seems both to be inherently flawed and a sign of madness. Supposedly respectable artistic success, on the other hand, is represented by the somewhat implausibly decent figure of Sandoz, complete with gastronomically gifted wife and lovable dog.

But Zola is 'doing something' more than merely showing off that he has succeeded where his artist friends have not. For, as its French title suggests, the novel is about 'working', about the human effort to create, about what Zola calls 'the struggle with the angel'. Nowadays we might say that it is a study of workaholics. Such a term may seem unacceptably anachronistic if applied to Claude Lantier. After all, is he not the gifted genius living in a garret (later a shed) and devoting himself to Art? But that, precisely, is the Romantic cliché. Compare Sandoz:

The thing is, work has simply swamped my whole existence. Slowly but surely it's robbed me of my mother, my wife, and everything that meant anything to me. It's like a germ planted in the skull that devours the brain, spreads to the trunk and the limbs and destroys the entire body in time. No sooner am I out of bed in the morning than work clamps down on me and pins me to my desk before I've even had a breath of fresh air. It follows me to lunch and I find myself chewing over sentences as I'm chewing my food. It goes with me when I go out, eats out of my plate at dinner and shares my pillow in bed at night. It's so completely merciless that once the process of creation is started, it's impossible for me to stop it, and it goes on growing and working even when I'm asleep. . . . Outside that, nothing, nobody exists. (pp. 302Ä3)

Like Claude at the end, Sandoz feels himself to be a human sacrifice: 'do what I will, I can't escape entirely from the monster's clutches, . . . in the end it'll devour me, and that will be the end of that!' (p. 303).

As Sandoz, like Lantier, sacrifices the present in the cause of a future masterpiece, he is keenly aware that such an achievement may in any case have no lasting value. The 'after-life' of posterity's acclaim may be as illusory as the Christian's paradise. What if all this effort is for nothing? 'What is the good of trying to fill the void? We *know* there's nothing beyond it, yet we're all too proud to admit it!' And Lantier agrees: 'When the earth falls to dust in space like a withered walnut, our works won't even be a speck among the rest!' (p. 374).

Here the central characters of *The Masterpiece* confront what twentieth-century writers would call the Absurd, the problem of finding a reason for living in the absence of religious faith. The novel thereby transcends the realm of art and poses a question about human activity in general, about man's 'work' here on earth. Is the human condition more accurately represented by Claude Lantier, with man-kind as mad fools wishing to achieve the unachievable, overreaching our limitations and coming inevitably face to face with death? Or by Sandoz who accepts that all his creations are imperfect and, though never satisfied, at least compromises with the ideal sufficiently to survive? Should we devote our time and energy to leaving a mark in some way (a painting, a sculpture, an opera, a fortune), or should we indeed 'spend more time with our family' and live for the present?

Sandoz's dilemma offers a more prosaic, modern version of the traditional theme of the artist's struggle for perfec-tion. It is difficult to imagine Victor Hugo worrying like this about neglecting his family, or Hector Berlioz sighing: 'As for my wife, she has no husband, poor thing' (p. 303). Zola is thus undermining a certain Romantic view of the artist, and yet all the while he is reinforcing the central Romantic notion of an unbridgeable dichotomy between art and life. The role of Christine in the novel is to represent the claims of life over art, of present involvement in the day-to-day activity of human beings versus self-absenting devotion to a quite possibly vain, and vainglorious, goal. From her initial disturbing physical presence, through the lovers' idyll at Bennecourt, to the final paroxysm of sexual passion, she is the life-force: 'Come with me . . . and love me. . . . Aren't you human? . . . Come with me, and you'll see life's still worth living. . . . ' (p. 408). Yet for Lantier the call of 'work' is too strong and, when finally he sees the folly of his 'masterpiece', the end is inevitable: 'But how can I go on living if there's no point in going on working?' (p. 409).

The antithesis of art and life is but one of many oppositions and parallels in the novel which Zola, a master of careful construction, uses to shape his story. Sandoz speaks patronizingly of 'Victor Hugo's mighty settings where dream figures immeasurably larger than life stalked through an everlasting battle of antitheses' (p. 36), but such a description might well be applied to the Rougon-Macquart novels in general and to *The Masterpiece* in particular. For in Zola's works 'science' and Romanticism continually compete for the upper hand. Many of the characters may be no larger than life, and indeed many are 'smaller', but the passion with which the central protagonists conduct their lives transcends the everyday. And antithesis is central to Zola's vision. Just as Lantier's great canvas depicts the duality of Paris at work and Paris at play, so Zola repeatedly presents both sides of every coin: birth and death, day and night, summer and winter, youth and age, success and failure, wealth and poverty, authenticity and sham, purity and prostitution. As the preparatory notes for the novel show (as do those for so many of the Rougon-Macquart novels), Zola sketched out both plot and characters with almost geometric precision.

Within this scheme of binary opposition human beings are generally divested of that traditional 'psychological' intricacy with which the standard nineteenth-century novel had previously tended to endow them. Like blotches on an Impressionist canvas, they lose their individuality and become ciphers, the passive victims of hereditary flaws, physiological needs, and environmental pressures. Ruled by desire (for sex, luxury, fame, artistic creation) they are subject to a natural rhythm of flowering and decay over which they seem to have little, if any, control. Many of Zola's narratives are organized so that for approximately the first third of the novel the main characters appear to be succeeding in their ambitions and to be achieving happiness, only to see the cup slowly and relentlessly recede from their lips. *The Masterpiece* is no exception, the riverine idyll of Bennecourt and the first healthy years of young Jacques being followed by a gradual descent into Parisian poverty and the eventual death of Lantier's and Christine's now monstrous child, 'the blemished offspring of genius' (p. 251).

This vision of human pettiness and frailty against a backdrop of malign fate, which is so powerful in Zola's novels, is reinforced by the hyperbolic treatment of the inanimate. In other Rougon-Macquart novels, physical objects—a mine, a still, a train—are variously transformed into devouring monsters requiring regular human sacrifice. Here the work of art—be it Mahoudeau's statue or Claude's final canvas—assumes this role; while Paris itself dominates the novel like some epic being, with the Seine flowing through it as blood along a vein and the Île de la Cité the seeming repository of its soul. The city takes on an other-worldly aura of impenetrable mystery as Zola, no less than Lantier, tries repeatedly to represent its shifting, manifold aspects; and the long passages devoted to urban landscape, with their careful notation of colour and perspective, demonstrate the novelist's desire to 'translate' Impressionist painting into literature with 'the palette . . . of my descriptions'. At such times the character, usually Claude, loses all identity and becomes the seeing eye of the novelist registering the tiniest nuances of light and shape.

Here Zola the Naturalist really is 'doing something'. Readers may vary in their response to the melodramatic nature of the plot of *The Masterpiece*, from the opening, apocalyptic thunderstorm to the final tumult of conjugal resentment and desire. They may take a more or less tolerant view of the frankness of certain scenes and of the voyeurism of the central character (and his creator). They may be impressed in differing degrees by the balanced patterning of incident and detail, by the alternating temporal rhythm of climactic moment and monotonous period. Few, however, will fail to find their imagination invaded by images of Paris and the Seine, which have the beauty and atmospheric charm of a Monet or a Sisley. For Zola, also, knew how to make an impression.

NOTE ON THE TRANSLATION

The Masterpiece (*L'Œuvre*) was first published in 1886.
Thomas Walton's excellent translation appeared in 1950 and
remained for many years the most reliable version available
in English. It has here been revised for the modern reader:
colloquialisms have been brought discreetly into line with
current usage, and bowdlerizations have been replaced by
more faithful renderings, especially of oaths. Other instances
of inappropriately dated usage have also been adjusted, and
some minor errors and infelicities removed.

SELECT BIBLIOGRAPHY

ALL twenty novels in the Rougon-Macquart series are available in English translation. *L'Assommoir, Nana, Germinal, Earth*, and *The Beast in Man* are generally acknowledged to be the best of these. The earlier masterpiece *Thérèse Raquin* is available in World's Classics in a new translation by Andrew Rothwell.

For an account of Zola's life the reader may wish to supplement the chronology which follows with F. W. J. Hemmings, *The Life and Times of Émile Zola* (London, 1977). Also available are Alan Schom's *Émile Zola: A Bourgeois Rebel* (London, 1987); and Philip Walker's *Zola* (London, 1985), which includes plot summaries. Graham King's *Garden of Zola* (London, 1978) is specifically subtitled 'Émile Zola and his Novels for English Readers' and ends with an informative section on English translations of Zola's novels.

The best literary critical introduction to Zola's work is still F. W. J. Hemmings, *Émile Zola* (2nd edn., Oxford, 1966; reprinted with corrections, 1970). Elliott M. Grant's *Émile Zola* (New York, 1966) may also be relied upon. Of further interest is Angus Wilson's *Émile Zola: An Introductory Study of His Novels* (New York, 1952). David Baguley's edition of *Critical Essays on Émile Zola* (Boston, 1986) presents a useful cross-section of essays and articles (in English or English translation) by leading writers and critics from Swinburne to the present day. Valuable contributions by leading Zola specialists of today have been edited by Robert Lethbridge and Terry Keefe in *Zola and the Craft of Fiction (Essays in Honour of F. W. J. Hemmings)* (Leicester, 1990).

Among several more closely focused studies, Brian Nelson's *Zola and the Bourgeoisie* (London, 1983) and Naomi Schor's *Zola's Crowds* (Baltimore, 1978) can be recommended.

Of specific relevance to *The Masterpiece* are Robert J. Niess's monograph *Zola, Cézanne, and Manet: A Study of 'L'Œuvre'* (Ann Arbor, 1968) and the collection of essays edited by Jean-Max Guieu and Alison Hilton, *Émile Zola and the Arts: Centennial of the Publication of 'L'Œuvre'* (Washington, DC, 1988).

Readers of *The Masterpiece* who wish to find out more about the background to the novel can do no better than consult John

Milner, *The Studios of Paris: The Capital of Art in the Late Nineteenth Century* (New Haven, Conn., and London, 1988). This mine of information is copiously illustrated, and it is of particular interest to see photographs of contemporary studios, the Salon Selection Committee at work, and other aspects of the world of Parisian art which feature in Zola's novel.

CHRONOLOGY

1840   (2 April) Born in Paris, the only child of Francesco Zola (b. 1795), an Italian engineer, and Émilie, née Aubert (b. 1819), the daughter of a glazier. The Naturalist novelist was later proud that 'zolla' in Italian means 'clod of earth'

1843   Family moves to Aix-en-Provence

1847   (27 March) Death of father from pneumonia following a chill caught while supervising work on his scheme to supply Aix-en-Provence with drinking water

1852–   Becomes a boarder at the Collège Bourbon at Aix. Friendship with Baptistin Baille and Paul Cézanne. Zola, not Cézanne, wins the school prize for drawing

1858   (February) Leaves Aix to settle in Paris with his mother (who had preceded him in December). Offered a place and bursary at the Lycée Saint-Louis. (November) Falls ill with 'brain fever' (typhoid) and convalescence is slow

1859   Fails his *baccalauréat* twice

1860   (Spring) Is found employment as a copy-clerk but abandons it after two months, preferring to eke out an existence as an impecunious writer in the Latin Quarter of Paris

1861   Cézanne follows Zola to Paris, where he meets Camille Pissarro, fails the entrance examination to the École des Beaux-Arts, and returns to Aix in September

1862   (February) Taken on by Hachette, the well-known publishing house, at first in the dispatch office and subsequently as head of the publicity department. (31 October) Naturalized as a French citizen. Cézanne returns to Paris and stays with Zola

1863   (31 January) First literary article published. (1 May) Manet's *Déjeuner sur l'herbe* exhibited at the Salon des Refusés, which Zola visits with Cézanne

1864   (October) *Tales for Ninon*

1865   *Claude's Confession.* A *succès de scandale* thanks to its bed-
         room scenes. Meets future wife Alexandrine-Gabrielle
         Meley (b. 1839), the illegitimate daughter of teenage
         parents who soon separated, and whose mother died in
         September 1849

1866   Forced to resign his position at Hachette (salary: 200
         francs a month) and becomes a literary critic on the
         recently launched daily *L'Événement* (salary: 500 francs
         a month). Self-styled 'humble disciple' of Hippolyte
         Taine. Writes a series of provocative articles condemn-
         ing the official Salon Selection Committee, expressing
         reservations about Courbet, and praising Manet and
         Monet. Begins to frequent the Café Guerbois in the
         Batignolles quarter of Paris, the meeting-place of the
         future Impressionists. Antoine Guillemet takes Zola to
         meet Manet. Summer months spent with Cézanne at
         Bennecourt on the Seine. (15 November) *L'Événement*
         suppressed by the authorities

1867   (November) *Thérèse Raquin*

1868   (April) Preface to second edition of *Thérèse Raquin*.
         (May) Manet's portrait of Zola exhibited at the Salon.
         (December) *Madeleine Férat*. Begins to plan for the
         Rougon-Macquart series of novels

1868–70 Working as journalist for a number of different news-
         papers

1870   (31 May) Marries Alexandrine in a registry office. (Sep-
         tember) Moves temporarily to Marseilles because of the
         Franco-Prussian War

1871   Political reporter for *La Cloche* (in Paris) and *Le Séma-
         phore de Marseille*. (March) Returns to Paris. (October)
         Publishes *The Fortune of the Rougons*, the first of the
         twenty novels making up the Rougon-Macquart series

1872   *The Kill*

1873   (April) *The Belly of Paris*

1874   (May) *The Conquest of Plassans*. First independent Im-
         pressionist exhibition. (November) *Further Tales for
         Ninon*

1875   Begins to contribute articles to the Russian newspaper *Vestnik Evropy* (*European Herald*). (April) *The Sin of the Abbé Mouret*

1876   (February) *His Excellency Eugène Rougon*. Second Impressionist exhibition

1877   (February) *L'Assommoir*

1878   Buys a house at Médan on the Seine, forty kilometres west of Paris. (June) *A Page of Love*

1880   (March) *Nana*. (May) *Les Soirées de Médan* (an anthology of short stories by Zola and some of his Naturalist 'disciples', including Maupassant). (8 May) Death of Flaubert. (September) First of a series of articles for *Le Figaro*. (17 October) Death of his mother. (December) *The Experimental Novel*

1882   (April) *Pot-Bouille*. (3 September) Death of Turgenev

1883   (13 February) Death of Wagner. (March) *Au Bonheur des dames*. (30 April) Death of Manet

1884   (March) *La Joie de vivre*. Preface to catalogue of Manet exhibition

1885   (March) *Germinal*. (12 May) Begins writing *The Masterpiece* (*L'Œuvre*). (22 May) Death of Victor Hugo. (23 December) First instalment of *The Masterpiece* appears in *Le Gil Blas*

1886   (27 March) Final instalment of *The Masterpiece*, which is published in book form in April

1887   (18 August) Denounced as an onanistic pornographer in the *Manifesto of the Five* in *Le Figaro*. (November) *Earth*

1888   (October) *The Dream*. Jeanne Rozerot becomes his mistress

1889   (20 September) Birth of Denise, daughter of Zola and Jeanne

1890   (March) *The Beast in Man*

1891   (March) *Money*. (April) Elected President of the Société des gens de lettres. (25 September) Birth of Jacques, son of Zola and Jeanne

1892   (June) *The Débâcle*

1893	(July) *Doctor Pascal*, the last of the Rougon-Macquart novels. Fêted on a visit to London
1894	(August) *Lourdes*, the first novel of the trilogy *Three Cities*. (22 December) Dreyfus found guilty by a court martial
1896	(May) *Rome*
1898	(13 January) 'J'accuse', his article in defence of Dreyfus, published in *L'Aurore*. (21 February) Found guilty of libelling the Minister of War and given the maximum sentence of one year's imprisonment and a fine of 3,000 francs. Appeal for retrial granted on a technicality. (March) *Paris*. (23 May) Retrial delayed. (18 July) Leaves for England instead of attending court
1899	(4 June) Returns to France. (October) *Fecundity*, the first of his *Four Gospels*
1901	(May) *Toil*, the second 'Gospel'
1902	(29 September) Dies of fumes from his bedroom fire, the chimney having been capped either by accident or anti-dreyfusard design. Wife survives. (5 October) Public funeral
1903	(March) *Truth*, the third 'Gospel', published posthumously. *Justice* was to be the fourth
1908	(4 June) Remains transferred to the Panthéon

The Masterpiece

CHAPTER 1

CLAUDE was passing the Hôtel de Ville and the clock was just striking two when the storm broke. He was an artist and liked to ramble around Paris till the small hours, but wandering about the Halles on that hot July evening he had lost all sense of time. Suddenly the rain began to fall so heavily and in such enormous drops that he took to his heels and careered madly along the Quai de la Grève; but then, at the Pont Louis-Philippe, furious at finding himself out of breath, he stopped. He was a fool, he thought, to be afraid of getting wet, so he made his way through the darkness—the violence of the rain was extinguishing the gas-lamps—and crossed the bridge at a more leisurely pace.

Besides, he had not very far to go. As he turned along the Quai de Bourbon, on the Ile Saint-Louis, a flash of lightning lit up the long straight line of big, old houses and the narrow roadway that runs along the bank of the Seine. It was reflected in the panes of their tall, shutterless windows and revealed for a moment their ancient, melancholy-looking façades, bringing out some of their details—a stone balcony, a balustrade, a festoon carved on a pediment—with amazing clarity. It was there Claude had his studio, in the garret of the old Hôtel du Martoy, on the corner of the Rue de la Femme-sans-Tête. The embankment, illuminated for a second, was plunged again into darkness and a mighty clap of thunder shook the whole neighbourhood from sleep.

When he reached his door, a low, old-fashioned, round-topped door encased in iron, Claude, blinded by the driving rain, groped for the bell-pull, but recoiled in amazement when he felt, huddled up in the corner, against the woodwork, a human body. Then, as the lightning flashed a second time, he caught sight of a tall girl, dressed in black, soaking wet and trembling with fright. The thunder made both of them start, then Claude cried:

'Well, I must say, I never expected. . . . Who are you? What do you want?'

He could not see her now, he could only hear her sobbing and stammering an answer to his question.

'Oh, monsieur! Please, please leave me alone! . . . It's the cabman I hired at the station . . . he left me here, near this doorway . . . he turned me out of the cab. . . . You see, there'd been a train derailed, near Nevers, monsieur, and we . . . we got in four hours late, so I . . . I didn't . . . find the person who . . . who should have been waiting for me at the station. . . . I don't know what I'm going to do . . . I . . . I've never been to Paris before, monsieur. . . . I don't know . . . where I am. . . .'

She stopped as the lightning flashed again and, wide-eyed with terror, caught a momentary glimpse of this unknown place, the purple-white vision of a nightmare city. The rain had ceased. On the far bank of the Seine the irregular roofs of the row of little grey houses on the Quai des Ormes stood out against the sky, while their doors and the shutters of the little shops made their lower half a patchwork of bright colours. On the left a wider horizon opened up as far as the blue slate gables of the Hôtel de Ville, and on the right to the lead-covered dome of Saint Paul's church. What really took her breath away though, was the Seine, the way it was built-in, and flowed so darkly through its narrow bed, between the solid piers of the Pont-Marie and the lighter arches of the new Pont Louis-Philippe, its surface peopled by a mass of extraordinary shapes—a dormant flotilla of skiffs and dinghies, a laundry-boat and a dredger moored at the wharf and, over against the other bank, barges loaded with coal, lighters full of millstone grit and, towering over them all, the iron jib of a gigantic crane. A flash, and all was gone.

'Humbug,' thought Claude. 'It's obvious what she is—a trollop, thrown out on to the street and looking for a man.'

He instinctively distrusted women. This story of an accident, of a train being late, of a bullying cabman, sounded to him like a ridiculous fabrication. When it thundered again, the girl had huddled further into the corner, terrified.

'But you can't spend the night there,' said Claude, aloud this time.

The girl started to cry again, and stammered:

'I beg you, monsieur, take me to Passy. That's where I'm going . . . Passy.'

He shrugged his shoulders. Did she really take him for a fool? Automatically, he turned towards the Quai des Célestins, where he knew there was a cab-rank. There was not the faintest glimmer of a lamp to be seen.

'Passy, my dear? Why not Versailles? . . . And where the devil do you think we're going to pick up a cab at this hour, on a night like this?'

She gave a little shriek of terror, dazzled as the lightning flashed again revealing the city once more, lurid this time, baleful and spattered with blood. It was one enormous trench hacked through the glowing embers of a fire, with the river flowing along it from end to end, as far as the eye could see. The minutest details were clearly visible. One could pick out the little closed shutters along the Quai des Ormes and the narrow slits of the Rue de la Masure and the Rue du Paon-Blanc breaking the line of the houses; near the Pont-Marie, where those huge plane-trees provide such a magnificent patch of greenery, one could have counted every single leaf. In the other direction, under the Pont Louis-Philippe, the flat river barges moored four deep along the Mail, piled high with yellow apples, were a blaze of gold. It was an amazing conglomeration, a whole world, in fact, besides the milling of the water—the tall chimney of the laundry-boat, the static chain of the dredger, the heaps of sand on the opposite wharf—that filled the enormous trough cut out from one horizon to the other. Then, with the sky blotted out again, the river was once more a stream of darkness amid the rattle of the thunder.

'Oh, dear God! It's no good . . . Oh, my God! What is to become of me?'

It began to rain again, hard. Driven by the gale, the rain swept along the embankment as if a flood-gate had been opened.

'Come along now, let me get indoors,' said Claude. 'This really won't do.'

Both of them were rapidly getting soaked to the skin. By the pale glimmer of the gas-lamp on the corner of the Rue de la Femme-sans-Tête, he could see the rain streaming off her clothes, her wet garments clinging to her body, as the rain beat against the door. He began to feel sorry for her. After all, he had once taken pity on a stray dog on a night like this! But he was annoyed with himself for letting himself be moved. He never took women to his room. He treated them all as if he neither knew nor cared about them, hiding his painful timidity behind an exterior of bluster and off-handedness. And this girl must have thought him unutterably stupid to try to waylay him with such a ridiculous, unconvincing tale. However, he ended up by saying:

'We've both had enough of this. Come on in. . . . You can sleep in my studio.'

This only increased her dismay and she made a move to get out of the doorway.

'Your studio! Oh no! No, I couldn't, really I couldn't. . . . I must get to Passy somehow, monsieur. Won't you please, please take me to Passy?'

At this he lost his temper. Why the devil was she making all this fuss? Wasn't he offering her shelter for the night? He had rung the bell twice already, and now the door swung open and he pushed the girl inside.

'But I can't, monsieur, I tell you, I . . .'

But a flash of lightning startled her again, and when the thunder roared once more she leaped inside, hardly realizing she was doing so. The heavy door swung to behind her and she found herself in total darkness in an enormous porch.

'It's me, Madame Joseph,' Claude called to the concierge. Then he whispered to the girl: 'Take hold of my hand. We've got to get across the courtyard.'

She offered no further resistance, but, worn out, bewildered, she gave him her hand and, side by side, they dashed out through the driving rain. It was a spacious baronial courtyard, with stone arcades faintly visible through the darkness. When they reached cover again, at a kind of narrow vestibule without a door, he let go her hand and she heard him swearing as he tried to strike match after match. These were all damp, so they had to feel their way upstairs in the dark.

'Keep hold of the rail, and go carefully. The steps are pretty steep.'

Wearily, and with many a stumble, she clambered up three inordinately long flights of narrow back stairs, and then, he told her, they had to go down a long corridor. He led the way and she followed, feeling her way along the wall, on and on, back towards the part of the house overlooking the river. At the end, there were more stairs, up to the attic this time, one steep flight of rough wooden steps without a handrail which creaked and swayed like a ladder. The landing at the top was so tiny that the girl collided with Claude as he tried to find his key. At last he opened his door.

'Don't go in,' he said. 'Wait, or you're sure to bump into something or other.'

So she stayed where she was, panting for breath, her heart pounding, her temples throbbing, worn out by her long climb through the darkness. She felt as if she had been climbing for hours through a mazy network of stairs and passages, and that she would never find her way down again. Inside the studio she could hear heavy footsteps, somebody groping around, something knocked over with a clatter, a muffled oath. There was a light in the doorway.

'There we are. You can come in now.'

She went in, looked about her, but really saw nothing. One solitary candle made a very feeble light in an attic fifteen feet high, crammed with unrecognizable objects which cast enormous eerie shadows on its grey-painted walls. She looked straight up to the attic window, for the rain was beating against it like the deafening roll of a drum. At that very moment, the lightning flashed across the sky, followed so closely by a clap of thunder that it felt as if the roof had been torn open. Speechless, white as a sheet, she collapsed on to a chair.

'That was a near one,' said Claude, himself a little pale. 'Just got in in time. We're better off here, don't you think, than out in the street?'

And he turned and slammed the door, double locking it, while the girl looked on in a daze.

'There,' he said. 'No place like home.'

The storm was now practically over; the thunder rolled farther and farther away in the distance, and before long the deluge, too, had ceased. Claude, conscious of a growing feeling of embarrassment, looked the girl up and down out of the corner of his eye. She wasn't bad-looking, he supposed, and she was certainly young, twenty at the outside. That put him more than ever on his guard, though he was not unaware of a certain feeling of doubt, a vague idea that she might not be telling a pack of lies after all. Anyhow, if she thought she'd been smart, if she thought she'd hooked him, she was making a sad mistake. So he exaggerated his toughness, put on a big voice for her benefit and said:

'Come on, let's turn in. Nothing like bed after a soaking.'

She stood up at once, terrified. She, too, had been taking stock of Claude, without looking straight at him, and she was afraid of this gaunt young man with a beard and bony knuckles, who might have been a brigand in a story with his big black hat and his old brown jacket weathered to a dingy green.

'Thank you,' she murmured, 'I shall be all right as I am. I can sleep in my clothes.'

'Sleep in your clothes when you're soaked to the skin! . . . Don't be a fool. Take 'em off and get into bed.'

He kicked a chair or two out of the way and drew aside a dilapidated screen. Behind it she saw there was a washstand and a small single bed. He began to turn back the counterpane.

'No, monsieur, please don't bother. I prefer to stay where I am. I assure you I do.'

This infuriated him.

'Stop acting the fool, for God's sake!' he cried, with an angry gesture. 'I'm offering you my bed, what more do you want? . . . And you can cut out all this modesty, too, because it will get you nowhere. I'm going to sleep on the divan.'

Standing over her, his fists clenched in anger, he appeared to be threatening her. She was petrified, convinced he was about to strike her and, with trembling fingers, she took off her hat, while the rain from her clothes formed a pool on the floor. Claude, after a moment of inarticulate rage, seemed to give in to a scruple of some kind, and blurted out, as a sort of concession:

'If it's me that puts you off, I can always change the bedding.'

And as he spoke, he began tearing the sheets off the bed and flinging them on to the divan at the far end of the studio. Then he brought out a clean pair from a cupboard and made up the bed afresh, with the deftness of a bachelor who is used to the job, carefully tucking in the blanket on the wall side, plumping up the pillow and finally turning back the sheets.

'There you are. Now off to sleep!'

Then, as she said nothing, but stood there aimlessly fingering the buttons on her dress without making up her mind to undo them, he closed the screen around her. My God! All this modesty! It did not take him long to turn in himself; he had soon tossed his clothes on to an old easel, arranged the sheets he had taken from the bed, and stretched himself out on the divan. Just as he was about to blow out the candle, he remembered the girl; she would not be able to see; so he waited. For a time he had not heard her moving about at all; perhaps she was still exactly where he had left her, standing by the bed. But now he could just make out the rustle of garments and imagine her slow, stealthy movements as if she, too, kept stopping and listening, wondering why the light was not put out. It was some considerable time before he heard the faint creak of the mattress, followed by a long silence.

'Are you all right, mademoiselle?' he called, in a much gentler voice.

Her reply was barely audible, for her voice still quavered with emotion.

'Yes, monsieur, thank you.'

'Good night, then.'

'Good night.'

He blew out the light. The silence seemed deeper than ever. In spite of his weariness, Claude could not keep his eyes closed, and he soon found himself wide awake, staring up at the window. The sky had cleared again and he watched the stars twinkling in the sultry July night. It was still very close, in spite of the storm, and he was so hot that he lay with his bare arms outside the sheets. His thoughts kept running on the girl and in his mind a lively battle was being fought out between the contempt he was only too happy to show, the fear of finding himself saddled for the rest of his days if he gave way, and the fear of looking ridiculous because he didn't take advantage of the situation. It was contempt that won in the end, and Claude chuckled as he congratulated himself on resisting the temptation, for he imagined the whole affair as some kind of plot to ruin his peace of mind. He was still too hot, so he kicked off the sheet and lay there, drowsy but half awake, straying through a glowing maze of stars in pursuit of the beauties he worshipped, women in all their naked loveliness. As his vision faded, his thoughts returned to the girl. What was she doing? he wondered. For a long time he had thought she was asleep, for she hardly seemed to be breathing. Now he could hear she was restless, like himself, though she stirred with infinite precaution, holding her breath as she did so. With what little he knew of women, he began trying to make some sense of the story she had told him, for he was perplexed by some of the details now that he came to think about them. But his mind refused to work logically, so what was the use of racking his brains to no purpose? Whether she was telling the truth or spinning a yarn, he had no use for her, so it was all one to him! In the morning she would take her leave; hail and farewell and that would be that; they would never see each other again. It was growing light, and the stars were paling when he finally dropped off to sleep. Behind the screen, the girl, exhausted though she was by her journey, was still unable to relax, for the room, being immediately under the zinc of the roof, was very stuffy. As dawn drew near, however, she stirred with less restraint, even giving vent, in a sudden spasm of nervous impatience, to a virgin's sigh of irritation at the irksome presence of this man asleep, so close to where she lay.

When he woke in the morning, Claude found he could hardly bear to open his eyes, for the day was well advanced and the sun was streaming in through his attic window. It was a theory of his that the young 'open air' painters* ought to take the studios the academic painters refused, the ones that were lighted by the full blaze of the sun. But the first slight shock made him sit for a moment on the edge of his couch, wondering how on earth he came to be sleeping there, on the divan. On looking about him, still bleary-eyed with sleep, he noticed a heap of petticoats on the floor, partly hidden by the screen. Then he remembered. That girl! He listened, and could hear her smooth, regular breathing, peaceful as a child's. That meant she was still so fast asleep that it would be a pity to wake her. He sat there, scratching his bare legs, not knowing quite what to do, rather annoyed with the situation he was in which was going to upset all his morning's work. He was obviously being far too soft-hearted. What he ought to do was rouse her and send her on her way as soon as possible. And yet, when he had put on his trousers and slid his feet into his slippers, there he was going about the room on tip-toe!

When the cuckoo-clock struck nine and there was still no sign of life behind the screen beyond the soft, regular breathing, Claude began to be worried. The best thing to do, he thought, would be to get on with his painting and make his breakfast later, when he was free to make a noise. But somehow he could not make a start. He was used to living in unspeakable disorder, but that heap of garments, slipped off and left lying on the floor, troubled him. They were still wet, too, lying in the pool of rain water which had seeped out of them during the night. Grumbling under his breath, he picked them up one by one and spread them out on chairs in the sunshine. How could anybody leave their things lying around like that? They'd never be dry and he'd never be rid of her! By the way he handled them and shook them out, he was clearly unused to women's things. He got very tangled up in the black woollen bodice and had to crawl about on hands and knees to retrieve the stockings which had dropped down behind one of his old canvases. They were grey lisle stockings, very long and very fine. He examined them closely before hanging them up. They were damp, from contact with the hem of the skirt, so he stretched them and smoothed them out between his warm hands, to make sure he would lose no time in packing her off.

Ever since he got up Claude had been wanting to move the screen, and his curiosity, which he admitted was foolish, only added to his ill-humour. At last, just as, with a characteristic shrug of the shoulders, he had decided to take up his brushes, a murmur and a rustle of bed linen interrupted the gentle breathing and this time he gave in, put down his brushes and looked round the edge of the screen. What he saw rooted him to the spot, and he stood there, gazing in ecstasy, with a gasp of mingled surprise and admiration:

'Good God!'

In the hothouse heat of the sunlit room, the girl had thrown back the sheet and, exhausted after a night without sleep, was now slumbering peacefully, bathed in sunlight, and so lost to consciousness that not a sign of a tremor disturbed her naked innocence. During her sleepless tossing the shoulder-straps of her chemise had come unfastened and the one on her left shoulder had slipped off completely, leaving her bosom bare. Her flesh was faintly golden and silk-like in its texture, her firm little breasts, tipped with palest rose-colour, thrust upwards with all the freshness of spring. Her sleepy head lay back upon the pillow, her right arm folded under it, thus displaying her bosom in a line of trusting, delicious abandon, clothed only in the dark mantle of her loose black hair.

'By God, she's a beauty!' Claude muttered to himself. Here it was, the very thing, the model he'd tried in vain to find for his picture, and, what's more, posed nearly as he wanted her! A bit on the thin side, perhaps, and still with something of the undeveloped child about her, but so supple, so fresh, so youthful! And yet her breasts were fully formed. How the devil had she managed to hide them last night? Why hadn't he even suspected what she was like? This was a find, and no mistake!

Softly he hurried to fetch his crayon-box and a big sheet of paper and, perching on the edge of a low chair, with a board across his knees, he began to draw. He looked profoundly happy. All his agitation, carnal curiosity, and repressed desire gave way before the spellbound admiration of the artist with a keen eye for lovely colouring and well-formed muscles. The girl herself was already forgotten in the thrill of seeing how the snowy whiteness of her breasts lit up the delicate amber of her shoulders, and in the presence of nature in all its beauty he was overcome with such apprehensive modesty that he felt like a small boy again, sitting to attention, respectful and well-behaved.

He went on drawing for about a quarter of an hour, stopping from time to time to look at her with half-closed eyes. He was afraid she would move, so he pressed on with his work, holding his breath for fear of disturbing her.

Absorbed as he was in his task, he nevertheless found himself indulging in vague speculations as to who she could be. She was certainly not the trollop he had taken her for, her bloom was too fresh for that. But whatever had made her spin such an incredible yarn? He thought over a number of other possible explanations for her escapade. Perhaps she had been seduced, brought to Paris by her lover and then abandoned. Perhaps she was a nice girl who had been led astray by one of her school friends and was afraid to go back to her parents. Or perhaps the whole affair was much more complicated, a case of some extraordinary girlish perversion, or even of horrors he would never be able to fathom. The more he guessed, the harder he found it to make up his mind about her, and it was in that uncertain state of mind that he began to sketch her face. He studied it very closely. The upper half was very kind and very gentle; the brow limpid, clear and smooth as a mirror, the nose small, the nostrils delicate and sensitive, and he could tell that, under their closed lids, the eyes wore a smile, a smile that would light up the whole face. The lower half, however, destroyed that impression of radiant tenderness, for the firm, strong chin, the blood-red lips, too full over the strong white teeth, were like a burst of passion—the stirrings of unconscious puberty—over features otherwise suffused with childlike delicacy.

Suddenly a faint shudder rippled the satin of her skin, as if she had unexpectedly become aware of masculine scrutiny, and she opened her eyes wide and gave a little cry of fright.

'Oh, my goodness!'

She was dazed and, for a moment, petrified with fear at finding herself in a strange place, with this young man in shirt sleeves devouring her with his eyes. Then, with one desperate gesture, she pulled up the sheet and hugged it to her bosom with both arms. So profound was the shock to her modesty that the blood rushed to her cheeks and her blush flowed, in a rosy tide, to the very tips of her breasts.

'Hey, what's up?' snapped Claude, his crayon poised, 'what's wrong?'

She neither spoke nor stirred, but lay there clutching the sheet to her throat, and making herself so small in the bed that she was hardly noticeable under the bedclothes.

'Don't worry, I'm not going to eat you. . . . Come on. Do me a favour and lie back the way you were.'

She flushed again and finally stammered:

'No! Oh, no! I couldn't, monsieur.'

He thought her obstinacy ridiculous and soon let fly in one of his characteristic outbursts of temper.

'What difference can it make to you? Why should you worry because I know what you look like undressed? You're not the first I've seen!'

At that she burst into tears and he, beside himself with anger, desperate because he thought he might never finish his drawing and this silly girl's prudery was going to deprive him of a good study for his picture, gave full vent to his rage.

'So you won't do it, eh? . . . Of all the damned silly things! What do you take me for? Have I as much as tried to lay a finger on you, tell me that? If I'd even thought of having a bit of fun, I've had plenty of opportunity since last night. . . . If you think I'm interested in that sort of nonsense, my girl, you're very much mistaken. You can show me all you've got, it won't upset me. . . . Besides, it doesn't show much gratitude, does it, refusing a little favour like that? . . . After all, I did take you in off the streets, and I did let you sleep in my bed.'

She was sobbing now, and had hidden her face in the pillow.

'I give you my word it's absolutely necessary, or I wouldn't be worrying you like this.'

All these tears surprised him, and he began to feel ashamed of his harshness. Not knowing what to do for the best, he said nothing for a few moments and then, when she had had time to calm herself, he said in a much gentler voice:

'If you really do mind, we'll say no more about it. . . . But if you only knew what it means to me . . . I have a picture there, you see, half finished, and likely to stay that way, and you were so exactly the type I've been looking for. . . . With me, the thing is, when it comes to damned painting I could kill my own mother and father! . . . Can you understand that? Forgive me. . . . You know, if you were really kind, you'd give me just a few minutes more. . . . No, you needn't be embarrassed, I don't mean the bust. I don't need that, I only want the head now. Just the head, that's all. If I could just finish that. . . . Will you do it? . . . Please . . .

Put your arm back as it was, and I'll be grateful to you as long as . . . oh, as long as I live!'

By the time he had finished he was almost praying to the girl, making vague, pitiful gestures with his crayon, so powerful was the urge he felt to draw. Otherwise, he had not stirred, he was still perched on the edge of his low chair, still at a respectable distance from her. At length she took a chance, now that she felt calmer, and uncovered her face. What else could she do? She was at his mercy, and he looked so downcast! One last moment of hesitation, one last touch of shyness and then, slowly, without saying a word, she slipped her arm back under her head, taking great care to keep the other out of sight, holding the sheets tightly up to her neck.

'Ah! Now that's what I call kind!' said Claude. 'I won't take long now. You'll be free in a matter of minutes.'

Bent over his drawing, glancing at her from time to time with the keen eye of the artist, he saw her no longer as a woman but simply as a model. Her faint blush lingered for a time in her confusion at exposing her bare arm, though it was no more than she would have innocently shown at a ball. But the young man seemed so reasonable that she soon regained her calm, the hotness left her cheeks, her mouth relaxed into a smile of confidence, while from under her half-closed lids she in her turn studied him. She had been terrified of him with his thick beard, his big head, his violent gestures, ever since she had set eyes on him; but she saw now he was not really ugly. There was a deep tenderness, she discovered, in his dark brown eyes, and above his bristly moustache the nose was surprisingly delicate, almost feminine. There was something inexplicably touching about his passionate intentness, sending a faint quiver through him as he worked, making a live thing of the crayon he held between his slim fingers. He could not be wicked, she thought. He bullied because he was shy. She would have found it difficult to explain what she felt, but her mind was at rest and she began to relax, as in the company of a friend.

The studio, however, still rather frightened her. Glancing discreetly about her, she was appalled by the disorder and apparent neglect. Last winter's ashes were still heaped up in front of the stove. Apart from the bed, the little wash-stand and the divan, the only other pieces of furniture in the place were a dilapidated oak wardrobe and a huge deal table littered with brushes, tubes of paint, unwashed crockery, and a spirit stove on which stood a saucepan still spattered with vermicelli. Chairs stood about, with holes in their seats, surrounded by rickety easels. Near the divan, on the floor, in a corner which was probably swept out less than once a month, was the candle he had used last night, and the only thing in the room that looked neat and cheerful was the cuckoo-clock, a large one of its kind with a resounding tick, ornamented with bright red flowers. But what unnerved her more than anything else were the unframed sketches hanging on the walls, covering them from ceiling to floor, where others lay heaped up in a disorderly landslide of canvas. She had never seen painting like it, so rugged, so harsh, so violent in its colouring; it shocked her like a burst of foul language bawled out from the steps of a gin-shop. She looked away, but her eyes were drawn towards one picture turned face to the wall. It was the big canvas the artist was working on and which he turned to the wall every night in order to judge it with a fresh, unbiased eye when he resumed his work in the morning. What could be on that one, she wondered, that he didn't even dare exhibit it?

By now the whole studio was flooded with sunshine, for there was no shade at the window, and it flowed like molten gold over the carefree poverty of its ramshackle furniture.

Claude found the silence oppressive. He wanted to say something, anything, partly in order to be polite, but largely to help her to forget she was posing. He racked his brains for a long time, but all he could find to say was:

'What's your name?'

Opening her eyes, for she had started to doze, she replied: 'Christine.'

Then he remembered he had never told her his own name. There they had been under the same roof since last night without even knowing each other's names.

'Mine's Claude.'

And, as he happened to look at her just at that moment, he saw her break into an enchanting laugh, the playful reaction of a girl not yet quite grown up. It struck her as very funny, this belated introduction and, following up her train of thought, she said:

'How odd! Claude and Christine. We both start with the same letter!'

There was another silence. His eyes half-closed, oblivious for a moment, he went on drawing, but then he thought he noticed her getting restless. He was so afraid she would lose the pose that to occupy her he ventured:

'A bit warm, isn't it?'

This time she restrained her laughter although now that she felt more at one with her surroundings her natural gaiety had revived and was not always easy to control. It was so hot that the bed was like a bath and her skin was damp and pale, with the milky paleness of camellias.

'Yes, it is rather warm,' she answered seriously, though her eyes were sparkling with merriment.

And Claude carried on in his simple, good-natured way:

'It's all this sun. . . . Still, it does you good, plenty of sun on your body. . . . We could have done with a bit of this last night in the doorway, couldn't we?'

That made them both laugh. Claude, delighted to have discovered a topic of conversation, began to ask her about her adventure, but not in any inquisitive spirit. He did not really care whether she told him the truth or not; all he wanted to do was to prolong the sitting.

Simply, in a few words, Christine told him what had happened. On the previous morning she had left Clermont to come to Paris to take up a post as reader to a Madame Vanzade, a wealthy old lady, the widow of a general, who lived in Passy. According to the time-table, her train was due into Paris at ten past nine, and all arrangements had been made for her to be met by one of Madame Vanzade's maids. They had even agreed that the maid should be able to recognize her by the grey feather in her black hat. But just on this side of Nevers the train had been held up. A goods train had been derailed and the main line was blocked by debris. That was the start of a long series of delays and setbacks. First they had waited an unconscionable time in the train, then they had been told to get out, leave their luggage behind and trudge three kilometres to the nearest station where a relief train had been formed. Two hours had been lost that way, and two more were lost through the general dislocation the accident had caused all along the line. So the outcome of it all was that they had only got into Paris at one o'clock in the morning, four hours late.

'Bad luck!' said Claude, breaking into her narrative, still not quite convinced, but staggered by the ease with which all complications were being smoothed out. 'And, of course, at that hour, the person who should have met you had gone.'

He was right. Christine had not been met by Madame Vanzade's maid, who must have given her up and gone home. She told him how scared she had been in the huge, poorly-lit concourse at the Gare de Lyon, practically deserted at that hour of the morning, and how for a long time she had not dared to take a cab but had wandered to and fro, clutching her tiny travelling bag, hoping somebody would turn up. When at last she had screwed up her courage it was too late, for there was only one cab on the rank, and the driver, who was very dirty and reeked of wine, had sidled up and leered as he asked her where she wanted to go.

'I know the sort,' said Claude, as interested now as if he were living a fairy-tale. 'And you let him pick you up?'

'He made me,' said Christine, her eyes fixed on the ceiling, still holding the pose. 'He called me dearie. I was scared to death. When I said I wanted to go to Passy he was furious and started off at such a rate that I had to hang on to the doors. After a time, I began to think he was harmless after all. He went at a reasonable pace along the

streets that were still lit up, and I could see there were
people about. Then I recognized the Seine. I've never been
to Paris before, but I knew what it looked like on the map,
so I thought he would simply follow the embankment. But
when I saw we were going over a bridge I was scared again.
It was just beginning to rain when the cab turned into a
patch of shadow, pulled up with a jerk and the driver
scrambled down from his seat. He wanted to get in with
me. He said it was too wet outside. . . .'

Claude started to laugh. He believed her now. She could
never have invented that cabby! She had stopped, embarrassed by his laugh.

'So that was his game, was it?' he said. 'And what did
you do?'

'I jumped straight out of the other door on to the roadway.
He started swearing at me then, pretended we were there
and said that if I didn't pay him he'd tear the hat off my
head. . . . It was pouring with rain and there wasn't a soul
about. I didn't know what to do, so I gave him a five-franc
piece and he drove off as fast as he could go, taking my
travelling bag with him. Fortunately there was nothing in
it but two handkerchiefs, a piece of brioche and the key to
the trunk I'd had to leave in the train.'

'But why didn't you take the number of the cab?' cried
the indignant painter.

He remembered now that a cab had whisked past him at
a breakneck speed as he was crossing the Pont Louis-Philippe
in the blinding rain, and he marvelled to think how often
truth is really stranger than fiction. Compared to the natural
course of life's limitless combinations, his version of the affair
was so simple and logical that it was completely stupid.

'You can just imagine how I felt when you found me in
the doorway!' said Christine. 'I knew very well I wasn't in
Passy; that meant that on my first night in this terrible city
I was going to have to sleep in the streets. Then there was
the thunder and lightning! Oh, those dreadful flashes, all
blue and red. I shudder to think what I saw when they lit
up the streets!'

Her eyes had closed again, and her face turned pale as she recalled the baleful vision she had seen the previous night; the embankment, a trench cut through a blazing furnace; the leaden waters of the river, a moat, congested with great black barges like so many dead whales, and stretching out over it all the gibbet-like arms of a host of motionless cranes. Could anyone call that a welcome? she reflected.

There was another gap in the conversation. Claude had resumed his drawing. At last his model had to move, for she felt her arm going to sleep.

'Could you keep the elbow just a little bit further back?' he said mechanically and, partly to show he was still interested, partly to excuse his abruptness, added:

'Your parents are going to be worried, aren't they, if they've heard about the train crash?'

'I haven't got any parents.'

'Neither father nor mother? Do you mean you're all alone in the world?'

'Yes. Quite alone.'

She was eighteen, she said, born at Strasbourg while her father, Captain Hallegrain, was waiting to be posted to another garrison. He was a Gascon, her father, from Montauban, and he had died, when she was nearly twelve years old, at Clermont where he had had to retire when he had become paralysed in both legs. For nearly five years more, her mother, who was a Parisian, had stayed on in Clermont, eking out her meagre pension by painting fans in order to bring up her girl like a lady. Fifteen months ago she, too, had died, leaving a penniless orphan whose only friend in the world was the Mother Superior of the Sisters of the Visitation, who had kept her on at the convent school. That was where she had come from now, as the Mother Superior had found her a place as reader to her old friend Madame Vanzade, who was practically blind.

Claude made no comment on these latest details. The thought of the convent, this nicely brought up girl whose story sounded more and more like a novel, had revived his embarrassment and made him clumsy again in his speech and gesture. He stopped drawing and sat there staring fixedly at his work, eventually asking:

'Is it a nice town, Clermont?'

'Not very. Rather gloomy. . . . But I hardly know, really. I didn't go out very much.'

Propped up on her elbow now, she went on in a low voice, deepened by the tears and emotion of bereavement, as if speaking to herself:

'Mamma wasn't very strong. She worked herself to death really. . . . She spoilt me. Nothing was too good for me. I had private tutors for everything, but I didn't make much headway. I was ill for a long time, but I wasn't very attentive either; I was far too unruly, much too fond of play. . . . I wasn't a bit fond of music-lessons; my arms simply ached when I had to play the piano. . . . I think I was best at painting. . . .'

Claude was alert at once, and broke in with:

'What? Do you paint?'

'Oh, no, not really. . . . Mamma was very clever. She taught me something about water-colours and I used to help her occasionally with the fans, painting in the backgrounds. She was a beautiful painter.'

As she said this, she instinctively cast a glance round the studio, at the terrifying pictures blazing on its walls; and a strange look came into her bright eyes, a startled, disquieted look occasioned by their stark brutality. From where she lay she could see, upside-down, the sketch Claude had made of herself. She was so taken aback by the violence of the colouring that slashed through the shadows that she did not dare to ask for a closer look. Besides, she was growing restless and uncomfortably hot in bed, and she was tortured by the idea of getting away once and for all from things which since last night had been like one long dream.

Claude, too, began to be aware of her restlessness and, feeling suddenly conscience-stricken, he put down his unfinished drawing and said hastily:

'Thanks for being so helpful, mademoiselle. I'm afraid I kept you rather a long time. . . . I'm sorry. . . . Do get up now, please. You have affairs of your own to attend to.'

And, not understanding why, when he was being so solicitous, she made no attempt to move, but drew her bare arm beneath the sheets and even blushed, he repeated his suggestion that she might now get up. Then, suddenly remembering, he made one wild gesture, swept the screen back round the bed and made his way to the other end of the studio where, in a bout of exaggerated modesty, he began to tidy up his pots and pans, making a deliberate clatter about it, so that she could get up and dress without thinking he was listening.

He made such a din that at first he did not hear her call out diffidently:

'Monsieur, monsieur . . . '

He stopped and listened.

'Monsieur, would you be so kind? . . . I can't find my stockings.'

Why, of course! What was he thinking of? How could he expect her to dress behind the screen when her stockings and the rest of her clothes were still spread out in the sun where he had put them? The stockings were quite dry; he rubbed them slightly to make sure. As he passed them to her over the thin partition, he had one last glimpse of her soft, round arm, as fresh and delicate as a child's. He tossed the rest of the garments on to the foot of the bed and pushed her boots round the edge of the screen, leaving only her hat still hanging on the easel. She thanked him, but that was all, and he heard nothing more for a time but the faintest possible rustle of garments and the discreet splash of water being poured into the basin. But he had not forgotten her needs.

'You'll find the soap in a saucer on the washstand,' he called. 'If you look in that drawer you'll find a clean towel. . . . Have you enough water? Wait a minute, I'll get you the jug.'

Then, suddenly annoyed with himself when he realized he was being tactless again, he hastened to add:

'There I go, making myself a nuisance again. . . . Don't mind me, just make yourself at home!'

With that he went back to his chores. But his mind was by no means at rest. Ought he to give her breakfast? he wondered. He could hardly send her away without, and yet, if he did, it would only drag things out and that would mean wasting the whole morning. Still undecided, he lit the spirit-stove, washed out the saucepan and started to make some chocolate. Chocolate, he thought, was more distinguished. Besides, he was secretly rather ashamed of his vermicelli, a pasta dish he prepared after the Provençal fashion, with bread and plenty of olive oil. But he had not even finished grating the chocolate into the saucepan when he exclaimed:

'What! Already!'

For there was Christine pushing aside the screen and standing all neat and tidy in her black, laced and buttoned and accoutred in the twinkling of an eye; her face fresh and rosy, her hair smooth and twisted into a heavy knot on the nape of her neck. Such a miracle of speed and housewifely efficiency filled Claude with amazement.

'Well!' he gasped. 'If you do everything else at that rate!'

She was taller and even lovelier than he had imagined, but what struck him more than anything else was her air of calm determination. She was not afraid of him now, that was very plain. She might have felt defenceless as long as she lay in that rumpled little bed, but once out of it, and fully clothed, she might have been wearing armour. She smiled, and as he looked her straight in the eyes he said what he had been hesitating to say for the last few minutes:

'You will have breakfast before you go, won't you?'

But she declined.

'Thank you, no . . . I must hurry to the station now. My trunk must surely be there by this time. . . . And then I shall make my way to Passy.'

He reminded her several times that she must be hungry and that it was hardly wise to start the day without breakfast, but all was in vain.

'Let me go down and find you a cab then.'

'No, please don't trouble.'

'But you can't possibly walk all the way. At least let me go with you as far as the cab-rank, as you don't know your way about Paris.'

'No, really, it's quite unnecessary. . . . It would be kind to let me go by myself.'

Her mind was made up. She could not bear the idea of being seen with a man, even by people who did not know her. She was going to say nothing about last night but would tell lies right and left and keep the memory of it all to herself. With an angry gesture Claude decided she could go to the devil and good riddance! It suited him not to have to go out and hunt for a cab. But he was hurt none the less; he thought her ungrateful.

'As you wish,' he said. 'I don't want to force you.'

At this, Christine's faint smile broadened, ever so slightly puckering the delicate corners of her mouth. She made no reply, but picked up her hat, glanced round for a mirror, but, as she did not see one, decided to tie the strings as well as she could without. As she stood with her elbows raised, twisting and pulling the ribbon calmly into a bow, her face was illuminated by the golden sunlight. Claude was surprised not to recognize the childlike softness of the features he had just been drawing, for now the upper part of the face, the candid brow, the gentle eyes, were less in evidence than the lower part, the strong jaw, the blood-red lips, and the fine white teeth. And still that enigmatic, girlish smile, which perhaps was mocking him.

'Anyhow,' he said irritably, 'you can't say I've done anything to offend you, can you?'

She had to laugh, a light, nervous laugh, as she replied:

'Oh, no, monsieur. I certainly can't say that.'

He could not take his eyes off her, though he was afraid he might have made himself look foolish, so powerless was he to combat his shyness and his ignorance. Just how much did she know, this tall young lady? No doubt what all girls at boarding-school know: everything and nothing. There is nothing so unfathomable as the first remote awakening of the heart and the senses. Perhaps in this artist's studio this modest though sensual young girl, in mingled fear and curiosity, had begun to open her eyes to the existence of the male. Now that she had stopped trembling was she surprised, even annoyed with herself, at having trembled for nothing? Nothing! Not even the faintest sign of gallantry, not so much as a kiss on the finger-tips! She had not been unaware of the young man's surly indifference, and the woman in her must have been vexed in consequence. She was probably going away a changed being, her nerves on edge, perhaps, but making light of her vexation, yet filled with unconscious regret for the terrible unknown things that might have, but had not, happened.

'Did you say,' she went on when she had recovered her gravity, 'that the cab-rank was over the bridge, on the opposite bank?'

'Yes. Just under all those trees.'

She was ready now; having tied her ribbons and put on her gloves, there was nothing else for her to do, yet she made no attempt to go, but stood looking vaguely about her. When her glance fell on the big canvas turned face to the wall, she wanted to ask if she might look at it, but her courage failed her. There was nothing more to stay for, yet she seemed to be looking for something, as if she felt she was leaving something behind, though what it was she would have been unable to say. At last she made a move towards the door.

Claude opened it and as he did so, a small roll of bread propped up against it fell into the room.

'There, you see, you might have had some breakfast. The concierge brings up a roll for me every morning.'

She shook her head in refusal, but on the landing she stopped for an instant, turned round and, with a cheerful smile, held out her hand and said:

'Thank you, thank you very much.'

He clasped her small, gloved hand in his large, colour-stained fingers and they stood for several seconds, close to each other, shaking hands like two good friends. She smiled, and he almost asked her: 'When shall I see you again?' But shyness prevented him. And so, when he said nothing, she released her hand.

'Goodbye, monsieur.'

'Goodbye, mademoiselle.'

Without looking back, Christine was already making her way down the narrow, creaking stairs as Claude flung back into the studio, slammed the door and cried:

'Blast these women!'

He was raging. Furious with himself and furious with everybody else, he vented his anger by kicking the furniture about and shouting. He was right never to bring any women back home. He knew he was. All the bitches were good for was to make a monkey of a man! The one who'd just gone, now, how could he be sure she hadn't been fooling him right and left, in spite of her innocent face? He'd certainly been silly enough to let himself be taken in by that incredible yarn she'd spun. But had he really? No, they'd never get him to swallow either the general's widow or the train crash, still less that impossible cabby! Things never happened like that. How could they? Besides, you'd only got to look at that mouth of hers . . . and that queer look as she went out. If only he could have known just *why* she was lying! But no. Just pointless, inexplicable lies, art for art's sake! He'd bet she was having a good laugh somewhere at his expense!

He folded the screen with a clatter and thrust it into a corner. She'd have left everything upside-down, he knew she would! But when he saw she had left everything neat and tidy, bowl, towel, soap, all where they ought to be, he flew into a rage because she had not made the bed. Exaggerating his efforts, he began to make it himself. The mattress, which he seized in both arms, was still warm; fragrance rose from the pillow as he thumped it with both his fists, and from the sheets there came the same clean, warm, pervading odour of youth. He washed in cold water to soothe his throbbing temples, but the old oppression returned when he found, in the damp face-towel, the same enveloping virginal scent that was now filling the entire studio with its sweetness. Muttering curses, he drank his chocolate out of the saucepan and gobbled great hunks of bread in his feverish haste to get back to his painting.

'This place is unbearable!' he cried. 'This heat's making me ill!'

The sun had moved on; the studio was really cooler.

Claude opened a small skylight and, with every sign of great relief, took a deep breath of the sultry breeze that floated in. He picked up his sketch of Christine's head and sat for a long time looking at it, lost in contemplation.

CHAPTER 2

TWELVE o'clock had struck and Claude was still working at his painting, when there was a loud and familiar knock on the door. Instinctively and despite himself he picked up the sketch of Christine's head, which he had been using in retouching the large female figure in his painting, and slipped it into a portfolio. Then he was ready to open the door.

'Pierre!' he exclaimed. 'Here already?'

Pierre Sandoz, his childhood friend, was twenty-two, very dark, with a round head, a square nose and gentle eyes in an energetic face framed in a short, scrubby beard.

'I lunched early on purpose,' he answered. 'I wanted to give you a good long sitting. . . . I say! It's coming along nicely!'

He stood and looked at the picture, then added, without a moment's hesitation:

'Oh look, you're altering the type of the woman!'

There was a long silence, during which they both stood contemplating the painting. It was a big canvas, five metres by three, all planned out, though parts of it were still hardly developed beyond the rough stage. As a sketch it was remarkable for its vigour, its spontaneity, and the lively warmth of its colour. It showed the sun pouring into a forest clearing, with a solid background of greenery and a dark path running off to the left and with a bright spot of light in the far distance. Lying on the grass in the foreground, among the lush vegetation of high summer, was the naked figure of a woman. One arm was folded beneath her head, thus bringing her breasts into prominence; her eyes were closed and she was smiling into space as she basked in the golden sunlight. In the background, two other nude women, one dark and one fair, were laughing and tumbling each other on the grass, making two lovely patches of flesh-colour against the green, while in the foreground, to make the necessary contrast, the artist had seen fit to place a man's figure. He wore a plain black velvet jacket, and was seated on the grass so that nothing could be seen but his back and his left hand upon which he was leaning.

'Coming on quite well, that woman,' said Sandoz at last. 'But heavens! It's all going to take a lot of work, you know.'

With a gesture full of confidence, his blazing eyes fixed on his work, Claude answered:

'Pah! I've got from now till the Salon. You can get through a lot in six months, you know. Maybe I really shall finish it this time, just to show myself I'm not completely hopeless!'

He started to whistle noisily, thrilled, though he did not say so, by the sketch he had made of Christine's head; he was carried aloft, for the moment, on one of those great waves of hope from which he was usually plunged deep into the agonies familiar to all artists with a devouring passion for nature.

'Come on then! No slacking!' he cried. 'As you're here, we might as well get started.'

Sandoz, out of friendship, and to save him the expense of a model, had offered to pose for the gentleman in the foreground. In four or five Sundays, his only free day, the figure would be practically finished. He was just slipping on the black velvet jacket when a thought suddenly struck him.

'I say, you can't have had much of a lunch, if you've been working all morning. . . . Off you go and get yourself a chop or something. I'll wait till you're back.'

Claude was indignant at the idea of losing any time.

'Of course I've had some lunch,' he replied. 'Take a look at the saucepan. Besides, I've still got a crust of bread here. I can eat that as I paint. So come on now, get settled and let me start.'

As, full of enthusiasm, he picked up his palette and seized his brushes, he added:

'Dubuche will be picking us up here later, will he?'

'Yes. He said he'd be here about five.'

'That's fine. We can go and have some dinner as soon as he comes. . . . Are you all right now? The hand a little further to the left, head a bit more on one side. That's it.'

After arranging the cushions on the divan, Sandoz settled himself on it in the desired pose. His back was turned to Claude, but they still went on talking, because that morning he had had a letter from Plassans, the little town in Provence where they had met as children in the infants' class at school. Then, after a time, the conversation petered out, for Claude, when he painted, was not of this world, and Pierre, in his efforts to retain the pose, grew more and more torpid as the sitting dragged on.

Claude was nine years old when he had the good fortune to be able to leave Paris and go back to his birthplace in Provence. His mother, a decent, hardworking laundress, whom his good-for-nothing father had practically driven on to the streets, had recently married an honest workman who had fallen madly in love with her pretty fair skin. Try as they might, however, they could barely make ends meet, so they had been heartily relieved when an old gentleman from Plassans had come and asked if he might take Claude to live with him and send him to the local school.* The generous, though somewhat eccentric, old art collector had been struck by some of the youngster's childish drawings. And so, for seven years, until he had practically finished his schooling, Claude had lived in the south, first as a boarder at the school, then as a day-boy, residing with his elderly patron. One morning, the old man was found dead on his bed, struck down by apoplexy. In his will he left an income of a thousand francs a year to Claude, with the power to draw on the capital when he was twenty-five. Claude, who was already consumed by the desire to paint, left school immediately, without even sitting his *baccalauréat*, and rushed off to Paris, whither his friend Pierre Sandoz had already preceded him.

From their earliest years at school in Plassans, Claude Lantier, Pierre Sandoz, and Louis Dubuche had been known as 'the three inseparables'.* Born within a few months of each other, but vastly different in both temperament and social background, they had soon become bosom friends, drawn together by subconscious affinities, the vague feeling of ambitions in common, the awakening of a higher intelligence among the vulgar herd of dunces and dunderheads they had to contend with in class.

Pierre's father, a Spaniard, had taken refuge in France after some political dispute and had opened a paper mill near Plassans, equipped with machines of his own invention. He had died, an embittered man, the victim of local prejudice and ill-will, leaving behind a series of such obscure and complicated lawsuits that his entire fortune was soon swallowed up in disastrous litigation. His widow, a Burgundian by birth, yielding to her resentment against the people of Provence, and suffering from creeping paralysis, for which she also held them responsible, had sought refuge in Paris, where Pierre now supported her, doing an ill-paid job and dreaming of literary triumphs. Dubuche, the eldest son of a Plassans baker, had joined his two friends in Paris later. Encouraged by his keen, ambitious mother, he was taking a course in architecture at the École des Beaux-Arts, living as best he could on the stingy allowance his determined parents invested in him, like Jews banking on a certain three per cent interest.

It was Sandoz who broke the silence, muttering under his breath:

'Confound this pose! It's breaking my wrist. I say,' he called to the painter, 'am I allowed to move now?'

Claude let him stretch himself, but did not answer. He was busy brushing in the black velvet jacket. He drew back a step, looked at his work through half-closed eyes, then suddenly laughed out loud, as a memory flashed through his mind.

'I say, do you remember the time Pouillaud lit a lot of candles in old Lalubie's cupboard? I shall never forget the look on Lalubie's face when he went to get his books to start his lesson and found the thing illuminated! Five hundred lines for the whole class!'

Sandoz laughed so much he had to lie flat on the divan for a moment before he could take up the pose again.

'Oh, he was a one, Pouillaud!' he said when he was settled again. 'Funnily enough, he says in this morning's letter that Lalubie's getting married. To a nice girl, too, the old slave-driver! One of Gallisard the draper's girls, the little fair one, remember? The one we used to serenade!'

The flood-gates opened, and Claude and Sandoz poured out recollections in an endless stream, the one painting away at fever-pitch, the other facing the wall, talking with his back, his shoulders shaking with excitement.

First it was the school itself they talked about; the mouldering ex-convent stretching away up to the town ramparts; its two playgrounds with their huge plane-trees; the muddy pond covered with green slime in which they had learned to swim; the downstairs classrooms where the damp ran down the walls; the refectory that always reeked of cooking and washing-up water; the juniors' dormitory, known as 'the chamber of horrors', and the sick-bay with its gentle, soothing nuns in their black habits and white coifs! What a to-do there'd been when Sister Angèle, the one with the virginal face who played such havoc with the hearts of the seniors, ran away with Hermeline, the fat boy in the top form who was so much in love that he used deliberately to cut his fingers so as to be able to go up and have her dress them for him!

After the school, the staff came under review, a terrible, a grotesque, a lamentable cavalcade of ill-natured and long-suffering figures; the headmaster who ruined himself giving parties in order to marry off his daughters, two fine, well turned-out girls, the subjects of endless rude drawings and inscriptions scribbled on every wall in the school; the senior master, 'Snitcher', whose famous nose, like a culverin, made his presence obvious from afar when he stood in ambush behind classroom doors; the whole gang of junior masters, each one labelled with a scurrilous nickname: 'Rhadaman-thus', never known to smile; 'Machine-Oil', who made chair backs filthy by perpetually rubbing his head on them. Then there was 'Adèle-how-could-you?', the physics master, the notorious cuckold, known to ten generations of pupils by the name of his wife, caught, it was said, *flagrante delicto* in the arms of a cavalryman. There were others, lots of others, from 'Spontini', the ferocious usher with the Corsican dagger he liked to exhibit, stained with the blood of three of his cousins, and little Chantecaille, who was so easy-going that he let them smoke when they were out walking, down to 'Paraboulomenos' and 'Paralleluca', a kitchen-boy and a scullery-maid, both monstrosities, who were accused of sharing an idyll among the saucepans and the garbage.

Next they talked about the 'rags' and those ridiculous practical jokes the memory of which could still reduce them to helpless mirth. Oh, the morning when they lit the stove with the boots of the boy who used to supply the whole class with snuff, 'Bones-the-Day-Boy', otherwise known as 'Death-warmed-Up', he was so thin! And that winter evening when they stole the matches from the chapel to smoke dried chestnut leaves in their home-made pipes. It was Sandoz who did it, and he now admitted how scared he had been as he scrambled down from the choir in the dark. Then there was the day Claude tried roasting cockchafers in the bottom of his desk, to see if they were good to eat like people said, and filled the place with such dense, acrid smoke that the usher had dashed in with a water-jug, thinking the desk was on fire. The onion fields they had robbed when out on school walks, and the windows they had broken and thought themselves very smart if the damaged pane looked anything like a map in the atlas; Greek lessons printed in large letters on the blackboard and rattled off by all the dunces without the master discovering how they did it; the playground benches sawn off and carried like corpses round the pond, in a long procession, complete with dirges. This last affair had been a great joke. Dubuche, as the priest, had slipped into the pond when he tried to fill his cap with 'holy' water. But the best joke of all, and the funniest, was the time when Pouillaud tied all the dormitory chamber-pots to one long string and then in the morning—it was the last day of term—raced along the corridor and down three flights of stairs dragging this long trail of domestic china clanking and smashing itself to atoms in his wake!

Claude laughed so much that he had to stop painting.

'Oh yes, he was a little monster, Pouillaud! Did you say he'd written to you? What's he up to now?'

'Nothing at all!' replied Sandoz, getting back on to his cushions. 'That's the trouble. I never read such a damned silly letter. He's finishing his Law and then he's going to follow in his father's footsteps and be a solicitor. . . . He sounds like one already in his letter. You ought to see it! Typical stodgy bourgeois settling down in his rut!'

There was another silence, then he added:

'You know, Claude, we've been lucky in a way.'

That released another spate of happy memories, and both their hearts beat faster as they recalled the carefree days spent out of school, in the fresh air and the sunshine of Provence. While they were still in the junior school the three inseparables had developed a passion for long walks. Not even a half-holiday went by without their covering a good few miles and, as they grew older and more venturesome, their rambles covered all the surrounding district and even on occasion took them away from home for days at a time. They would spend the night wherever they happened to be, under a hollow rock, on the hot, flagged threshing-floor of a barn, with the new-made straw for bedding, or in some deserted hut where they would make themselves a couch of lavender and thyme. In their unthinking, boyish worship of trees and hills and streams, and in the boundless joy of being alone and free, they found an escape from the matter-of-fact world, and instinctively let themselves be drawn to the bosom of Nature.

As he was a boarder, Dubuche could only join these excursions during holidays. Besides, he could never cover the ground as they could; his were the leaden limbs and unwilling flesh of the diligent goody-goody. Claude and Sandoz never tired; every Sunday they would be up and one would be throwing pebbles at the other's bedroom shutters by four o'clock in the morning. In summer especially their dream was the Viorne, the mountain torrent that waters the low-lying meadows of Plassans. They could swim when they were scarcely twelve, and they loved to splash about in the deeper parts of the stream; they would spend whole days, stark naked, lying on the burning sand, then diving back into the water, endlessly grubbing for water-plants or watching for eels. They practically lived in the river, and the combination of clear water and sunshine seemed to prolong their childhood, so that even when they were already young men they still sounded like a trio of laughing urchins as they ambled back into Plassans on a sultry July evening after a day on the river. Game-shooting had been their next enthusiasm, game-shooting as practised where there is no game, as in Provence, and where it means tramping six leagues to bag half a dozen sparrows. They would often come back from a whole day's 'shooting' with nothing in their bags but some incautious bat, brought down when they were discharging their guns on the way back home. The memory of those country walks always brought tears to their eyes. They went along the long white roads once more, roads covered with dust like a thick fall of snow and ringing with the tramp of their heavy boots; they cut across the fields again and roamed for miles where the soil was rusty-red with iron deposits, and there was not a cloud in the sky, not a shadow, and nothing but a few stunted olive trees and the sparse foliage of almonds. They recalled their homecomings, the delicious sense of weariness, their boasting about having walked even farther than last time, the thrill it gave them to feel they were carried over the ground by sheer momentum, their bodies spurred into action and their minds lulled into numbness by some dreadful troopers' song.

Even in those days, Claude used to carry about with him, besides his pellets and his powder-flask, an album in which he would sketch bits of scenery, while Sandoz, too, always had a book of poetry in his pocket. They lived in a kind of fine, romantic frenzy of high-flown verses, barrack-room ribaldry, and odes poured out into the shimmering heat of the summer air. And when they found a brook and half a dozen willows to cast a patch of grey on the blinding earth, they would lose all sense of time, staying there till the stars were out, acting the plays they knew by heart, booming the heroes' parts, piping the parts of the queens and the ingénues. Those were the days when they left the sparrows in peace. That was how they had lived from the time they were fourteen, burning with enthusiasm for art and literature, isolated in their remote province amid the dreary philistinism of a small town. Victor Hugo's mighty settings where dream figures immeasurably larger than life stalked through an everlasting battle of antitheses, had carried them away by their epic sweep and sent them gesticulating to watch the sun go down behind ruins or to watch life go by in the false but superb lighting of a Romantic fifth act. Then Musset had come and over-whelmed them with his passion and his tears; they had felt their own hearts beat with his and a new, more human world had opened before them, conquering them through pity and the eternal cry of anguish they were to associate henceforth with every mortal thing. On the whole they were not over-discriminating, but swallowed the good with the de-testable, with the healthy gluttony of youth; such was their appetite for reading, so eager were they to admire, that they were often as thrilled by trash as by an acknowledged masterpiece.

It was, as Sandoz was now saying, that love for long country walks, that insatiable appetite for literature that had saved them from becoming as stolid as their fellows. They never set foot in a café, they professed a strong dislike for streets, where, they pretended, they pined away like eagles in a cage, while their contemporaries were already wearing out their elbows on café tables, playing cards for drinks. Provincial life, luring children early into its toils—the club habit, the local paper read to the last letter of the last advertisement, the everlasting game of dominoes, the same walk at the same time along the same avenue, the ultimate degradation of the brain ground down by its inescapable millstone—filled them with indignation, spurred them to protest, sent them clambering up the neighbouring hills in search of solitude, declaiming verses in the pouring rain, deliberately refusing shelter in their hatred of cities. They planned to camp on the banks of the Viorne, running wild and bathing all day, with five or six books, not more, to satisfy their needs. Women were banned, for they elevated their shyness and their inexperience into the austerity of boys who are above such things. For two years Claude was eaten up with love for a girl apprenticed to a local hatmaker; he followed her home, at a safe distance, every evening, but he was never bold enough to speak to her. Sandoz, too, had dreams he cherished, of damsels met on his travels, of handsome creatures springing to life in mysterious woods, being his for a day, then flitting away like shadows in the twilight. The one 'adventure' they did have they still regarded as a great joke. It consisted of serenading two young misses on the instruments they played in the school orchestra. Night after night they stood under the window, one blowing a clarinet, the other a cornet, rousing the entire neighbourhood with their cacophonous efforts until that night of nights when the girls' parents emptied every water-jug in the house over them.

They had been happy days, and the memory of them always brought them to the verge of tears amid their laughter. Just now the studio walls happened to be covered with a series of sketches Claude had made on a recent visit to the haunts of their boyhood. It made them feel that they had all around them the well-known landscapes, the bright blue sky above the rust-red earth. One sketch showed a stretch of plain with wave after wave of little grey olive trees rolling back to the irregular line of rosy hills on the skyline. Another showed the dried-up bed of the Viorne crossed by an ancient bridge white with dust, joining two sun-baked hillsides red as terra-cotta, on which all green things had withered in the drought. Farther along there was the Gorge des Infernets, a yawning chasm in the heart of a vast wilderness of shattered rocks, a stony, awe-inspiring desert stretching away to infinity. There was a host of other well-known places, too; the deep shady 'Valley of Repentance', fresh as a bunch of flowers among the burnt-up meadows; the 'Wood of the Three Gods', where the pine trees, green and glossy as varnish, shed tears of resin in the blazing sun; the Jas de Bouffan, white as an oriental mosque in the centre of its enormous fields that looked like lakes of blood. There were glimpses of dazzling white roads, of gullies where the heat seemed to raise blisters on the very pebbles, strips of thirsty sand greedily drinking up the last drops of the river, molehills, goat tracks, hills against the sky.

'Hello,' exclaimed Sandoz as he looked at one of the sketches. 'Where's this?'

Indignant, Claude waved his palette.

'What?' he cried. 'You don't remember? . . . We nearly broke our necks there! You must remember the day, with Dubuche, when we climbed up from Jaumegarde, and the rock was like glass. We had to claw our way up with our finger-nails, then half-way up we got stuck. When we did get to the top, we thought we'd cook some chops, and you and I nearly came to blows about it.'

Now Sandoz remembered. 'Oh yes! Yes! We were each to cook his own chop over a fire of rosemary twigs, and my twigs burnt too quickly, so you made fun of me, because the chop was being burnt to a cinder.'

They laughed loud and long over that incident. Then Claude, who had started painting again, remarked very solemnly:

'That's all over, my friend! No time for messing about now in this place.'

It was quite true. Since the dream of the three inseparables had come true and they had been able to meet in Paris and set about its conquest, they had found life incredibly hard. They had made a bold attempt to revive their long cross-country walks and on Sundays they would sometimes set out from the toll-gate at Fontainebleau, make their way through the spinneys at Verrières, push on as far as Bièvres, then through the woods at Bellevue and Meudon, and come back into Paris via Grenelle. But they said Paris spoilt them for rambling; so absorbed were they by their notion of conquest that they hardly ever strayed now beyond the city's pavements.

From Monday to Saturday Sandoz fretted and fumed in a gloomy corner of the office of the Registrar of Births for the Fifth Arrondissement, a thraldom he accepted solely for his mother's sake, although his hundred-and-fifty a month did not exactly keep her in luxury. Dubuche, anxious to reimburse the funds his parents had invested in him and his education, did odd jobs for architects as well as his work for the École des Beaux-Arts. Claude, thanks to his private income of a thousand francs, was a free man, though after sharing his funds with his friends he was often in sore straits at the end of the month. Fortunately, he was beginning to sell small canvases to old Malgras, an astute dealer, who gave him ten or twelve francs a time for them. He would have starved, however, rather than commercialize himself by doing bourgeois portraits, trumpery religious subjects, painting awnings for restaurants or signboards for midwives. When he had first returned to Paris he had had a huge studio in the Impasse des Bourdonnais; then, to save money, he had moved to the Quai de Bourbon. There he led a rough-and-ready existence disdaining everything but paint-ing. Sheer disgust had made him break with his family and he had also severed connection with his aunt, who kept a pork-shop in the Halles and, he thought, was making too good a thing of it. But in his heart of hearts he suffered at the thought of his mother being exploited and dragged into the gutter by men.

Abruptly he called to Sandoz:

'Have a care! You're slumping!'

But Sandoz swore he had cramp and jumped off the divan to stretch his legs. He was granted ten minutes' rest, during which they talked of other things. Claude was in a good mood now. When his work was going well he gradually warmed up and grew talkative, though he painted with clenched teeth, fuming to himself as soon as he felt nature was escaping him again. So Sandoz had hardly taken up the pose again before Claude was busily painting and providing an uninterrupted flow of talk.

'Now we're getting somewhere! And you're going to cut quite a figure, the way things are shaping. . . . Ah, the old fools! Just let them refuse this one! I'm much harder on my own work than they are on theirs, believe me. When I say a thing's good, it means a hell of a lot more than the opinion of all the selection committees in the world. . . . You know the one I did of the Halles, two kids on top of the piled-up vegetables . . . well, I've scrapped it.* No kidding. It just refused to come, so I gave it up. . . . Got more involved than I bargained for . . . bitten off more than I could chew again. . . . I'll go back to it one day, see if I don't, when I feel I can do it. . . . I'll show 'em yet. . . . Give 'em something to lay 'em out flat!'

And he flung out his arm in a gesture to sweep aside a crowd. Then, squeezing a tube of blue on to his palette, he grinned to himself as he wondered what old Belloque would have thought of his painting. Old Belloque, his first drawing master, the one-armed ex-army captain who used to impart the subtleties of shading to his pupils at the Plassans Museum! Had not Berthou, famous for his 'Nero at the

Circus', in whose studio he had worked for six months, told him scores of times that he would never do anything worth while? He regretted them now, those six months feeling his way like an idiot and doing those stupid exercises under the iron rule of a despot with whom he could never possibly have seen eye to eye. It had set him for ever against working at the Louvre. He would rather have cut off his hand, he said, than have gone back and spoilt his eye turning out another of those copies which prevent you from ever seeing anything as it really is. What was Art, after all, if not simply giving out what you have inside you? Didn't it all boil down to sticking a female in front of you and painting her as you *feel* she is? Wasn't a bunch of carrots, yes, a bunch of carrots, studied directly and painted simply, personally, as you see it yourself, as good as any of the run-of-the-mill, made-to-measure École des Beaux-Arts stuff, painted with tobacco-juice? The day was not far off when one solitary, original carrot might be pregnant with revolution! That was why he was now content to go and paint at Boutin's, a free studio run by an ex-model in the Rue de la Huchette. Once he had paid his twenty francs to the treasurer, he could go there, sit in his corner and draw all the nudes he wanted, men, women, enough for an orgy. And draw he did, for all he was worth, spurning meat and drink, working like a madman in an endless struggle with nature, while his superior fellow-students accused him of laziness and ignorance and boasted of their own achievements because they were satisfied with copying noses and mouths under the watchful eye of a master.

'Look,' he said, 'when one of those teacher's pets can knock together a torso like this fellow, he can come and tell me, and then I'll talk to him.'

He pointed with his brush to a nude study hung on the wall near the door. It was a superb piece of work, drawn with a master touch. Alongside it were other equally admirable pieces; the feet of a little girl, of exquisite delicacy; the belly of a woman, with a texture like satin, pulsating with life. In his rare moments of contentment, he was proud of his handful of studies, the only ones that really satisfied him, the ones that revealed a painter remarkably gifted, but impeded by sudden, inexplicable fits of impotence.

Boldly brushing in the velvet jacket, and at the same time working up the fury of his intransigence, he went on talking, almost shouting, to Sandoz:

'A lot of cheapjack dabblers, that's all they are! Every one of 'em either a fool or a knave, ready to pander to the bad taste of the general public. Not one of 'em worth his salt. Not a man among 'em bold enough to smack the philistines clean between the eyes! Not one! . . . Look at old Ingres,* now. You know, he makes me feel sick, the way he smears his paint on! Well, I still take my hat off to the old devil. Know why? Because he had guts enough to do what *he* wanted and thrust that thundering good drawing of his down the throats of the idiots who now claim to understand him! . . . After him, there are only two, two, do you hear? of any consequence at all: Delacroix and Courbet.* The rest are a gang of sharpers . . . Delacroix, the old Romantic lion, there's a figure for you! There's a decorator who put some warmth in his colouring. And look at his energy! He'd have covered every wall in Paris if he'd had to; his palette simply boiled over. Boiled over, that's what it did. Oh, I know he painted a lot of fantastical stuff, but I don't mind that, I even get a bit of a kick out of it. Besides, it was just what was wanted to set fire to the École and all its works. . . . Then there's Courbet, a sound workman if ever there was one, the only real painter of the century, one with the true classical technique. And not one of the numskulls spotted it. They howled themselves hoarse about "profanity" and "realism", when the only realism there was was in the subjects. The vision was the same as the old masters', the treatment simply carried on the tradition of our accepted museum pieces. . . . But both Courbet and Delacroix arrived just at the right moment. They both took a ·real step forward. But now! Now! . . .'

He stopped and stepped back to look at his work, and was lost for a moment in contemplation. Then he went on:

'Now we need something else. . . . Just exactly what I don't really know! If I did, and if I *could* . . . I should be very smart . . . and I should be the one person to be reckoned with! But I do feel that the grand, Romantic pageantry of Delacroix is just about played out, and Courbet's "black" painting is already beginning to feel stuffy and reek of a musty studio where the sun never enters. . . . Do you see what I mean? Perhaps that's what we need now, sunlight, open air, something bright and fresh, people and things as seen in real daylight. I don't know, but it seems to me that that's our sort of painting, the sort of painting our generation should produce and look at.'

Words failed him again; he began to stammer in his unsuccessful attempt to express the first vague stirrings of the future he could feel within himself. While he finished feverishly brushing in the black velvet jacket, there was a long silence.

Sandoz had listened to him without dropping the pose and now, still with his back turned, as if addressing the wall, he answered in a dreamy voice:

'We don't know, that's the trouble. We don't know . . . but we ought to know. . . . Every time a teacher has wanted to impose a truth on me, I've been filled with revolt and defiance. Either he's deceiving himself, I've thought, or he's deceiving me. Their ideas simply exasperate me. . . . Truth must surely be broader and deeper than that. . . . Wouldn't it be wonderful to devote one's whole life to one work and put everything into it, men, animals, everything under the sun! But not in the order prescribed by philosophy text-books, not according to the idiotic hierarchy so dear to our personal pride, but in the mighty universal flow of a life in which we should be a mere accident, completed, or explained by a passing dog or a stone on the roadway . . . the mighty All, in a word, in working order, exactly as it is, not all ups and not all downs, not too dirty and not too clean, but just as it is. . . . Science, of course, is what poets and novelists are going to have to turn to; science is their only possible source these days. But there you

are again! What are they to get out of it? How are they to
keep up with it? As soon as I think of that, my mind
goes blank. If I knew, if only I knew, I'd turn out a series
of books that would give the world something to think
about!'

He, too, fell silent. The previous winter he had published
his first book, a series of pleasant sketches of life in Plassans,
in which a harsh note here and there was the only indication
of the author's revolt, of his passion for truth and power.
Since then he had been groping his doubtful way through
the mass of still confused notions that besieged his brain.
He had started by toying with the idea of a gigantic
undertaking and had projected an 'Origins of the Universe'
in three phases: the creation, established according to scientific research; the story of how the human race came to play
its part in the sequence of living beings; the future, in which
beings succeed beings, completing the creation of the world
through the ceaseless activity of living matter. He had cooled
off, however, when he began to realize the hazardous nature
of the hypotheses of this third phase, and was now trying
to find a more limited, a more human setting for his
ambitious plan.

'The ideal would be,' said Claude, after a while, 'to see
everything and paint everything. To have acres of walls to
cover, to decorate the railway stations, the market-halls, the
town-halls, whatever they put up when architects have at
last learnt some common sense! All we'll need then will be
a good head and some strong muscles, for it isn't subjects
we'll be short of. . . . Think of it, Pierre! Life as it's lived
in the streets, the life of rich and poor, in market-places,
at the races, along the boulevards, and down back streets in
the slums; work of every kind in full swing; human emotions
revived and brought into the light of day; the peasants, the
farmyards and the countryside. . . . Think of it! Then they'll
see, then I'll show 'em what I can do! It makes my hands
tingle only to think of it! Modern life in all its aspects,
that's the subject! Frescoes as big as the Panthéon! A series
of paintings that'll shatter the Louvre!'

Claude and Sandoz were never together for long before they reached this pitch of excitement; they goaded each other into it in their obsession with glory and success. Behind it all there were such flights of youthful enthusiasm, such a passion for hard work that they often smiled themselves at their ambitious dreams, though they found them a cheering source of flexibility and vigour.

Backing away from his easel, Claude leaned up against the wall, relaxed. Sandoz, tired of posing, got up from the divan and went across to him. Without a word they both stood looking at the picture. The man in the black velvet jacket was now completely brushed in; his hand, which was farther advanced than the rest, showed up well against the grass, while the dark patch of his back stood out with such force that the two little shapes in the background, the two women tumbling each other in the sunshine, looked as if they had withdrawn far away into the shimmering light of the forest clearing; the big reclining female figure, however, was still only faintly sketched in, still little more than a shape desired in a dream, Eve rising from the earth smiling but sightless, her eyes still unopened.

'Tell me,' said Sandoz, 'what are you going to call it?'

' "Open Air",' was the curt reply.

Such a title sounded over-technical to Sandoz who, being a writer, often found himself being tempted to introduce literature into painting.

' "Open Air"! But it doesn't mean anything!'

'It doesn't need to mean anything. A man and a couple of women resting in the woods, in the sunshine. What more do you want? Seems to me there's enough there to make a masterpiece.'

Then, throwing back his head, he added between his teeth:

'Damn it! It's still too dark! Delacroix, that. Can't get away from him. And the hand there, look at it. That's Courbet, pure Courbet! . . . That's what's wrong with all of us, we're still wallowing in Romanticism. We dabbled in it too long when we were kids, and now we're in it up to the neck. What we need is a thorough scrubbing!'

Sandoz made a gesture of despair. He, too, complained that he had been born 'at the confluence of Hugo and Balzac'. Still, Claude was satisfied, happy and excited at the result of a good sitting. If Sandoz could let him have two or three more Sundays like this, his man in black velvet would be finished, really finished. Today he'd done enough, he said, and that made them both laugh, for generally he nearly killed his models, and only released them when they fainted clean away from fatigue. Today it was he who felt ready to drop; his legs were tired and he had not had a decent meal all day. The cuckoo-clock was singing five as he fell on the remains of his breakfast roll and devoured it. Dog-tired, breaking off bits with his trembling fingers and gulping them down unchewed, he went back and stood in front of his picture, so completely obsessed that he was not even aware he was eating.

'Five o'clock,' said Sandoz, stretching his limbs. 'Time we had some dinner . . . and here's Dubuche on the dot.'

There was a rap on the door and in came Dubuche. He was a thick-set young fellow, dark, respectable-looking, with puffy features, cropped hair and, for his age, a heavy moustache. He shook hands with Sandoz and Claude, then stopped, nonplussed, in front of the picture. Such unbridled painting brought him up with a jolt; it disturbed his sense of balance, it jarred with his respect for established formulas; usually it was only his old friendship for Claude that made him keep his criticism to himself. But this time, it was plain to see, his whole being rebelled.

'Well, what's up? Don't you like it?' asked Sandoz, who had seen his reaction.

'Oh yes, yes. . . . Nice bit of painting. But . . . '

'Come on, out with it! What's worrying you?'

'It's . . . it's the man. . . . Fully dressed and the women naked. It's so . . . so . . . unusual!'

At once the other two burst out laughing. Weren't there scores of pictures in the Louvre composed exactly like this? Besides, if it was unusual now, it jolly soon wouldn't be. Who cared a twopenny damn for the public anyhow?

Unperturbed by the vehemence of his friends' retorts, Dubuche answered quietly:

'The public won't understand that. . . . They'll think it's just smutty. . . . And it *is* smutty.'

'Philistine!' cried the furious Claude. 'A rare old die-hard you're getting to be since you went to the Beaux-Arts. You used to be a reasonable human being!'

This, the stock rejoinder to any of Dubuche's remarks since he went to study at the École des Beaux-Arts, together with the disturbingly violent turn the discussion had taken, caused him to beat a retreat, but not without some parting shots at painters in general. One thing was quite certain, the painters at the Beaux-Arts were a fine collection of numskulls, but for architects, well, the situation was rather different. Where else could he go to study architecture, he'd like to know? He had to go to the Beaux-Arts, it was the only place he *could* go to. But that didn't mean he wasn't going to have ideas of his own, later. As he said this he put on the most revolutionary air he could muster.

'Good,' said Sandoz. 'Now you've made your excuses, let's go and have some dinner.'

But Claude had automatically picked up his brush and set to work again. The woman's face looked all wrong somehow in relation to the man, so now, in a moment of impatience, he was drawing a sharp line round it, to fix it in what he now thought was its proper place.

'Are you coming?' Sandoz repeated.

'In a minute, I'm busy. What's the hurry, anyhow? . . . Just let me finish this, and I'm with you.'

Shaking his head, Sandoz added, gently, for fear of exasperating him even more:

'It's a mistake to stick at it like that, Claude. . . . You're tired, you're hungry, and all you're going to do is spoil it again like you did last time.'

An irritated gesture from Claude, and he said no more. It was the usual story: Claude never knew when to stop working, he let himself be carried away by the desire for immediate certitude, the urgency of proving to himself that this really was his masterpiece. Now, after a momentary feeling of satisfaction with the sitting, he was being assailed by doubt and despair. Ought he to have given so much prominence to the velvet jacket? Was he going to be able to find the note he wanted to give the nude figure of the woman? And he would rather have died on the spot than not have the answer at once. He whisked the drawing of Christine's head from the portfolio in which he had hidden it, and began comparing his picture with the document he had copied direct from nature.

'Hello!' exclaimed Dubuche, 'where did you draw that? Who is it?'

Claude, startled by the question, made no reply; then, without any compunction, although he usually told them everything, he lied, overcome by a strange sense of reserve, a delicate feeling that he wanted to keep his adventure to himself.

'Do you hear? Who is it?' the architect insisted.

'Oh, nobody. A model.'

'A model! Really? Very young, isn't she? Not bad either. . . . You must let me have her address. . . . Not for myself, for a sculptor I know who's looking around for a Psyche. Is it here, with the rest?'

And Dubuche turned to a patch of the studio wall where addresses of models were chalked up at all angles. Women in particular left their 'cards' there, in sprawling, childish hands: 'Zoé Piédefer, 7 Rue Campagne-Première', a big brunette, now inclined to sag round the middle, cut clean across little 'Flore Beauchamp, 32, Rue de Laval', and 'Judith Vaquez, 69 Rue du Rocher', a Jewess; two nice, fresh girls, though both a little on the skinny side.

'I say, have you her address?' Dubuche repeated.

Claude was furious.

'For God's sake be quiet!' he bellowed. 'How should I know her address? . . . And stop making a damned nuisance of yourself when somebody's working!'

Sandoz had not spoken. Claude's outburst had startled him at first, but now he smiled. He was subtler than

Dubuche, to whom he gave a knowing wink as they both turned on Claude. Beg your pardon. Sorry, I'm sure. If Monsieur wanted to keep her for his own private use, they would not dream of asking Monsieur if they might borrow her. What a rascal, treating himself to beauties like this! Who would have thought it now? And where had he picked her up? In a low dive in Montmartre, or in the gutter in the Place Maubert?

Claude, whose irritation increased with his embarrassment, could contain himself no longer.

'Don't be such fools!' he said. 'Don't be such fools! . . . And stop it, anyhow, I can't bear it just now!'

His voice sounded suddenly so different that the other two stopped at once, while he, after scraping off the head of his nude figure, drew it afresh and painted it in again after the drawing of Christine, though his hand was feverish, uncertain and often clumsy. From the head he went on to the breasts, which as yet were barely sketched in. This keyed him up even more, for, chaste as he was, he had a passion for the physical beauty of women, an insane love for nudity desired but never possessed, but was powerless to satisfy himself or to create enough of the beauty he dreamed of enfolding in an ecstatic embrace. The women he hustled out of his studio he adored in his pictures. He caressed them, did them violence even, and shed tears of despair over his failures to make them either sufficiently beautiful or sufficiently alive.

'Give me ten minutes, will you?' he asked. 'I just want to go over these shoulders ready for tomorrow, and then we can be off.'

Knowing that it was useless to try to prevent him from slaving away, Dubuche and Sandoz resigned themselves. The former lit his pipe and flung himself on the divan. He was the only smoker of the three. The other two had never really taken to tobacco; they still felt sick at the smell of a good strong cigar. Lying flat on his back, gazing aimlessly through the puffs of smoke, he began rambling on in his monotonous way, about himself. What a place Paris was, the way you had to work yourself to the bone to get anywhere at all! He talked about his fifteen months' apprenticeship with the famous Dequersonnière, ex-Grand Prix, now architect to the Government, Officer of the Legion of Honour, Member of the Institut, whose masterpiece, the Church of St. Mathieu, was a cross between a jelly-mould and an Empire clock; a decent sort, at bottom, whom Dubuche made fun of from time to time, though he still shared his respect for the old-established formulas. Without the other students, however, he would never have learned very much at the studio in the Rue du Four, where the *patron* only made fleeting appearances three times a week. They were a tough lot and they had led him a pretty hard life when he was a newcomer, but they had at least taught him how to make a mount and how to draw and wash a plan. The times he'd lunched off a roll and a cup of chocolate in order to pay his twenty-five francs fee, the paper he'd spoilt, tinkering away at his drawing, the hours he'd spent at home poring over his books before he'd sat for the Beaux-Arts entrance exam! Even then he'd nearly failed, in spite of his tremendous effort. It was imagination he lacked. In the drawing test, a caryatid and a summer dining-room, he had come out bottom. At the oral, it is true, he had fared better, with his logarithms, geometry, and history, as he was particularly keen on the scientific side. Now he was at the Beaux-Arts as a second-class pupil, he was having to wear himself to a shadow to pull off a first-class diploma. A hell of a life! Sort of thing that might go on for ever!

On he went, sprawling all over the cushions, puffing away at his pipe:

'The lectures you have to attend, perspective, descriptive geometry, stereotomy, building, history of art! And the reams of notes you're expected to make! . . . Then there's the monthly architecture test, sometimes a draft, sometimes a working drawing. No time for playing around if you want to get through your exams decently, especially when you've to do as I have and earn your keep out of school hours. . . . Honestly, it's killing. . . .'

A cushion had slipped off the divan. He picked it up with his feet.

'Still, I've been lucky, I suppose. I know plenty of fellows on the look-out for jobs who can't get a thing. Day before yesterday I came across an architect who works for a big contractor. Never met an architect who knew so little about his job. He'd be useless as a mason's labourer and can't make head or tail of a drawing if he sees one! He pays me twenty-five sous an hour, and I sort out his houses for him. . . . Couldn't have been more convenient. Mother'd just written to say she was stony again. Poor mother! The money I owe to that woman!'

As Dubuche was obviously talking for his own benefit, chewing over his usual ideas, his everlasting preoccupation with making money, Sandoz was not taking the trouble to listen. He had opened the little window, finding the heat in the studio almost overpowering, and was sitting down looking out over the roof. After a time he did break in on the architect.

'Coming to dinner on Thursday, Dubuche? . . . The others are all coming, Fagerolles, Mahoudeau, Jory, Gagnière.'

Every Thursday a whole gang of young men used to meet at Sandoz's flat, friends from Plassans, others they had made in Paris, all revolutionaries, every one animated by the same passion for art.

'Next Thursday? I don't think so,' Dubuche replied. 'I have to go and call on some people; they're giving a dance.'

'And what do you expect to get out of that, a handsome wife with a nice fat dowry?'

'I could do worse, I expect. That's quite an idea!'

He tapped his pipe in his left palm to empty it, and then suddenly announced:

'I was forgetting! . . . I've had a letter from Pouillaud.'

'You too! . . . He's certainly been pouring his heart out by the look of it. . . . Pity he's gone to the bad as he has.'

'What do you mean? He'll carry on his father's business and get through his money in comfort at Plassans. What's wrong with that? I always said he'd teach us all a lesson, even though he did play the fool. . . . He was a one, was Pouillaud!'

Sandoz, furious, was just about to retort when a despairing oath from Claude cut him short. Since he had insisted on going on working, Claude had never opened his lips; he did not even seem to notice the presence of his two friends.

'To hell with the thing! Missed it again! . . . I'm hopeless, I must be! Never will be any good!'

In his blind fury he was about to put his fist through his canvas, but his friends restrained him just in time. It was childish, they said, to flare up like that. What good would it do him to ruin his work and regret it ever afterwards? Claude, quivering with wrath, made no reply, but stood glaring at the picture, his eyes burning with the unspeakable torture of his impotence. His hands had refused once more to produce anything clear or lifelike; the woman's bosom he had been painting was simply a dauby mess of dull colour, the flesh he worshipped and had dreamed of reproducing with such brilliance was drab and lifeless. He could not even set it in its proper plane. What could be wrong with his brain that he almost thought he could hear it snap under the strain of his futile efforts? Could there be something wrong with his eyes that impaired his vision? Were his hands no longer his, since they refused to carry out his intentions? What drove him to distraction was the infuriating thought of the hereditary something, he did not know what, that sometimes made creation a sheer pleasure and at other times reduced him to such complete sterility that he forgot the very basics of drawing. It was like being swept up into some sickening vortex and filled with the urge to create while everything was being swirled away from one—pride in one's work, hopes of success, the very meaning of one's life!

'Listen, Claude,' said Sandoz, 'we're not blaming you, but it's half-past six and we're both famished. . . . Be a good fellow and come out with us.'

But Claude was busy cleaning a corner of his palette. He squeezed out more colours and replied, in a voice like thunder:

'No!'

For ten whole minutes nobody uttered a word, while the artist, beside himself, struggled with his painting. The other two sat there, anxious and downcast, wondering what they could do to calm him. There was a knock on the door. It was the architect who got up to open it.

'Hello! If it isn't Malgras!'

The dealer was a big man with white, cropped hair and a red face mottled with purple which, combined with the old, very dirty green greatcoat in which he was enveloped, made him look like a down-at-heel cabby.

'I happened to be passing,' he said in his husky, drinker's voice, 'when I spotted monsieur at the window, so I thought I'd come up. . . .'

He stopped short, receiving no response from the painter who, with a gesture of impatience, had turned firmly towards his canvas. Otherwise, Malgras was in no way perturbed; quite at his ease, he just stood there and ran his bloodshot eyes over the unfinished picture. He appraised it candidly in a sentence compounded of irony and sympathy.

'There's a creation for you!'

Then, as nobody said a word, he ambled quietly round the studio, looking at the walls.

Under his thick shell of dirt, old Malgras was a smart dealer with a taste and a flair for good painting. He never wasted his time on second-raters, but instinctively went straight for the original, though still unrecognized painters whose future his flamboyant, drunkard's nose could sniff out from afar. What was more, he drove a very hard bargain and would stop at nothing to acquire a coveted picture dirt cheap. After that he would be satisfied with a relatively honest profit, twenty per cent or at most thirty, as he ran his business on a basis of quick returns, never buying anything in the morning without knowing which of his customers would buy it in the evening. As a liar, he was superb.

Near the door, he stood for a long while contemplating the nude studies painted at Boutin's; his eyes lit up with

the pleasure of a connoisseur, though he kept them carefully
shaded under his heavy lids. He had talent, great talent, and
a real feeling for life, this young maniac, if only he wouldn't
waste his time on things that nobody wanted!

Those little girl's legs, that woman's body, they were a
delight to look at, but they wouldn't sell. He had already
made his choice—that little landscape, a bit of the Plassans
country, both forceful and delicate, but he pretended not to
be looking at it. Then, after a time, he went up to it and
said, in his off-hand way:

'What's this? Oh, one of the little things you did in
Provence. . . . Too crude. I still haven't sold the last two.'

Then he rambled on lackadaisically:

'You may refuse to believe me, Monsieur Lantier, but
they just don't sell, they just don't. At home I've a room
crammed with that sort of thing, so full that I'm afraid
I'll put my foot through something every time I turn
round. I can't carry on like that, you know, I really can't.
I shall have to sell them off cheap, and that means the
poor-house. . . . Now you know me, Monsieur Lantier. You
know my heart's bigger than my pocket and there's nothing
I like better than to oblige young men of talent like yourself.
And *you* have talent, no doubt about it, and don't I keep
telling 'em you have? But they won't bite. Believe it or not,
they just won't bite!'

He piled up the emotion very cleverly, then, with the
impulse of someone who cannot resist extravagance, added:

'Ah well, I can't go away empty-handed. . . . How much
for this little thing?'

Claude, angry and still very agitated, went on painting
and did not even look round as he snapped out:

'Twenty francs.'

'Twenty francs! You're mad! You let me have the others
at ten francs a time. . . . I'll give you eight, take it or leave
it.'

Usually Claude gave way at once. He had no patience
with bargaining and at heart he was only too glad to make
a little money. But this time he stood firm and told the

dealer to his face what he thought about him; to which Malgras replied in kind, stripped him of all his talent, cursed him roundly, and called him an ungrateful young puppy. Then, taking out of his pocket, one at a time, three five-franc pieces, he pitched them one after the other on to the table where they fell chinking among the dirty crockery.

'One, two, three! . . . and that's the last, understand! There's one too many already. But you'll pay it back; I'll knock it off something else, you see if I don't. . . . Fifteen francs for that bit of a thing! You'll be sorry for this, my lad! You'll wish you'd never done it.'

Claude was exhausted. He let the old dealer take down the picture himself, and it disappeared as if by magic into the green greatcoat. Had he slipped it into some special pocket, or tucked it away under the lapel? Wherever it was, it did not show.

Having worked his trick, Malgras, suddenly calm, made as if to go, then turned back and said good-naturedly:

'Look, Lantier, I want a lobster. . . . Can you manage one? It's the least you can do, surely, after skinning me like this. Good, I'll provide the lobster, you'll do me a nice still-life and you can keep it for your trouble and eat it with your friends. How's that? Agreed?'

At this proposal, Sandoz and Dubuche, who had been taking everything in, burst into such peals of laughter that Malgras had to laugh with them. Oh, these good-for-nothing painters! Starving, every one of them. What would they do, the lazy spongers, if old Malgras didn't show up now and again with a nice leg of lamb or a fine fresh brill, or a lobster complete with bunch of parsley?

'I get my lobster then, Lantier? . . . Good. . . . Many thanks.'

He was back again in front of the big canvas. He gave a smile of mocking admiration, then took his leave, repeating:

'There's a creation for you!'

Claude would have picked up palette and brushes again, but his legs gave way beneath him and his arms dropped heavily to his sides as if bound to his body by some irresistible force. He staggered blindly across to his half-formed picture and, through the dreary silence that followed Malgras's departure, he stammered:

'No, impossible! . . . I'm finished! . . . That swine's finished me!'

The cuckoo had just called seven o'clock, which meant that he had worked for eight solid hours with nothing to eat but a crust, without a moment's rest, on his feet the whole time and trembling with fever. Now the sun was going down, and the studio was filling with shadows, imparting a feeling of overpowering melancholy to the end of the day. When the light filtered away like this after a bout of fruitless labour, it felt as if the sun had disappeared for ever and taken with it all the life and gaiety and harmony of colours.

'Come on, Claude,' begged Sandoz, moved almost to tears by his friend's despair. 'Come and have some dinner.'

'Yes, come and have some dinner,' repeated Dubuche, and added: 'You'll get it all sorted out in the morning.'

For a time Claude refused to give in. He stood riveted to the floor, deaf to their friendly voices, in grim determination. What he wanted to do now that his fingers were so numb they could not grip the brush, he did not know, but he refused to acknowledge his impotence, burning with the mad desire to do something, to create something in spite of it. Even if he did nothing, he was going to stay where he was, he was not going to retreat before his difficulties. Finally, a tremor ran through his body like some long sob, and he made his move. Seizing a broad palette knife, with one slow, deliberate stroke he scraped off the head and shoulders of the reclining woman. It was murder he was committing, total obliteration in a mess of pulpy, muddy pigment. So all that remained, stretched out beside the man in the powerful jacket while in the background two lively female figures rolled and frolicked on the bright green turf, was a naked woman's body with neither head nor shoulders, a mutilated trunk, a vague, corpselike shape, the dead flesh of the beauty of his dreams.

Dubuche and Sandoz were already clattering down the wooden stairs. Claude went after them, suffering unspeakable torture at the thought of leaving his picture as it was, disfigured by an ugly, gaping wound.

CHAPTER 3

THE week had started with disaster. Claude was plunged in one of his fits of doubt which made him hate painting with the hatred of a betrayed lover who curses his false mistress though tortured by the knowledge that he loves her still. On Thursday, after three horrible days of fruitless, solitary struggle, he was so disheartened that by eight o'clock in the morning he had walked out of his studio, slamming the door behind him and swearing he would never touch a brush again as long as he lived. Whenever he succumbed to a fit of depression he knew there was only one way of throwing it off: by getting away from himself, either by having a good healthy argument with some of his friends or, better still, by walking it off, tramping the streets of Paris till the heat and the smell of battle that rises from their paving stones had given him heart again.

This Thursday he was dining as usual with Sandoz, who was at home to his friends every Thursday evening. But what was he going to do until then? He could not bear the idea of being alone with his gnawing despair, and would have gone straight to look up Sandoz if he had not remembered that the latter would be engaged at his office. He wondered about Dubuche, then hesitated, as their old friendliness had been cooler of late. The brotherly sympathy in times of stress had weakened; Dubuche had other ambitions now, and Claude was not unaware of a certain obtuseness, not to say hostility, in his attitude. Still, whom else could he turn to? So he decided to take the risk and made for the Rue Jacob where the architect occupied a box of a room on the sixth floor of a big cold house.

Claude had already reached the second floor when the concierge shrieked up to him that Monsieur Dubuche was out and had not been in all night. He was so staggered by this outrageous announcement—the idea of Dubuche having an 'affair'!—that it was some moments before he emerged on to the street again. This was a stroke of ill-luck he had not bargained for. What should he do now? Hovering on the corner of the Rue de Seine, wondering which way to go next, he suddenly remembered that Dubuche had talked of working all night at Duquersonnière's studio, the night before the last day for sending in drawings for the Beaux-Arts Diploma competition. So he turned up towards the Rue du Four in the direction of the studio. Up to now he had always avoided going there for Dubuche, because of the jibes and cat-calls which always greeted outsiders. But today, emboldened by his agonizing solitude, he cast shyness to the winds and made straight for it, ready to face all manner of abuse to gain a companion in his troubles.

The studio was at the back of an old, weather-beaten building in the narrowest part of the Rue du Four. To reach it he had to go through two filthy courtyards into a third, across which had been built a sort of hut of lath and plaster, formerly occupied by a packing-agent. From outside all that could be seen through the four big windows was the bare, whitewashed ceiling, for the lower panes had been rubbed with whitening.

Claude went in, closed the door behind him, but stopped where he was, on the threshold. It was a huge place, with rows of students sitting at four wide, double tables set at right-angles to the windows and cluttered with damp sponges, paint-pots, jars of water, iron candlesticks and the wooden boxes in which the students left their white overalls, compasses and colours. In one corner, which was obviously never swept out, stood a large, rusty stove and the remains of last winter's coke. On the wall at the other end, between a pair of hand-towels, hung a big zinc water-cistern. The walls themselves, in this vast, bare, unkempt barn of a place, afforded a remarkable spectacle. Around their upper half ran shelves loaded with a nondescript collection of plaster casts; the lower half was hidden behind a barricade of drawing boards strapped together in bundles and a forest of T-squares and set squares; while the spaces which were left uncovered had gradually been filled up with drawings and scribblings, like scum splashed over the margins of an ever-open book. These were caricatures of people, sketches of unmentionable objects, expressions to make a gendarme blench; there were maxims, calculations, and addresses, the whole outshone by the plain, laconic statement chalked up in big letters in the place of honour: 'On the seventh of June Gorju said, "To hell with Rome": signed, Godemard.'*

Claude was welcomed by a sort of general growl, the growl of wild beasts disturbed in their lair, and he stood in amazement at the sight of the place on the morning after 'tumbril night', as the architecture students call their last night of work for their diploma. Since the previous evening the entire studio, sixty students, had been shut up in this place, the ones who were not competing, the 'slaves', giving a hand to the ones who were behind with their drawings and trying to squeeze a whole week's work into twelve hours. At midnight they had feasted on cold meats and cheap wine. About one a.m., for dessert, they had sent out for three ladies from a neighbouring brothel. And so, without interrupting the work, the feast had developed into a Roman orgy thinly veiled in tobacco smoke. The last traces of it were still in evidence, strewn about the floor, greasy papers, broken bottles, sinister little pools now slowly sinking into the boards, while the whole place reeked of a mixture of burnt-out candles, the pungent musk used by the ladies, cold sausage, and wine.

'Outside! Outside! . . . What an idiot! . . . What's he after? . . . Who is this dummy? . . . Outside!' they bawled, like a lot of savages.

Claude, somewhat daunted by the outburst, wavered for a moment, wondering what to do. But by the time they had reached the refined stage of seeing who could bring out the most disgusting epithets, he had rallied and was just about to retaliate when Dubuche recognized him and blushed furiously, for he hated to be involved in situations of this kind. He was ashamed of Claude, and received his own share of jeers as he rushed up to him, spluttering with rage:

'How could you? ... I told you never to come inside! ... Wait for me in the yard.'

As he backed out, Claude was nearly bowled over by a small handcart which two bearded giants were just rushing into the yard. This was the 'tumbril' to which last night's work owed its name and to which for the past week the students whose outside jobs had made them behind with their studio work had been referring when they groaned they were 'booked for the tumbril'. Now it was here, there was pandemonium. It was a quarter to nine, just time to get to the Beaux-Arts. The studio emptied in a general stampede; everybody elbowing his way out with his mounted drawing; the ones who wanted to hang back and put on the odd finishing touch were soon hustled out with the rest. In less than five minutes all the drawings were piled up in the cart, and the two bearded giants, the most junior members of the studio, harnessed between the shafts, raced away with their load while the rest of the mob streamed after them, shouting and pushing behind. They roared through the other two yards like a river in spate and poured out into the roadway, flooding the street with their din.

Claude, too, was with them, running alongside Dubuche, who brought up the rear, very annoyed because he had not been able to spend another quarter of an hour to finish tinting his drawing.

'What are you doing afterwards?'

'Oh, I have a whole host of things to do today.'

Discouraged, realizing that his friend was not to be detained, Claude answered reluctantly.

'I'll leave you to it then. ... You'll be at Sandoz's tonight, I expect.'

'Well, yes. If I'm not asked to stay to dinner elsewhere.'

They were both getting out of breath. The mob was keeping up a goodish pace and, for the fun of prolonging its racket, was going the longest way round. At the bottom of the Rue du Four it had swept across the Place Gozlin and dashed into the Rue de l'Échaudé. In front, the handcart, pushed and pulled with increasing vigour, bumped madly over the uneven pavings giving its load of drawings a dreadful shaking; behind it, the students racing hell-for-leather forced everyone else to stand well out of the way to avoid being run down, while tradesmen stood open-mouthed in their shop doorways, thinking revolution had broken out. The entire neighbourhood was roused. In the Rue Jacob the din and confusion reached such a pitch that some people closed their shutters. As they turned at last into the Rue Bonaparte, one fair-haired youngster scooped up a little servant-girl who stood gaping on the pavement and carried her along, a straw on the waters.

'I'll say goodbye then,' said Claude. 'See you tonight.'

'See you tonight.'

Completely breathless, Claude broke away at the end of the Rue des Beaux-Arts. The others surged into the open forecourt of the School. He watched them until he had got his breath again, and then made his way back to the Rue de Seine. His bad luck was getting worse; it was clearly not intended that he should lead any of his friends astray that morning. He walked slowly up the street and on as far as the Place du Panthéon, without any particular plans in his mind. Then, as he happened to be so near, he thought he might just as well call on Sandoz at his office. It would be ten minutes well spent. To his amazement he was told that M. Sandoz had asked for a day off, to attend a funeral. He knew what that meant. Sandoz always made the same excuse when he wanted to do a good day's work at home. He had already turned in that direction when a sudden fellow-feeling for an artist absorbed in his work stopped him in his tracks. It would be a crime to go and disturb an honest workman, to break in on him with a tale of discouragement just when he was probably making splendid progress himself.

Resigned to spending the day in his own company, Claude trailed gloomily along the riverside until noon, his brain throbbing with the persistent thought of his impotence, but otherwise so numb that he perceived his favourite views of the Seine only as through a veil of mist. As he found himself back again in the Rue de la Femme-sans-Tête, he stopped to lunch at Gomard's, the wine-shop with the sign '*Au Chien de Montargis*' that always intrigued him. Some masons, their smocks caked with plaster, were already at table; he joined them and, like them, took the eight-sous 'ordinary': the bowl of broth into which he broke up his bread, and the slice of boiled beef and beans served on a plate still wet with washing-up water. Still too good, he thought, for a dud who can't even do his own job! Whenever he had spoilt a piece of work he always set himself below the meanest labourer who at least had brawn enough to do his job. He lingered there for over an hour in the stultifying atmosphere of the general conversation before he resumed his leisurely, aimless walk along the streets.

In the Place de l'Hôtel de Ville an idea struck him which made him quicken his pace. Why had he never thought of Fagerolles? Fagerolles was a nice chap even though he *was* at the Beaux-Arts; he was jolly, and no fool. You could talk to him, even when he was trying to defend bad painting. If he'd been home for lunch, he was probably still there, in the Rue Vieille-du-Temple.

It was cooler, Claude noticed, when he turned into that narrow street, for the day was now very hot. But in that busy little thoroughfare steam was still rising from the pavings; it was still damp and even slippery under foot, in spite of the cloudless sky. Every moment drays and wag-gonnettes threatened to run him down when the crowd forced him to step off the pavement. Still, as a street, it amused him. He liked the happy-go-lucky arrangement of the houses, their flat fronts plastered to the eaves with sign-boards, pierced with narrow slits of windows, each one of them a hive of busy craftsmen. At one of the narrowest points in the street his attention was arrested by a tiny paper-shop, with a barber's on one side and a tripe-shop on the other and its window full of ridiculous prints remarkable either for their mushy sentimentality or their barrack-room lewdness. Feasting their eyes on the amazing display were a dreamy-looking youth and a couple of giggling, precocious little girls. He could have slapped their faces. Fagerolles lived just opposite in an old, dark house that stood out further than its neighbours and was, in consequence, more thickly splashed with mud from the gutter. As Claude turned to cut across the street, an omnibus came bearing down upon him; he had just time to leap on to the pavement, at that point merely a kerb, as the wheels brushed past and splashed him up to the knees.

Fagerolles senior dealt in ornamental zinc-work and had his workshops on the ground floor, using as his showrooms, because they were better lighted, the two big first-floor rooms overlooking the street. He lived at the back of the shop in a set of gloomy, stuffy little rooms like a cellar. There his son Henri had grown up, a true child of the Paris streets, on that narrow strip of pavement worn by the wheels of the traffic, drenched by the water from the gutter, across the street from the paper-shop, the tripe-shop and the barber's. His father had started by making him design ornaments for the shop. Then, when the lad had begun to have higher ambitions, had gone in for painting and started to talk about going to the Beaux-Arts, there had been quarrels and even blows, periods of estrangement and eventual reconciliations. And even now that Henri had begun to make his way, his father still treated him harshly and, although he was resigned to letting the boy do what he liked, was still convinced he was going to the bad.

Claude brushed the filth off his clothes and plunged into the entry, through a long archway opening into a yard about which there hung the same greenish light and stale, musty smell one might expect to find at the bottom of a water-tank. The stairs ran up the outside of the building, protected by an awning and a balustrade crumbling with rust, and as Claude was passing the showrooms on the first floor he saw

M. Fagerolles through the glass panel of a door, bending over some of his wares. Not wishing to appear rude, he went in, though he knew nothing more nauseating than the hideous, deceptive prettiness of M. Fagerolles's zinc masquerading as bronze.

'Good afternoon, Monsieur Fagerolles. Is Henri still with you?'

The zinc-ornament dealer, a big, sallow-complexioned man, straightened up in the midst of his urns, flower-vases and statuettes, clutching in his hand the latest thing in thermometers, a woman juggler squatting on her heels and balancing the fine glass tube on the end of her nose.

'Henri hasn't been home for lunch,' he said curtly, leaving the young man somewhat disconcerted by his welcome.

'Oh, I see. He hasn't been home. . . . Sorry, monsieur. Good afternoon.'

'Good afternoon.'

Outside, Claude cursed to himself. No luck again! Fagerolles had escaped him too. He was annoyed with himself now for coming, and especially for taking an interest in the picturesque street, for that meant that he still harboured within him the canker of Romanticism. Perhaps that was his trouble; perhaps that was the false idea he could feel obstructing his brain! By the time he had reached the river again he was beginning to wonder whether to go back to his studio and see whether his picture was really as bad as he thought. But the very idea made him shudder. His studio struck him as a place of horror where he could never bear to live again now that it housed the mutilated corpse of something he had loved. No! No! Climbing those three flights of stairs, opening his door and shutting himself up with *that* was more than he could bear to contemplate. He crossed the Seine and walked from one end of the Rue Saint-Jacques to the other. There was nothing else for it; he was so miserable he could stand it no longer! He was going to the Rue d'Enfer to distract Sandoz from his work!

The little fourth-floor apartment consisted of a dining-room, a bedroom and a small kitchen which Sandoz himself occupied, and, across the landing, another room where his mother, hopelessly paralysed, spent her days in doleful, self-imposed solitude. The street was deserted and the windows of the flat looked out over the vast gardens of the Sourds-Muets, across the rounded tree-tops to the square belfry of Saint-Jacques-du-Haut-Pas.

Sandoz was in his room, sitting at his table, poring over a page of manuscript when Claude arrived.

'Am I disturbing you?'

'Not at all. I've been at it since this morning. I've done enough. . . . Believe it or not, but I've been struggling for the last hour trying to knock one sentence into shape; it haunted me all through lunch.'

A gesture from Claude, together with his look of blank despair, and Sandoz summed up the situation at once.

'So you're in a bad way, too, are you?' he said. 'Come on. Let's go out; a good long walk will brighten the pair of us up. What do you think?'

As he was passing the kitchen he was detained for a moment by an old woman, his daily who came for two hours in the morning and two in the afternoon, but on Thursdays stayed on for the evening because of the dinner.

'It's all settled, then, is it, monsieur?' she asked. 'Skate, and then roast leg of lamb and potatoes?'

'Yes, if you would.'

'For how many tonight, monsieur?'

'That's one thing I never know. . . . Set for five, anyhow. . . . For seven o'clock. We'll try to be back in time!'

Then, leaving Claude on the landing for a moment, Sandoz slipped in to see his mother. When he came out again, with the same solicitous discretion, the pair of them went downstairs without a word. On the doorstep, after a glance to right and left to take their bearings, they went up the street to the Place de l'Observatoire and then turned down the Boulevard du Montparnasse. It was their usual walk; they chose it instinctively, for there was nothing they loved better than a leisurely stroll down the long, broad stretches of the outer boulevards. Neither had spoken yet, for both were still preoccupied, but they gradually recovered their good spirits in each other's company. It was not until they were passing the Gare de l'Ouest that Sandoz suddenly had an idea.

'I know,' he said, 'let's go and look up Mahoudeau and see how that thing of his is getting on. I know he's giving his saints and angels a miss today.'

'Good idea!' Claude answered. 'We'll call on Mahoudeau.'

They turned at once into the Rue du Cherche-Midi, where, only a short walk from the boulevard, Mahoudeau the sculptor had rented a shop from a fruiterer who had gone bankrupt, rubbed a thick coat of whitening on the windows and called it a studio. There is something pleasantly provincial about this particular bit of the broad, quiet Rue du Cherche-Midi, and even just the faintest dash of the odour of sanctity. There are great open gateways leading to long strings of courtyards, a cow-byre that sends out wafts of bed-straw and manure, and a convent wall that seems to go on for ever. It was there, between the convent and a herbalist's, that Mahoudeau had opened his studio which was still marked by the signboard with 'Fruit and Vegetables' painted on it in great yellow letters. Claude and Sandoz were nearly blinded more than once by little girls skipping in the road, for they had been forced off the pavement, which was blocked by chairs where people sat sunning themselves on their doorsteps. They lingered a moment outside the herbalist's. Between the two windows with their show of enemas, bandages, and a host of other intimate and delicate objects, under the bunches of dried herbs hanging over the doorway shedding their spicy odours on the passers-by, a thin, dark woman stood staring at them, while behind her, in the half light of the shop, they could make out the figure of a pallid little man apparently coughing out his lungs. They nudged each other and there was a roguish look in their eyes as they turned the handle of the studio door.

It was a roomy shop, but it appeared to be completely filled by an enormous heap of clay, a colossal Bacchante reclining on a rock. The planks which supported it sagged beneath the weight of the still more or less shapeless mass with its gigantic breasts and legs like twin towers. There was water all over the floor, buckets of muddy liquid about the place and a nasty, plastery mess in one corner, and the shelves which had once been used to display fruit and vegetables were now cluttered with casts after the antique, already assuming a thin, grey veil of accumulated dust. The place was as damp as a wash-house and reeked of wet clay, and the wan light from the whitened windows made it look even dirtier and more dismal than the average sculptor's studio.

Mahoudeau, whom they discovered sitting smoking his pipe in contemplation of his giantess, welcomed them with a cheerful 'Hello! Come in!'

He was a thin little man with a bony face already, at twenty-seven, deeply furrowed with wrinkles. His narrow forehead was crowned by a bush of crisp, black hair, and the ferocious ugliness of his sallow face was tempered by the disarmingly childish smile in his pale, vacant eyes. He was the son of a Plassans stone-cutter and, having been brilliantly successful in the art competitions organized by the local Museum, had been sent to Paris with an annual grant of eight hundred francs for four years. But in Paris he had found himself out of his element, had failed at the Beaux-Arts and frittered away his allowance doing nothing, with the result that at the end of his four years, when he had found himself obliged to earn his living, he had hired himself out to a dealer in religious statuary for whom he slaved ten hours a day making Saint Josephs, Saint Rochs, Mary Magdalenes, and all the Saints in the calendar. During the last six months, since he renewed contact with his friends from Provence, his juniors from the days when they all attended 'Auntie' Giraud's nursery school and now a lot of red-hot revolutionaries, his ambition had begun to revive. The more he saw of his rabid artist friends who fuddled his brain with their outrageous theories, the more his ambitions favoured the colossal.

'I say!' Claude gasped. 'What a piece!'

Mahoudeau, delighted, took out his pipe and blew a cloud of smoke.

'Yes, isn't it?' he said. 'I'm going to show 'em some real flesh, not those bladders of lard they're all so fond of!'

'What's she doing, bathing?' Sandoz asked.

'Bathing! Of course she isn't. She's a Bacchante . . . will be when she gets her vine leaves.'

This was too much for Claude.

'A Bacchante!' was his indignant exclamation. 'What do you take us for? A Bacchante! Is there such a thing? A grape-picker, if you like, and a *modern* grape-picker, what's more! I know it's a nude, but what does that matter? She can be a peasant girl undressed, can't she? People have got to feel that she's alive!'

Mahoudeau merely trembled and said nothing for a moment; he was rather afraid of Claude's censure and usually ended by accepting his ideal of strength and truth in art; so now, to make up for his shortcomings he blurted out obsequiously:

'Yes. Of course. That's what I meant, really, a grape-picker. And she'll be alive, you'll see. She'll *reek* of woman when I've finished with her!'

Just then Sandoz, who was making his way round the great mass of clay, gave a cry of surprise:

'Well! If sly old Chaîne isn't here, too!'

And there, completely obscured by Mahoudeau's gigantic work, sat the stolid Chaîne, silently copying on to a diminutive canvas the rusty old studio stove. It was easy to discern his peasant origins in his slow, deliberate gestures and his thick bull-neck, tanned brown as leather by the sun of Provence. His only other prominent feature was his forehead, a forehead bulging with obstinacy, for his nose was so short that it was lost between his rosy cheeks, and his powerful jaws were hidden by his vigorous beard. He came from Saint-Firmin, a village near Plassans where he had been a shepherd until he was old enough to draw for conscription.* His undoing had been the enthusiasm of a local art-collector for the walking-stick handles he used to carve out of roots with his clasp knife. Once 'discovered', he became the shepherd-boy genius, the artist with a future, according to his patron, who happened to be on the Museum Committee and who pushed him, flattered him and turned his head with hopes for the future. That had not prevented him from failing all along the line, in his class-work, in the Beaux-Arts entrance competition, in the local scholarship test; but he had come to Paris nevertheless. He had got his father, an impoverished peasant, to advance him his share of his patrimony, a mere thousand francs, on which to live for a year, until his undoubted success was achieved. The thousand francs lasted eighteen months. Then, when he had only twenty francs left, he had joined forces with his friend, Mahoudeau. They shared the same bed in the gloomy back premises of the shop; they shared the same loaf of bread, and they bought their bread once a fortnight only, so that it would be thoroughly stale and they would be unable to eat more than a small portion at a time.

'Very accurate, that stove of yours, Chaîne,' said Sandoz.

Chaîne did not answer, but smiled through his beard, a smile of triumph that lit up his face like a ray of sunshine. To cap everything his patron's advice had made him take up painting, in spite of his genuine talent as a wood-carver. And a clumsy job he made of it, succeeding only in reducing the purest and most vibrant colours to the same oppressive drab. But, for all his lack of skill, his great gift was accuracy. His infantile mind, still of the earth earthy, delighted in minute detail which he reproduced with the meticulous simplicity of a primitive. His stove, its perspective completely askew, was precise and lifeless and the colour of mud.

Claude went over and looked at it and in a moment of pity, he who was usually so hard on bad painting, found a word to say in its favour:

'They'll never be able to call you a charlatan, anyhow, Chaîne. You do at least paint as you feel, and that's how it ought to be!'

The door had opened again and a young man stepped into the shop. He was tall, with fair hair, a big pink nose and large blue eyes, and was obviously short-sighted. He was laughing.

'That herbalist next door,' he said. 'There she is touting for customers . . . and with a face like that!'

They all laughed then, except Mahoudeau, who appeared very embarrassed.

'Jory, the prize brick-dropper!' laughed Sandoz, as he shook the newcomer's hand.

'Why, what have I said now? Oh, you mean Mahoudeau here goes to bed with her!' Jory went on, when he finally grasped the situation. 'And why not? What's wrong with that? Who ever said "No" to a woman?'

'It looks as if you said something to yours,' said Mahoudeau simply. 'She's taken a piece out of your cheek.'

They all laughed again, but this time it was Jory's turn to blush. He had indeed two long, deep scratches down his cheek. The son of a Plassans lawyer, Jory had driven his father to despair by his amorous adventures, which he had brought to a sensational climax by running away with a singer from a café-concert while pretending to be going to Paris to take up literature. For the past six months the pair of them had been camping out in a disreputable hotel in the Latin Quarter, and his companion literally skinned him alive every time he left her for some trollop or other he picked up on the street. That explained his perpetual scars, bloody noses, thick ears, and black eyes.

While the others talked, Chaîne alone went on solidly painting, with the determination of an ox yoked to a plough. Jory went into ecstasies over the 'Grape-Picker'. He, too, adored fat women. At Plassans he had made his literary debut by turning romantic sonnets to the ample bosom and ampler hips of a local butcher's wife, the cause of many a restless night. In Paris, where he had joined up with the rest of the Plassans gang, he had branched out as an art critic, trying to make a living selling articles at twenty francs a time to an obstreperous little paper *Le Tambour*. One of his articles, a study of a picture of Claude's exhibited by old Malgras, had just stirred up a terrific scandal by praising his friend at the expense of 'the public's favourites' and proclaiming him the leader of a new school, the 'open-air' school. Fundamentally extremely practical, he had no use for anything which was not to his own advantage and simply repeated the theories he heard the others expound.

'We must have an article on you now, Mahoudeau,' he cried, 'to launch this buxom wench of yours . . . God! Just look at those thighs! Talk about a treat, eh!'

Then, suddenly changing the subject, he added:

'By the way, my old skinflint of a father repented! He's afraid I might blot the family copy-book, so he's sending me a hundred francs a month. I'm paying my debts.'

'Debts!' said Sandoz with a quiet smile. 'What do you know about debts?'

Jory's hereditary avarice was a standing joke with his friends. He never paid his women, and somehow managed his riotous living without money and without a slate. With his instinctive knowledge of how to get everything for nothing, he combined perpetual duplicity, the habit of lying he had contracted in the pious atmosphere of his home, where he was so anxious to conceal his vices that he lied all the time about everything, even when it was quite pointless. He had a superb reply for Sandoz, a reply worthy of a sage who has seen life:

'And what do any of you know about the value of money?'

The others booed, called him a 'dirty bourgeois' and were on the point of using even more powerful epithets when a gentle tapping on a window pane reduced them all to silence.

'Damn that woman!' growled Mahoudeau.

'What woman?' said Jory. 'The herbalist next door? Let's have her in. We'll have some fun.'

The door was open already and there on the doorstep was the woman, Madame Jabouille, known to them all as Mathilde. She was only thirty, but her thin, flat face was already deeply lined, while her eyes burned with passion under their dark blue lids. It was said that the priests had arranged her marriage to the little herbalist Jabouille, who was a widower

and who did good business in that church-going neighbourhood. It was certainly possible, on occasion, to catch sight
of a figure in a cassock gliding through the mysterious little
shop which the herbs and spices filled with the fragrance
of incense, where the sale of sprays was negotiated with
discreetness worthy of the cloister and unction reminiscent
of the vestry, and where customers whispered as devoutly
as in a confessional, slipping the enemas unobtrusively into
their reticules and departing with eyes cast modestly down.
There had been unfortunate rumours of abortions, but
right-minded people attributed them to the malice of the
wine-merchant across the street. Since Jabouille had remar-
ried, business had begun to decline. The coloured bottles
seemed to be losing their brightness and the dried herbs
hanging from the ceiling were falling to dust while Jabouille
himself, reduced to little more than a shadow, was coughing
himself to death. Even though Mathilde herself was a
regular churchgoer, the church-going customers fell away,
for they thought she made herself too obvious with other
men now that Jabouille was worn out.

She stood in the doorway for a moment, her sharp eyes
taking everything in, and soon the room was filled with her
all-pervading perfume, the strong smell of simples that
impregnated her clothes and scented her greasy, always
untidy hair—the sickly sweetness of mallow, the sharpness
of elderberry, the bitterness of rhubarb, all dominated by
that warm odour of strong peppermint which seemed to be
the very breath of her lungs, the breath she breathed into
the faces of her men.

'Oh dear! You have visitors,' she exclaimed, feigning
surprise. 'I didn't know. I'll come back later.'

'Yes, do,' replied Mahoudeau angrily. 'I'm going out,
anyhow. You can give me a sitting on Sunday.'

In amazement, Claude looked first at Mathilde and then
at the 'Grape-Picker'.

'What!' he exclaimed. 'Do you mean to say it's Madame
Jabouille who poses for those muscles? Piling it on a bit,
aren't you?'

The others laughed as Mahoudeau concocted an explanation. No, not for the bust or the legs, only the head and hands, and only for the odd details even then. But Mathilde shrieked with laughter too, for she had now come brazenly into the room, closed the door behind her and was quite at home with all the men, sidling up and sniffing them like a dog on the scent. When she laughed, she showed the gaps in her mouth where teeth were missing, and that, added to her generally wizened appearance, made her look frighteningly ugly. Jory, whom she had not seen before, was the one who attracted her; he was plump and fresh and there was something promising about his big pink nose. She nudged him; then, hoping to arouse his interest, dropped into Mahoudeau's lap with all the abandon of a prostitute.

'Don't,' said Mahoudeau as he rose to his feet. 'I'm busy. . . . Isn't that so, boys, somebody's expecting us?'

He gave them a wink. He was looking forward to a nice long walk in their company, so they all replied that somebody was expecting them and set to work helping him to cover up his sculpture with old wet dusters.

Mathilde, meanwhile, looking rather quelled and disappointed, did not go, but stood about, moving when she found herself in the way. Chaîne, who had stopped painting, sat glaring at her over the top of his canvas, shy but greedy with pent-up desire. Until now he had not opened his lips, but as Mahoudeau was starting out with the other three he said in his thick, muffled voice:

'Will you be back?'

'Not till late. Get yourself some supper and don't wait up. Goodbye.'

So Chaîne was left alone with Mathilde in the damp shop among the heaps of clay and the pools of water, the poverty and disorder, under the crude and chalky daylight that poured in through the whitened windows.

When they got outside, Claude and Mahoudeau walked on ahead, followed by Sandoz and Jory, who protested loudly when Sandoz teased him by saying he had made a conquest of Mathilde.

'Oh, no! She's awful. Old enough to be mother to the lot of us. A toothless old bitch, that's all she is, and stinks like a medicine-chest!'

Sandoz laughed at Jory's exaggerated picture:

'Don't overdo it,' he said. 'Besides, you are not usually so fussy. She can probably still give points to some of your conquests.'

'Which ones, I'd like to know? . . . Now we're out of the way, you can bet she's pounced on Chaîne. Just think of the fun they're having, the pigs!'

Mahoudeau, who, to all appearances, was deep in discussion with Claude, suddenly turned round in the middle of a sentence and said:

'As if I cared!'

He finished what he had been saying to Claude, then called again over his shoulder:

'Besides, Chaîne's too dense anyway!'

The subject was dropped, and as the four of them strolled gently along they seemed to take up the whole width of the Boulevard des Invalides. The gang usually spread out like that, as friends tacked themselves on to it until it looked like a horde on the war-path. As they squared their broad young shoulders, these twenty-year-olds took possession of the entire pavement. Whenever they were together, fanfares cleared the way before them and they picked up Paris in one hand and put it calmly in their pocket. Victory was theirs for certain, so what did they care about down-at-heel boots and threadbare jackets when they could be conquerors at will? Their disdain went hand-in-hand with a boundless contempt for everything outside their art, for society, and, above all, for politics. What use had they for such sordid nonsense? Nothing but a lot of brainless old dodderers. Their youthful arrogance set them above all sense of justice and made them deliberately ignore all the claims of social life in their mad pursuit of their dreams of an artists' Utopia. There were times when it turned their heads completely, but it also gave them both strength and courage.

In the warmth of their hope and enthusiasm, Claude
began to take heart and cheer up. All that remained of the
morning's tortures was a remote feeling of numbness as he
launched into a discussion of his picture with Sandoz and
Mahoudeau, swearing, of course, that he was certainly going
to destroy it in the morning. Jory, flashing defiant though
myopic glances at all the old ladies they encountered, was
holding forth on his theories of artistic production. You
should produce exactly as you feel, in the first burst of
inspiration. He himself never crossed out so much as a line.
As they talked the four friends made their way down the
boulevard, and the quietness and the long endless rows of
trees made a perfect setting for their arguments. But as they
came out into the Esplanade des Invalides, their argument
flared up into so violent a quarrel that they came to a halt
in the very middle of that spacious thoroughfare, with
Claude furiously telling Jory he was an idiot, arguing that
it was better to destroy one's work than sell third-rate stuff,
and swearing that nothing disgusted him more than a mer-
cenary commercial attitude, while Sandoz and Mahoudeau
stood by, both talking at once at the tops of their voices.
Passers-by, wondering what it was all about, first turned
and stared, and finally began to gather round the four young
men who looked as if they might fly at each other's throats
at any moment. But they had to turn away disappointed,
feeling they had been fooled when the four friends suddenly
forgot their quarrel and turned as one man to rhapsodize at
the sight of a nursemaid in a light dress and long cherry-
coloured ribbons. Well, they were damned! Just look at that
for colour! They were enraptured. Half closing their eyes
to appreciate the full effect, they moved off after the girl
among the trees, like men suddenly aroused from a dream
and surprised to be down to earth again. They adored the
Esplanade, open as it was to the whole sky, bounded only
on the south side by the Invalides, so quiet and yet so vast,
allowing room for their expansive gestures; they looked on
it as a kind of breathing space in a Paris that was too small,
too stuffy for the ambition in their breasts.

'Are you two going somewhere?' Sandoz asked Mahou-deau and Jory.

'No, not really,' the latter answered. 'We were going with you. Where are *you* going?'

It was Claude who replied, with a strange, blank look in his eye:

'I hadn't thought. . . . Along here.'

And they turned and walked along the Quai d'Orsay as far as the Pont de la Concorde. As they passed the Corps Législatif, he added with a look of disgust:

'Of all the filthy-looking buildings!'

'That was a damned good speech Jules Favre made a couple of days ago,' said Jory. 'Old Rouher wasn't half riled!'

The three others refused to let him go on, and the quarrel broke out again. Who was Jules Favre, they wanted to know? Who ever heard of Rouher?* Did they even exist? Couple of windbags nobody would think of mentioning ten years after they were dead! And as they crossed over the bridge, they shook their heads pityingly at Jory. By the time they had reached the middle of the Place de la Concorde they were quiet again. It was Claude who broke the silence again.

'That,' he declared as he looked around him, 'is *not* so filthy-looking.'

It was four o'clock, and the day was just beginning to wane in a golden haze of glorious sunshine. To right and left, towards the Madeleine and the Corps Législatif, the lines of buildings stretched far into the distance, their rooftops cutting clean against the sky. Between them the Tuileries gardens piled up wave upon wave of round-topped chestnut trees, while between the two green borders of its side avenues the Champs-Élysées climbed up and up, as far as the eye could see, up to the gigantic gateway of the Arc de Triomphe, which opened on to infinity. The Avenue itself was filled with a double stream of traffic, rolling on like twin rivers, with eddies and waves of moving carriages tipped like foam with the sparkle of a lamp-glass or the glint of a polished panel, down to the Place de la Concorde with its enormous pavements and roadways like big, broad lakes, crossed in every direction by the flash of wheels, peopled by black specks which were really human beings, and its two splashing fountains breathing coolness over all its feverish activity.

Claude was quivering with delight.

'Ah! this Paris!' he cried. 'It's ours! All ours for the taking!'

Each one of them was thrilled almost beyond words as they looked on the scene with eyes that shone with desire. Did they not feel glory being wafted over the whole vast city from the top of that Avenue? Paris was here, and they meant it to be theirs.

'And we'll take it,' asserted Sandoz, with his look of stubborn determination.

'Of course we will!' added Jory and Mahoudeau.

They moved on again and, after walking some time at random, found themselves behind the Madeleine. As they came into the Place du Havre from the Rue Tronchet, Sandoz suddenly called out:

'So we're going to Baudequin's, are we?'

The others looked surprised, but agreed they must have been going to Baudequin's.

'What day is it?' Claude asked. 'Thursday? . . . Fagerolles and Gagnière'll be there. . . . Come on, let's go to Baudequin's.'

So they turned up the Rue d'Amsterdam. They had just walked right across Paris, one of their favourite jaunts, although they had other favourites too; all along the riverside, for example, or over part of the fortifications, from the Porte Saint-Jacques, say, to Les Moulineaux; or perhaps out to Père-Lachaise and back round the outer boulevards. For a whole day at a time they would roam the streets and squares, as long as their legs would carry them, as if they wanted to conquer one district after another by flinging their startling theories in the face of its houses. The pavements they tramped were their battlefield, the very soil of which produced an ecstasy which drugged their fatigue.

The Café Baudequin was on the Boulevard des Batignolles, at the corner of the Rue Darcet. The gang had made
it its regular meeting-place; why, they could never say,
for Gagnière was the only member who lived near it.
There they met every Sunday evening, and on Thursdays
about five o'clock any of them who happened to be free
usually looked in at least for a moment or two. On this
particular Thursday, as it was so sunny, the little tables
outside under the awning were all occupied and their
double rank of customers filled the entire pavement. But
the gang detested all such cheek-by-jowl ostentation, so
they pushed their way through the crowd into the cool,
deserted café.

'Why, Fagerolles is all by himself!' said Claude, as he
made his way to their usual table and shook hands with its
one occupant, a pale, slim young man with a girlish face
and a waggish, inveigling look in his steely grey eyes. They
all sat down and ordered beer, while Claude went on talking
to Fagerolles.

'I went looking for you at your father's place this afternoon. I can't say he welcomed me with open arms.'

Fagerolles, who fancied himself as a tough, laughed and
slapped his thigh.

'Oh, he makes me sick, the old man!' he said. 'I cleared
out this morning, after a bit of a dust-up. He *will* try to
make me design a lot of junk for his damned zinc. As if I
didn't do enough junk at the Beaux-Arts!'

His easy joke at the expense of his teachers delighted his
friends. He amused them, and his ceaseless flow of both
flattery and disparagement won their undying affection. He
smiled disarmingly, first at one and then at another, while
with inborn facility his long, supple fingers worked out
intricate little sketches with the drops of beer spilled on the
table. His art came easily to him and he had a happy knack
of making a success of everything.

'Where's Gagnière?' asked Mahoudeau. 'Haven't you seen
him?'

'No. And I've been here an hour.'

Jory said nothing, but nudged Sandoz and motioned with his head in the direction of a girl sitting with her gentleman at a table at the far end of the room. There were only two other customers in the place, a couple of gendarmes busy playing cards. She looked little more than a child, a typical product of the Paris streets, where youngsters still look spare and immature even at eighteen. Her bang of short blonde hair, her delicate little nose and the big smiling mouth in her quaint, rosy face made her look rather like a well-brushed dog. She was turning over the pages of a picture-paper while her escort solemnly sipped his madeira. Every now and then she flashed a lively glance at the gang over the top of her paper.

'How's that? Not bad, eh?' muttered Jory, already more than interested. 'Who the devil's she after? . . . She's looking straight at me.'

Fagerolles instantly retorted:

'Look here, there's no question about it. She's mine! . . . You don't think I've been here an hour just waiting for *you*, do you?'

The others laughed, and Fagerolles lowered his voice to tell them about Irma Bécot. Quaint little thing, and screamingly funny! He knew her whole history. She was the daughter of a grocer in the Rue Montorgueil. Well educated; at school till she was sixteen; reading, writing, arithmetic, scripture, and what not; she used to do her homework in the shop between a couple of bags of lentils, and finished her education at street level, living in the rush and bustle of the pavements, learning about life from the everlasting gossip of the local cooks who laid the dark secrets of the neighbourhood bare as they waited for their quarter of Gruyère. Her mother was dead and her father had, very sensibly, taken to sleeping with his maids, as it saved him the trouble of seeking satisfaction elsewhere. But it also developed his taste for women; much wanted more, so in next to no time he was launched upon such an orgy of dissipation that the grocery business was frittered away too, all the dried vegetables, jar upon jar, drawerfuls of sweet-

meats, everything. Irma was still a schoolgirl when one of
her father's assistants rolled her over on a basket of figs one
evening as he was closing the shop. Six months later the
business was ruined; her father died of a stroke and Irma
sought refuge with an aunt who ill-treated her. Three times
she ran away with a boy who lived opposite, and three times
she came back. The fourth time she ran away for good and
roved around all the low haunts of Montmartre and the
Batignolles.

'Another trollop!' said Claude, with a look of contempt.

All at once, after a whispered leave-taking, her escort got
up and went out. Irma watched him go and then, like a
child let out of school, dashed across and sat herself on
Fagerolles's lap.

'See what he's like? Can't shake him off! . . . Kiss me
quick, he's coming back!'

She kissed him full on the lips and then took a drink
from his glass. She included all the others in her embrace
and laughed engagingly at all of them, for she adored artists
and was only sorry they were not rich enough to afford
women just for themselves.

Jory seemed to be the one who attracted her most. He
was very taken and his eyes burned like coals of fire as he
looked at her. As he was smoking, she took his cigarette
from his mouth and put it into her own, chattering all the
time like a mischievous magpie.

'So you're all painters, eh? How funny! What are those
three looking so glum about? Laugh, can't you? Or do you
want me to come and tickle you? That'll learn you!'

True enough, Claude, Mahoudeau, and Sandoz were so
taken aback that they just sat looking on without even a
smile. She was still on the alert, and as soon as she heard
her escort coming back she said hastily to Fagerolles:

'How about tomorrow night? Pick me up at the Brasserie
Bréda.'

Then, pushing the wet cigarette back into Jory's mouth,
she made off to her own table, taking ridiculously big
strides, making wild gestures, and pulling an unexpectedly

funny face. By the time her escort arrived, looking very
serious and rather pale, she was exactly as he had left her,
her eyes still fixed on the same picture. The whole of this
scene had been enacted so rapidly, at such a rollicking speed,
that the two policemen, good sorts the pair of them, were
ready to choke with laughter as they shuffled their cards.

Irma had obviously made the conquest of the whole gang.
Sandoz said her name, Irma Bécot, would sound well in a
novel; Claude wondered whether he could get her to pose
for him, and Mahoudeau saw her as a statuette, a Street-
Urchin, a subject bound to sell. After a while she departed,
throwing kisses behind her escort's back to every one, a
whole shower of kisses that roused Jory's excitement to fever
pitch. But Fagerolles was unwilling to lend her to any of
them. It amused him, unconsciously, to think he had found
in her another child of the streets like himself; he was tickled
by the thought of the pavement depravity he sensed in her.

At five o'clock, the gang called for more beer. Local
habitués had filled up the neighbouring tables and, half in
scorn, half in uneasy deference, were now beginning to look
askance at the artists' corner. They were well known and
even beginning to acquire some notoriety. But now they just
talked banalities; the heat, the difficulty of getting a seat on
the bus to the Odéon, the discovery of an eating-place run
by a wine-merchant where they served decent meat. One of
them wanted to start an argument about a lot of dud pictures
recently accepted by the Musée du Luxembourg,* but
everybody agreed that the pictures were not worth the gilt
they were framed in, so the subject was dropped and they
sat for a time just smoking, exchanging the odd word or
sharing a laugh in unspoken complicity.

'Look here,' said Claude at last, 'are we waiting for
Gagnière or not?'

The rest of them complained, too, that Gagnière was a
nuisance, but they were sure he would turn up as soon as
there was any soup going.

'Yes, come on,' said Sandoz. 'Let's go. There's leg of
lamb tonight, so let's try to be on time.'

Each of them paid for his own drinks and then they left. Their departure caused something of a stir in the café. Some of the young men, who were probably painters, whispered to each other and pointed at Claude, as if he were the chief of some terrible tribe of savages. Jory's famous article was taking effect; the public was co-operating and creating the 'open-air' school on its own account. The gang still looked on the whole thing as a joke and said that the Café Baudequin had no idea of the honour they were doing it by making it the probable cradle of a revolution.

Their number had increased to five, for Fagerolles had joined them, when they left the café and started back across Paris with the calm and certainty of conquerors.

They went down the Rue de Clichy, along the Rue de la Chaussée-d'Antin into the Rue de Richelieu, crossed the Seine by the Pont des Arts, jeering at the Institut as they passed, and reached the Luxembourg by the Rue de Seine, where a poster in three glaring colours, advertising a fairground circus, made them shout with admiration. Evening was coming on and the flow of traffic slowing down, as if the tired city was lingering in the shadows, like a woman ready to give herself to the first man with vigour enough to claim her.

When they reached the Rue d'Enfer, Sandoz showed the others into his room and then went in to see his mother in hers; he spent a few moments there, came out smiling tenderly as he always did, and joined his friends without a word. They were soon making a terrible din, everybody laughing, arguing, and shouting at once. Sandoz tried to set a good example by helping the daily woman, who was complaining bitterly because it was half-past seven and her lovely joint was drying up in the oven. The five were already at table eating their excellent onion soup when a new guest arrived.

'Gagnière!' they yelled as one man.

Vague little Gagnière, with his chubby, startled face fringed with a blond and wispy beard, stood for a moment in the doorway blinking his green eyes. Gagnière came from

Melun, where his wealthy parents had just left him a couple of houses. He had learnt to paint all by himself in the Forest of Fontainebleau, and painted conscientious, well-meaning landscapes. But his real passion was for music. It was a kind of mania with him, an unquenchable fire in his brain that put him on a par with the rest of the hotheads in the gang.

'Am I one too many?' he asked, in a quiet voice.

'Of course you're not! Come in!' replied Sandoz.

The woman was already setting another place.

'Don't you think we might set a place for Dubuche at the same time?' Claude asked. 'He said he was almost certain to come.'

But the suggestion was shouted down. Dubuche was beyond the pale; he had gone into Society. Jory told how he had seen him out driving with an old lady and her daughter and carrying their sunshades.

'What have you been up to that makes you so late?' Fagerolles asked Gagnière.

Gagnière, who was just going to take his first spoonful of soup, put it back in his plate.

'I've been in the Rue de Lancry, listening to chamber music,' he said. 'Schumann. Things . . . oh! you can't imagine what they were like! Things that get you here, somehow, at the back of your head, like a woman breathing down your neck. . . . Not like a kiss. . . . No, more insubstantial than that . . . a breath, a soft, faint breath. Oh! it's like . . . like feeling your soul going out of your body!'

His eyes glistened with tears and his face turned pale in his ecstasy.

'Have your soup,' put in Mahoudeau, 'and tell us all about it afterwards.'

When the skate was served, the vinegar bottle was brought on to the table for those who wanted to give an extra fillip to the black-butter sauce. They attacked the simple meal with great gusto, devouring large quantities of bread, but being careful to put plenty of water with their wine. They had just greeted the leg of lamb with a hearty cheer, and the master of the house had just begun to carve, when the door opened again. This time the late comer was received with furious protests:

'Full up! No more room! . . . Outside! . . . Turncoats not wanted!'

It was Dubuche. He was out of breath with running and, astounded by his hostile reception, pushed his great pale face round the door and tried to stammer out some kind of excuses.

'It isn't my fault, really. It's the buses. . . . I had to let five go past, all full up, in the Champs-Élysées.'

'Don't believe him! He's fibbing! Send him away! Don't give him any lamb! Send him away! Send him away!'

When he did manage to get inside the room, they saw he was very formally dressed, all in black: black trousers, black frock-coat, spick and span and meticulous as a bourgeois going to dine in town.

'Hello! He's missed his party!' cried Fagerolles. 'His society friends didn't ask him to stay, so he's come here to eat our lamb as he's nowhere else to go!'

Dubuche blushed and stammered.

'Oh! What a thing to say! . . . That's just not fair! Shut up, the lot of you!'

Sandoz and Claude, who were sitting next to each other, looked at him and smiled; Sandoz motioned to him as if to say:

'Get yourself a plate and a glass and come and sit here between us two. They'll leave you alone then.'

But all the time they were eating the lamb they never stopped teasing him. He took it all in good part, like a good fellow, and when the woman had brought him a plate of soup and a portion of skate, he began to play up to their jokes, pretending to be ravenous, mopping up his plate with his bread, telling how one mother had turned him down as a prospective son-in-law because he was an architect. The meal ended in pandemonium, with everyone talking at once. The last course, a choice piece of Brie, was particularly well received, not a trace of it was left. The bread nearly ran out and the wine actually did, so everybody washed the meal down with a good long draught of water, with much smacking of lips and clicking of tongues, accompanied by hearty laughter. And so, with faces flushed and paunches full, and with that blissful feeling experienced by people who have dined on the richest viands, they moved into the bedroom.

It was just another of Sandoz's pleasant gatherings. Even at his poorest he had always had a bite to share with his friends. He liked doing it; he liked to be one of a band, all good friends, all living for the same ideals. Although he was the same age as his friends, he beamed with a pleasant, fatherly sort of kindness to see them about him, under his own roof, all intoxicated with the same ambitions. He had no drawing-room, so he threw his bedroom open to the gang and, as space there was limited, two or three of them had to sit on the bed. Through the windows, flung wide open on hot summer evenings, they could see two dark shapes against the clear sky, towering over the neighbouring house-tops, the belfry of Saint Jacques-du-Haut-Pas and the tree in the garden of the Sourds-Muets. When they were in funds there was beer to drink and everyone brought his own tobacco, so the room was soon so thick with smoke that they could hardly see each other as they sat talking far into the night, in the vast and melancholy silence of that out-of-the-way corner of the city.

On this particular evening, the daily woman was tapping on the door by nine o'clock to say, 'I've finished, Monsieur Sandoz. May I go now?'

'Yes, off you go,' was the answer. 'You have left some water on, haven't you? . . . I'll make the tea.'

Sandoz got up and went out when she had gone, and stayed out for about a quarter of an hour. He had been saying good night to his mother; he tucked her up in her bed every night before she settled to sleep.

The talk was getting noisier. Fagerolles was just telling them something that had happened to him.

'Yes, my friend,' he was saying, 'at the Beaux-Arts they actually correct the model! . . . The other day Mazel came up to me and said: "Those two legs aren't properly bal-

anced." So I said: "I know they aren't, neither are hers."
It was little Flore Beauchamp, and you know what she's
like. He was furious, and what do you think he said! He
said: "Well, if they aren't they ought to be!" '

They were all convulsed, especially Claude, for whose
benefit Fagerolles had told the story, as a form of flattery.
He had been influenced by Claude for some time and,
although he still painted with the slickness of a conjuror,
all he talked about now was solid painting, chunks of nature
flung raw on to the canvas, pulsating with life—which did
not prevent him from making fun of the 'open-air' school,
when he was in other company, and accusing them of
putting on their paint with a ladle.

Dubuche, who had not laughed because he was so
shocked, screwed up the courage to retort:

'Why do you stay on at the Beaux-Arts if you think it's
so stupid? If you don't like it, leave! . . . Oh, I know you've
all got a down on me because I stand up for the Beaux-
Arts, but you see I happen to believe that if you want to
do a job you can't do better than learn to do it properly.'

The others roared in derision, and Claude had to assert
himself very firmly to make himself heard.

'He's right,' he said. 'You ought to learn your job. But
it isn't perhaps the best thing to learn it from a lot of
hide-bound teachers who want to impose their point of view
on you at all costs. . . . Mazel's a fool! Saying Flore Beauchamp's legs aren't properly balanced! You've seen 'em for
yourselves, haven't you? They're amazing! They tell everything there is to know about her, fast living included!'

He lay back on the bed and, as he gazed into space, talked
on, his voice warm with enthusiasm.

'Life! Life! Life! What it is to feel it and paint it as it
really is! To love it for its own sake; to see it as the only
true, everlasting, ever-changing beauty, and refuse to see
how it might be "improved" by being emasculated. To
understand that its so-called defects are really signs of
character. To put life into things, and put life into men!
That's the only way to be a God!'

His faith in himself was reviving, aroused by the long walk across Paris, and now he was warming again to his passion for full-blooded nature. The others listened in silence, then, after one last, wild gesture, he went on in a quieter voice:

'Ah, well, everybody has a right to his own ideas, but the trouble is, at the Institut, they're even less tolerant than we are ... and the Institut *is* the Salon Selection Committee, so I'm sure that fool Mazel's going to turn me down again.'

That released all their wrath; the question of the Selection Committee always did. They wanted reforms, and each had his own ready-made solution, varying from the election by universal suffrage of a very liberal committee to complete freedom, with the Salon open to all comers.

While the others were deeply involved in their discussions Gagnière had drawn Mahoudeau towards the open window, and as he looked away out into the night he was murmuring in a vague, far-away voice:

'It's hardly noticeable, really, just the faintest impression, a matter of four bars. But it's the amount of meaning he's got into it! ... It makes me think first of a fleeting landscape, with the shadow of a hidden tree at the turn of a melancholy bit of road, and then of a woman passing by, just the faintest glimpse of a profile as she goes away, away into the distance, never to be seen again ...'

Just then Fagerolles called out.

'Gagnière, what are you sending to the Salon this year?'

But Gagnière did not hear; he was too enraptured.

'In Schumann,' he went on, 'there's everything. He's infinite. ... And Wagner! ... They hissed him again last Sunday!'

Another shout from Fagerolles brought him up with a start.

'What? Eh? What am I sending to the Salon? Oh, a landscape, probably, a bit of the Seine. It's hard to know, really. I've got to feel satisfied with it myself first,' he replied, suddenly shy and diffident again.

His scruples of artistic conscience often kept him for months working over a canvas no bigger than a man's hand. Following the example of those masters who first made the conquest of nature, the French landscape painters, his chief preoccupations were accuracy of tone and exact observation of values, but he worked as a theorist whose integrity made him heavy-handed with his brush. It often happened that he was too timid to risk a really vibrant note and produced something surprisingly grey and sad, in spite of his revolutionary passion.

'Wait till they see my piece,' put in Mahoudeau. 'That'll give 'em something to think about.'

'Oh, you'll get in all right,' said Claude. 'The sculptors are always more open-minded than the painters. Besides, you know what you're after, and you're bound to bring it off . . . you've got it in your fingers. . . . She's going to be worth looking at, that grape-picker of yours.'

Claude's compliment gave Mahoudeau something to think about, for although power was what he aimed at in his work it was not really his natural bent, and he despised grace, though it sprang from his rough, uneducated workman's fingers, invincible and persistent as a flower sown in hard ground by the wind.

Fagerolles, smart as usual, was not exhibiting, in case his teachers did not like it, so he poured out all his contempt on the Salon—'a filthy old junk-shop where good painting went as mouldy as the bad.' Though he would never admit it, what he wanted was the Prix de Rome, though he ridiculed that along with the rest.

Jory planted himself in the middle of the floor, his glass of beer clutched in his fist, and punctuated his remarks with sips.

'I've had just as much as I can stand of that famous Selection Committee!' he exclaimed. 'It's got to be smashed, and I'm going to smash it! I shall open the attack in our next number, and I'll give it hell, so don't forget to let me have a note or two, and between us we'll do for it. It'll be fun.'

Amid the general enthusiasm Claude regained his self-esteem completely. The battle was on, and he was in it!

They were all in it, elbow to elbow, to march to the fray. Not one among them at that moment had any thought of his own personal glory, for as yet nothing had come between them, neither their fundamental disparities, which they had not yet realized, nor the spirit of rivalry which was one day to set them at variance. The success of one, surely, meant success for them all! Bubbling over with youth and brotherly devotion, they were launched again into the old, old dream of banding together to conquer the earth, each making his own contribution, each supporting the other, the whole band in a firm and serried rank to the very end. Claude, as acknowledged leader, was already distributing the victors' laurels. Even Fagerolles, in spite of his Parisian cynicism, believed in the need for banding together, while Jory, duller in appetite than his friends, still not quite free of his slough of provincialism, was nevertheless doing all in his power to help them, making mental notes of what they said and already planning his articles in his mind. Mahoudeau, deliberately exaggerating, was making violent, convulsive gestures, like a baker kneading the whole world like a lump of dough; Gagnière, now freed from the shackles of his pale grey painting, was rhapsodizing about subtleties of feeling, tracing them to disappearing point in the remotest realms of intelligence, while Dubuche, with his solid convictions, amid the general hubbub, placed an occasional word here and there, but every word smashed through its obstacle like the blow of a club. Sandoz himself was so happy, beaming with pleasure at seeing his friends so united, 'all in the same shirt', as he put it, that he opened another bottle of beer. He would have given them the last drop in the house.

'Now we know what we're after,' he cried, 'let's see that we get it! There's nothing better in the whole wide world than understanding each other when you've got ideas in your noddle, and letting fools go to the devil!'

He was cut short, much to his amazement, by a ring at the door-bell. All the rest stopped talking too, and in the sudden silence he went on:

'Who on earth can that be? It's eleven o'clock!'

He ran to open the door, and the others heard him give a shout of joy. He was back in a moment, flinging the door wide open as he said:

'Now that is decent of you, to give us such a pleasant surprise! . . . Gentlemen, Bongrand!'

The great painter, announced with such respectful familiarity by the host, came in holding out both hands to greet the party. They were all on their feet in a second, pleased and touched by his cordial gesture. Bongrand was a big man with a deeply-lined face and long grey hair. He was forty-five and had just been made a Member of the Institut, and in the button-hole of his plain alpaca jacket he was wearing the rosette of the Legion of Honour. He was fond of young people, and there was nothing he liked better than to drop in now and again and smoke a pipe with these friendly novices and share the warmth of their enthusiasm.

'I'll go and make the tea,' cried Sandoz.

And when he came back from the kitchen with the cups and the teapot, he found Bongrand settled in, sitting astride a chair smoking his short clay pipe in the middle of a renewed outburst of chatter, and talking himself in a voice like thunder. His grandfather was a farmer from the Beauce; his father a middle-class townsman of peasant stock refined by his mother's sound artistic taste. He was rich, so he had no need to sell and had remained a true Bohemian both in taste and opinions.

'Selection Committee!' he was saying, 'I wouldn't be seen dead on it.' And he emphasized his assertions by vigorous gestures. 'I couldn't be so inhuman as to turn down a lot of poor beggars who almost certainly have their living to earn.'

'Still,' said Claude, 'you could do us a jolly good turn by standing up for our pictures.'

'Not I! All I should do would be to compromise you! I cut no ice really, you know. I'm a mere nobody.'

There was an outburst of protest, and Fagerolles fairly shrieked: 'You can't tell us the man who painted "The Village Wedding" cuts no ice!'

Bongrand was on his feet in a moment, his face flushed with temper.

'Don't even mention "The Wedding" to me! I've heard just as much as I can stand about "The Wedding", so now you're warned. Ever since the thing was put in the Luxembourg it's haunted me like a bad dream.'

His 'Village Wedding' was, nevertheless, his masterpiece. It represented a wedding party straggling across a cornfield, a series of closely studied peasant types to whom he had managed to impart an epic quality worthy of Homer himself. It was an artistic landmark, a turning-point in the evolution of painting; it presented a new formula. Following Delacroix, and parallel with Courbet, it was Romanticism tempered by logic, more precise in observation, more perfect in treatment, although it did not make a frontal attack on nature in the full crudity of the open air. And yet the younger school of painting claimed descent from Bongrand's painting.

'I don't know anything lovelier,' said Claude, 'than the two first groups, the fiddler and the bride and the old peasant.'

'What about the big peasant woman,' cried Mahoudeau, 'the one that's turning round and beckoning to the others? . . . I wanted to do it as a statue.'

'And the wind blowing through the corn,' Gagnière added, 'and those two lovely patches of colour away in the distance, the boy and the girl cuffing each other.'

Bongrand listened, looking embarrassed and with a long-suffering smile. When Fagerolles asked him what he was doing at the moment he replied with a casual shrug of the shoulders:

'Nothing much really. A little thing here and there . . . not for exhibition. I'm trying something out. . . . If only you knew how lucky you all are to be able to be still at the bottom of the slope. While you're still climbing, you've plenty of both strength and courage. But when you've got to the top it's then the trouble begins. Torture, that's what it is; one long struggle, one effort after another to keep yourself from coming a cropper before your time. . . . Oh, believe me, I'd rather be at the bottom again, with the grade still to make. . . . Oh, you can laugh now, but you'll see, you'll see one day, take my word for it!'

They were laughing, too, thinking it was just one of Bongrand's paradoxes, the great man posing, which they were ready to forgive. No joy could be greater, they knew, than that of being acknowledged a master, as he was. So he gave up trying to make himself understood and sat listening to them, without a word, resting his arms on the back of his chair and puffing slowly away at his pipe.

Dubuche meanwhile, as he had his domestic side, was helping Sandoz serve the tea, while all the others went on talking at once. Fagerolles was telling a priceless story about old Malgras, who used to lend out his wife's cousin as a model to anyone who agreed to do a nude for him. From that the conversation turned to models. Mahoudeau was furious because good bellies were a thing of the past; it was impossible, he said, to find a girl with a belly worth looking at. The din became suddenly louder when they began to congratulate Gagnière on the collector he'd met while listening to the band in the Palais Royal, a crank with a little money whose one vice was buying pictures. Laughingly everyone asked for his address. Dealers they had no use for. It was a pity collectors had so little faith in painters that they insisted on buying through a dealer, in the hope of getting a discount. The daily-bread question led to further arguments. Claude was supremely contemptuous; if they rooked you, he said, what did it matter so long as you knew you'd produced a masterpiece, even if you had to live on nothing but water? Jory's avowed interest in filthy lucre was received with indignant shouts of 'Journalist!' and 'Throw him out!' followed by a volley of ticklish questions. Would he sell his pen for money? Would he cut off his right hand rather than write the opposite of what he believed to be true? His answers were not listened to, however, as the general excitement now worked up to fever-pitch in the fine frenzy of twenty-year-olds pouring out their scorn on the

world in general, unanimous in their passion for the work
of art unmarred by any human frailties and set high in their
heaven like a sun. They would willingly have flung themselves into the fire they were starting.

Bongrand had not stirred for some time, but faced with
all this boundless confidence, all the joyful clamour of
attack, he made a vague gesture of forbearance. Forgetting
all the scores of paintings that had established his reputation, thinking only of the birth pangs of the sketch he had
just left standing on his easel, he took out his little pipe
and, with tears in his eyes, murmured quietly:

'What it is to be young!'

Until two o'clock in the morning Sandoz kept on plying
his guests with tea. Outside, the only sound that rose from
the sleeping streets was the angry wailing of an amorous
cat. Inside, everyone was talking at random, carried away
by the flow of their own words, though throats were hoarse
and eyes burning from lack of sleep. When, at last, the party
did decide to break up, Sandoz picked up the lamp and
lighted them down the stairs, leaning over the banister to
whisper:

'Don't make a noise, mother's asleep.'

And when they had picked their way stealthily down the
stairs and the sound of their footsteps had died away, the
house was silent.

When it struck four, Claude, who was seeing Bongrand
home through the deserted streets, was still talking. He had
no desire to go to bed, he was burning with impatience for
the sun to come up so that he could get back to his picture.
This time, warmed by his day of good fellowship, his head
aching and seething with ideas, he was certain to produce
a masterpiece. He felt he could paint now and saw himself
going back to his studio, as to a woman he loved, his heart
pounding with excitement, regretting he had left her even
for a day which he now felt was like total desertion. He was
going straight back to his picture, and after one sitting his
dream would have come true. Bongrand meanwhile kept
stopping him every few yards, under the fading glimmer of

the street-lamps and, holding him by one jacket button, telling him that if ever there was a god-forsaken job it was painting. He, Bongrand, might think he was smart, but he still hadn't got to the bottom of it. Every picture he painted was like starting again from scratch. It was like bashing one's head against a stone wall. And they wandered along side by side, each talking at the top of his voice, for his own benefit, as the stars grew paler and paler in the morning sky.

CHAPTER 4

ONE morning, six weeks later, Claude was painting in the sunshine that came streaming in through his studio window. The middle of August had been dull and wet, but now the sky was blue again his heart was back in his work. His big canvas was making only slow progress, but he was putting up a determined fight and spending long, silent mornings working on it.

There was a knock at the door. He thought it was the concierge, Madame Joseph, bringing up his lunch, so, as the key was always in the lock, he simply called out:

'Come in!'

The door opened; he was aware of a faint, barely perceptible movement, and that was all. He went on painting without even turning to look. But after a time the tense silence, broken only by the soft sound of somebody breathing, began to disturb him, so he looked to see what it was. He was dumbfounded, for there stood a woman he did not recognize, wearing a light dress, her face half hidden under a white veil and, what was most amazing, she was carrying a bunch of roses.

Suddenly he realized who it was.

'It's you, mademoiselle! . . . The very last person I should have thought of!'

It was Christine. His last, hardly complimentary remark, though it had slipped out almost before he was aware of it, was really perfectly true. For a time her memory had occupied his thoughts incessantly; then, as two months went by without her giving any sign of life, she had become merely a fleeting vision, a pleasant face unfortunately never to be seen again.

'Yes, it's me, monsieur,' she said. 'I thought it was not nice of me not to have thanked you.'

She blushed, and her speech was hesitant, as if she could not find her words. Maybe the long climb up the stairs from the street had made her out of breath, for her heart was beating very fast. Had she done the wrong thing, she wondered, to pay this call which she had discussed with herself so often until at last it had appeared to her quite a natural thing to do? What made things worse was her having bought those roses as she came along the embankment, to give the young man as a kind of thank-offering. Now she found them simply embarrassing. How should she give them to him? What was he going to think of her? The indecorousness of all these things had only dawned on her once she had opened the door.

But Claude was even more embarrassed than she, and his politeness was exaggerated in consequence. He put down his palette and practically turned the studio upside-down in his efforts to produce a chair for her.

'Do sit down, mademoiselle, please. . . . This is such a surprise. . . . It really is charming of you . . . '

Having sat down, Christine regained her calm, and Claude looked so funny, making his floundering gestures, which she recognized as a sign of his shyness, that she had to smile. Then, her own shyness forgotten, she offered him the flowers.

'Look,' she said, 'they're for you, to show you I'm not ungrateful.'

He said nothing for a moment, but simply stood looking at her. Then, when he saw she was quite serious, he seized both her hands and almost crushed them in his own as he said:

'Now I know what you are, you're a real good sort! A real good sort, do you hear?' And he added as he was putting the flowers in his water-jug, 'And believe me, it's the first time I've paid *that* compliment to a woman!'

Coming back to her, he asked, looking straight into her eyes:

'Is it true, you hadn't forgotten me?'

'Why, of course I hadn't,' she answered with a laugh.

'Then why did you wait two months?'

That made her blush again, embarrassed for a moment by the lie she had just told.

'Because I'm not free to do as I like, you know. . . . Oh, Madame Vanzade is very kind to me, but she's a helpless invalid and never goes out. It was she who had to make me come out for an airing today, as she thought it would do me good.'

She did not tell him of the shame she had suffered for days after their encounter on the Quai de Bourbon, or how, when she found herself in the shelter of the old lady's household, the memory of the night she had spent in a strange man's room tortured her with remorse, like a sin, or how, at last, she had managed to put the man out of her mind and the whole episode, like the aftermath of an unpleasant dream, had gradually melted away. Then, she did not know how, through the measured calm of her new life, the image had risen again from the shadows and grown clearer and more precise until it obsessed her every moment of the day. Why should she have forgotten him? She had nothing to hold against him. On the contrary, she had reason to be grateful to him. The thought of seeing him again, completely repressed at first and held at bay for a long time later, had gradually become an *idée fixe*. Every evening when she was alone in her room temptation had haunted her in the form of an irritating, unsettled feeling, a vague, unacknowledged desire; and she had only been able to ease her mind a little by explaining away her restlessness as the need to express her gratitude. She felt so alone, so stifled in that sleepy household, while the pulse of youth was beating fast within her, and her heart was so eager for friendship.

'So I thought I would make the most of my first outing,' she said. 'Besides, it was so lovely this morning, after all that depressing rain!'

Claude, still standing looking at her, was very happy; he, too, made his confession, for he had nothing to hide.

'I didn't dare go on thinking about you,' he said. 'You see, you were like one of those fairies who come up through the floor, or melt into the wall, just when you least expect them to. So I said to myself: "It's all over; perhaps it isn't even true that she came into this studio." But here you are, and I'm so pleased! More pleased than I can possibly tell you!'

Smiling, but rather ill at ease, Christine turned away, pretending to look about her. Her smile soon disappeared, however, for the savage-looking painting she saw all around her, the flamboyant sketches of Provence, the terrifying anatomical precision of the studies from the nude made her blood run cold, as they had done the first time she saw them. She suddenly felt afraid again, really afraid, and in a different, much more serious voice, said:

'I'm afraid I'm in your way. I must go.'

'Oh, no!' cried Claude at once. 'You mustn't go!' He gently pushed her back on her chair. 'I'd just about worked myself to a standstill, so it'll do me good to talk to you. . . . The torments I suffer for that wretched picture!'

Christine looked up and saw the big canvas, the one that had been turned to the wall the last time she was there, and which she had so badly wanted to see.

The background and the dusky forest clearing, broken by a patch of sunshine, were still only roughly sketched in, but the two little female figures, one dark, the other fair, were practically finished and stood out remarkably clearly in the sunlight. In the foreground the man had been attempted three times and then left unfinished. It was the central figure, the reclining woman, that had received most attention. The head Claude had left untouched, but he had worked persistently on the body, using a fresh model every week until at last, despairing of ever finding one to his satisfaction, for the last two days he had been working from memory instead of from nature, in spite of his contention that his power of invention was non-existent.

Christine recognized herself immediately in the woman stretched out on the grass with one arm beneath her head and her eyes closed, smiling into space. The woman was naked, and the face was hers! She was as revolted as if the body had been hers too, as if it were herself lying there, stripped to her virgin nakedness. What hurt her more than anything else was the vehemence, the uncouthness of the painting itself; it pained her as if she had been outraged and beaten. She could not understand such painting; she thought it was abominable; she hated it instinctively, as an enemy.

She rose and repeated curtly:

'I must be going.'

Claude looked at her, surprised and disappointed by her sudden change of mood.

'What, so soon?'

'Yes. They're expecting me back. Goodbye.'

She was at the door already when he managed to take her hand and ask her tentatively:

'When shall I see you again?'

Her little hand melting in his, she hesitated for a second and then replied:

'I really don't know. I'm kept so busy, you see.'

And, withdrawing her hand from his, she left him, with a quick:

'Some day, when I can . . . Goodbye!'

Claude stood still where he was, in the doorway, wondering what had come over her this time; why her sudden reserve, why that veiled irritation? He closed the door and stalked about the room, baffled, trying in vain to think what he had said or done to offend her. Then perplexity gave way to anger in the form of a violent oath and a vigorous shrug of the shoulders, as if to shake off his senseless preoccupation. You never knew where you were with women! But the sight of the bunch of roses filling up his water-jug calmed him down, it smelt so sweet. It filled the whole studio with its perfume and, without another word, he set to work again in the scent of the roses.

Two more months went by. The first few days after Christine's visit, at the slightest sound, or when Madame Joseph brought him up his lunch or his mail, Claude would look sharply round and could never conceal his disappointment. He never went out now before four in the afternoon, and when the concierge told him one evening that a young lady had called about five he had been unable to set his mind at rest until he realized that his caller must have been Zoé Piédefer, the model. Then day had followed day in a long bout of feverish activity during which he had been so unapproachable, his theorizing had been so alarmingly violent, that none of his friends had dared to argue with him, so sweeping was he in his condemnations. Painting alone was worthwhile, and everything should be sacrificed to that, parents, friends, and particularly women! From his burning fever he had slipped into excruciating despair, a whole week of impotence and doubt, a whole week tortured by the thought of his bungling stupidity. He was gradually recovering and had gone back to his usual routine, his resigned and solitary struggle with his painting when, one misty October morning, he started and hastily put down his palette. No one had knocked at the door, but he had recognized a footstep on the stairs. He opened the door, and she entered. She had come at last.

She was wearing a big grey woollen cloak which completely enveloped her and a little dark velvet hat with a black lace veil beaded with moisture from the mist outside. There was a nip of winter in the air, but Christine was in excellent spirits. She apologized for having delayed her visit so long, and smiled her frank, open smile as she admitted she had been reluctant to come; that she had even thought she did not want to come; ideas of hers, she said, things he surely understood. But he did not understand, and did not try to

understand, because there she was. It was enough to know
that he had not offended her and that she was willing to
come and see him now and again as a good friend. There
was no explanation between them. Neither of them spoke
of the torment and the struggle of the preceding days; they
chatted for nearly an hour, in perfect agreement, without
dissembling or hostility, as if, while they were apart, they
had unconsciously come to understand each other. The
sketches and the life studies on the walls meant nothing to
her now. She looked for a moment at the big picture, at
the nude figure reclining on the grass in the blazing golden
sunshine, and concluded it was not herself. It could not be;
the woman in the picture had neither her face nor her limbs.
How could she possibly have recognized herself in that
frightful mess of colours? And a dash of pity was added to
her friendship for this well-meaning young man who could
not even paint a likeness. Taking her leave in the doorway,
it was she who held out her hand with a cordial: 'I shall
come again, you know.'

'I know, in another couple of months.'

'No, next week. . . . You see if I don't. . . . Till Thursday,
then.'

And on Thursday she was there, just as she had said.
From that day on she never failed to call once a week,
though not always on the same day at first, but just on
whatever day she happened to be free. Then, after a time,
she settled on Monday, as Madame Vanzade had decided
she should have Monday mornings for going out and taking
the air in the Bois de Boulogne. She had to be in again by
eleven, so she walked very quickly and often even ran, with
the result that she was quite pink with exertion when she
reached the studio, for it was quite a way from Passy to the
Quai de Bourbon. For four months that winter, between
October and February, she came every week through pelting
rain, fogs from the Seine, or pale winter sunshine doing its
best to warm the pavements. After the first month or so, if
she happened to have an errand to do in Paris, she would
pay an unexpected call on some other day of the week,

dashing up to the studio with only a moment or two to spare, the time to say 'good morning' and call out 'goodbye' as she ran down to the street again.

Claude was getting to know Christine better now. With his everlasting distrust of women, his suspicion that she had been involved in a love affair back in the provinces had persisted for some time, but her gentle eyes and her crisp laugh had at last dispelled it, and now he felt she was as innocent as a child. As soon as she came in now she was at home, at her ease, without the faintest trace of embarrassment, ready to start her ceaseless flow of chatter. She had recounted her childhood at Clermont a score of times already, but she always came back to it. The evening her father, Captain Hallegrain, had his last stroke and dropped like a log from his chair, she and her mother were out at church. She remembered their homecoming perfectly, and the terrible night that ensued, with the Captain, who was very strong and heavily built, laid out on a mattress; she remembered so well the way his lower jaw protruded that it was impossible for her to think of him otherwise. She herself had the same shape of jaw, and when her mother was at her wits' end to call her to order she used to say: 'You've got your father's chin, my girl. You'll come to a sad end, like he did!'

'Poor mother!' Christine would say as she recalled how often she had nearly deafened her by her rowdy games. As far back as she could remember her, her mother had always sat at the same window painting her fans, a slim, silent little figure with gentle eyes, the only one of her mother's features she had inherited. People often used to say to the dear soul, knowing it would please her: 'She has *your* eyes.' And then she would smile, happy to feel that she was at least responsible for that one touch of gentleness in her daughter's face. After her husband's death, she worked so hard that her sight began to fail. But she had to live somehow. The six hundred francs she drew as a widow's pension were barely enough to keep the child. So for five years the child had watched her mother grow a little paler, a little thinner every day, wasting away to a mere shadow, so that now she could never forgive herself for not having been a good child, for driving her mother to despair by not persevering with her work, starting every week with the best of intentions, swearing she would soon be helping her to earn their living. But do what she might, her limbs would not keep still and every time she tried to make herself settle down she began to be ill. Then one morning her mother had been unable to get up, and had died, without a parting word, her eyes brimming with tears. That was how she could still see her mother, with eyes wide open, staring at her, weeping even after death.

At other times, when Claude asked her about Clermont, Christine would forget her sorrows and call up happier memories. She laughed heartily as she told him about what she called their 'camp' in the Rue de l'Éclache: herself born in Strasbourg, her father from Gascony and her mother from Paris, all dumped in Auvergne, and all hating it. The Rue de l'Éclache, which runs down to the Jardin des Plantes, was narrow and dank and dismal as a cellar; not a single shop, never a passer-by, nothing but dreary houses with the shutters always closed; but, as their apartment had a southern aspect and overlooked the inner courtyards, it fortunately got plenty of sun. Even the dining-room opened on to a wide balcony, a sort of wooden gallery with arches buried in the foliage of an enormous wistaria. That was where she had grown up, first with her invalid father, then cloistered with her mother, who was exhausted by even the shortest venture out of doors. She knew so little about the town and the surrounding district that both she and Claude had to laugh at the number of his questions she had to answer by her inevitable 'I don't know'. Were there any mountains? Oh yes, there were mountains on one side, you could see them at the ends of some of the streets. On the other side, if you went along other streets, you could see great flat fields stretching away into the distance; but you never went to them, it was too far. The only mountain she could identify was the Puy de Dôme, because it looked like a hump. In the town itself, she could have found her way to the cathedral with her eyes closed; you went round by the Place de Jaude and along the Rue des Gras. But it was useless to expect more of her. The rest was an inextricable tangle of narrow streets and sloping boulevards in a city of black lava creeping down a hillside, along which rain rushed like a torrent in thunderstorms. And they were formidable storms they had in Auvergne; she still shuddered at the thought of them. The lightning-conductor on the Museum, which she could see over the roofs out of her bedroom window, never seemed to be without its tongue of flame. In the dining-room, which was also the drawing-room, she had her own special window, in a deep recess, almost another little room, where she had her work table and kept her most cherished possessions. It was there that her mother had taught her to read; it was there that, later, she had so often dropped off to sleep, tired and bored by listening to her teachers. So now she made a joke of her ignorance: the well-educated young woman who could not even give the names of all the kings of France with the appropriate dates; the famous musician who never got beyond '*Les Petits Bâteaux*'; the marvellous water-colourist who spoilt all her trees because she found leaves were so hard to paint! From there she would suddenly leap to the fifteen months she had spent after her mother's death in the big Convent of the Visitation in its magnificent gardens on the outskirts of the town. She would tell endless stories about the nuns and tremble to think how jealous, or foolish, or innocent they were. She herself was to have become a nun, though she felt stifled inside any church. Just when she was thinking it was too late to break away, the Mother Superior, who was very fond of her, had headed her away from convent life by getting her this place with Madame Vanzade. One thing about it still surprised her: how had the Mother of the Holy Angels been able to see through her so clearly? For since she had been in Paris she had grown completely indifferent to religion.

When the memories of Clermont appeared exhausted, Claude wanted to know what sort of life she led at Madame Vanzade's, and every week she supplied him with fresh details. Life in the silent, secluded little mansion in Passy was as smooth and regular as the gentle ticking of its antiquated clocks. Two ancient retainers, a cook and a butler, who had been with the family forty years, were the only people who moved about the empty rooms, with silent, slippered tread, like ghosts. Visitors were few and far between, and then only some eighty-year-old general, so dry and shrivelled that he hardly made an impression on the carpet. It was a house of shadows, where the sunshine was filtered down to a guttering night-light strength between the laths of the window-shutters. Since the old lady had gone blind and lost the use of her legs, her sole entertainment had been to have someone read pious literature to her indefinitely. How dreary they seemed to the girl, those endless readings! If only she had known how, she would have loved to spend her time cutting out dresses, trimming bonnets or making artificial flowers. It was hard to think that she was really good for nothing, that she should have been taught so many things and yet be qualified to do little more than any simple hired girl! Besides, she felt too repressed in such a stern, secluded house that smelt of death and decay, and that same reckless feeling she had known as a child, when she wanted to force herself to work to please her mother, returned and filled her with revolt, making her want to shout and jump and dance for the sheer joy of living. But Madame treated her so gently, relieved her of her duties in the sick-room and told her to go out for long walks, and she was often conscience-stricken when she came back from the Quai de Bourbon and had to lie about having been in the Bois de Boulogne, or invent some religious service or other when she never so much as set foot inside a church. Madame seemed to grow fonder of her every day and was always giving her presents, a silk dress, an antique watch, even linen. She for her part was very fond of Madame, and had cried one evening when Madame called her her little girl, and had then sworn she would never leave her now she was so old and infirm.

'Oh well, anyway,' said Claude one morning. 'Your devotion will not go unrewarded. She'll make you her heiress!'

Christine could not believe it.

'Do you think she will? . . . They say she's worth three million. . . . Oh, no! I couldn't think of it, I shouldn't want it. Besides, what should I do if she did?'

Claude, who had turned away, said shortly:

'You'd be rich, of course! . . . Besides, she'll probably marry you off first, who knows?'

At that, Christine broke in with a laugh:

'Yes,' she said, 'to one of her nice old friends. The colonel with the silver jaw-bone, for example! . . . That would be very funny!'

So they remained, on a sound footing of good friendship. He was almost as inexperienced as she was; his knowledge of women he had gleaned from casual affairs, for he lived beyond the pale of reality, in a world where love was a romantic passion. It appeared both simple and natural to both of them to go on meeting as they did, in secret, but as friends merely, with a handshake for greeting on arrival and another handshake for leave-taking. He had even stopped wondering just how much this nicely brought-up girl really knew about life in general and men in particular, and it was she who found him shy, and would often look at him with that tremor of surprise and uncertainty in her glance that springs from passion undisclosed. But so far the pleasure of being together was still unspoilt by any hint of emotional stress. Their handshakes were honest and frank, their conversation varied and lively, and when they argued it was as two friends who know they will never quarrel. But their friendship was becoming so vital that they could no longer live without each other.

As soon as Christine arrived Claude would take the key out of the door. Christine insisted that he should, so that no one should come and disturb them. After the first few visits she had soon taken possession of the studio and made herself at home in it. She was sorely tempted to try to tidy up the place, for she suffered torments surrounded by such neglect. But it was no easy undertaking, as Claude refused to let Madame Joseph sweep the floor lest the dust should settle on his wet canvases. So Christine's first attempts at tidying were looked upon with a worried and anxious eye. What was the good of moving things around? he asked. Wasn't it enough to have them handy? And yet she seemed to be so happy doing her little chores that he let her jolly him into giving her the run of the place, so that now she no sooner arrived than she took off her gloves, pinned up her skirt to keep it clean, pushed everything everywhere, and had the place straightened up in no time. The heap of accumulated cinders had gone from in front of the stove, the bed and the washstand were hidden by the screen, the divan had been brushed and dusted, the wardrobe polished, the deal table cleared of dirty crockery and paint stains; and over the chairs arranged in pleasing symmetry and the wobbly easels propped against the walls the enormous cuckoo-clock with its blaze of bright red flowers sent out a tick which seemed to have gained in resonance. The result was marvellous. The studio was unrecognizable. Claude could hardly believe his own eyes when he saw her bustling round the room, singing as she worked. Could this possibly be the girl who said she was lazy and that work gave her terrible headaches, he wondered? She laughed. Brain work did give her headaches, but working with her hands and feet did her a world of good, she said, and kept her from wilting. She confessed, as if it were some sort of vice, her fondness for the really heavy work of a house, a taste deplored by her mother, whose ideal in education was the white-handed governess disdainful of anything but the most ladylike accomplishments. The talkings-to she had had, even when she was quite small, for being caught sweeping up, or dusting, or enjoying herself playing at cooking! Even now, if only she could have beaten the dust out of something, she would have found life at Madame Vanzade's much less boring. The question was, what would they have thought of her? It would have meant she was no longer a lady; so she used to go and indulge her fancy at the studio, where she bustled around until she was quite breathless with a look in her eye like a sinner tasting forbidden fruit.

In time even Claude grew to appreciate her feminine tidiness, and occasionally, to get her to sit down for a quiet chat, he would ask her to put a stitch or two in a shirt cuff or mend a tear in a jacket. She herself had volunteered to go over his linen, but mending was not among the foremost of her housewifely accomplishments. She did not know how to sew, to start with; that was obvious from the way she held her needle. Besides, she did not like sitting still, and it maddened her to have to concentrate on a darn. The studio was as spick and span as any drawing-room, but Claude was still in rags, and that amused the pair of them; they thought it a great joke.

How happy they were during those four months of rain and frost they spent in the studio, with the stove drawing red and roaring like an organ-pipe! Winter cut them off completely from the rest of the world. While the snow lay thick on the neighbouring roofs and sparrows came and fluttered at the attic window, they smiled to think how cosy they were and yet how isolated in the silent heart of the great city. In time, however, their happiness ventured outside the studio's narrow limits, when at last she gave him permission to escort her on her way home. For a long time she had insisted on going back alone, still ashamed at the idea of being seen abroad in the company of a man. Then one day there was a sudden heavy shower and she was obliged to let him escort her with an umbrella. But as it stopped raining as soon as they had crossed the Pont Louis-Philippe she told him to go back, so they simply stood for a moment or two on the embankment, looking down on the Mail, happy to be together under a cloudless sky. Alongside the wharf below, great river barges loaded with apples were drawn up four deep and so closely packed that the gang-planks connecting them were like alleyways thronged with women and children unloading the fruit in

big round baskets. They were thrilled by the sight of such
an avalanche of fruit piling up and completely blocking the
wharf, giving out a strong, almost unpleasant smell of
fermenting apple juice which rose to their nostrils mingled
with the dank breath of the river. The following week, as
the sun was shining and Claude had·been saying how few
people one met on the embankment in the Ile Saint-Louis,
she agreed to take a walk. So they went up the Quai de
Bourbon and the Quai d'Anjou, stopping every few yards,
attracted by the various activities along the Seine, the
dredger with its grating buckets, the laundry-boat loud with
the shouts of a quarrel, a crane in the distance busy
unloading a barge. Christine was amazed; she could not
believe that the busy Quai des Ormes on the far bank, and
the Quai Henri-Quatre she was on, with its broad strand
like a beach, and dogs and children rolling about on the
heaps of sand, and the whole sky-line of this city so full of
life and activity, was the sky-line of that accursed city, lurid
and spattered with blood, she had glimpsed the night of her
arrival. They moved on then, round the tip of the island,
lingering to savour the silent, forsaken atmosphere of its
stately old houses; they watched the water seething among
the forest of piles at the breakwater and came back round
by the Quai de Béthune and the Quai d'Orléans. They were
closer to each other now than when they started out, forced
together by the broadening of the stream, until they stood
shoulder to shoulder looking over its huge current across to
the Port-au-Vin and the Jardin des Plantes. Against the sky
domed roofs of buildings were turning a deeper blue. As
they approached the Pont Saint-Louis, he had to tell her it
was Notre-Dame she could see since she did not recognize
it from the east end, from which it looked like some
enormous crouching beast with flying-buttress legs, raising
its head of twin towers at the end of its lengthy monster's
spine. But their great discovery on that particular day was
the westerly end of the island, like the prow of a vessel
eternally at anchor, straining towards Paris without ever
reaching it. At the foot of a steep flight of steps they found

a wharf planted with huge trees and not a soul about, a pleasant refuge, a sanctuary in the heart of the crowd, for all around on the bridges and embankment Paris roared while they, on the water's edge, tasted all the joy of being alone and ignored by the rest of the world. From that moment the wharf was their little strip of countryside, their bit of open air where they made the most of the sunshine when the oppressive heat of the studio with its red-hot, roaring stove grew too stifling for them and began to make their hands tingle with a fever they instinctively distrusted. Even then Christine still refused to let Claude escort her any further than the Mail. At the Quai des Ormes she always sent him back, as if Paris, its crowd, and all its possible encounters began at that long stretch of embankment that lay ahead of her. But Passy was such a long way off, and she was beginning to be so bored by making the entire journey alone, that little by little she relented and allowed him first to go as far as the Hôtel de Ville, then as far as the Pont-Neuf, then to the Tuileries. She began, too, to forget the danger she had imagined, and in the end they would go off together arm in arm, like a pair of newlyweds, and with time the same leisurely walk along the same pavements, along the riverside, had assumed an infinite charm and filled them with a keen sense of happiness the like of which they were never to know again. They belonged to each other heart and soul, though neither had embraced the other physically, and the soul of the great city, rising from the waters, wrapped them in all the tenderness that had ever pulsed through its age-old stones.

When the weather turned really wintry, in December, Christine started coming only in the afternoon, so that the sun was going down when Claude started out with her, about four o'clock, in the direction of Passy. On clear days, as soon as they came out on to the Pont Louis-Philippe, the whole vast stretch of the embankment, apparently endless, lay open before them. Along its entire length the slanting rays of the sun cast over the houses on the right bank a dusting of warm gold, while on the left bank and the islands the buildings stood out black against the flaming glory of the sunset. Between these two margins, one ablaze with light, the other gloomy with shadow, the spangled Seine flowed, cut across by the narrow stripes of the bridges, the five arches of the Pont Notre-Dame under the single span of the Pont d'Arcole, then the Pont au Change and beyond that the Pont-Neuf, each narrower than the other, the shadow of each followed by a stripe of bright light where the satin-blue water faded to white. While the twilit silhouettes on the left bank culminated in the pointed towers of the Palais de Justice harshly blacked on the cloudless sky, on the right a gentle curve swung through the sunlight running away into the distance so far that the Pavillon de Flore standing out like a citadel yonder at its utmost tip, looked like a dream castle rising, smoky blue, airy and quivering against the rosy mists on the horizon. But Claude and Christine, drenched in sunshine under the leafless plane-trees, did not look for long at the mighty splash of colour in the west, but took pleasure in other sights, and always the same ones, especially the ancient houses that stand above the Mail. There were little one-storey ironmongery or fishing-tackle shops surmounted by balconies gay with green shrubs and virginia creepers and backed by taller houses, all badly in need of repair, all sporting washing at their windows, the whole making an amazing pile of odd-looking buildings, a surprising jumble of beams and masonry, crumbling walls and hanging gardens through which balls of glass lit up like stars.

Following the embankment, they soon left behind the next batch of big buildings, the barracks, the Hôtel de Ville, and turned their attention to the other bank of the Seine, the Cité, packed tight inside its straight, smooth walls rising sheer from the water. Above the houses dark in shadow the towers of Notre Dame stood resplendent, as though freshly gilded. Booksellers' boxes were beginning to take over the parapets along the embankment; under an arch of the Pont Notre-Dame, a lighter laden with coal was straining against the powerful current. There, on flower-market days, they

would stop, whatever the weather, to smell the first violets
and the early wallflowers. On the left, the embankment was
now more open, and another long stretch of it came into
view. Beyond the pointed towers of the Palais de Justice
they could see the pallid little houses on the Quai de
l'Horloge, leading to the terrace with its clump of trees.
Further along, other parts of the embankment began to show
through the mist; the Quai Voltaire away in the distance,
and the Quai Malaquais, the dome of the Institut, the square
edifice that was the Mint, then a long grey strip of houses
where the windows were quite indistinguishable, and a
promontory of roof-tops made by the chimney-pots to look
like a rocky headland jutting into a phosphorescent sea. On
the opposite bank, meanwhile, the Pavillon de Flore was
losing its dreamlike quality and solidifying into reality in
the final burst of glory of the setting sun. Now, to right,
to left, on either bank of the river, opened the endless vistas
of the Boulevard de Sébastopol and the Boulevard du Palais
and, further ahead, the new buildings on the Quai de la
Mégisserie, with the new Préfecture de Police opposite, then
the old Pont-Neuf with its statue that resembled an ink-blot
against the sky, and beyond that, the Louvre, the Tuileries
and, rising above Grenelle, the heights of Sèvres and the
open country flooded in early evening sunshine. Claude was
never allowed to go beyond the Pont-Royal; Christine always
stopped him near the big trees next to Vigier's bathing
establishment, and when they stopped to exchange a final
handshake and looked back along the river in the red gold
of the sunset they could see that over the Ile Saint-Louis,
their starting-point, the other nebulous boundary of the
capital, night was already coming down from the slate-blue
sky in the east.

The lovely sunsets they watched on those weekly strolls
along the Seine, when the sun shone ahead of them all the way
through the many lively aspects of embankment life: the
Seine itself, the lights and shadows dancing on its face,
the amusing little shops, each one as warm as a greenhouse,
the pots of flowers on the seedsmen's stalls, the deafening

twitter from the bird-shops, and all the joyous confusion of sounds and colours that makes the waterfront the everlasting youth of any city. As they strolled along, the glowing embers of the sunset turned a deeper red above the dark line of the houses on their left, and the sun seemed to wait until they had passed the Pont Notre-Dame and reached the wider stretch of river before it began to glide slowly down behind the distant rooftops. Never, over ancient forest, mountain pathway, or meadow in the plain does day depart in such a blaze of triumph as over the dome of the Institut, when Paris retires to rest in all its glory. They never saw it twice the same; there was always some new furnace adding its fire and flame to the diadem. One evening, in an unexpected shower, the sun, as it reappeared through the falling rain, lit up every cloud in the sky, making the rain overhead glow like liquid fire shot through with pink and blue. On days when the sky was clear, the sun like a ball of fire would sink majestically into a waveless lake of sapphire. For a moment, as it passed behind the black dome of the Institut, it was horned like a moon on the wane; then as its disc reddened to deepest purple it would pass out of sight in the depths of the lake transformed into a pool of blood. After February, as the curve of the decline increased, it would fall straight into the Seine, which seemed to boil on the horizon at the touch of the red-hot disc. But the most theatrical effects, the most magnificent transformation scenes were only produced in a cloudy sky. Then, according to the whim of the prevailing wind, they would see waves of sulphur breaking on boulders of coral, palaces, towers, and buildings piled up in a blazing heap or crumbling down as torrents of lava poured through the gaps in their walls. Or, at other times, the sun already out of sight, hidden by a veil of mist, would suddenly break through with such a mighty thrust of light that a tracery of sparks would be sent shooting clear across the sky like a flight of golden arrows. And twilight would come down as they took leave of each other, their eyes still dazzled by the glory of the sky, and felt that Paris in its triumph had its share in the boundless joy that was theirs every time they wandered along the old stone parapets of the Seine.

The day came at last when the thing happened that Claude had always feared, though never expressed. Christine seemed to have given up the idea that they might meet someone they knew. Who knew her, anyhow? she asked. She could go about for ever and meet no one she knew. But he never quite forgot his artist friends and often felt a slight shock when he thought he recognized somebody's back in the near distance. He was obsessed by a strange sense of modesty; he suffered unspeakable torments at the thought of anyone staring at the girl, accosting her, or maybe going so far as to make fun of her. And on the day in question, with her clinging to his arm, they were just approaching the Pont des Arts when they came upon Sandoz and Dubuche coming down the steps. It was impossible to avoid them, since they met practically face to face. It was even possible his friends had seen him first, for they were both smiling. He went pale, but did not turn aside, though he thought all was lost when he saw Dubuche make a move in his direction; then Sandoz held him back and led him firmly ahead. They passed, apparently quite indifferent, and disappeared into the courtyard of the Louvre without even looking back. They had both recognized the original of the pastel head that Claude had kept hidden out of sight, like a jealous lover. Christine was far too happy to have noticed anything, but Claude, his heart thumping in his breast, answered her with difficulty as he choked back tears of gratitude for the thoughtful gesture of his two old friends.

A few days later he received another shock. He was not expecting Christine, and had told Sandoz to call, when she ran up to spend an hour with him and give him one of the surprises they both enjoyed. They had just taken the key out of the lock, as they always did, when someone gave a friendly thump on the door. Claude recognized the knock at once and was so flustered that he knocked over a chair. That made it impossible not to answer the door. But Christine turned deathly pale and with a frantic gesture begged him not to stir. He did not move, and held his breath. The knocking continued and someone shouted: 'Claude! Claude!' He still did not move, but stood there, overcome, pale to the lips, his eyes cast down. There was a long silence, then footsteps going down the creaking wooden stairs. His heart was suddenly filled with a tremendous sadness and he felt ready to burst with remorse at every receding footstep, as if he had denied his oldest friendship.

Then, one afternoon, someone knocked again and Claude had only time to whisper in dismay:

'The key's still in the lock!'

Christine had forgotten to take it out. In alarm she rushed behind the screen and dropped on to the edge of the bed, stuffing her handkerchief into her mouth to cover the sound of her breathing.

As the banging grew louder and somebody laughed outside, Claude was forced to call out:

'Come in!'

His discomfiture increased when he saw it was Jory who, with a great show of gallantry, ushered in Irma Bécot. Fagerolles had passed her on to him a fortnight ago, or, to be exact, he had agreed to her whim rather than lose her altogether. Out of sheer physical exuberance she was squandering her youth and beauty right and left, in one studio after another, packing her three chemises every week and moving on, but prepared to go back for the odd night if the fancy took her.

'She wanted to come, so I've brought her,' was the way Jory explained their visit.

Without waiting to be invited, she at once made herself at home and began to explore, exclaiming:

'I say, this *is* a funny place! . . . Oh! What funny painting! My! . . . Come on, now, be kind and show me all there is to see. That's what I've come for. . . . I say, where do you sleep?'

Claude was terrified lest she should move the screen, thinking of Christine behind it and grieved already at what she was hearing.

'You know what she's come to ask you, don't you?' went on the gallant Jory. 'Don't say you've forgotten. You promised you'd let her pose for something or other. . . . She'll pose for anything you like, won't you, darling?'

'You bet! Now, if you like!'

Claude was embarrassed.

'Well, you see, this picture's going to keep me pretty busy up to the Salon. . . . There is one figure in it that's giving me a bit of trouble. I don't seem to get what I want from any of those damned models!'

'What, this nude on the grass?' she asked, standing in front of the canvas and tilting her little nose with an air of understanding.

'I wonder if there's anything I can do to help?'

Jory was on fire with enthusiasm in a second.

'Why, of course! Marvellous idea! You're looking for a good model and can't find one. . . . Why not have a look at Irma? . . . Come along, dear, slip your things off and let him see what you're like.'

Irma whipped off her hat with one hand and with the other began to undo the hooks on her dress, undeterred by Claude's emphatic refusals and his violent attempts to extricate himself from the outrageous situation.

'No, no,' he said. 'Thanks very much, but it's quite useless. . . . Madame is not large enough. . . . Not at all the type I want, really, not at all the type.'

'What does that matter?' she said. 'Have a look all the same.'

Jory, too, insisted.

'Yes, go on! Have a look. The pleasure's hers. She doesn't model generally, doesn't need to, but she gets a great kick out of showing herself. . . . Wouldn't mind if she never wore a stitch. Come on, darling, undo your frock. We'll just have the bust, as he obviously thinks you're going to eat him!'

In the end Claude did manage to prevent her from undressing, stammering excuses meanwhile: he would be delighted, later, but not now; he was afraid that at this stage a new model might only confuse him still further. And so she merely shrugged her shoulders, fixed him with her pretty eyes sparkling with vice and an air of smiling contempt.

Then Jory began talking about the gang. Why had Claude not been at Sandoz's last Thursday? They never saw him these days, and Dubuche accused him of being kept by an actress. There'd been a fine old scrap between Fagerolles and Mahoudeau about modern dress in sculpture. The Sunday before, Gagnière had come out of a Wagner concert with a black eye. He himself had nearly had a duel at the Café Baudequin on account of one of his latest articles in *Le Tambour*. Oh, he treated 'em rough, all the twopenny-ha'penny daubers and their overrated reputations. The campaign against the Selection Committee was creating a devil of a fuss. By the time he'd finished with them there'd be nothing left of that band of self-appointed excisemen who put an embargo on nature and impounded ideals as if they were contraband. Claude listened with unveiled irritation and impatience. He picked up his palette and kept hovering about his easel until at last Jory took the hint.

'You're wanting to work. We'll leave you to it.'

Irma, still vaguely smiling, never stopped looking at the painter, surprised that he could be silly enough not to want her and stung now by the whim of getting him in spite of himself. It was no show-place, this studio of his, and you could hardly say he was handsome himself, so why all the virtue? Shrewd, intelligent, with her happy-go-lucky youth for a fortune, she could not resist just one other joke at his expense. So, as she was leaving, making him a final offer over her long, warm, enveloping handshake:

'Any time you like.'

When they had gone Claude had to go and move the screen, for Christine remained where she was, on the edge of the bed, as if she had not the strength to stand up. She made no comment on his lady visitor, but simply said she had been rather frightened. She wanted to leave at once; she trembled at the idea of anyone else calling and had no desire to betray her distress by even so much as a look.

From the first she had been disturbed by the violent atmosphere of Claude's studio, lined as it was with his vigorous paintings. She had never been able to get used to the outspoken studies from the nude and she was repelled, not to say physically pained, by the crude reality of the sketches of Provence. To her, they did not make sense, but then she had been brought up to admire another, and gentler, art: her mother's water-colours, the dreamlike delicacy of her fan designs, where lilac lovers sauntered in pairs through gardens of misty blue. Even now she often amused herself by doing little schoolgirl landscapes, a lake with a ruin, a water-mill, or a chalet with pine trees in the snow, her three stock subjects. So she was amazed to think how anyone as intelligent as Claude could possibly do such ugly, wrong-headed, false-looking painting. For she thought his pictures not only monstrous and hideous, but also quite beyond the pale of any acceptable truth, the work of a madman, in short.

One day Claude insisted on her showing him her little sketch book, the little album she had often mentioned she had had in Clermont. For a long time she had refused to bring it, but at last she gave way, partly because she felt flattered, but largely because she was curious to know what he would have to say. Claude went through it and smiled, but said nothing, so she broke the silence.

'You think it's bad, don't you?' she murmured tentatively.

'No. It's not bad, it's innocent.'

The word annoyed her, though his intonation showed it was kindly meant.

'Well, what can you expect? I only had a few lessons from Mamma. . . . What I like is something nicely done and pleasant to look at.'

Her last remark made him laugh outright.

'You can admit now,' he said, 'that my painting makes you ill. I know it does, by the way you tighten your lips and go pop-eyed, you're so scared. . . . Oh, it's no painting for ladies, and certainly not for young ladies. . . . But you'll get used to it; it's only a matter of training your eye and then you'll see it's sound, healthy stuff, really.'

And in the event Christine gradually did get used to it, but not, be it said, through any artistic conviction. For Claude, with his disdain for female opinion, made no attempt to put ideas into her head, but even avoided talking art with her, as if he wanted to keep that passion in his life completely separate from the new passion that was creeping into it. No, Christine simply slipped into the habit and began to take some interest in Claude's appalling pictures when she realized the supremely important place they held in his life. That was the first stage, when she began to be moved by his passion for work and by the way he hurled himself into it, body and soul. It *was* touching, she thought; it was even wonderful. Then, as she realized how he was either elated or depressed after a good or an unsuccessful sitting, she began to feel that she, too, had a share in his work. She sympathized if she found him depressed, she was lively when he greeted her with a smile. And from then it became her one preoccupation, wondering whether he had been working hard and whether he was satisfied with what he had done since their last meeting. At the end of two months her conquest was complete; she could look at the pictures without flinching, and, although she did not always thoroughly approve of the way they were painted, she began to repeat artists' expressions she had heard Claude use, and say things were 'vigorous', or 'luminous', or 'well put together'. She found him so kind, and she was so fond of him, that once she had excused him for producing such terrible daubs she began to look out for their good points, so that she could try to grow fond of them too.

There was one picture, however, the one for the forthcoming Salon, that she still found difficulty in accepting. She could look at the nudes painted at Boutin's and the sketches of Plassans now without any feeling of distaste, but the naked woman lying on the grass still irritated her beyond words. It was a personal dislike, the outcome of the shame of having thought for a moment she recognized herself, and the vague embarrassment she still felt when she looked at the picture, though the features seemed to grow less and less like her own. At first she had protested by looking away. Now she would stand for minutes on end gazing at it in silent contemplation, wondering how the resemblance could have disappeared. The more Claude worked over it, for he was never satisfied and came back scores of times to the same points, the less like her it became. And, though she would have been unable to analyse her feelings, still less *admit* them, even to herself, she was more and more grieved to see less and less of herself in it, in spite of her original revulsion. With each little detail that changed, their friend-ship seemed to be diminished, she felt less close to him. Did he not like her, she wondered, that he should let her fade out like that? Who was the other woman? Whose was the nebulous, unknown face that was beginning to show through her own?

Claude, very dejected at having spoilt the head, was won-dering how he could bring himself to ask her to pose for an hour or two. Even if she had just sat as she was, he could have noted the essentials, but having seen her in one rage he had no desire to provoke another. He had made up his mind to ask her nicely and pleasantly, but when the moment came words failed him and he was as overcome with shame as if he had been going to say something improper.

He came to the point, however, one afternoon, in a fit of anger he could not control even for her sake. Nothing had gone well the whole week, and he was talking of scrapping the whole canvas, stalking furiously about the room and kicking the furniture about. Suddenly he gripped her by the shoulders and sat her down on the divan as he said:

'Please do me a kindness, or, if you don't, by God, I'm finished!'

Taken by surprise, she did not understand at once.

'Kindness?' she said. 'What is it you want?'

Then, seeing him pick up his brushes, she added, almost before she was aware of it:

'Oh, *that*! . . . Why didn't you ask me before?'

Of her own accord, she lay back against a cushion and folded her arm beneath her head. But the surprise and confusion at having consented so quickly made her turn suddenly very serious, for she had not known she was going to do this thing, in fact she would have sworn, a few minutes previously, that she was never going to pose for him again.

Delighted, he cried at once:

'Are you really going to do it? . . . Now I'll show them how to paint a woman, by God I will!'

Then again without thinking, she said:

'Only the head, of course.'

And he, suddenly afraid that he might have gone too far, stammered apologetically:

'Oh, of course, only the head.'

Both rather disconcerted, they said no more, and Claude began to paint while she lay still, gazing into space, annoyed with herself for having made that last remark, yet already filled with remorse for being even so obliging. There was something reprehensible, she felt, in allowing her likeness to be painted on that nude body lying there resplendent in the sun.

In two sittings the head was finished. Claude was delirious with joy. It was the best bit of painting he'd ever done, he cried. And he was right. He had never painted anything more alive or more genuinely lighted. Happy to see him happy, Christine cheered up too and even went as far as to say the head was very good; still not a very good likeness, but full of expression. They stood a long time looking at it, half closing their eyes and standing back against the wall.

'Now,' he said at last, 'I can polish off the rest with a model. . . . Thank God I've settled *her*! She was nearly too much for me.'

And in a fit of childish merriment he seized the girl in his arms and they danced together what he called the 'victory dance'. Christine enjoyed it as much as he did, and laughed heartily, with all her doubts and scruples and worries flung to the winds.

At the end of a week, Claude was as gloomy as before. He had got Zoé Piédefer to pose for the body and she was not giving him what he was looking for. The head was too delicate, he said, to fit on to such common shoulders. He refused to give in, however, scraped his canvas and started afresh. About the middle of January, in utter despair, he gave it up and turned the picture to the wall. A fortnight later he set to work again, with another model, big Judith this time, which meant that he had to revise completely his tone values. Things went wrong again, so he fetched Zoé back and then lost his grip once more, quite ill with anguish and uncertainty. The unfortunate thing about it all was that it was only the central figure that proved such a difficulty; the rest of the work, the trees, the two small female figures, and the man in the black velvet jacket were all finished and satisfied him in every way. February was drawing to a close; there were only a few days left if the thing was to go to the Salon. It looked like a disaster.

One evening, beside himself with fury, he shouted at Christine:

'How in God's name can you put one woman's head on another woman's body? . . . I ought to cut off my right hand for trying to do it!'

There was only one thought now at the back of his mind: to get her to consent to pose for the whole figure. It had grown, slowly, out of a simple wish, which he had immediately repressed as absurd, through a long, recurrent argument with himself, into a definite desire stimulated by the spur of necessity. He was haunted now, obsessed by the memory of her bosom as he had glimpsed it that morning, radiant with the freshness of youth, and he knew he had to paint it. If she refused him now, it would be useless to go on with the picture, for he knew no one else could satisfy his need. And he would sit for hours, slumped on a chair, tortured by his own impotence, his inability to decide where to place his next brush-stroke, and all the time trying to make bold resolutions. As soon as she came in he thought he would tell her his troubles, and in such moving terms that she would be sure to give in. But when she did come in, with her frank, friendly laugh and her dress so chaste that it revealed nothing of her figure, his courage failed

completely and he looked away from her lest she should
notice him trying to trace, beneath her bodice, the supple
line of her torso. No, you could not make such demands of
a friend like her. He, at least, would never have the courage
to do it.

Then, one evening, as he was getting ready to escort her
and she was putting on her hat, they stood for a second
looking into each other's eyes, just as the upward movement
of her arms moulded her dress closely to the shape of her
breasts. A thrill went through him, and he knew by the
sudden serious look and the way the colour left her cheeks
that his thoughts had been divined. As they walked along
the river the sun was setting in a sky of burnished bronze,
but they hardly exchanged a word, as though they sensed
there was something between them. Twice he saw from her
look that she knew what was haunting his mind. Indeed, his
thoughts had affected the train of hers, now fully awake to
the most unintentional allusions, and, although at first she
had hardly noticed the effect, it was soon brought clearly
home to her. But even then she felt there was no call to be
on the defensive, for it was just something that had no place
in real life, but was one of those things one dreamed and
blushed to think of afterwards. The fear that he might make
the request of her never even crossed her mind. She knew
him so well now that she could have silenced him with a
look, in spite of his sudden flashes of temper, even before
he could have managed to stammer out the first few words.
The whole idea was mad. Nothing could possibly come of
it, ever!

Days went by, and the fixed idea they shared in silence
grew. No sooner were they together than they felt bound
to think of it. No mention of it ever passed their lips, but
their very silences were full of it. Behind every gesture they
made and every smile they exchanged they felt the presence
of the thing they could never bring themselves to express,
though it now filled every corner of their minds. Soon it
was the only thing left in their relationship as friends. She
felt as if he was undressing her with every look; the most

innocent words began to resound with equivocal overtones; every handshake went a little further than the wrist and sent a thrill of emotion through the entire body. And the thing they had so far avoided in their friendship, the disturbing factor, the awakening of the male and female in them, was unleashed at last by this constant preoccupation with virgin nudity. They each became aware, in time, of a secret fever raging in the other; their cheeks would flush and burn if their fingers chanced to meet, and every moment held its potential thrill, while the excruciating torments they could neither speak nor hide, the gradual invasion of their entire being, choked them and racked their bodies with immeasurable sighs.

When Christine called one day about the middle of March, she found Claude sitting in front of his canvas, overcome with despair. He did not even hear her come in and simply sat quite still, his wild, blank stare fixed on his unfinished painting. He had only three days left to finish it in time for the Salon.

'Well,' she said gently, dismayed to see him dismayed. 'What do you think of it?'

He started and turned towards her.

'What do I think of it?' he repeated. 'I think it's useless. I'm not sending it in this year. . . . And I'd set such store by this Salon.'

They both relapsed into their despondency with its deep, disturbing undercurrents. Then, suddenly, thinking aloud, Christine murmured:

'There's still time.'

'Still time? Of course there isn't, short of a miracle. Where do you expect I'm going to find a model now? . . . Listen, I've been weighing things up ever since this morning, and I thought for a moment I'd found a way out. I thought I'd call in Irma, the girl who came here once, do you remember? Oh, I know she's short and a bit on the plump side, and I might have to alter everything. But she's young. I think she might do. . . . Anyhow, I'm going to give her a trial. . . . '

That was all he said, but his burning eyes as he looked at her said quite plainly: 'There's still yourself, and that would be the real miracle; success would be a certainty if only you would make this supreme sacrifice for my sake. I beg you, I beseech you as a friend, a friend I worship, the loveliest, the purest friend I have!'

And Christine, head held high and pale with emotion, heard every word and was moved by the force of the prayer in his burning look. With slow, deliberate fingers she took off her hat and her pelisse, then, without more ado, continued the same calm gesture, undid and removed her dress and her corsets, slipped off her petticoats, unbuttoned the shoulder-straps, and let her chemise slip down over her hips. She did all this without saying a word, as if she were elsewhere, or in her own room undressing herself without thinking while her mind wandered off in pursuit of a dream. Why should she let a rival give him her body when she herself had already given him her face? She wanted it to be *her* picture, hers entirely, the token of her affection, and as she realized that, she realized also that she had been jealous all along of that strange, nondescript monster on the canvas. And so, still silent, virgin in her nudity, she lay on the divan and took up the pose, eyes closed, one arm beneath her head.

Petrified with joy, Claude watched her undress. It all came back to him now, the momentary vision, so often conjured up in his mind, was come to life again, a little childlike and frail, but supple, youthful, and fresh. Again he wondered how she managed to dissemble such a well-formed bosom so that it could hardly be suspected beneath her dress. He did not speak either, but started to paint in the rapt silence that had settled on them both. For three long hours he lost himself in work, and in one virile effort finished a superb sketch of the whole figure. No woman's form had so enraptured him; his heart pounded in his breast as it might have done in the presence of a naked saint. He made no attempt to approach, but stood amazed at the transfiguration of the face, its heavy, sensual jaw softened and outshone by the soothing calm of the cheeks and brow. Throughout those three hours she never stirred or even appeared to breathe, but made the sacrifice of her modesty without a tremor and without embarrassment. Both were aware that if either of them spoke so much as a word they would be overwhelmed by shame. All she did from time to time was to open her bright eyes and fix for a moment some vague point in space, revealing nothing of her thoughts the while, then closing them again, assuming once more the remoteness of a lovely marble statue but never losing the fixed, mysterious smile that was part of the pose.

With a gesture Claude indicated he had finished, immediately regained his clumsiness and knocked over a chair in his haste to turn his back while Christine, blushing violently, rose from the divan. Shivering now, and so flustered that she did up the hooks all awry, she hurried on her clothes, pulling down her sleeves and even turning up her collar in her anxiety to leave no portion of her skin uncovered. She was already enveloped in her pelisse before he dared to turn his face from the wall and risk a glance in her direction. When he did turn round he walked over to her, but they could only stand and look at each other in silence, for both were so overcome by emotion that speech was impossible. Was it sorrow they felt, infinite, unconscious, unspoken sorrow? For the tears welled in their eyes as if they had both made a wreck of their lives and plumbed the depths of human misery. Shattered, heartbroken, unable to utter so much as a word of thanks, he planted a kiss on her brow.

CHAPTER 5

ON the fifteenth of May, Claude, who had come home from Sandoz's at three o'clock in the morning, was still asleep at nine when Madame Joseph brought him up a big bunch of white lilac. He knew what it meant. It was Christine celebrating in advance the success of his picture. For this was his great day, the opening of the 'Salon des Refusés', the first of its kind, where his picture, which had been turned down by the Selection Committee of the official Salon, was being hung.*

He was touched by her delicate thought of sending fresh, sweet lilacs to greet him on awaking, like the promise of a happy day. Barefoot in his shirt, he took them and put them in his water-jug. Then, bleary-eyed still, he hustled into his clothes, grumbling because he had slept so late. The night before he had promised Dubuche and Sandoz he would pick them up at eight o'clock at the latter's flat, so that they could all go together to the Palais de l'Industrie where they were to meet the rest of the gang. And he was an hour late already!

He might have known he would be unable to lay his hand on anything, since the studio had not been tidied up since the big picture was taken away. It took him five minutes to find his shoes, crawling around on his knees among a lot of old frames, with gold dust floating in the air all round him. As he had not known where to find the money for a frame, he had got the local joiner to knock together four pieces of wood and he had gilded them himself, assisted by Christine, who had proved a very inexpert gilder. Fully dressed at last, and his hat sparkling with constellations of gold dust, he was just about to go when a superstitious thought called him back to the flowers left standing alone in the middle of the table. He had to kiss those lilacs or meet with a setback; so he kissed them and filled his nostrils with their heavy springtime scent.

Down in the porch he handed his key to the concierge as usual and said:

'I shall be out all day, Madame Joseph.'

In less than twenty minutes he was on Sandoz's doorstep in the Rue d'Enfer. Sandoz, whom he hardly expected to find, was also late. His mother had not been well; nothing serious, just a bad night. It had worried him and kept him awake, but now his mind was at rest. Dubuche had written to say they were not to wait for him, he would meet them at the exhibition, so the two of them started out together. As it was nearly eleven they decided to lunch at a quiet little dairy in the Rue Saint-Honoré. They lingered over their meal, as if their eagerness had suddenly given way to inaction and left them to revel in sentimental recollections of their childhood.

One o'clock struck as they were crossing the Champs-Elysées. It was a beautiful day, with a clear blue sky made brighter somehow by a breeze which, for the season, was still cool. Under the corn-coloured sun the long rows of chestnuts spread the delicate green of their newly-opened, freshly-varnished leaves; the fountains spouting their watery sheaves, the well-kept lawns, the endless avenues and vast open spaces all gave the city landscape an air of luxury. A few carriages—it was still early for them—were making their way up the Avenue, but crowds were pouring, like ants, in a never-ending stream towards the Palais de l'Industrie and being swallowed up by its enormous arcade.

Claude shuddered when he found himself in its gigantic entrance hall, for it was as cold as any cellar and on its damp flagstones footsteps resounded as on the floor of a church. Looking up, right and left, at the monumental staircases, he said scathingly:

'What do we do, trudge through all the rubbish in *their* Salon?'

'I should think we don't!' replied Sandoz. 'Let's cut through the garden to the west staircase. That leads straight to the "Refusés".'

They passed scornfully by the little tables of the catalogue sellers, between the great red velvet curtains and through a porch full of shadow to the glass-roofed garden.

It was the moment of the day when the garden was practically empty, apart from the crowd flocking to lunch at the buffet under the clock. Everybody else was on the first floor, looking at the pictures, and the only figures to be seen near the yellow sanded pathways that cut smartly round the green of the turf were the white marble statues—permanent, motionless visitors bathed in the diffused light that filtered through the glass and settled on them like dust. At the southern end the centre aisle was blocked by sun blinds, making it golden when the sun was out, with a splash of bright red and blue at either end from the stained-glass in some of the windows. One or two visitors who were already feeling the strain were sitting about on the brand new chairs and benches bright with paint, while flocks of the sparrows which roosted in the forest of girders overhead kept swooping and wheeling in noisy pursuit, or boldly scratching about in the sand.

Claude and Sandoz made a point of hurrying ahead without looking at anything: they had been so irritated by the first thing they saw, a stately but graceless Minerva in bronze, by a Member of the Institut. But, as they were racing past an interminable row of busts, they recognized Bongrand, alone, walking slowly round a massive recumbent figure of colossal proportions.

'Why, hello!' he exclaimed when they went to shake his hand. 'I was just looking at friend Mahoudeau's effort. They did at least have the intelligence to accept it and put it in a good place. . . .'

He stopped suddenly, then asked:

'Have you been upstairs?'

'No,' said Claude, 'we've just come in.'

Then, very slowly, he talked to them about the 'Salon des Refusés'. He was a Member of the Institut himself, though he had little in common with his fellow members, but he found the whole thing very amusing; the everlasting dissatisfaction of the painters, the campaign launched by the smaller papers such as *Le Tambour*, the protests, the endless complaints which had eventually begun to worry the Emperor himself; the artistic *coup d'état* for which he had been solely responsible, silent dreamer though he was; the shock and commotion he had caused, well and truly setting the cat among the pigeons.

'You have no idea,' he went on, 'of the indignation among the members of the Selection Committee! . . . And they don't say too much in front of me, you know; they don't quite trust me. The full blast of their fury, of course, is meant for those awful Realists. It was against them, you remember, that the doors of the temple were systematically barred, and it's for their benefit that the Emperor wanted to give the public a chance to revise its opinion. And the Realists have won! Oh, the things I heard said! If half of them were true, I should think the outlook's going to be pretty black for you youngsters!'

And with a big, kindly laugh he flung wide his arms as if to embrace all the youth he felt was springing up about him.

'Your pupils are growing up,' said Claude.

Bongrand silenced him with a gesture, as though suddenly embarrassed. He had nothing in the exhibition, and all these things he was walking round and looking at, all this effort of human creation, the pictures, the statues, filled him somehow with regret. It was not jealousy, for he was a good man and his soul was above such emotions; rather they gave him pause and stirred that unspoken fear of gradual decline that he was never able to escape.

'What about the "Refusés"?' asked Sandoz. 'Are they a success?'

'Superb. You'll see.' Then, turning to Claude, and clasping both his hands, he said:

'You, my lad, have got something. . . . They tell me I'm smart, but believe me, I'd give ten years of my life to have painted that buxom wench of yours upstairs.'

Such praise, from such a source, moved the young artist to the verge of tears. So he had done something worth while at last! Unable to utter a word of thanks, he suddenly switched the conversation to another subject, to cover up his emotion.

'Good old Mahoudeau!' he cried, 'he's done a good job here! Talk about temperament, eh!' he added, as he and Sandoz walked round Mahoudeau's figure.

'Temperament enough,' said Bongrand with a smile, 'but too much leg and too much bust. Still, look at the joints of those limbs, how delicate; beautifully done! . . . Ah well, goodbye. This is where I leave you. I'm worn out. I'm going to sit down.'

Claude, meanwhile, was looking up, listening, suddenly aware that the air was filled with a terrific noise, a persistent rumbling, like the pounding of a storm against rocks, or the ceaseless roar of some untiring onslaught from out of the infinite.

'Listen,' he said. 'What's that?'

'That,' said Bongrand, as he moved away, 'is the crowd upstairs at the show.'

And the two young men hurried across the garden and up to the 'Salon des Refusés'.

It was all very well set out; the setting quite as luxurious as that provided for the accepted pictures: tall, antique tapestry hangings in the doorways, exhibition panels covered with green serge, red velvet cushions on the benches, white cotton screens stretched under the skylights, and, at the first glance down the long succession of rooms, it looked very much like the official Salon, with the same gold frames, the same patches of colour for the pictures. But what was not immediately obvious, was the predominant liveliness of the atmosphere, the feeling of youth and brightness. The crowd, already dense, was growing every minute, for visitors were flocking away from the official Salon, goaded by curiosity, eager to judge the judges, convinced from the outset that they were going to enjoy themselves and see some extremely amusing things. It was hot; there was a fine dust rising from the floor; by four o'clock the place would be stifling.

'Damn it!' said Sandoz, elbowing his way in. 'It's going to be no easy job getting through this crush and finding your picture.'

In the warmth of his friendship for Claude, Sandoz wanted to lose no time; this day he was living only for Claude, Claude's work and Claude's success.

'Don't worry!' cried Claude, 'we'll get to it in time. It won't fly away!'

And he deliberately pretended to be in no hurry, in spite of his overwhelming desire to run. Head high, he began to look about him. Soon, through the mighty voice of the crowd that had dazed him somewhat at first, he detected laughter, restrained still, and drowned by the trampling of feet and the hubbub of conversation. Visitors were making humorous comments in front of some of the pictures. That disturbed him, for beneath his rugged revolutionary's exterior he was as credulous and sensitive as a woman, always expecting martyrdom, always suffering tortures, always amazed to find himself rebuffed or ridiculed.

'They seem to be having fun in here,' he said, half to himself.

'I should think they are, and no wonder,' Sandoz pointed out. 'Look at the nags there. Can you beat those?'

At that moment, just as they were preparing to linger a moment in the first room, Fagerolles walked straight into them. He had not seen them, and started slightly, as if the meeting annoyed him, but he was soon his amiable self again.

'Hello!' he said. 'I was just thinking about you two. . . . I've been here for the last hour.'

'What have they done with Claude's picture?' Sandoz asked.

Fagerolles, who had just spent twenty minutes in front of the picture, studying it and studying the reactions of the public, answered smoothly:

'I've no idea. . . . Let's all look for it together, shall we?'

With that, he joined them. He was as big a humbug as ever, and had now exchanged his former raffish garb for clothes of more formal cut, and, though devastating irony was still never far from his lips, he now assumed the serious, pursed-up expression that indicates the young man bent upon success.

'I'm sorry now I didn't put something in this year, too,' he said, with great conviction. 'Then I could have been on the line with the rest of you. . . . There are some startling things here, believe me. Look at those horses now.'

He pointed at the huge canvas ahead of them, and at the crowds milling in front of it and laughing. It was the work, they said, of a retired vet, and showed a lot of horses in a meadow. They were life-size horses, painted in the most fantastic blues and mauves and pinks, with their bones sticking through their hides in a most astonishing manner.

'What do you mean?' said Claude suspiciously. 'What do you take us for?'

Fagerolles feigned enthusiasm.

'No, seriously,' he said, 'it has its points. The chap knows his horses! He paints like nothing on earth, of course, but what does that matter? He is at least original. He does offer something new.'

There was not a trace of a smile on his girlish face, but only in his bright eyes just the faintest spark of mockery. Then he threw out another remark, the unkindness of which he alone was able to appreciate:

'If you're going to attach any importance to a lot of ignoramuses laughing, you're going to have your eyes opened in a minute or two.'

The three friends moved on and were soon ploughing their way laboriously through the sea of shoulders. When they reached the second room they cast their eyes round, but the picture they were looking for was not there. What they did see, however, was Irma Bécot on Gagnière's arm, crushed close against the wall. He was inspecting a very small canvas, and she, with a smile on her comic little face, was looking about her, thoroughly enjoying being jostled by the crowd.

'Hello,' said Sandoz, surprised. 'She's with Gagnière now, is she?'

'Just a passing fancy,' explained Fagerolles calmly. 'It's very funny really. . . . You know somebody's furnished a flat for her, of course? Oh, yes, the very last word. It's that young duffer of a marquis there was such a fuss about in the papers, remember? Oh, she's a girl with a future, is Irma; I've always said she was. You can put her in a four-poster in a mansion, but there are times when you can't keep her out of a camp-bed in a studio. That's what she was after on Sunday night. She dropped in at the Café

Baudequin about one o'clock in the morning; we'd just gone, and there was only Gagnière left, asleep over his beer. . . . So she picked up Gagnière!'

Irma had noticed them at once and was already making affectionate gestures to them, so they could not escape. When Gagnière turned round, looking even more generally colourless than usual, with his light hair and beardless cheeks, he showed no surprise at finding them standing behind him.

'It's amazing,' he faltered.

'What is?' asked Fagerolles.

'This picture. . . . A little masterpiece. . . . Honest, simple, painted with real conviction.'

And he pointed to the tiny canvas in which he had just been so absorbed. It was such an infantile effort that it might have been painted by a child of four: a little house with a little path in front and a little tree on one side, all very badly askew, all outlined firmly with black, with the inevitable corkscrew of smoke twirling out of the chimney.

Claude looked impatient, but Fagerolles, completely self-possessed, murmured:

'Subtle, very subtle,' and added: 'But what about your picture, Gagnière? Where's that?'

'Mine? There,' replied Gagnière.

And indeed there it was, not far from the little masterpiece. It was a landscape, all pearly grey. A bit of the Seine, very carefully painted, pretty, though rather heavy in tone, perfectly balanced and completely free from all revolutionary crudity.

'So they were fools enough to turn this down, were they?' said Claude, now full of interest. 'But why?' he went on, for there was no obvious reason for the Selection Committee's action. 'Why, I ask you, why?' And indeed there seemed to be no reason why the Committee should have refused it.

'Because it's Realist!' declared Fagerolles in a voice so decisive that it was impossible to tell whether his remark was directed against the Selection Committee or the picture.

Irma, meanwhile, left to her own devices, was simply staring at Claude, smiling unconsciously, as she always did, at his rather bungling shyness. To think he had never had the gumption to look her up! He looked different today, she thought, funny somehow, certainly not at his handsomest, dishevelled as he was and blotchy about the face, as if he had had a high fever. Grieved by his lack of interest, she tugged his sleeve as she said:

'Isn't that a friend of yours over there, looking for you?'

It was Dubuche. She recognized him as she had met him once at the Café Baudequin. He was pushing laboriously through the crowd and looking vaguely about him, over the sea of heads. Suddenly, just as Claude was waving wildly to attract his attention, he turned round and bowed very low to a group of three people; the father, very short and stout and red in the face with blood pressure; the mother, very thin with a complexion like wax, wasted by anaemia; the daughter, so puny for her eighteen years that she looked as frail and spindly as a very young child.

'Now he's nicely entangled,' said Claude quietly. 'The fellow certainly has some ugly friends! I wonder where he dug up those beauties?'

Gagnière, unperturbed, said he knew the man by name. It was old Margaillan, a big building contractor, a millionaire five or six times over already and making another fortune out of the rebuilding of Paris, contracting for whole boulevards at a time. Dubuche had most likely made his acquaintance through some of the architects whose plans he overhauled.

Sandoz felt sorry for the girl, she was so thin.

'Poor thing!' he said. 'Like a skinned rabbit. Of all the sad sights!'

'Enough of that!' said Claude harshly. 'They're every one of 'em stamped with all the crimes of their class; they reek of stupidity and scrofula . . . and serve 'em right, too. . . . There! He's dropping us and going off with them. We might have known he would, he's an architect! Ah, well, good riddance! If he wants us now, he can look for us.'

Dubuche, who had not even noticed his friends, had just offered his arm to the mother and was moving away, explaining the pictures with a wealth of obsequious and exaggerated gestures.

'Come on,' said Fagerolles. 'It's time we moved, too.'

Then, turning to Gagnière, he added:

'Do you happen to know where they've stuck Claude's picture?'

'I don't,' replied Gagnière. 'I was looking for it. . . . I'll go along with you.'

So he joined the party, but forgot to include Irma Bécot. It had been her idea that it would be nice to go round the Salon on his arm, but he was so unused to having a woman with him that he was continually losing her and was always surprised to find her at his side, since he could not think how, or why, they came to be together. She ran after him now and clutched his arm again, though she really wanted to be with Claude, who was just moving into the next room with Fagerolles and Sandoz.

All five of them wandered around taking in what they could, forced apart one moment, crushed together the next, but carried along by the general surge of the crowd. An abominable effort of Chaîne's, 'Christ and the Woman taken in Adultery', brought them to a momentary halt with its stiff, wooden figures, all skin and bones, painted in the drabbest of colours. Next to it was something they admired; a beautiful study of a woman from the back, her haunches well in evidence, and her head turned towards the painter. On every side the walls were covered with a mixture of the excellent and the execrable, in every possible style; last-ditchers of the 'historical' school cheek by jowl with youthful fanatics of Realism, colourless mediocrity with blatant originality, a 'Jezebel Dead' that looked as if she had mouldered away in the cellars of the Beaux-Arts hung next to a 'Woman in White', a curious vision, but seen by the eye of a great artist; opposite an immense 'Shepherd contemplating the Sea (Fable)', a tiny picture of Spaniards playing *pelota*, a marvel of intensity in lighting. The execrable was very fully represented; nothing was left out, neither military subjects complete with toy soldiers, wishy-washy Classical subjects nor medieval subjects heavily scored with bitumen. Superficially, it was an incoherent jumble, but there was truth and sincerity enough about the landscapes and sufficient points of technical interest in most of the portraits to give it a healthy atmosphere of youthful passion and vigour. There may have been fewer frankly bad pictures in the official Salon, but the general level of interest and attainment was certainly lower. Here there was a scent of battle in the air, a spirited battle fought with zest at crack of dawn, when the bugles sound and you face the foe convinced you will defeat him before nightfall.

The warlike atmosphere put new life into Claude and roused him to such anger that he listened to the swelling laughter of the crowd with a look on his face as defiant as if he were listening to the whistle of bullets. The laughter, which had sounded very discreet at first, grew louder as he advanced through the various rooms. When he reached the third the women had stopped stifling their merriment with their handkerchiefs, and the men, completely unrestrained, were holding their sides and roaring with laughter. It was the contagious hilarity of a crowd bent on amusement, gradually working itself up to the point where it would laugh loudly at nothing and be just as convulsed by beautiful things as by ugly ones. Chaîne's Christ provoked less laughter than the nude woman whose prominent buttocks, which seemed to stand out from the canvas, were apparently thought to be screamingly funny. The 'Woman in White' provided some amusement, too, for she was rarely without her group of grinning admirers digging each other in the ribs and going off into fits of helpless mirth. Every picture had its peculiar attraction; people would call to each other to come and look at this or that, and pithy remarks were heard on every lip, until at last, by the time Claude had reached Room No. IV, one old lady's chortles so exasperated him that he nearly slapped her face.

'Of all the idiots!' he cried, turning to the others. 'Enough to make you want to take a masterpiece and knock them on the head with it!'

Sandoz, too, was becoming hot under the collar now, but Fagerolles merely added to the general merriment by singing the praises of the most detestable paintings, while Gagnière simply floated through the throng and in his wake trailed Irma, delighted to feel her skirts wrapping round the legs of the men.

Suddenly they recognized Jory away in the distance, blond and handsome as ever, his fine, pink nose resplendent in his beaming face, thrusting his way through the crowd, waving his arms and hurrahing as if he had just had some personal triumph. As soon as he saw Claude he exclaimed:

'So there you are at last! I've been looking for you for the last hour. . . . Talk about a success, my friend! I've never seen anything like it!'

'Success? What success?'

'Your picture, of course! . . . Come on, I must show you. No, go and see for yourself. It's stunning!'

Overjoyed, Claude turned pale and he felt a lump in his throat, although he pretended to be unmoved by his friend's announcement. Recalling what Bongrand had said, he was now convinced of his genius.

'Good afternoon all!' Jory ran on, shaking hands all round. Then he, Fagerolles, and Gagnière settled round the good-natured Irma, who dispensed her smiles evenly among the three of them; it was, as she said, 'quite a family gathering'.

Sandoz was impatient.

'Where is the thing?' he asked. 'Take us to it, can't you?'

So Jory took the lead and the others followed. They practically had to fight their way into the last room, and Claude, who was well behind the rest, heard the laughter growing louder and louder, mounting like a tide. Then, when at last he did manage to get inside the room, he saw one enormous confused mass of humanity seething and milling in front of his own picture. It was there that everybody was laughing loudest and longest: in front of *his* picture.

'There!' cried the triumphant Jory. 'How's that for success?'

Gagnière, cowed and feeling almost as ashamed as if he had taken a smack in the face, murmured:

'It's the wrong sort. . . . I'd rather have seen something else.'

'Something else! Don't be a fool!' cried Jory in a burst of impassioned conviction. 'That's success, I tell you! Who cares a damn if they laugh? We're launched, no doubt about it. The papers'll be full of us tomorrow!'

'Idiots!' was all Sandoz could say; he was choking with grief.

Fagerolles said nothing, but assumed the dignified, detached look of a family friend at a funeral. The only one who could still smile was Irma; she thought it was funny. Then, with a soothing gesture she leaned on the shoulder of the wretched Claude and whispered gently:

'Don't take on because of them, love. It's only meant in fun, you know, so cheer up.'

Claude never stirred. He felt frozen. His heart had stopped beating for a moment in his bitter disappointment. As if drawn and held by some invisible force, he stood glaring in astonishment at his picture. He hardly recognized it hanging there in that room. It was certainly not the work he had seen in his studio. It looked yellower in the light that filtered through the white cotton screen; it looked somehow smaller, too, and cruder, and yet at the same time more laboured. And now, either by comparison with the pictures hanging near it, or simply on seeing it for the first time in this new setting, he took in all its faults at a glance, after looking on it with blind eyes for months on end. In a few strokes he was already painting it all afresh, altering all the planes, rearranging a limb here, changing his tone value there. Without a shadow of doubt, the man in the black velvet jacket was all wrong, he was over-painted and badly posed; the best thing about him was his hand. In the far distance the two little female figures rolling together on the grass were not sufficiently developed, not solid enough, only amusing to the trained eye of the artist. The trees and the sunlit glade he liked, and the naked woman lying on the grass he found so resplendent with life that she looked like something above and beyond his capacities, as if she had been painted by someone else and he himself had still to see her as she really was.

He turned to Sandoz and said:

'No wonder they're laughing. The picture's unfinished. . . . Still, the woman's good. Bongrand wasn't fooling.'

Sandoz tried to get him outside, but he refused to be led and moved even closer to the picture. Now he had passed judgment on his own work, he wanted to watch and listen to the crowd. It was one long-drawn-out explosion of laughter, rising in intensity to hysteria. As soon as they reached the doorway, he saw visitors' faces expand with anticipated mirth, their eyes narrow, their mouths broaden into a grin, and from every side came tempestuous puffings and blowings from fat men, rusty, grating whimperings from thin ones, and, dominating all the rest, high-pitched, fluty giggles from the women. A group of young men on the opposite side of the room were writhing as if their ribs were being tickled. One woman had collapsed on to a bench, her knees pressed tightly together, gasping, struggling to regain her breath behind her handkerchief. The rumour that there was a funny picture to be seen must have spread rapidly, for people came stampeding from every other room in the exhibition and gangs of sightseers, afraid of missing something, came pushing their way in, shouting 'Where?'—'Over there!'—'Oh, I say! Did you ever?' And shafts of wit fell thicker here than anywhere else. It was the subject that was the main target for witticisms. Nobody understood it; everyone thought it 'mad' and 'killingly funny'. 'There, do you see, the lady's too hot, but the gentleman's wearing his jacket, afraid of catching a cold.'—'No, that's not it! She's green, can't you see! Must have been in the water some time when he pulled her out. That's why he's holding his nose.'—'Pity he painted the man back to front, makes him look so rude, somehow!'—'I know what it is, it's a Young Ladies' Academy having a picnic. Don't you see those two playing leap-frog?'—'I say, what's this, washing day? People blue, trees blue, he's blued up the whole thing, if you ask me!' The ones who did not laugh lost their tempers, taking the overall blueness, Claude's original way of rendering the effect of daylight, as an insult to their intelligence. It was an outrage and should be stopped, according to elderly gentlemen who brandished their walking sticks in indignation. One very serious individual, as he stalked away in anger, was heard announcing to his wife that he had no use for bad jokes, while another visitor, a finicky little man who searched through the catalogue for an explanation to enlighten his daughter, read out the title: 'Open Air', and released a fresh outburst of hooting and shouting. The word was picked up, repeated, passed on for comment. 'Open Air'! Well, well, it was certainly open, and there was plenty in the air, too much in the air, it was all in the air! It was beginning to look like a riot. More and more people kept forcing their way up to the picture, and as the heat grew more intense faces grew more and more purple, the stupid, gaping faces of ignorant people pretending to appreciate painting and voicing all the nonsense, all the preposterous remarks, all the gibes and taunts that the sight of an original work never fails to elicit from the mouths of bourgeois imbeciles.

The last blow had still to fall. The commotion was at its height when Claude saw Dubuche coming back with the Margaillans still in tow. As soon as he came up to the picture the cowardly Dubuche, overcome with shame and embarrassment, tried to hurry past, pretending he had seen neither the picture nor his friends. But the building contractor had already planted himself in front of the picture, his stubby legs well apart and his eyes starting from their sockets as he bawled in his great, raucous voice:

'I say! Does he call himself a painter, the fellow who did this?'

The millionaire parvenu's good-humoured coarseness, summing up as it did the average opinion of the crowd, raised a tremendous guffaw. Then Margaillan, flattered by his reception and tickled by the unfamiliarity of the painting before him, began to laugh, too, an unrestrained, full-throated laugh that boomed over all the rest—the grand *finale* on the great organ, with all the stops full out.

'Please take Régine outside,' pale Madame Margaillan whispered to Dubuche, who immediately began to clear a passage for the daughter, whose eyes were modestly cast down, and he put so much muscular vigour into the task that he might have been rescuing the poor little creature from certain death. Then, when he had taken his leave of the Margaillans in the doorway, with many handshakes and a rare display of social graces, he came back to join his friends and said bluntly to Sandoz, Fagerolles, and Gagnière:

'How could I help it? It wasn't my doing. . . . I'd told him what to expect, that people wouldn't understand it. And besides, say what you like, it's smutty and you can't deny it.'

Sandoz turned pale and clenched his fists with rage.

'They jeered at Delacroix,' he cried, 'and they jeered at Courbet! Philistines, that's what they are! An enemy race of cruel, mindless executioners!'

Gagnière, remembering his Sunday battles for real music at the Pasdeloup concerts, shared Sandoz's indignation.

'It's the same lot who hiss at Wagner,' he cried. 'I know their faces. . . . Look. That fat one over there. . . . '

Jory had to hold him back, though he himself would have liked to stir the excitement of the crowd even more. He kept on saying it was a capital show, with a hundred thousand francs' publicity value! Meanwhile Irma, who had been running loose among the crowd, had picked up two young stockbrokers she knew, a pair of the most unbridled scoffers, and was trying to make them see reason, slapping their fingers to make them say the picture was good.

So far Fagerolles had not opened his lips. He was still examining the picture, with occasional glances at the public. With his Parisian's flair, his slickness, and his supple conscience, he realized at once where the discrepancy lay, and he had the vague feeling that some slight attenuation, a rearrangement of the subject and a general toning-down of the treatment were all that was needed to make the picture an unqualified popular success. The influence Claude had had on him persisted; it had soaked deep into him, left its mark upon him; but he still thought Claude was an unutterable fool for submitting a picture like this. Wasn't it sheer stupidity to believe in the intelligence of the public? What was the point of the woman being naked and the man fully clothed? What was the sense of the two small female figures wrestling in the background? Here was a piece of painting without its equal in the Salon, the work of a master, but for all that he could not help feeling a profound contempt for a painter who, though so admirably gifted, set all Paris laughing as if he was the craziest of crazy daubers.

His feeling of contempt was so strong that he could hide it no longer, and in an outburst of irrepressible candour he said to Claude:

'Between you and me, old fellow, you asked for it. If anyone's a fool here, it's you!'

Claude did not answer, but turned his eyes from the crowd and looked at him. He was pale and his lips twitched occasionally, but otherwise the laughter had not affected him; nobody knew who he was; it was his work, not he, that had been outraged. For a short while, then, he looked back at the picture and then, very slowly, at all the other paintings in the room, and, amidst the ruins of his illusions and the pain of the wound inflicted on his pride, there came to him, out of all that painting, so gay and brave and reckless in its challenge to out-of-date routine, a breath of youth and sanity. It both consoled him and gave him strength, it freed him from all sense of remorse or self-reproach and urged him rather to make an even firmer stand against the public. Some of the efforts were clumsy, inevitably, and some of them childish, but the general tone was admirable and so was the light, a fine, silvery, diffused light, with all the verve and sparkle of the open air! It was like a window flung open on all the drab concoctions and the stewing juices of tradition, letting the sun pour in till the walls were as gay as a morning in spring, and the clear light of his own picture, the blue effect that had caused so much amusement, shone out brighter than all the rest. This was surely the long-awaited dawn, the new day breaking on the world of art! As he looked around he saw one critic stop, but not to laugh; he saw famous painters, obviously surprised, but interested; and he watched old Malgras, unwashed as usual, and lips pursed as becomes a connoisseur, after going from canvas to canvas, stop dead in front of his and stand rapt in contemplation. It was then he turned to Fagerolles and surprised him by his delayed retort:

'Fools are born, my dear chap, not made, so my fate seems to be sealed. How lucky you must feel to be so clever!'

Fagerolles slapped him on the back to show there was no ill-feeling, and Claude let Sandoz take him by the arm to lead him away. They had all decided that on leaving the 'Salon des Refusés' they would go through the Architecture room, as Dubuche had had a plan for an art-gallery accepted, and he had been hovering around with such a humble, beseeching look on his face that they felt they could hardly refuse him the satisfaction of showing it to them.

'Ah! What an ice-box!' said Jory with a laugh as they entered the room. 'At least you can breathe in here!'

They all took off their hats and mopped their brows in relief, for it was like coming into cool shadow after a long trek in the broiling sun. The room was empty. The soft, even, rather dismal light that filtered through the white holland blind stretched across the sky-lights, was reflected like a stagnant pool in the mirror of the highly polished floor. Against the faded red of the walls the plans, large and small, with their pale blue borders, stood out in rectangles of palest water-colour. And alone, absolutely alone in the heart of this desert was one man, a man with a beard standing lost in contemplation in front of a project for a charity institution. Three ladies who looked in took fright and trotted hastily into the next room.

Dubuche was already explaining his exhibit to his friends. It consisted of a single drawing, a sorry little project for an art-gallery, sent in at the last moment, merely to satisfy his ambition and contrary both to accepted custom and to the wishes of his teacher, who had, however, as in honour bound, arranged to have it accepted.

'What's it intended to house, this gallery of yours,' asked Fagerolles with a very straight face, 'painting of the Open-Air School?'

Gagnière nodded his head in admiration, thinking all the time of something else, while Claude and Sandoz, out of loyalty to Dubuche, showed a genuine interest in the work.

'It's not at all bad,' said Claude. 'The decoration looks a bit mongrel to me, but that's a mere detail.'

Jory broke in then; he was getting impatient.

'Let's get a move on,' he said. 'I'm catching my death in this place.'

So the gang moved on. The one drawback was that, to make a short cut, they had to go through the official Salon; this they resigned themselves to doing, although they had sworn that, as a protest, they would not even set foot in it. Cutting through the crowd they went firmly from end to end of the rooms casting only the occasional indignant look to right or left. There was nothing here to recall the lively riot of *their* Salon, with its fresh colours and its exaggerated rendering of bright sunlight. It was one long succession of gold frames filled with shadow, black, ungraceful shapes, jaundiced-looking nudes in gloomy half-lights, all the paraphernalia of Classical Antiquity, historical subjects, genre paintings, landscapes, each one thoroughly soaked in the train-oil of convention. Every picture oozed unfailing mediocrity; every one showed the same dingy, muddy quality typical of anaemic, degenerate art doing its best to put on a good face. They hurried ahead, ran almost, to escape from this place where bitumen still reigned supreme, condemning everything wholesale with the injustice of all good partisans and swearing there was nothing worth while in the place, nothing, absolutely nothing.

They managed to escape at last and were just going downstairs to the garden when they ran into Mahoudeau and Chaîne. The former flung himself into Claude's arms exclaiming:

'What a picture, old fellow! Full of character! Full of character!'

Claude immediately replied with a word of praise for the 'Grape-Picker'.

'You've given them something of an eye-opener, too!' he said.

Then, seeing Chaîne hovering in the background without a word from any of them about his 'Woman taken in Adultery', Claude felt sorry for him. There was something inexpressibly sad about Chaîne's abominable painting and the way his whole peasant's life had been spoilt by the misguided admiration of a foolish bourgeois amateur, so Claude always tried to cheer him with a word of approval.

'Good bit of work, too, that little thing of yours,' he said, giving Chaîne a friendly slap on the back. 'You can still teach 'em a thing or two when it comes to drawing.'

'Yes, I believe I can,' replied Chaîne, blushing purple with vanity under his scrubby black beard.

Now he and Mahoudeau tagged on to the rest, and Mahoudeau asked them if they had seen Chambouvard's 'Sower'. It was amazing, the only decent bit of sculpture in the show, he said, as he led them into the garden which was now also being overrun by the crowds.

'Look!' he said, stopping in the middle of the centre alleyway. 'There it is, and Chambouvard himself standing in front of it!'

And there, indeed, firmly planted in front of the statue, admiring his own work, was a big fat man with a bull neck and the heavy handsome face of an Indian idol. He was said to be the son of a veterinary surgeon from Amiens or thereabouts. At forty-five he had already produced a score of masterpieces, simple, lifelike statues, modern in texture, modelled by a workman of genius, without any refinements, all part of his routine production, for he brought forth statues as a field produces grass, good one day, bad the next, with no idea of the value of the thing created. His lack of critical faculty was such that he drew no distinction between the most glorious works of his hands and the abominable gimcrack figures he sometimes turned out. Never worried or dubious about his work, but always firmly convinced of its worth, he had the pride of some divine creator.

'Stupendous!' Claude remarked as he examined 'The Sower'. 'Look at the size—and the gesture!'

Fagerolles did not even look at the statue; he was much more amused by the great man and the train of open-mouthed young disciples he always dragged around.

'Just look at them!' he said. 'You'd think they were at Holy Communion! And look at him! The great brute trans-figured by the contemplation of his own navel!'

Isolated, completely unaffected by the general curiosity, Chambouvard stood gaping at his Sower with the shattered look of a man who cannot quite believe he ever fathered such a work. He might have been viewing it for the first time and finding it more than he could take in. Then a look of ecstasy spread over his broad features, his head began to nod and he broke into a soft, irrepressible laugh as he murmured over and over again to himself:

'Funny . . . funny . . . funny.'

Behind him his entire train was almost swooning in rapture, but that was the only word he could find to express his boundless admiration of himself.

There was a moment of tension when Bongrand, who was walking round with his hands behind his back, looking at nothing in particular, came up against Chambouvard. A whisper ran through the crowd as it watched the two famous artists, one short and sanguine, the other tall and diffident, shake hands and exchange a few friendly words:

'Still producing marvels, I see.'

'As usual! What about you, have you nothing in this year?'

'Not a thing. I'm having a rest, looking for a new idea.'

'Don't be funny! You don't need to *look* for new ideas!'

With that they parted. Chambouvard and his courtiers made a measured progress through the crowd, like a sovereign very satisfied with life. Bongrand, on seeing Claude and his friends, came up to them, his hands now fluttering with agitation, and said, indicating the sculptor with a movement of his chin:

'There's a fellow I envy! Always convinced he produces masterpieces!'

He complimented Mahoudeau on his 'Grape-Picker' and treated them all with a fatherly good humour that well became an old Romantic who had made his peace with the world and received the blessings of officialdom. Turning to Claude, he said:

'Now, what did I tell you? You've seen for yourself, now you've been upstairs. . . . You've founded a new school.'

'Well, they certainly didn't mince matters upstairs,' said Claude, then added: 'But the master of all of *us* is *you*.'

Bongrand made his usual vague, pained sort of gesture:

'What do you mean?' he said as he hastened away. 'I'm not even my own master yet!'

The gang strolled round for a little longer and had gone back to look once again at the 'Grape-Picker' when Jory noticed that Gagnière no longer had Irma Bécot on his arm. Gagnière was flabbergasted; he could not think how he had lost her. But when Fagerolles told him she had gone off in the crowd with a couple of young men he stopped worrying and followed the others around feeling considerably lightened and relieved by the loss of his embarrassing conquest.

By this time it was almost impossible to move at all. All the benches were full and the crowds blocked the pathways, so that the slow progress of the visitors was punctuated with stops and starts marked by the most popular of the bronzes and marbles. Round the refreshment bar the general clamour that filled the vast, church-like nave swelled into a tremendous babel of voices, accompanied by the rattle of crockery and the tinkle of spoons. The sparrows had sought refuge in the forest of girders, chirping and chattering at the sinking sun through the warm glass panels in the roof. The atmosphere was static, damp and close as in a greenhouse, and with the same insipid smell of leaf-mould freshly turned, while over the seething tide of humanity in the garden the din from the upstairs rooms, the tramping of feet on the cast-iron floors, roared on and on like the beating of a gale against cliffs.

Claude was keenly aware of the tempest raging in the background and reaching a point where it blotted out all other sounds and howled and shrieked with all its might. It was the gaiety of the crowd, the cat-calls and the laughter released like a hurricane by the sight of his picture. He could bear it no longer:

'What are we hanging round here for?' he asked. 'Surely not for refreshments? The place reeks of the Institut! Let's go and have a drink outside, shall we?'

Footsore and weary, but with contempt marking every feature, they left the exhibition. Outside they breathed again, noisily, to indicate their joy at renewing contact with nature and the spring. It was only four o'clock or thereabouts, and the sun was shining straight down the Champs-Élysées, setting everything alight, the serried ranks of carriages, the young leaves on the trees, the jets of the fountains as they leaped into the air and broke into spray of purest gold. Sauntering down the Avenue they stopped at last at a small café, the Pavillon de la Concorde, on the left just before the Place itself. It was so cramped inside that they sat down at the tables near the side-avenue, although it was already almost cold under the thick, dark canopy of the leaves. Beyond the belt of dark green shadow under the two double rows of chestnut trees, the sunlit roadway of the Avenue lay before them, and they could see Paris going by in a cloud of glory, the carriages with wheels like radiant stars, the great yellow omnibuses more heavily gilded than triumphal cars, riders whose glossy mounts seemed to shoot out sparks, while the very passers-by were transfigured and resplendent in the blaze of the sun.

For close on three hours Claude sat there, his beer untouched, talking, arguing, in an ever-rising fever, worn out physically, but his brain seething with ideas after all the painting he had just seen. What usually happened after their visit to the Salon was greatly intensified this year as a result of the Emperor's liberal gesture; the tide of theories rose even higher, their voices grew thicker as they grew more and more intoxicated with far-fetched theories and gave vent to their burning passion for art and beauty.

'What does it matter,' he cried, 'if the public laughs? All we have to do is to educate the public! . . . After all, it really amounts to a victory. Take out a couple of hundred duds and *our* Salon knocks theirs into a cocked hat. We've got guts! We've got courage! We *are* the future! . . . Oh yes, the day will come when we'll kill their Salon stone dead. We'll ride into it as conquerors, with masterpieces for weapons. If Paris is silly enough to laugh, let it laugh! We'll have it at our feet yet!'

He broke off only to make a prophetic gesture embracing the great triumphal Avenue, alive with all the gaiety and luxury of the city and sweeping down to the Place de la Concorde, the view of which, through the trees, was composed of one of its splashing fountains, a stretch of balustrade, and two of its statues, Rouen with her enormous breasts, and Lille advancing her gigantic naked foot.

'They think it's amusing, the open air,' he went on. 'Good! If it's open air they want, let 'em have open air, the Open-Air School, eh! Yesterday nobody had heard of it except you and me and one or two artists. Today the name's well launched, the new school's founded, and *they* founded it. . . . After all, why not? Open-Air School's a good name, so I've no objection.'

Jory meanwhile was slapping his thighs with satisfaction.

'What did I tell you?' he said. 'After those articles of mine they'd *got* to bite, they'd got to swallow it, the numskulls! We've got 'em at our mercy now, and they're going to know it!'

Mahoudeau joined in the victory chorus, too, repeatedly bringing in his 'Grape-Picker' and explaining its bold originality to the silent Chaîne, the only one who was listening. Gagnière, ruthless like all timid people let loose on pure theory, was talking glibly of sending the entire Institut to the scaffold, while Sandoz, an ardent sympathizer with all sound workmanship, and Dubuche, succumbing to the contagion of his friends' revolutionary ideas, were both seething with indignation, thumping the table and drowning Paris in every draught of beer they took. Fagerolles, very calm and collected, just smiled. He had followed the others round out of sheer amusement, for his own peculiar pleasure in inciting his friends to do things he knew would have disastrous results. While egging them on to rebel, he was making the firm resolve to work from now on for the Prix de Rome. The day's events had made up his mind for him; he would be a fool, he thought, to compromise his talent any longer.

The sun was dipping now to the horizon, shedding its paler gold upon the downward flow of carriages returning from the Bois. The Salon, too, must have been closing, for among the steady stream of passers-by there were numbers of gentlemen who looked like critics, with catalogues tucked under their arms.

'If you want to know who invented landscape, look at Courajod,' said Gagnière in a sudden burst of enthusiasm. 'Have you seen his "Pool at Gagny" in the Luxembourg?'

'A perfect gem!' said Claude. 'It's thirty years old, and still nobody has done anything to beat it. Why do they leave it in the Luxembourg? It ought to be in the Louvre!'

'Because Courajod isn't dead,' said Fagerolles.

'What! Courajod not dead? But nobody ever sees him, nobody ever talks about him!'

They were all astounded to learn from Fagerolles that the seventy-year-old landscape painter was still living quietly somewhere in Montmartre with his dogs and his poultry. That was one of the sad things about elderly artists; they could outlive their reputations, they could be lost sight of during their own lifetime. An awed silence fell on the little group as Bongrand, with flushed face and diffident gestures, greeted them as he went by on the arm of a friend. Close on his heels, surrounded by his disciples, came Chambouvard, laughing loudly, forging ahead, an absolute master, confident of eternity.

'Hello, you leaving us?' said Mahoudeau to Chaîne, who was moving away from the table.

Chaîne mumbled some vague reply into his whiskers, shook hands all round and made off.

'You know where he's going,' said Jory to Mahoudeau. 'He's off for another bit of fun with your midwife friend, the herbalist, the lady who smells of seasoning! . . . I know he is; I saw that burning look come into his eyes. Look at him, practically running. Comes over him suddenly evidently, like a touch of toothache!'

Some of them laughed; Mahoudeau shrugged his shoulders; Claude was not listening, he was busy talking architecture to Dubuche. The art-gallery Dubuche had shown was not at all bad, but there was nothing new about it; it was simply a patient piecing together of Beaux-Arts formulas. Surely all the arts were intended to march forward together, and the process of change which was taking place in literature, painting, and even music, was going to lead to a renewal of architecture too. If ever there was a century in which architecture should have a style of its own, it was the century shortly to begin, the new century, new ground ready for reconstruction of every kind, a freshly sown field, the breeding ground of a new people. Down with the Greek temples; there was no use or place for them in modern society! Down with the Gothic cathedrals; belief in legends was dead! Down, too, with the delicate colonnades and the intricate tracery of the Renaissance, that Classical revival crossed with medieval art, which produced architectural jewels but could never house modern democracy! What was wanted, and he emphasized his words with vigorous gestures, was an architectural formula to fit that democracy, the power to express it in stone, building which it could feel to be its own, something big and strong and simple, the sort of thing that was already asserting itself in railway-stations and market-halls, the solid elegance of metal girders, developed and refined still further, raised to the status of genuine beauty, proclaiming the greatness of human achievement.

'Yes, quite,' Dubuche kept saying, swept off his feet by Claude's enthusiasm. 'Yes, quite. That's exactly what I want to do. You wait. Give me a chance to get where I want to, and as soon as I'm free, the moment I'm free, you'll see what I can do.'

It was growing darker, and Claude's increasing animation made him more eloquent than his friends had ever known him. It excited them all to listen to him, and all showed their rowdy appreciation of the outrageous remarks he fired off at them. He had returned to the subject of his own picture now and enjoyed himself thoroughly, talking about it, mimicking the bourgeois visitors looking at it, imitating every note of their imbecile laughter. On the Avenue, now ashen grey, there was nothing to see but the shadow of an occasional carriage. The side-avenue was quite dark, and it was bitterly cold under the trees. From somewhere in the clump of trees behind the café a solitary voice came floating on the air, probably from a rehearsal at the Concert de l'Horloge, the maudlin voice of a woman running through a sentimental song.

'Oh, the fun those fools have given me!' laughed Claude in a final outburst of merriment. 'I wouldn't have missed today for ten thousand francs!'

He had talked himself out. The others, too, had dried up, and in the consequent lull in the conversation, they all shuddered in the icy breeze that had sprung up. With an exchange of weary handshakes the party broke up in a kind of stupor. Dubuche was dining in town. Fagerolles had an appointment. Jory, Mahoudeau and Gagnière tried in vain to drag Claude off to a cheap meal at Foucart's, but Sandoz, worried at seeing him so abnormally cheerful, had already taken his arm and was leading him away.

'Come along with me,' he said. 'I promised Mother I'd go home. You can have a bite of food with us. It'll be nice to end the day together.'

They started off along the embankment by the Tuileries, arm in arm, like two brothers, but at the Pont des Saints-Pères Claude would go no further.

'You're not going to leave me!' Sandoz exclaimed. 'I thought you were coming to dinner!'

'No, Pierre, thank you. . . . I've too much of a headache. . . . I'm going home to bed.'

To get him to change his mind was impossible, so Sandoz left him with a smile and said:

'Very well then, as you please. Withdraw from the world, wrap yourself in mystery, I won't stop you.'

Claude managed to repress a movement of impatience, and, after watching his friend across the bridge, he went on his way straight down the embankment. Oblivious to everything, his eyes fixed on the ground, he swung along like a sleepwalker guided by instinct. Opposite his own door on the Quai de Bourbon he looked up, surprised to find a cab in his way, drawn up at the kerb waiting for someone. With the same mechanical step he went up to the concierge's lodge to pick up his key.

'I've given it to the lady,' Madame Joseph called out from the depths of her retreat. 'She's gone upstairs.'

'Lady!' he exclaimed in amazement. 'What lady?'

'The young lady, of course! You know very well who I mean, the one that comes here regular.'

He had no idea what she meant, his mind was so confused, so he decided to go and investigate. He found the key in the lock, went in, and closed the door behind him, very gently.

He stood where he was for a moment. The studio had been invaded by shadow, a deep violet shadow, that poured through the skylight in a melancholy twilight, drowning everything. He could not even see the floor clearly; furniture, pictures, and everything else that happened to be lying about seemed to have merged into one even mass, like the stagnant water of a pool. One thing, however, stood out against the dying light of day, a dark shape sitting on the edge of the divan, a tense, anxious figure desperately awaiting his return. He recognized her now; it was Christine.

She stretched out her hands to him and murmured in a low, broken voice:

'I've been here three hours, three whole hours, listening for you. . . . When I came out of that place I took a cab, because I only wanted to look in and then hurry home. . . . But I couldn't go away without shaking your hand, even if I'd had to wait all night.'

She went on to tell him of her burning desire to see his picture and how she had slipped away to the Salon and found herself caught in the storm of laughter and derision. It was at her the hisses of the crowd were aimed, her nudity that was being spat upon, her nudity so brazenly exposed to all the wits and wags of Paris that it had taken her breath away as soon as she entered the room. Panic-stricken, overcome by shame and mortification, she had run away, feeling as if the laughter were pounding down upon her naked flesh, drawing blood like the merciless lashing of whips. But now she could forget about herself and think only of him, for she was keenly aware of the depth of his grief and her feminine sensitiveness intensified the bitterness of his disappointment and filled her heart to overflowing with a tremendous need to share her sympathy.

'Don't take it so much to heart,' she said. 'I had to come and see you and tell you I think they're just jealous, and that I think it's a wonderful picture, and that I am so proud and so happy I was able to help you and have my little share in it too.'

He never stirred as he listened to her warm, kind words, her faltering voice. Then suddenly he collapsed in front of her, with his head on her knees, and burst into tears. All the excitement of the afternoon, his dauntless courage before the hisses of the crowd, his gaiety, all his violence broke down in a burst of choking sobs. From the moment when the laughter of the crowd had struck him, like a slap in the face, he had felt it pursuing him like a pack of hounds in full cry, down the Champs-Élysées, all along the embank-

ment, and still now, at his heels, in his own studio. His
strength gave way in the end, leaving him helpless as a child,
and he kept on saying, in a weary, toneless voice as he rolled
his head on her knees:

'Oh God, how it hurts!'

Then, in a sweep of passion, she took hold of him with
both hands, raised him up to her lips and kissed him.

'Don't cry,' she said. 'Don't cry, my dearest. I love you.'

And her warm breath carried her words to his very heart.

They were both in love, and it seemed fitting that their
love should be consummated there in the studio as part of
the story of the picture that had gradually drawn them
together. Night closed in around them, and they lay in each
other's arms, weeping tears of joy in the first outpourings
of their passion. Near them, on the table, the lilacs she had
sent that morning filled the evening air with their perfume,
and on the floor flecks of gilt from the picture-frame caught
the last of the daylight and shone out like a galaxy of stars.

CHAPTER 6

IT was quite dark now, and she was still in his arms.

'Stay here with me,' he said.

But she withdrew, reluctantly, from his embrace.

'No,' she said. 'It's impossible. I must go home.'

'Tomorrow, then. . . . Come back tomorrow. . . . Please.'

'Tomorrow's impossible too . . . but I'll come again soon.
Goodbye.'

The following morning she was back again by seven o'clock,
still blushing at the thought of the lie she had told Madame
Vanzade. She was supposed to have gone to the station to meet
a friend from Clermont who was spending the day in Paris.

Claude was delighted to have her with him for a whole
day and suggested taking her to the country, feeling he
wanted her all to himself, far away from everything, in the
sunshine.

Christine was thrilled by the idea, so they rushed out like a pair of mad things and reached the Gare Saint-Lazare just in time to jump into the train for Le Havre. He knew a small village just on the other side of Mantes, Bennecourt, where there was an artists' inn on which he had descended more than once with his friends, and, without a thought for the two-hour journey, he took her there for lunch with as little fuss as if he had been taking her no farther afield than Asnières. She thought the long journey was great fun; the longer the better! It seemed impossible that the day itself could ever come to an end.

By ten o'clock they were at Bonnières. There they took the ramshackle old ferry boat, worked by a chain, across the river to Bennecourt. It was a lovely May morning; the little waves glittered like spangles in the sun and the tender young leaves shone green against the cloudless blue of the sky. Then, when they had passed the islands that lie scattered across the river at that particular point, they came to the intriguing little country inn and grocery store, with its big general room that smelt of washing and its vast farmyard full of manure heaps and dabbling ducks.

'Hello there, Faucheur!' Claude called to the landlord. 'Can you give us some lunch? . . . An omelette, sausage, cheese. . . . '

'Will you be staying the night, monsieur Claude?'

'No, not this time. . . . And some white wine, eh? Something with a kick in it!'

Christine was already out in the farmyard with Faucheur's wife who, when she came back with the eggs, smiled at Claude in her knowing peasant way and said:

'So you're married now, then, are you?'

'I am,' Claude replied without a moment's hesitation. 'Must be, as I've brought the wife with me!'

The lunch was delicious, though the omelette was over-cooked, the sausage fatty, the bread so hard that Claude had to cut off snippets to save Christine from spraining her wrist. They drank two bottles of wine and part of a third, and became so gay and so noisy that they talked themselves into a whirl, alone over their lunch in the big general room of the inn. Christine, her cheeks on fire, swore she was tipsy; she had never been tipsy before and thought it was so very funny that she was soon helpless with laughter.

'Let's go out and get some air,' she said at last.

'Good idea, a short walk. . . . We start back at four, so we've got three hours to play with.'

They walked to the top of Bennecourt past all its little yellow cottages straggling for a couple of kilometres or more along the riverside. The whole village was at work in the fields; all they met were three cows and the little girl who was driving them. Claude apparently knew his way about and kept pointing out things as they went along; then, when they reached the last of the houses, a rambling old place on the bank of the Seine, just across from the slopes of Jeufosse, he skirted right round it and led her into a dense oak wood. This was the faraway place they had both been looking for; turf like velvet, a canopy of leaves pierced only by slender shafts of blazing sunlight. Their lips met at once in a devouring kiss, and there, amid the perfume of the freshly trampled grasses, she was his. Then, for a long time they lay where they were, too much in love to do more than breathe an occasional word, gazing ecstatically at the flecks of gold each saw sparkling in the depths of the other's brown eyes.

As they came out of the wood two hours later they were startled to find a peasant with wizened little eyes like an old wolf's standing at the open door of the house as if he had been watching for them. Christine blushed and Claude, to hide his embarrassment, exclaimed:

'Why, if it isn't old Poirette! . . . So this old shack is yours, is it?'

The old man explained, with tears in his eyes, that his tenants had cleared out and paid no rent, but left him their furniture. Then he asked them inside.

'You can always have a look . . . maybe you'd know somebody who. . . . There must be plenty of folk in Paris who'd be glad of a place . . . three hundred francs a year, furnished . . . If that isn't cheap, what is?'

Intrigued, they followed him round. It was a large, roomy old place that might easily at one time have been a barn. Downstairs there was an enormous kitchen and a living-room big enough for a ballroom; upstairs were two more rooms, both so huge that they felt lost in them. The furniture consisted of a walnut bed in one of the upstairs rooms and a table and household utensils in the kitchen. In front of the house, the garden, badly neglected, was planted with magnificent apricot trees and overrun with giant rose-bushes, all in full bloom; at the back, running up to the oak wood, was a small potato field surrounded by a hedge.

'And I'll leave the potatoes in,' added old Poirette.

Claude and Christine looked at each other in one of those sudden desires for solitude and escape that often overtake lovers. How wonderful it would be to be there, in the back of beyond, far removed from everyone they knew, alone with their love! But could they do it? They looked at each other and smiled; they had only just time to catch the train back to Paris. The old peasant, who happened to be Madame Faucheur's father, went with them along the river-bank to the ferry, and as they were getting into the boat he called to them, much against his better judgement:

'Listen! I'll take two hundred and fifty, so don't forget to send somebody!'

Back in Paris, Claude escorted Christine all the way to Madame Vanzade's mansion. They were now both very downcast and parted with a long, silent, despairing hand-clasp, for they were afraid to kiss each other good night.

It was the beginning of a life of torment for both of them. In the next fortnight Christine was able to go to the studio only three times, and then always in a breathless hurry, with only a few moments to call her own, as the old lady was making more and more demands on her time. Claude was worried about her, for she was looking very pale and enervated, and her eyes were bright and feverish. Never, she said, when he questioned her, had she found Madame

Vanzade's pious household so unbearable, like a family vault
without either daylight or fresh air; it was killing her with
boredom. Her old fits of dizziness had come back again, and
lack of exercise sent the blood rushing to her head. One
night in her room, she said, she had fainted outright, just
as if a heavy hand had suddenly choked her. But she did
not have a bad word to say against her mistress; she was,
on the contrary, very sorry for her, the poor old creature,
so helpless, but so very kind, who called her 'my little girl'.
It pained her as if she were committing some heinous crime
every time she deserted the old lady to run and join her
lover.

Two more weeks went by, during which the lying with
which she had to pay for every hour of freedom grew to be
unbearable. She quivered with shame now every time she
returned to Madame Vanzade's strict world, where her love
seemed to her like some ugly stain. She had given herself
to her lover, and she would willingly have cried it from the
rooftops; her honesty rebelled against having to hide the
truth as if it were a sin and tell such abject lies, like a
servant afraid of being dismissed.

The end came one evening in the studio. Just as she was
ready to leave, she turned and, in despair, flung herself into
Claude's arms, sobbing with pent-up emotion.

'I can't!' she cried. 'I can't! . . . Let me stay here! Don't
let me go back!'

Holding her close in his arms, he stifled her sobs with
kisses.

'Do you love me as much as that? . . . Oh, my dear! My
dear, dear love! . . . But I have nothing to offer you, and
you have everything to lose. . . . How can I let you ruin your
expectations for me?'

Still sobbing bitterly, she tried to answer, but the words
she managed to bring out were broken with tears:

'Her money, you mean? . . . Or whatever she might leave
me. . . . Do you think I'm worried about that? I've never
even thought about it; I swear I haven't. . . . Let her keep
her money. What I want is to be free. . . . I'm beholden to

nobody, I have no family, so surely I have a right to do as I like! I'm not asking you to marry me, all I want is to live with you. . . . '

Then, in one last, heartrending sob, she added:

'Oh, but you're right! It would be wrong to leave her, poor woman! Oh, I despise myself! . . . If I only had the strength! . . . but I love you too much, and it hurts me too much. I can't go on suffering like this.'

'You shan't go!' he cried. 'Stay with me, and let others do the suffering. It's our happiness that counts!'

He had drawn her down on to his knees, and they sat laughing and crying at the same time, swearing between their kisses that they would never leave each other again, never.

In one foolish moment it was done. Christine packed her trunk and, without more ado, left Madame Vanzade's the very next day. Both she and Claude at once turned their minds to the old derelict house at Bennecourt with its giant rosebushes and enormous rooms. If only they could get away, at once, without wasting a moment, and live their simple domestic bliss far away at the end of the world! She clapped her hands for joy. He, still smarting after his failure at the Salon, felt that nothing would help him to recover so much as the peace and quiet of nature. Out there he could have the real open air, he could work out of doors to his heart's content and come back to Paris loaded with masterpieces. In a couple of days they were ready to go, they had given up the studio and packed their few bits of furniture off to the station. They had had a stroke of luck, a windfall, five hundred francs old Malgras had paid for a batch of twenty-odd pictures he picked out from the flotsam and jetsam of the removal. They were going to live like royalty; Claude had his thousand francs a year, and Christine brought some small savings, her linen, and a few dresses. So off they went; one might even say they fled, for they carefully avoided all their friends and did not even write to tell them they were going away. Paris meant nothing to them now and they were only too happy to leave it.

It was nearing the end of June, and for a whole week after their move the rain came down in torrents. They discovered, too, that before signing their lease old Poirette had taken away half the kitchen utensils. Disappointment had no effect on them however; they thought nothing of paddling through the rain as far as Vernon, three kilometres away, to buy pots and pans and bring them back in triumph. They were in their own home and they were happy, that was all that mattered. Upstairs they used only one of the rooms and left the other to the mice; downstairs they turned the dining-room into an enormous studio, and they were as pleased as two children to eat in the kitchen on the big deal table, near the hearth with the pot simmering on the hob. They had taken on as a daily help a girl from the village called Mélie, a niece of the Faucheurs' and delightfully stupid. They would have had a long way to go to find one denser, they said.

When the sunny weather returned their life was one long succession of blissful days; the months went by in mono-tonous felicity. They never knew the date or even the day of the week. In the mornings they lingered in bed long after the sun, shining through the slits in the shutters, had begun to cast bars of deep red light on the whitewashed walls of their bedroom. Then, after breakfast, the day was spent in rambling over the hilltop planted with apple-trees, down grassy lanes, along the banks of the Seine, through the meadows as far as La Roche-Guyon, or even farther afield, away on the opposite bank of the river, exploring the way through the cornfields round Bonnières and Jeufosse. They had developed a wild passion for the river itself, and, having bought an old boat for thirty francs from someone who had had to move away from the district, they would spend whole days on voyages of discovery, rowing up and down, or lying up in dusky little backwaters, under the willows. Among the islands strung along the Seine like a mysterious floating city they explored the whole network of narrow waterways, floating gently through them, stroked as they passed by the low, overhanging branches, alone with the wood-pigeons and kingfishers. Claude, with his trousers rolled up to the knee, would occasionally have to leap out on to the sand and push the boat along. Christine, full of determination and very proud of her strength, loved to handle the oars and always wanted to row against the strongest currents. Back home in the evening they would eat their cabbage soup in the kitchen and laugh at Mélie's stupidity, just as they had laughed at it the previous night. By nine o'clock they were in bed, in the great walnut bed, big enough for a whole family, where they spent twelve hours of every day, pillow-fighting in the early morning, then going off to sleep again, their arms round each other's neck.

Every night Christine would say:

'Now, my darling, you're going to promise me one thing. Say you'll do some work tomorrow.'

'I promise. I'll do some work tomorrow.'

'And remember, this time I shall be cross if you don't. I don't keep you from it, do I?'

'You! Of course you don't. I came here to work, didn't I? So just you wait till tomorrow, you'll see what I can do.'

The following morning they would be out boating again. She would look at him with an uneasy smile when she saw him starting out with neither paints nor canvas; then she would kiss him and laugh at the thought of the power she had over him, touched by the perpetual sacrifice he was making for her. Then there would be more tender reproaches, and she would swear that tomorrow, yes, tomorrow she would tie him in front of his easel.

Claude did eventually make the odd attempt to work. He started a study of Jeufosse, with the Seine in the foreground, but when he went and set up his easel on one of the islands Christine would go with him. She would lie in the grass at his feet, her lips slightly parted, gazing into the blue, and there, amidst the greenery, in the wilderness where only the murmur of the river broke the silence, she appeared so desirable that he continually left his painting to lie down beside her and let the sweetness of the earth lull them both into oblivion. Another time it was an old farm above

Bennecourt that took his fancy, in the shade of some ancient apple-trees that had grown to the size of oaks. Two days running he went there, but on the third Christine carried him off to Bonnières market to buy hens; the next day, too, was wasted, for the canvas had dried; he lost his patience over setting to work on it again, and in the end gave it up. Throughout the entire summer all he did was work in fits and starts, sketching in part of a picture, leaving it on the slightest pretext, without any attempt at perseverance. His feverish passion for work which once used to get him out of his bed at dawn to wrestle with his recalcitrant paint, seemed to have departed and given way to indifference and idleness. So, like a man recovering from a serious illness, he allowed himself to vegetate and revelled in it, for the sheer joy of living through his physical functions alone.

Christine was all that mattered to him now. It was she who enveloped him in a searing flame that caused his artistic ambitions to shrivel up to nothing. Ever since she had so heedlessly placed that first burning kiss upon his mouth the girl had given way to the woman, the lover had sprung to life in the virgin, pursing her lips above her fine, firm chin. Now she was showing herself as she was meant to be, in spite of her long integrity, one of those physically, sensually passionate beings who are so profoundly disturbing once they are aroused from their dormant state of modesty. Immediately, and without any teaching, she knew what love should be, and brought to it all the fervour of her innocence, while the pair of them, she who until now had had no experience, and he who had had next to none, discovered ecstasy together and were carried away by the rapture of their mutual initiation. Claude now blamed himself for his previous disdain. He had been a fool, he said, and very childish, to spurn delights he had never experienced. Henceforth, all his fondness for female beauty, all the desires he used to work out in his painting, were concentrated in the one warm, living, supple body he had made his own. He used to think that what he loved was the light as it skimmed over satin-smooth breasts, the downy contours and the fine pale amber tones that gilded shapely loins. What idle fantasy! Now at last his dream, the dream that his painter's fingers had been powerless to grasp, had come to life, now it was his to clasp in both his arms. Christine gave herself up to him entirely, and he possessed her entirely, from her throat to the tips of her toes, holding her in an embrace so close as to make her flesh melt into his own. Having killed off his painting, and delighted to have rid herself of her rival, she determined to prolong their nuptials. It was her plump arms and her smooth legs that made him linger in bed in the mornings, binding him as with chains in happiness and lassitude. When they were out boating and Christine plied the oars, he simply let himself be carried along, helpless, intoxicated by the movements of her hips. On the islands he would lie on the grass all day, his eyes gazing into hers, absorbed by her completely, drained of both strength and feeling. Anywhere, and at any time, they would take each other, so insatiable was their desire to possess and be possessed.

One thing that surprised Claude was to see Christine blush whenever he let slip a coarse word. Once she had adjusted her skirts, she would smile uncomfortably and look away if he made any jocular allusion to their love-making. She did not like such talk, and one day it almost led to a quarrel.

They were in the little oak wood at the back of the house where they often used to go in memory of the kisses they exchanged there on their first visit to Bennecourt. Out of sheer curiosity he was questioning her about her convent days. With his arm round her waist, and tickling her behind the ear with his breath, he was trying to confess her, asking her what she knew about men in those days, how she used to discuss them with her friends, what she had thought it would be like to be with a man.

'Surely you can tell me something, my pussy-cat! . . . Had you any idea what it might be like?'

She laughed rather irritably and tried to break away.

'Don't be so silly,' she said, 'and leave me alone! . . . Why are you so interested, anyway?'

'But it amuses me. . . . Come on, now, say how much you knew.'

'Oh . . . as much as the others, I suppose,' she answered, her cheeks flushed with embarrassment. Then, suddenly burying her face on his shoulder, she added:

'But it's a bit of a surprise all the same!'

He roared with laughter as he hugged her madly to him and showered her with kisses. Then, when he thought he had won her round and was hoping she would confide in him, like a friend who has nothing more to hide, she eluded him by giving empty answers and ended up by sulking and refusing to say another word. She never did tell him more than that, even though she adored him. The first awakening of sex even the most outspoken women keep to themselves, buried deep within them and somehow sacred, and Christine was very much a woman; she retained just that much reserve even though otherwise she abandoned herself completely.

For the first time, that day, Claude felt that they were still strangers to each other. He felt chilled by the cold from another body. Could it be impossible, he wondered, for each to become part and parcel of the other when they lay breathless in each other's arms, each clinging tighter and tighter to the other in their burning desire to attain something beyond mere possession?

The days drifted by, and solitude was never irksome to them. The desire for a change, to pay a call or receive a visit, had still not come between them. The time she did not spend with Claude, in his arms, Christine spent in a whirl of domestic occupations, turning the place upside-down, forcing Mélie into great bouts of house-cleaning, and even, in her thirst for activity, joining in herself and marshalling their few pots and pans in the kitchen. It was gardening, however, that kept her really busy. Armed with a pair of pruning-shears, scratching her hands on the thorns, she reaped bumper harvests from the giant rosebushes. On one occasion, when she had made herself ache all over by picking them, she sold the entire crop of apricots for two hundred francs to the English buyers who scour the country-side for them every season. She was inordinately proud of her achievement, for her dream was to make a living out of their garden produce. Claude was less keen on gardening. He had put his divan in the big room they had made into a studio and would often stretch out on it in front of the wide-open window, watching Christine busy sowing and planting out seedlings. Their peace was absolute, they were sure that no one would call, that the door bell would never disturb them from one end of the day to the other. Claude, in his fear of the outside world, went so far as to avoid passing the Faucheurs' inn, as he was always afraid he might come up against a party of his friends come out from Paris. But the whole summer passed and not a soul appeared, and every night as he went up to bed Claude murmured to himself that they had been damned lucky.

There was just one secret wound bleeding quietly away under all their happiness. After their flight from Paris Sandoz had discovered their address and wrote asking if he might come and see Claude, but Claude had never replied. In the consequent misunderstanding their old friendship seemed to have died. Christine was sorry for what had happened, as she felt that Claude had broken with his friends on her account, and she talked about it continually. She had no wish to set him at loggerheads with his friends and insisted on his making contact with them again. Claude promised to set matters right, but in fact did nothing. All that was finished now; what was the use, he said, of going back to the past?

Towards the end of July, as money was getting scarce, he had to go to Paris to sell half a dozen old sketches to Malgras, and, as she accompanied him to the station, Christine made him swear to go and see Sandoz. When he came back in the evening, there she was at Bonnières station, waiting for him.

'Well,' she cried, 'did you see him? Have you made up?'

For a moment he could say nothing, and then, as they walked along side by side, he mumbled:

'No. I'd no time.'

Two big tears welled into her eyes.

'You're being very unkind,' she said.

As they were under the trees he kissed her cheeks and even wept as he asked her not to make him sadder than he was. Such was life, and he could do nothing to alter it. Was it not enough that they should both be happy together?

Only once in those first few months did they meet any strangers, and that was up above Bennecourt as they were coming up from La Roche-Guyon. They were going along a quiet, leafy lane when, at a sudden bend, they came upon three townsfolk, father, mother and daughter, taking an airing. At that very moment, thinking they were alone, they had their arms round each other's waist and, heedless like any pair of lovers behind a hedge, Christine was just offering her lips to be kissed and Claude was laughingly bending over to meet them. They were so surprised that they simply behaved as if the others were not there, and walked straight by them, at the same slow pace, without interrupting their embrace. Dumbfounded, the other three stood back jammed against the bank, the father gross and apoplectic, the mother thin as a rake, the daughter a mere slip of a girl, skinny as a sickly bird, and all three of them ugly, mean examples of a thoroughly vitiated stock. They were a blot on the landscape, teeming as it was with freshness and vigour in the blaze of the sunshine. Suddenly, the wretched child, wide-eyed with amazement at the sight of love passing by, found herself bundled along by her father, dragged along by her mother, both beside themselves at the sight of such an embrace, asking why there were no police patrolling the countryside these days. The lovers, meanwhile, moved along undaunted, triumphant in their glory.

Claude was busy racking his brains, however, wondering where on earth he had seen those people before, decadent bourgeois types with their mean, squat features, and dripping with ill-gotten wealth. It had certainly been at some crucial moment in his career, he thought; and then he remembered and recognized the Margaillans. Margaillan was the building contractor whom Dubuche had shown round the 'Salon des Refusés', and who had laughed his raucous, imbecile laugh in front of his picture. A little farther along, when he and Christine came out of the lane, opposite a big white house with vast, beautifully wooded grounds, they asked an old peasant woman what it was. It was known as 'La Richaudière', she told them, and had belonged to the Margaillans for the last three years; they had paid fifteen hundred thousand francs for it, and they had just spent over a million on improvements.

'We shan't be round that way again in a hurry,' said Claude as they were going back down to Bennecourt. 'They quite spoil the countryside, monsters like that!'

The middle of August brought an important change in their lives. Christine was pregnant, and, since she was in love and consequently heedless, she had not noticed her condition until the third month. Both she and Claude were rather taken aback at first; the idea of such a thing happening had never crossed their minds. Then, at length, they resigned themselves to the situation; rather reluctantly, however, for Claude was worried by the thought of the complications a child would make in their way of living, and Christine was overcome by a strange inexplicable anxiety, as if she felt that this unforeseen event would mean the end of their love-affair. She wept for a long, long time with her head on his shoulder and he tried in vain to console her, though he himself was choking with the same indefinable sorrow. Later, when they had grown used to the idea, their hearts softened towards the little being they had created on that tragic day she gave herself to him as he wept by her side in the mournful twilight of the studio. The dates fitted; their child would be the child of suffering and pity, scorned from conception by the brainless mockery of the crowd. So, as they were both kind-hearted, they began to look forward to it and to busy themselves with preparations for its coming.

The winter was bitterly cold and a serious chill kept Christine indoors for a long time, though the house was incredibly draughty and almost impossible to warm. She was often sick, too, and spent long periods huddled over the fire; and she had even to lose her temper occasionally to make Claude go out without her and take long walks on the hard, ringing frost-bound roads. And Claude, when he did go out walking, alone after months of sharing all his activities with Christine, was surprised at the turn his life had taken, almost of its own accord. He had never wanted to set up house like this, even with Christine; he would have been horrified at the idea if anyone had suggested it to him; but now it was done and could clearly not be undone, for, apart from the fact that a child was on the way, he was not the kind who has courage to break away. Obviously this was the fate that was meant for him, so he might as well stick to the first woman who would not be ashamed of him. The frozen earth resounded under his heavy boots and the icy wind froze his random thoughts at the point where he realized how lucky he had been to come across a decent girl, and how much suffering and disgust he would have had to face if he had taken up with a model who had had her share of the hectic life of the studios. That made him take a kinder view of his new life, and he hastened back home to take Christine in his arms and hold her close, as if he felt he had been going to lose her. Her cry of pain: 'Not so tight! You're hurting me!' rather disconcerted him as she freed herself from his embrace and clutched her swollen body which filled him still with anxiety and surprise.

The child was born in the middle of February. A midwife came in from Vernon and all went well. Christine was up and about again at the end of three weeks. The child, a sturdy boy, was so greedy for his mother's milk that she often had to get up five times in the night to keep him from crying and rousing his father. From the moment of his arrival the little fellow turned the whole household upside-down. Christine, though a keen housekeeper, was not so good a nurse. Motherhood did not come naturally to her, in spite of her kind heart and her ready sympathy with childish discomforts. She was soon tired and easily discouraged and too ready to call in Mélie, whose gawping stupidity only made things even more difficult, so that Claude in the end had to come and give a hand, though he was even more inexpert than either of the women. Her morbid dislike for sewing and her general aversion from all such feminine activities came out again when the child required attention. He was not well looked after and grew up more or less casually, scrambling about the garden or the house, where tidiness had been abandoned in despair and the floors were a clutter of napkins, broken toys, and the general dirt and mess so easily made by a young gentleman who is cutting his teeth. When things got completely out of hand, all she could do was to fling herself into her dear love's arms and take refuge on the bosom of the man she loved, the only place where she could forget and be happy. She was a lover still, not a mother, still twenty times fonder of the father than of his child. All her old ardour had returned once the child was born and her body had regained its slimness and her beauty bloomed afresh, renewing her love like the rising sap in spring, and making her physical passion more intense and her desire keener than ever before.

It was about this time, however, that Claude began to paint a little again. The winter was coming to an end and he did not know what to do with the bright sunny mornings, since Christine was unable to go out before noon on account of Jacques. They called the boy after his maternal grandfather, but did not trouble to have him baptized. For lack of something better to do Claude started painting in the garden; he dashed off a sketch of the apricot-trees, started on one of the rosebushes and did some still-lifes of four apples, a bottle, and an earthenware pot standing on a table-napkin. He did it to keep himself occupied; then, as he gradually warmed to his work, he began to be obsessed by the idea of painting a figure, fully clothed, in the sunshine. From that moment Christine was his victim, and a willing one, since she wanted to make him happy and was as yet unaware of the terrible rival she was creating for herself. He started a score of pictures of her, in a white dress, in a red dress against a background of greenery, standing still, walking, reclining on the grass, wearing a big straw hat, bare-headed under a sunshade, her face all pink with the light shining through the cherry-coloured silk. As he was never completely satisfied he scraped his canvases after two or three sittings and set to work again at once on the same subject. A handful of studies, unfinished but full of engaging vigour, were saved from the palette knife and hung on the dining-room walls.

After Christmas Jacques had to pose. They stripped him naked as a cherub and, when it was warm enough, laid him on a blanket and tried to make him keep still. But it was well-nigh impossible. Tickled and excited by the sunshine, he laughed and wriggled and waved his little pink feet in the air and rolled about and nearly turned head over heels. His father laughed, but ended by losing his temper and cursed the 'damned brat who couldn't be sensible for a single minute', and wondered how anybody could think of painting as a laughing matter! Thereupon Christine would put on a severe look too, and hold the child so that his father could hastily sketch in an arm or a leg. He clung doggedly to the subject for weeks on end, captivated by the delicacy of the baby's colouring. It was a feast for his artist's eye, a motif for the masterpiece he had at the back of his mind every time he looked at it through half-closed lids. He tried again and again, gazing at the child for hours on end, exasperated because the young rascal would not even go to sleep just when it would have been the best time to paint him.

One day, when Jacques was crying and refusing to pose for his father, Christine said gently:

'You tire him, poor darling. That's what's the matter with him.'

Then Claude was angry with himself and overcome with remorse.

'Why yes, I suppose I do,' he said. 'I'm a fool to insist. Children aren't made for that sort of thing.'

Spring and summer went gently by, though Claude and Christine did not go about so much now and practically never went boating at all, as it was quite a problem taking the child out to the islands; so the boat was left to rot in the water. One thing they often did, however, was to wander slowly down the river bank, though rarely very far afield. Claude had tired of painting the garden and turned now to the riverside for subjects. On the days he was out painting Christine and the boy would go out to meet him and all three would saunter gently back home in the growing dusk. One afternoon she surprised him by turning up with her own old painting-book. She made a joke of it and pretended it reminded her of old times to be sitting behind him, painting her own picture. Her voice trembled a little as she spoke, for the truth was that she felt she had to claim a share in his work, as she felt that work was taking him from her more and more every day. With her meticulous school-girl hand she did a little drawing and a water-colour or two, then, discouraged by his smiles and feeling that this was ground on which they would never really meet, she stopped bringing her painting-book, but forced him to promise he would give her painting lessons later, when he had time.

What was more, she liked his latest canvases. After a whole year's rest in the open country and in pure, unsullied daylight, he was painting as with a renewed vision, producing something lighter, livelier, more harmonious in tone. Never before had he shown such handling of reflections, such a true feeling for people and things bathed in diffused light. Now, won over by the feast of colour he provided, she would have been prepared to say his painting was good if only he would finish it off a little more, and if she had occasionally not been taken aback to see him paint mauve soil and blue trees, which rather upset her firm ideas about colouring. One day, when she ventured to criticize him for painting in a blue poplar, he showed her on the spot the delicate blue cast of the leaves, and she had to agree with him that the tree really did look blue. In her heart of hearts, however, she refused to accept the fact. She was convinced that, in nature, there was no such thing as a blue tree.

She was always very serious now when she talked about the pictures he hung on their dining-room walls. Art was regaining its place in their lives, and it gave her much to think about. Sometimes, when she saw him ready to start out with his bag, his stick, and his sunshade, she would fling her arms round his neck and say:

'You do love me, don't you, Claude?'

'Don't be silly, of course I do. Why should you think I don't?'

'Kiss me then, and show me you do! Kiss me! Kiss me!'

As she accompanied him out into the road she would say:

'Off you go and work now. I've never tried to stop you working, you know. . . . I like it when you work.'

During their second autumn in the country, with the first nip in the air and the first yellow leaves on the trees Claude began to grow more and more restless. The weather was atrocious; for a whole fortnight he was kept hanging about the house because of torrential rain; after that, fog began seriously to hinder his work out of doors. So he would sit gloomily in front of the fire, and, although he never spoke about Paris, he could feel it was there, on the horizon, winter Paris, with its gas-lamps all ablaze at five in the afternoon, its gatherings of friends and their keen competitive spirit, its wealth of production unhindered even by December's icy blasts. Three times in one month he went there on the pretext of seeing Malgras, to whom he had sold a few more pictures. He stopped going out of his way to avoid the Faucheurs' inn; he even let himself be held up by old Poirette and now and then accepted a glass of white wine. In the inn he would peer about the place as if he expected to come upon some of his old friends, out from Paris that morning, in spite of the weather; he would linger there in expectation, only to have to go back home in desperate solitude, stifling with what was boiling up inside him, sick with the need for someone to whom he could cry aloud what was ready to burst his brain.

Winter came and went, and Claude had at least the consolation of being able to paint some lovely snow effects. A third year was beginning when, towards the end of May, he was profoundly upset by an unexpected meeting. It happened one morning when he had gone up to the plateau in search of a subject, having tired of the banks of the Seine. At a sudden bend in the lane that ran between two hedges of elder bushes he was dumbfounded to find himself face to face with Dubuche wearing a silk hat and looking very correct in a tight-waisted frock-coat.

'Well, of all people!' cried Claude.

Dubuche was so flustered he hardly knew what to say.

'I'm just going to pay a call,' he mumbled. 'Sounds silly, doesn't it, calling in the country? Still, there are things that have to be done, so there we are! . . . What about you? Do you live up this way? I thought you did . . . at least I'd heard something of the sort, but I thought it was further down, somehow, on the other bank.'

Claude was very agitated but he managed to help Dubuche out of his difficulty.

'Now there's no need for you to make excuses, old fellow. I'm the one who ought to apologize. . . . It's a long time since we last met, isn't it? You can't imagine the way my heart thumped when I saw you nosing your way through the greenery!'

Grinning with pleasure, he took Dubuche's arm and began to walk along beside him. Full of his own affairs as usual, Dubuche could never stop talking about himself, so he started at once to talk about his future. He had taken a first-class pass at the Beaux-Arts, after working his way painfully through all the usual intermediary grades. But success had not solved his problems. His parents never sent him a penny now; all they did was to cry poverty in the hope that he would help to support them. He had given up the idea of trying for the Prix de Rome as he was sure he would be beaten, and he was in a hurry to start earning his living. But he had had enough of it already; he was sick of doing odd jobs at one franc twenty-five an hour for ignorant architects who treated him simply as a drudge. He did not know what to do for the best, which was the shortest route to take. If he left the Beaux-Arts, he would be well backed by his tutor, the powerful Duquersonnière, who liked him because he was docile and a plodder, but that would only mean a lot more hard work, as there was no obvious future in it. He complained bitterly of State schools where you could slave away for years, but which did not even promise jobs for all the pupils they turned out.

Suddenly, he stopped in the middle of the path; the elder hedges were petering out into the open plain, and 'La Richaudière', with all its big trees, was coming into view.

'Ah, of course!' cried Claude. 'I might have known! You're going to the lair, to see those disgusting-looking monsters!'

Very annoyed by Claude's outburst, Dubuche bridled as he answered:

'You may think old man Margaillan's a fool, but he's a good man at his job. You ought to see him at it, supervising his building, you'd be surprised at his energy. Besides, he has an amazing gift for good management and a marvellous flair for picking his site and knowing exactly what materials to buy. Anyhow, to make millions, like he does, you've got to have something about you. I know one thing, and that is I should be a fool not to be polite to a man who can be useful to me.'

As he spoke, he took up his stand in the middle of the narrow lane, preventing his friend from going any further, clearly because he was afraid he would be compromised if they were seen together and also to make him understand that this was where they had to take their leave.

Claude was going to ask him about their friends in Paris, but he did not. Not a word was said about Christine either. He had quite made up his mind to leave Dubuche and was ready to shake his hand when, in spite of himself, the question slipped out:

'How's Sandoz?'

'Oh, all right. . . . I don't see much of him. . . . He mentioned you last time I saw him, a month ago. He's still sorry you turned your back on us.'

'But I didn't turn my back on you!' retorted Claude angrily. 'I want you to come and see me! You can't imagine how pleased I'd be!'

'If that's what you want, we'll come! I'll tell Sandoz to come, too! . . . I must be off now, I haven't much time. Goodbye, goodbye,' said Dubuche as he made off towards 'La Richaudière', while Claude stood watching the glint of his silk hat and the black patch of his frock-coat grow smaller and smaller as he hurried across the fields. Claude ambled slowly back home, his heart inexplicably heavy. He said nothing to Christine about his encounter.

About a week later Christine had been down to the Faucheurs' to buy a pound of vermicelli and was dawdling on the way back talking to a neighbour with the child on her arm when a man who had just come over by the ferry came up to her and said:

'This is the way to Monsieur Claude Lantier's house, I believe?'

She was surprised, but answered simply:

'Yes, it is, monsieur. If you would care to follow me. . . .'

They walked on side by side for a time, and the stranger, who appeared to know her, gave her a friendly smile; but as she tended to hurry ahead, hiding her confusion by looking very serious, he did not try to make conversation. She opened the door and showed him into the living-room, saying as she did so:

'Claude, here's someone to see you.'

With one great shout of joy the two men fell on each other's neck.

'Dear old Pierre! How splendid of you to come! . . . Where's Dubuche?'

'Detained on business at the last minute. He sent me a telegram telling me to start out without him.'

'I see, but I'm not surprised really. . . . You're here, and God knows I'm glad to see you!' said Claude. Then, turning towards Christine, who was smiling now to see them both so happy, he went on:

'Why, it's true, of course, I never told you. I met Dubuche the other day on his way up to the big house to call on the monsters. . . . But what am I thinking about?' he cried, clutching his brow as if he had suddenly remembered something. 'You two don't know each other, and here am I doing nothing about it! . . . Darling, the gentleman you see before you is my old friend Pierre Sandoz. I love him as a brother. . . . And this, Pierre old fellow, is the woman in my life. . . . And now you're going to kiss each other and be friends!'

With a jolly laugh Christine readily offered her cheek. She had taken to Sandoz at once. She liked his affability, his staunch sincerity, and the sympathetic, almost fatherly way he looked at her. Tears welled into her eyes as he held both her hands in his and said to her:

'I'm glad to know you're fond of Claude. You must always be fond of each other. It's the finest thing that can happen to anybody.'

Then, as he bent down to kiss the baby in her arms, he said:

'So this is the first, already.'

'Yes, that's the first,' said Claude, with a vague, apologetic gesture. 'What can you do? The creatures seem to be there almost before you know they're coming!'

Claude and Sandoz stayed talking in the living-room, whilst Christine was turning the kitchen upside down in preparation for lunch.

In a few words Claude told their story, who she was, how he had met her, what had led them to set up house together. He seemed most surprised when his friend wanted to know why they did not get married.

Married? Why, they had never so much as mentioned the subject, and Christine did not even seem keen on it. Besides, what difference would it make so long as they were happy? Did it matter, anyhow?

'It's your affair,' said Sandoz, 'and it certainly doesn't worry me. Still, she's been yours from the start, you ought to make an honest woman of her.'

'I'm ready when she is,' said Claude. 'Though I shouldn't think of leaving her in the lurch with a youngster on her hands.'

Sandoz changed the subject and began to sing the praises of the pictures hanging on the walls. The rascal hadn't wasted his time, obviously! There was colouring for you, and look at that now for sunlight! Delighted, and with occasional laughs of conscious pride, Claude listened to Sandoz's eulogies, and was on the point of asking him about the rest of their friends and their doings when Christine came in calling:

'Come quickly now, the eggs are on the table!'

They had lunch in the kitchen and an extraordinary lunch it was. Boiled eggs followed by fried gudgeon, then last night's boiled beef done up in a salad with potatoes and a red herring. It was delicious, eating in the strong, appetizing odour of the herring which Mélie had tossed on the coals, with the coffee splashing slowly but noisily through its filter on the hob. By the time dessert was brought on, strawberries fresh from the garden, cheese from a neighbouring dairy, all three had their elbows on the table, engrossed in conversation. Paris? What were the others doing in Paris? Oh, nothing particularly new, really. Still, they were putting up a pretty good fight to see who would get to the top of the tree first. Of course, people who stayed away from Paris were making a sad mistake; Paris was the place to be if you didn't want to be forgotten altogether. But surely talent would out, wherever it was, and didn't success depend to a great extent on strength of will? Oh, there was no doubt about it that the ideal was to live in the country and pile up masterpieces and then go back to Paris and swamp it with them!

In the evening, as Claude was escorting him to the station, Sandoz said to him:

'By the way, I'm going to let you into a secret. . . . I think I'm going to get married.'

Immediately Claude laughed.

'So that's your game, is it? That accounts for your sermon this morning!'

They went on talking till the train was due. Sandoz explained what he thought about marriage. It was the essential condition, he said, for the good, solid, regular work required of anyone who meant to produce anything worth while today. Woman seeking whom she may devour, Woman who kills the Artist, grinds down his heart, and eats out his brain was a Romantic idea and not in accordance with the facts. He himself felt the need of an affection to safeguard his peace of mind and a sympathetic home in which he could live in cloistered seclusion and give up his whole life to the vast work he had so long dreamed of. Everything, he added, depended on the wife one chose, and he thought he had found what he was looking for: a simple girl, the orphan of small business people without a penny to her name, but good-looking and intelligent. Since he gave up his office job six months ago, he had made some headway in journalism and found it more remunerative too. He had just settled his mother into a little house in the Batignolles where he was looking forward to having the two women to cherish him and to being able to support the three of them by his own efforts.

'You get married by all means,' said Claude. 'One should always do what one thinks is best. . . . Well, goodbye for the present; here's your train. Don't forget, now, you promise to come and see us again.'

Sandoz did go to see them again many times. He would often drop in uninvited when his newspaper left him any leisure and while he was still single; he was not to be married until the autumn. It meant happy days again for them all, whole afternoons spent exchanging confidences, a re-awakening of their old desire for fame.

One day, when he was alone with Claude, lying out on one of the islands, gazing into the blue, he confessed his great ambition.

'A newspaper is simply a battleground, if you see what I mean. A man has to live, and to live he has to fight. The

Press, whatever one thinks of it, and however much you may dislike working for it, is a power to be reckoned with, an invincible weapon in the hands of a chap who has the courage of his convictions. . . . Just now I'm forced into using it myself, but I don't intend to spend the rest of my days in journalism. Far from it! No, my plans are made. I've found what I've been looking for for a long time. It may turn out to be killing work, and once I've plunged into it I may never get out of it, but I'm going to do it.'

There was a silence, for not even the leaves stirred in the heat, and then he spoke again, more slowly now, and in more disjointed sentences:

'Look. This is the idea: to study man as he really is. Not this metaphysical marionette they've made us believe he is, but the physiological human being, determined by his surroundings, motivated by the functioning of his organs. . . . Don't you think it's a farce, the way they've concentrated their studies exclusively on the brain and its functions and pretend that the brain is the noblest of the human organs? . . . Thought, now. What is thought, in God's name, but the product of the entire body? Can they get a brain to think all by itself? What happens to the "nobility" of the brain when its owner has belly-ache? . . . No, the whole thing's ridiculous! Philosophy's behind the times. So is science. We call ourselves positivists and evolutionists, and yet our man is still the literary manikin of the classicists and we still go on trying to comb out the tangled hairs of pure reason! To be a psychologist is to be a traitor to truth. Besides, "psychology", "physiology", what do they mean really? Just nothing. They've overflowed into each other to such an extent that they've become one, and human mechanism has come to be the sum total of human functions. . . . That's the point we start from, the only possible basis for our modern revolution. The inevitable death of the old conception of society and the birth of a new society, and that means a new art is bound to spring up in the new ground. . . . Oh, that's bound to happen! A new literature for the coming century of science and democracy!'

His cry rose and was lost in the heavens. There was not a breath of wind, only the river slipping silently by beneath the willows. Turning sharply to his companion, Sandoz spoke full into his face:

'I know now exactly what I'm going to do in all this. Oh, nothing colossal, something quite modest, just enough for one lifetime even when you have some pretty exaggerated ambitions! I'm going to take a family and study each member of it, one by one, where they come from, what becomes of them, how they react to one another. Humanity in miniature, therefore, the way humanity evolves, the way it behaves. . . . I shall place my characters in some definite period that will provide the milieu and the prevailing circumstances and make the thing a sort of slice of history, if you see what I'm getting at. . . . I shall make it a series of novels, say fifteen or twenty, each complete in itself and with its own particular setting, but all connected, a cycle of books that will at least provide a roof in my old age, if they don't prove too much for me in the meantime!'

He stretched out on his back on the ground and spread his arms wide, as if he wanted the earth to embrace him, and then began to laugh as he launched into a comic tirade.

'Good earth!' he cried. 'Take me to thy bosom, thou who art the mother of us all, the only, the unique source of life! Thou, the immortal, the eternal, through whom the very soul of the world doth circulate, the sap which floweth even through thy stones, and maketh the trees themselves the brothers of us all! . . . Let me lose myself in thee, good earth, as I feel thee now beneath my limbs, embracing me, filling me with thy warmth! In my work thou alone shalt be the great moving force, the means as well as the end, the mighty ark in which all things shall draw life from the breath of all beings!'

Started as a joke, on a note of mock lyricism, his invocation ended as a cry of burning conviction quivering with the poet's true emotion. There were tears in Sandoz's eyes, and, to hide his feelings, he added in a deliberately hard voice and with a vague gesture that embraced the whole horizon:

'Of all the damned silly notions! One man one soul, when there's this universal soul for all of us!'

Claude, almost completely hidden in the grass, lay still where he was. Then, after another silence, he broke out with:

'Good old Pierre! Go ahead and slay the lot of 'em. . . . But be ready for a few hard knocks yourself.'

'I'm not worrying about that,' replied Sandoz, scrambling to his feet and stretching himself. 'My hide's too thick. They'd only break their wrists. . . . Time we were making a move now, don't you think? I don't want to miss my train.'

Christine had taken a great liking to Sandoz; she admired his healthy, straightforward attitude to life, so one day she found the courage to ask him to do her a favour and be godfather to Jacques. She never entered a church herself these days, but she saw no reason for penalizing the child. What really decided her was the desire to provide him with a firm support in life in the shape of a godfather whose steady reliability she had not been slow to discern in the midst of his powerful outbursts. Claude was clearly surprised at her idea, but agreed with a casual shrug, and so the child was baptized. They managed to find him a god-mother, a neighbour's daughter, and they all feasted on lobster brought specially from Paris.

That day, when goodbyes were being said, Christine took Sandoz on one side and beseeched him to come and see them again:

'Come again soon,' she said. 'He gets so bored out here.'

She was right. Claude was slipping back into his fits of black despair, dropping his painting, going out alone, hanging round the Faucheurs' inn near where the ferry-boat landed its passengers, as if he expected to see Paris itself step ashore at any moment. Paris haunted him. He went there regularly, once a month, and always came back depressed and unable to work. Autumn came, and then winter, a wet, muddy winter, and he let himself sink into a kind of

surly torpor, accompanied by occasional recriminations
against Sandoz who, since he married in October, had been
unable to make such frequent trips to Bennecourt. Sandoz's
visits were the only thing that seemed able to arouse him;
they would keep him in a state of great excitement for a
whole week and provoke an endless flow of feverish talk
about the latest news from Paris. For a long time Claude
had been able to hide his longing for Paris, but now he
talked about it from morning till night, and, as they sat by
the fireside after Jacques was asleep, made Christine's brain
reel with a spate of talk about things she had never heard
of and people she had never seen. The more he talked the
more his excitement grew, and Christine was called upon
to express her opinion and side with this person or that as
they cropped up in his never-ending commentary.

Didn't she think Gagnière was a fool to throw himself
away on music when he might have been developing his
talent as a painter of landscapes? He was going to a young
lady for music lessons now, it appeared. At his age! What
did she think of that? Didn't she think he was mad? Then
there was Jory, trying to make it up with Irma Bécot ever
since she got herself a nice little place of her own in the
Rue de Moscou. She knew those two, of course; a fine pair,
and well matched, didn't she think so? But the smartest of
the smart was Fagerolles. He'd tell *him* what he thought
about him next time he met him. He'd let down the whole
gang by entering for the Prix de Rome, even if he *had* been
turned down! A bounder who used to have nothing to say
in favour of the Beaux-Arts and wanted to wipe tradition
off the face of the earth! There was no getting away from
it, all this itching for success and being hailed by a lot of
numskulls even if it meant riding rough-shod over one's
friends, made people do the dirtiest tricks. Say what she
liked, she couldn't defend him, could she? She couldn't be
bourgeois enough to do that! And when she had agreed with
him on that point, he would revert to another story he
thought extremely funny and that always provoked him to
fits of noisy, nervous laughter, the story of Mahoudeau and

Chaîne. Between them they had killed little Jabouille, the husband of the terrible Mathilde who kept the herb-shop. Oh, yes, they killed him, the little consumptive cuckold, one night when he had one of his fits; his wife called in the pair of them, and between them they massaged the life out of the poor little beggar!

When Christine showed no sign of being amused, Claude would get up and grumble:

'Nothing ever makes you laugh! . . . Come on, we'd be better off going to bed.'

He adored her as much as ever and claimed her body with the desperate urge of a man who means love to be a joy unto itself, blotting out the memory of all else. But now love in itself was not enough, he wanted to go beyond even that, for another old, unconquerable urge had come over him once more.

When spring came he began to show a lively interest in the Salon, though he had previously pretended to disdain it and had sworn he would never submit a picture again. Whenever he met Sandoz he asked him what the others were sending in. On opening-day he went to see it and came back in the evening very excited and very critical. There was a bust of Mahoudeau's, not bad but not outstanding; a little landscape by Gagnière, a make-weight really, but nicely lighted. That was all, except a thing by Fagerolles, an actress in front of a mirror making up her face. He did not mention it at first, but later referred to it with a certain amount of indignant laughter. Just like Fagerolles, always with an eye to the main chance! Now he had missed his Prix de Rome he had no qualms about exhibiting his work and breaking away from the Beaux-Arts; but the way he was doing it had to be seen to be believed. He was simply producing a sort of slick compromise, painting that appeared daring on the surface but without a single original quality about it! What's more, he was certainly going to make a success of it, for there's nothing the bourgeois likes better than being stroked when he thinks he's being manhandled. It was time a real painter showed up in that dreary wilderness of a Salon, among that crop of smart young men and brainless idiots! If ever a citadel was worth storming, this was, by God it was!

Christine, realizing how furious he was, finally ventured to break in quietly with:

'If you like, we can go back to Paris.'

'Who's talking about going back to Paris?' he cried. 'It's impossible to talk to you without your getting the wrong end of the stick!'

Six weeks later he heard something that kept him occupied for a whole week. . . . His friend Dubuche was going to marry Mlle. Régine Margaillan, the daughter of the owner of 'La Richaudière'. It was a complicated story, full of surprising details which kept him tremendously amused. In the first place, Dubuche had gone and won himself a medal with a project he had exhibited for a pavilion in the middle of a park. And the funny part about *that* was that his teacher, old Duquersonnière, had apparently remodelled the whole thing himself and then coolly arranged for the Selection Committee, of which he was chairman, to award it the medal! And, to crown all, it was the award that settled the wedding. A pretty state of affairs, eh, when medals were used for placing poor but deserving pupils in conveniently wealthy families! Like all *parvenus*, old Margaillan wanted nothing more than a son-in-law who could be of use to him in his business, a son-in-law complete with the right sort of diplomas and the latest cut in morning coats.

For some time he had had his eye on the young man from the École des Beaux-Arts who always got such very good marks and was so diligent and so highly commended by his teachers. The medal brought his enthusiasm to a head; he gave him his daughter on the spot and took him into the firm as a partner who could not fail to turn millions into tens of millions, since he knew all there was to know about good building. Besides, he was just what poor, sickly, little Régine needed, a good healthy husband.

'A chap would have to be pretty keen on the cash, don't you think, to marry a skinned rabbit like Régine?' was Claude's inevitable comment.

When Christine, who felt sorry for her, tried to say something in her favour, he would retort:

'But I'm not running her down! If married life doesn't prove too much for her, all well and good. It's certainly no fault of hers if her father's a mason who was silly and ambitious enough to marry a bourgeois. With generations of drunkards on one side and the worn-out, disease-ridden blood of a degenerate race on the other, no wonder the girl's what she is! There's decrepitude for you, in spite of the money-bags! What's the good of piling up wealth? I ask you, what is the good of it if all it leads to is a generation of foetuses in pickle-bottles?'

He showed signs of becoming so violent that Christine had to take him in her arms and hold him there as she kissed him and laughed him back to his old kind-hearted self. Then, in a quieter mood, he understood and even approved of the marriages his two old friends had made. It meant three of them had found wives for themselves, really! What a funny thing life was, after all!

Once more summer went by, the fourth they had spent at Bennecourt, and the happiest they were ever to have, for living was a quiet, easy affair in the depths of the country. Since they went there they had never been short of money; Claude's thousand francs a year and the money they got for the few pictures he sold were enough for their needs. They even managed to put a certain amount aside as well as buy some linen. Country life was ideal, too, for young Jacques. He was two and a half now, sturdy and rosy-cheeked, and spent all his days out of doors, tearing his clothes to tatters and getting so dirty that his mother very often did not know where to start getting him clean. So long as he slept well and enjoyed his food she did not worry over much about him, but kept all her tenderness and anxiety in reserve for her grown-up child, her artist husband whose humours and depressions kept her nerves constantly on edge.

The position was growing worse every day. They led a quiet life and should have been free from cares, and yet they felt themselves slipping into a restless, depressing state of mind which expressed itself in a sense of perpetual exasperation.

The joy they had known in the early days of their country life was over. Their boat had rotted, fallen to pieces and sunk to the bottom of the Seine, and they never even thought of making use of the one the Faucheurs had placed at their disposal. They had grown tired of the river and lost all taste for rowing, and although they still repeated their old cries of enthusiasm over certain favourite beauty-spots on the islands, they never had any inclination to go and visit them again. Even their rambles along the river-bank had lost their charm; it was too hot down there in summer, and in winter it was where you caught colds. As for the plateau overlooking the village with its vast stretches of apple orchards, it might have been some far distant county, so completely off the beaten track that it would have been foolish even to try to get there on foot. Even the house was getting on their nerves, with its living-room like a barracks where they had to eat in a perpetual smell of stale cooking, and a bedroom that seemed to be the rallying-ground of all the winds of heaven. To make things even worse, the apricot crop had failed and the finest of the giant rosebushes, being so old, had fallen easy victims to blight and died. It was familiarity breeding dreary contempt, making even eternal nature appear to grow old through over-contemplation of the same landscape. The worst thing about it was that Claude the painter was tired of it all, totally unable to find a single subject to fire his imagination. He plodded wearily about the countryside as if it were devoid of all interest and drained of all life, and there was not a single tree he did not know or a play of light he had not seen. No, it was all over, cold, lifeless; he would never do anything worth while now in such a god-forsaken backwater!

October came with its watery skies, and on one of the first wet evenings Claude flew into a rage because his dinner was late. He pushed the stupid Mélie out of the house and slapped Jacques because he happened to get into his way. Christine, in tears, put her arms around him and said:

'It's time we left this place. Please let us go back to Paris.'

'So you're at that again, are you?' cried Claude furiously, tearing himself from her embrace. 'We shall never go back to Paris! Never! Do you hear?'

'For my sake,' Christine went on gently. 'Do it for my sake, please. Do it to please me.'

'Why, don't you like being here?'

'No, I shall die if we stay here. Besides, I want you to work, and I know your place is in Paris, not here. It would be a crime to bury yourself in this place any longer.'

'That's enough! We're staying here.'

He was trembling with emotion, for Paris was calling him, just on the horizon yonder, Paris lighting up on a winter evening. He could feel the mighty effort his friends were making there; he was back with them, sharing their triumph, being their leader again, since there was not one among them strong enough or proud enough to claim their leadership. Yet, for all his hallucinations, for all the need he felt to hasten back to join them, by some ungovernable contradiction which sprung he knew not how from the very depths of his being, he persisted in his refusal to go. Was it the fear that is known to attack even the brave, or the unconscious revolt of happiness against the force of destiny?

'Listen!' cried Christine. 'I'm going to pack and you're going to come with me!'

Five days later they were on their way to Paris, after packing up all their things to be forwarded by rail.

Claude was already outside in the road with little Jacques when Christine suddenly had an idea that she had forgotten something. She went back into the house alone, and when she saw it completely empty began to cry; she felt it somehow tearing at her, as if she were leaving behind some part of herself. How willingly she would have stayed on there, how keenly she felt she could have lived there for ever, though it was she who had insisted upon them leaving it and going back to that passionate city in which she had always sensed a rival! Still looking around for what she thought she had forgotten, she picked a rose she found growing outside the kitchen window, the one last rose, nipped by the frost. Then she closed the gate on the deserted garden.

CHAPTER 7

NO sooner was Claude back on the Paris pavements, among the feverish bustle and the din, than he was all eager to be out and about, to go and look up his friends. As soon as he was up in the morning he was out of doors, leaving Christine alone to settle into the studio they had rented in the Rue de Douai, near the Boulevard de Clichy. Thus, two days after their return, he dropped in on Mahoudeau at eight o'clock on a dull, cold, grey November morning. He found the shop the sculptor occupied in the Rue du Cherche-Midi already open, and Mahoudeau, only just out of bed, pale-faced, bleary-eyed and shivering with cold, was just taking down the shutters.

'Why, it's you, is it?' he said. 'Bit early for Paris, aren't you? . . . Have you left the country then? Back in town?'

'Since the day before yesterday.'

'Good! We'll be seeing more of you now. . . . Come in. Bit chilly outside this morning.'

Inside the shop Claude felt colder than before. He kept his overcoat collar turned up and plunged his hands deep into his pockets as he met the sudden chill of the damp streaming down the bare walls and the mud, the heaps of clay and the endless pools of water that covered the floor. The wind of poverty had blown through the place since his last visit, sweeping the casts after the Antique from the studio shelves, playing havoc with the work-tables and tubs which were now held together by rope. It was simply a messy, disreputable hole, like a mason's yard gone to rack and ruin, and in the whitening that had been rubbed over the glass panel in the door some derisive finger had drawn a sun with rays all round and a face in the middle with a grinning semicircle for a mouth.

'Wait a bit,' went on Mahoudeau, 'we'll soon have the fire going. These damned studios soon get clammy with all the water and wet rags and what not.'

On turning round, Claude saw that Chaîne was there, kneeling in front of the stove pulling the straw out of the seat of an old stool to use as a fire-lighter. He greeted him, but Chaîne did not even look up; all he did was to give a sort of low growl.

Claude turned back to Mahoudeau.

'What are you doing these days?' he asked.

'Oh, nothing particularly startling! It's been a rotten year really; worse than last, and that wasn't up to much! . . . There's a bit of a slump in saints and angels, you know. Oh yes, religion doesn't sell like it did, so that means I've had to tighten my belt. Look, this is what I'm reduced to in the meantime,' he said, and began to unwrap a bust he had been working on. He revealed a long face made still longer by side-whiskers, a monstrosity of pretentiousness and boundless stupidity.

'It's a barrister from round the corner,' he explained. 'Did you ever see such a revolting mug in all your life? You should hear the fuss he makes about having his mouth just as he wants it! . . . Still, what can you do? A man has to eat.'

He had an idea for the Salon, he said, an upright figure, a 'Woman Bathing', trying the water with her toes, with just that faint shudder of cold that looks so lovely on a woman's skin. The model he showed Claude was already showing signs of cracking; Claude looked at it in silence, surprised and angry to notice the artist's concessions, a certain obvious prettiness showing through the persistent exaggeration of the limbs, a natural desire to please without deviating too far from his natural prejudice in favour of the colossal. Mahoudeau's complaint was that it was no simple matter producing an upright figure. It meant using metal supports, and they were pretty dear, and a turntable, as he had not got one already, besides a lot of other equipment. So he thought, after all, he might decide to have her reclining on the water's edge.

'What do you think?' he asked Claude. 'Do you like her?'

'Yes, in a way,' Claude replied. 'A little bit sugary, in spite of her hefty thighs. Still, one can't really tell until it's finished. . . . But she *must* stand up, old chap; she's *got* to stand up, or the whole thing's lost!'

The fire was roaring in the stove now, so Chaîne got up and began to move around. He went into the dark back room where he shared the bed with Mahoudeau, and came out again in a moment with his hat on. He still did not open his lips, and in deliberate, oppressive silence he slowly took a piece of crayon in his clumsy, peasant's fingers and scrawled on the wall: 'Off to buy baccy, put more coal on stove', and walked out.

Claude watched him in astonishment; then, when he had gone, turned to Mahoudeau.

'What's all this?' he asked.

'We're not on speaking terms,' was the sculptor's quiet explanation. 'We always write.'

'Since when?'

'The last three months.'

'And you share the same bed?'

'Yes.'

Claude roared with laughter. Of all things! What a couple of stubborn mules they must be to carry on like that! And what, he asked, was the cause of their little tiff? The indignant Mahoudeau replied by saying exactly what he thought about Chaîne. The hound! Hadn't he come home unexpectedly one evening and caught Chaîne with Mathilde, the herbalist next door, both in their underclothes, tucking into a pot of jam? It wasn't their being half-dressed that upset him, he didn't care a damn about that. No, what upset him was the jam! He couldn't ever forgive them for treating themselves behind his back. Disgusting, he thought, when he had to eat his bread dry! God's truth, if you share your woman, you can surely share your jam!

So for the last three months or so, without any explanation, they had been steadily sulking at each other. Their life had organized itself in consequence and their strictly necessary relations had been reduced to the short messages they scrawled about the walls. They still shared the same woman just as they still shared the same bed, having reached a tacit agreement about the times they were to be with her, each arranging to go out when the other's turn came round. After all, it wasn't absolutely necessary to talk; they understood each other well enough without.

As he finished making up the fire Mahoudeau poured out all his resentment to Claude.

'You may not believe it,' he said, 'but when you're half starved it isn't unpleasant not to have to talk. Silence helps you to vegetate somehow. It acts as a sort of a damper on the hunger pains. . . . But Chaîne! . . . You've no idea how grasping he can be; it's the peasant in him, of course. When he found he'd spent his last sou and was still no nearer making the fortune he'd expected to make out of painting, he went into business, in a small way, to be able to pay for his education. What do you think of that for keenness? And what do you think his scheme was? He used to have olive oil sent from Saint-Firmin, from home, you know, and then he went round collecting orders for it among the well-to-do Provençal families who have houses in Paris! Unfortunately, his scheme didn't last long. He's so uncouth, people would have no more dealings with him. So, as there's one jar left that nobody wants, we're living on it ourselves. We dip our bread in it . . . when we have any bread, that is.'

He pointed to the jar in a corner of the shop. The oil had run and made big, black stains on the wall and the floor.

Claude stopped laughing now at the thought of such poverty and discouragement, wondering how anyone could be hard on people who gave way under it. As he walked round the studio his anger against the models with their tame concessions died away, and he even began to feel he could tolerate the frightful bust. In the midst of his meditations he came upon a copy Chaîne had made at the Louvre, a Mantegna, all its native stiffness reproduced with amazing exactitude.

'The rascal!' he muttered to himself. 'He's nearly brought it off! . . . Certainly never done anything better. . . . Perhaps that's what's wrong with him; he was born four hundred years too late!'

Then, as the place began to warm up, he took off his overcoat and remarked as he did so:

'He's a long time fetching his "baccy".'

'Oh, I know his "baccy",' said Mahoudeau, busy on the side-burns of the bust. 'His "baccy's" just there, on the other side of this wall. When he sees I'm busy he slips off to see Mathilde, hoping to pinch a bit of my share of her too. The man's a fool!'

'Has it been going on long, this affair with Mathilde?'

'Oh, yes. It's got to be a habit now. If it wasn't her it would be somebody else. . . . But it's she who comes back for more. . . . She's too much for me to handle alone, believe it or not!'

There was no ill-will in what Mahoudeau said about Mathilde. She must be ill, he thought, to behave as she did. Since little Jabouille's death she had taken up religion again, but that did not prevent her from scandalizing the neighbourhood. There were still a few of the local church-going ladies who patronized the shop because they could not face the initial embarrassment of asking for their delicate and intimate purchases elsewhere; but the business was going rapidly downhill, and bankruptcy appeared unavoidable. One night, when the gas company had cut off supplies because she had not paid her bills, she had come round to borrow some olive oil, but she had obviously been unable to get it to burn in her lamps. She never paid any bills these days, and to save the expense of a workman she used to get Chaîne to repair the sprays and syringes her pious customers brought in carefully done up in newspaper. In the wine-merchant's across the street they *did* say that she sold syringes second-hand to convents. In a word, the place was heading for disaster; the mysterious little shop with its cassocks hovering in the shadows, its murmurings, discreet as any confessional, its vestry atmosphere of stale incense and all it stood for in the way of intimate care and attention which could never be mentioned above a whisper, was all going to rack and ruin. The decay of poverty had already such a firm hold that the dried herbs hanging from the ceiling were a mass of cobwebs, and the leeches in their bottles were dead and mouldering on the top of their water.

'Here he comes,' said Mahoudeau. 'That means she'll be here, too, in a minute. See if it doesn't.'

Chaîne came in as he spoke and ostentatiously brought out a packet of tobacco, filled his pipe and settled down to smoke in front of the stove, without speaking a word, as if there was no one else present. Almost immediately Mathilde appeared, to pass the time of day, as any neighbour might do. Claude thought she looked thinner than ever; her face was blotchy, though there was the same fire in her eyes, and her mouth looked wider as she had lost two more teeth. The smell of spices that always clung to her unkempt hair seemed staler, the sweet freshness of camomile and aniseed had gone. She still filled the place with the peppermint that seemed to be her natural breath, but that, too, was tainted by the stricken body that produced it.

'Working already!' she cried, then added: 'Good morning, my sweet,' and kissed Mahoudeau before she even acknowledged Claude. Then she did go and shake his hand in her usual brazen fashion, with her belly thrust well forward, which made her appear to be offering herself to every man she met.

'Guess what I've found!' she said. 'A box of marshmallows! We'll have it as a treat for breakfast, shall we? . . . Come on, now, let's share it out.'

'Thanks all the same,' said the sculptor, 'but it's a bit too cloying for me. I'd rather have a pipe.'

Then, seeing Claude putting on his overcoat, he added: 'You're not going?'

'Yes, I'm going,' said Claude. 'I want to get back into the old ways again and fill my lungs with Paris air.'

He lingered for a moment or two, watching Chaîne and Mathilde stuffing themselves with marshmallows, first one dipping into the box, then the other. And, in spite of being forewarned, he was again amazed to see Mahoudeau pick up the crayon and scribble on the wall: 'Give me baccy out of coat pocket.'

Without a word, Chaîne pulled out the packet and handed it to the sculptor, who filled his pipe from it.

'See you soon, I suppose,' he said to Claude, who replied: 'Hope so. . . . Next Thursday, at Sandoz's, if not before.'

He was unable to repress an exclamation of surprise when, on leaving the shop, he bumped straight into a man busily engaged in peering between the dusty old bandages in the herbalist's window, trying to see what was going on inside the shop.

'Why, it's Jory!' he cried. 'What are you doing here?'

'I? . . . Oh, nothing. . . . I happened to be passing . . . just having a look in,' said the startled Jory, twitching his big, pink nose. Then, having decided to laugh the matter off, he dropped his voice, as if he thought somebody might overhear him, and said:

'She's next door with the others, I expect, isn't she? In that case, let's go. I'll call another day.'

As he walked along with Claude he told him of the goings-on at the herb-shop. The whole gang visited Mathilde these days, he said; they had told each other about her, so now they called on her in turn, or sometimes even in a group, if they thought it might be more amusing that way; and he held up Claude in the middle of the jostling crowd on the pavement to tell him, in a confidential undertone, of the marvellous orgies. The revival of an ancient Roman custom, what? Couldn't he just imagine it all, behind the barrier of enemas and bandages, under the shower of scents from the herbs on the ceiling! What could be smarter? A brothel for priests, old fellow, complete with all the dubious perfumes of corruption, in a setting of cloistered calm!'

Claude laughed.

'But you used to say that woman was a fright!' he said.

'She's good enough for that particular job,' Jory answered, with a nonchalant gesture. 'That why I thought I'd pop in and see her this morning. I happened to be passing the shop after seeing somebody off at the Gare de l'Ouest. . . . It was handy, you understand. I wouldn't go out of my way for it.'

He was clearly embarrassed to provide an explanation at first; then, in what was, for him, an unexpected flash of truth, he suddenly launched into a frank revelation of his depravity.

'Oh, what the hell does it matter? I think she's an amazing creature, so you might as well know it. . . . She's no beauty, I'll admit, but there's something bewitching about her, the sort of woman you pretend you wouldn't even touch with a barge-pole and yet you do the craziest things for her.'

It was only at this point that he expressed surprise at seeing Claude in Paris, and, as soon as he had heard Claude's plans and learnt that he was in Paris to stay, he ran on again:

'Now I'll tell you what you're going to do,' he said. 'You're coming with me to lunch with Irma!'

The idea frightened Claude; he refused the invitation with brusque firmness, and pretended he could not accept as he was not dressed for the occasion.

'What the devil does that matter?' was Jory's retort. 'That's all to the good, much more amusing. Irma'll be delighted. . . . I think she has a bit of a soft spot for you, she's always talking about you. . . . Come along, now, and don't be silly about it. I tell you she's expecting me this morning, and she's sure to do both of us proud, so come on.'

He had taken Claude's arm and refused to let it go as they walked along together up to the Madeleine. Generally Jory kept his love affairs to himself, just as drunkards avoid talking about drink, but that morning he was overflowing, joking about them and describing them in detail. The singer from the café-concert with whom he had eloped from Plassans and who used to tear his face to ribbons with her nails, had been abandoned a long time ago. Now, year in year out, his life was just one endless cavalcade of women, the maddest and most unexpected collection; the cook at a house where he used to dine with friends; the legitimate spouse of a member of the police force, which meant he had to remember when the husband was out on the beat; a girl who worked for a dentist, earning sixty francs a month letting herself be put to sleep and brought round again before every patient, just to inspire confidence. There were others too, lots of others, odd girls picked up in low dives, respectable women in search of excitement, the girls who brought his laundry, the charwomen who made his bed, any woman who showed she was willing; the whole street and everything it offers in the way of pick-ups, chance meetings, women to buy and women to steal. He did not choose his women but took them as they came, young or old, pretty or ugly, sacrificing quality to quantity to satisfy his insatiable appetite for female flesh. Whenever he happened to be alone at night, the idea of a cold, unshared bed filled him with horror and urged him to go out on the prowl scouring the pavements until the sinister small hours and only going back to his room when he had captured his woman. As he was so short-sighted, he occasionally went astray, so that one morning, for example, he found the white head of a hag of sixty sharing his pillow, whom, in his haste, he had taken for a blonde.

In general, he was satisfied with life. His skinflint of a father had cut him off again and cursed him for sticking to the primrose path, but that made no difference to him now that he was making seven or eight thousand francs a year in journalism, where he had made quite a niche for himself as an art critic. The rowdy days of *Le Tambour* were over; articles at a louis a time were a thing of the past. He was settling down, collaborating with two widely read periodicals, and although he was still, at bottom, as cynical as ever in the pursuit of his own ends, in his desire for success at all costs, he had assumed a certain bourgeois pomposity and distributed praise and blame with solemn finality. He had inherited his close-fistedness from his father, and every month now he put money aside, but always in mean little investments the secret of which he kept firmly to himself. His vices had never cost him less than they did now, for the only treat he offered his women was a cup of chocolate, and that only when he was feeling especially generous and particularly well satisfied.

As they were approaching the Rue de Moscou, Claude said:

'So you're keeping the Bécot girl now, are you?'

'I!' exclaimed Jory, profoundly shocked. 'You forget, my dear chap, that she now pays twenty thousand a year in rent and is talking about building herself a mansion that's going to cost five hundred thousand! No, all I do is lunch with her, or dine with her once in a while, and that's more than enough for me.'

'Apart from sleeping with her, of course?'

Jory laughed and avoided a direct answer.

'Fathead! Who wouldn't? . . . Here we are now. In you go!'

But Claude made yet another attempt to get away. He could not, he said; his wife was expecting him home for lunch. It meant that Jory had to ring the bell and push him into the vestibule, insisting that he would accept no excuses and that they would send a footman to the Rue de Douai with a message. Suddenly a door opened and there was Irma Bécot herself. When she saw Claude she exclaimed:

'Well, well! The wanderer's return!'

She put him at his ease immediately, welcoming him as an old friend, and he was relieved to see that she did not even notice his old overcoat. He found her so altered he would hardly have recognized her. In four years she had become a different woman. With all the cunning of a hardened actress she had narrowed her brow with a fringe of frizzled hair, made her face look long and thin, by sheer will-power presumably, and changed herself from the lightest of blondes into a violent red-head, so that the former guttersnipe appeared to have grown into a courtesan by Titian. As she used to say in her more confiding moments, this was 'the mug she put on for the mugs'. The house itself, which was smallish, was luxuriously appointed, but not free from lapses of taste. There were some good pictures on the walls; a Courbet and a notable sketch by Delacroix prompted Claude to remark to himself that little Irma was no fool, in spite of the frightful cat in coloured *biscuit* so prominently displayed on a side-table in the drawing-room.

When Jory mentioned sending the footman to let Claude's wife know where he was, Irma, taken completely by surprise, exclaimed:

'You married? Not really!'

'Yes, really,' replied Claude simply.

She turned to Jory for confirmation; he smiled; she understood, and added:

'You're living with somebody, that's what you really mean, isn't it? ... To think that they used to say you had no use for women! ... Do you know I'm very cross with you? I am really! You used to be so scared of me, do you remember? You still are, or you wouldn't be backing away as you're doing now. Am I as ugly as all that?'

She had taken both his hands in hers and smiled as she raised her face to his and looked him straight in the eyes, for she was hurt, profoundly hurt, she was so keenly determined that he should like her. He shuddered slightly as he felt her warm breath through his beard, and as she let go his hands she said:

'Never mind, we'll talk about that some other time.'

It was the coachman who was sent to the Rue de Douai with a note from Claude, for by this time the footman was already at the drawing-room door announcing that lunch was served. The meal, a particularly choice one, passed off very properly under the cold eye of the domestic. They talked about the vast rebuilding scheme that was causing such an upheaval in Paris, and that led them to discuss the price of land, and from that they went on to discuss the sort of people who have money to invest. But when they had reached the dessert and the three of them were left alone with their coffee and liqueurs, which they had decided to drink where they were, at table, they soon livened up and became as free and easy in their talk as if they had met over drinks at the Café Baudequin.

'Say what you like, boys,' said Irma, 'there's nothing better than a good laugh and feeling you don't give a damn for anybody!'

She kept on rolling cigarettes as she talked, and, having taken charge of the nearest bottle of Chartreuse, was rapidly emptying it. Her face grew redder and redder, and her hair more out of control as she reverted to her own natural, amusing vulgarity.

'I was just going to buy it,' said Jory, excusing himself for not having sent her that morning a book she had asked for. 'I was just going to buy it, I say, last night about ten o'clock when I ran into Fagerolles.'

'You're lying,' she broke in curtly. Then, to cut short any further denials from Jory, she added:

'Fagerolles was here last night, so now you know you're lying. He's disgusting,' she said, turning to Claude. 'You've no idea what a liar he is. . . . He's like a woman. He lies for the sake of lying, or for a lot of sordid bits of nonsense that don't matter anyhow. The truth of the whole matter is this, simply this: he didn't want to fork out three francs to buy me a book. He's always the same. Every time he was supposed to buy me a few flowers he'd either dropped them under a cab or there wasn't a flower to be had in Paris! If there was ever a man who had to be loved for his own sake, Jory's the man!'

Jory, completely unruffled, simply lolled back in his chair, puffed his cigar and grinned maliciously as he said:

'Now that you've taken up with Fagerolles again . . . '

'But I haven't,' she screamed angrily. 'And if I had, it's none of your business. . . . Fagerolles means nothing to me, do you hear, but he does know it's useless to lose your temper with me. Fagerolles and I understand each other; we both grew out of the same gap in the pavement. . . . Listen to me. If I wanted your Fagerolles, I'd only have to raise my little finger and he'd be there, on the floor, licking my feet. He's mad about me, your Fagerolles is, mad about me!'

Seeing she was preparing for a battle, Jory thought it wiser to retreat. All he said was:

'*My* Fagerolles?'

'Yes, *your* Fagerolles! Surely you don't imagine I can't see through your little game, the pair of you? He soft-soaping you in the hope you'll write an article about him; you pretending to be generous and broad-minded and working out how much you're likely to make for yourself by boosting an artist the public fancies!'

To this Jory could find no answer. He was very annoyed it should have been said in front of Claude, but he made no attempt to defend himself and tried to turn the quarrel into a joke. Irma was very entertaining, wasn't she, when she let herself go like that, with that vicious glint in her eye and that twist to her mouth that meant she was ready for a row?

'The trouble is, my dear, that it doesn't do much for your Titian image.'

Completely disarmed by this last remark, she started to laugh.

Claude meanwhile, completely at peace with the world, went on drinking glass after glass of cognac. Like the others, he let himself glide smoothly through the mist of tobacco smoke into the rising tide of intoxication, that very hallucinating intoxication produced by liqueurs. The talk rambled on for two hours and had reached the subject of the high prices that painting was beginning to fetch when Irma, who had dropped out of the conversation and had been sitting for some time with a burnt-out cigarette stub on her lip, staring fixedly at Claude, suddenly turned to him and asked him, in a dreamy, intimate voice:

'Where did you come across this "wife" of yours?'

The question did not appear to surprise him; his thoughts by now were completely out of control.

'She came up from the provinces,' he replied, 'into service with an old lady. Not a fast girl, either.'

'Pretty?'

'Of course she's pretty.'

Irma slipped back into her dream for a moment, and then with a smile added:

'Consider yourself lucky! I thought there were no more girls like that. They must have found one specially for you.'

Then, pulling herself together, she rose from the table, exclaiming:

'Nearly three o'clock! . . . This is where I turn you out, boys. I have an appointment with an architect. I'm going to look at some land near the Parc Monceau where they're building all those new houses. I have a feeling it's going to be a good proposition,' she said as they went back into the drawing-room, where she stopped in front of a mirror, annoyed at finding her cheeks so flushed.

'Going about this house you've been talking about, I expect?' said Jory. 'Does that mean you've found the money then?'

Irma was busy arranging her hair over her forehead, smoothing away the flush from her cheeks, making her face look long and oval again, changing herself back into the auburn-haired courtesan with all the intelligent charm of a work of art. Then, turning her back on the mirror, she answered him with:

'There now! The Titian's restored!'

They were still laughing as she shepherded them into the vestibule where, once again, she took both Claude's hands in hers and, with eyes bright with desire, looked deep into his, without a word. Out in the street Claude began to feel uneasy. As the cold air sobered him up he began to be tortured with remorse for talking about Christine to Irma Bécot, and he swore he would never set foot in her house again.

'Not a bad sort, Irma, is she?' said Jory, lighting a cigar he had picked out of the box on his way out. 'And no obligations, that's the point. You lunch with her, dine with her, sleep with her, and that's that. Afterwards you go your separate ways.'

By this time Claude was so overcome with shame that he felt he could not possibly go straight back home, and when his companion, full of energy after his lunch and ready for a walk, suggested going to call on Bongrand, he was delighted with the idea. So the pair of them made for the Boulevard de Clichy where for the last twenty years Bongrand had had a huge studio. Bongrand had made no concessions to the taste for sumptuous hangings and valuable curios which was beginning to prevail among the younger painters. His was the plain, bare studio of the older school, with nothing on the walls but the master's own paintings, unframed, and packed as close together as *ex-votos* in a church. The only luxuries he allowed himself were a cheval-glass in Empire style, a huge Norman wardrobe, two armchairs in Utrecht velvet, very threadbare, and a bearskin, completely devoid of hair, which was thrown over a big divan in one corner. One habit he had retained from his Romantic youth was wearing a special costume for working in, which explained why he received his visitors in baggy trousers, a dressing-gown with a cord round the waist like a monk, and the top of his head encased in an ecclesiastical skull-cap. He answered the door himself, palette and brushes in hand.

'So it's you! What a good idea of yours to call! I've been wondering about you. Somebody, I don't know who, said you were back in town, so I thought it would not be long before I saw you,' he said to Claude, offering him his free hand in a burst of genuine affection. Then, as he shook Jory's he added:

'Welcome, too, young pundit! I've just read your latest article. Thank you for the kind things you said about me. . . . Come in, both of you. You won't disturb me. I'm making the most of every minute of daylight. There's plenty of time left for doing nothing, now the days are so damnably short.'

He set to work again at once, standing at an easel on which was a small canvas showing two women, mother and daughter, sitting sewing at a bay window in full sunlight. The two young men stood behind him, watching.

'Exquisite,' said Claude after a time.

Bongrand shrugged his shoulders, without turning round.

'It's not much really. Just something to keep me occupied. ... I did it from life when I was staying with some friends. I'm just tidying it up a bit.'

'But it's a gem!' cried Claude with growing enthusiasm. 'It's got everything, truth, light, simplicity. Just look at it for simplicity; that's the overwhelming thing about it, in my opinion.'

Bongrand stepped back at once, half closed his eyes and said with obvious surprise:

'Is it really? Do you really like it then? ... Because when you came in I was just thinking it was downright bad! ... Oh yes, I was! I was feeling indescribably miserable, thinking I'd spent the last ounce of talent I ever had!'

His hands trembled as he spoke, for his whole body was in the painful throes of creation. He put down his palette and moved over towards Jory and Claude, beating the air with helpless gestures.

'It may surprise you,' he said, for he had been successful from an early age and his place in French painting was now firmly established, 'but there are days when I question my ability to draw a simple thing like a nose. ... Every picture I paint, I'm as excited as the rawest novice; my heart thumps like mad, my mouth goes dry out of sheer emotion. Funk, that's what it is, plain, unvarnished funk! You youngsters think you know all about that, but you don't begin to suspect what it's like. The reason's simple. If you make a mess of a picture, all you have to do is try to do better next time, and nobody slates you for it. But we old stagers, who have shown what we can do, are forced to keep up our standard, to improve it even. If we weaken we drop clean into an open grave. . . . It's all very well being a celebrity, a great artist, but it means sweating blood and still more blood to climb higher and higher till you get to the top; and once at the top, if you can keep on marking time where you are, consider yourself lucky and keep on marking time as long as you can, till your feet drop off, if you must. But once you feel you're going downhill, let yourself drop, and smash yourself to pieces in the death agonies of your talent that's out of keeping with the times, your failure to remember how you produced your immortal masterpieces and the staggering realization that your efforts to produce any more have been, and always will be, entirely fruitless!'

His voice swelled up to a roar and a final burst of thunder, and there was anguish in his broad, red face, but he went on talking, striding up and down the room in a surge of uncontrollable violence.

'Haven't I told you scores of times that you're always beginners, and the greatest satisfaction was not in *being* at the top, but in *getting* there, in the enjoyment you get out of scaling the heights? That's something you don't understand, and can't understand until you've gone through it yourself. You're still at the stage of unlimited illusions, when a good, strong pair of legs makes the hardest road look short, and you've such a mighty appetite for glory that the tiniest crumb of success tastes delightfully sweet. You're prepared for a feast, you're going to satisfy your ambition at last, you feel it's within reach and you don't care if you give the skin off your back to get it! And then, the heights are scaled, the summits reached, and you've got to stay there. That's when the torture begins; you've drunk your excitement to the dregs and found it all too short and even rather bitter, and you wonder whether it was really worth the struggle. From that point there is no more unknown to explore, no new sensations to experience. Pride has had its brief portion of celebrity; you know that your best has been given and you're surprised it hasn't brought a keener sense of satisfaction. From that moment the horizon starts to empty of all the hopes that once attracted you towards it. There's nothing to look forward to but death. But in spite of that you cling on, you don't want to feel you're played out, you persist in trying to produce something, like old men persist in trying to make love, with painful, humiliating results. . . . If only we could have the courage to hang ourselves in front of our last masterpiece!'

He seemed larger than life now, and the lofty studio rang with his voice, as he shook with emotion and his eyes filled with tears. Dropping on to a chair in front of his picture, he asked, in the anxious voice of a pupil seeking encouragement:

'So you really think it looks all right? . . . I daren't let myself believe it does. It must be my misfortune to have both too much and not enough critical sense. As soon as I set to work on a picture I think there's nothing like it, and then, if it isn't well received I'm tortured to death. It would be far better to be completely uncritical like Chambouvard there, or else to have no illusions at all and stop painting. . . . Frankly, do you like this little thing?'

Claude and Jory stood petrified with surprise and embarrassment before such a revelation of the birth-pangs of a work of art. They wondered just at what point of the crisis they had arrived to make an acknowledged master like Bongrand cry aloud in his sufferings and ask their opinion as equals. And the worst of it was that they had not been able to conceal their moment's hesitation from those great, burning, supplicating eyes, behind which they could clearly discern his secret fear of waning talent and failure. For they knew what was being said about him and they themselves shared the current opinion that he had never produced anything to equal his famous 'Village Wedding'. Even though he had managed to keep up his standard in a certain number of subsequent pictures, he was drifting towards something far too lifeless and sophisticated. The spark of genius had gone and every work seemed less good than the last. But those were things it was impossible to say, so Claude, when he felt sufficiently collected, declared:

'It's the most powerful thing you've ever done!'

Bongrand looked at him again, straight in the eyes, then turned back to his picture, looked at it thoughtfully for a moment and, after making a terrific effort with his great, brawny arms, as if he were straining his muscles to breaking point to lift such a very small canvas, he murmured softly to himself:

'My God, it's a weight, but it shan't get me down, not if it kills me!'

Picking up his palette, he found peace again in the first brush stroke, and as he settled to work he rounded his broad, honest shoulders, which still revealed something of that crossing of burly peasant obstinacy with bourgeois delicacy of which he was the offspring.

There was silence for a time, then Jory, who could not take his eyes off the picture, said:

'Is it sold?'

Bongrand replied in a leisurely way, as an artist who worked only when it pleased him to do so, and never for profit:

'No. . . . I'm paralysed if I know there's a dealer in the background goading me on.'

Still painting, he went on talking, now in a more bantering vein.

'Painting these days is getting to be more and more of a business proposition. . . . All this trafficking in works of art is beyond an old stager like me. . . . Our journalist friend here, for example, handed out bouquets right and left in that article in which he so kindly mentioned me. Two or three of the youngsters he talked about were geniuses beyond a shadow of doubt.'

'That's what a newspaper's for,' replied Jory, laughing, 'to be put to good use. There's nothing the public likes better than having great men pointed out to it.'

'Oh, there's nothing more brainless than the general public, I grant you that, and I've no objection to your playing up to it. . . . But I was thinking about the way *we* started! We weren't pampered, believe me. Far from it! Every one of us had ten years of gruelling hard work behind him before he could get the public to so much as look at his pictures. . . . But now any little whipper-snapper who shows he can handle a brush is greeted with all the fanfares of publicity. And what publicity! Alarums and excursions the length and breadth of the country, reputations that blow up overnight and go off with a bang before the gaping admiration of the populace! To say nothing of the works themselves, poor little things, announced with salvos of artillery, awaited with unbridled impatience, a nine days' wonder in Paris and then they're forgotten as irrevocably as if they'd never existed!'

'That's the case against the Press in a nutshell,' said Jory, who had stretched himself out on the divan and was lighting another cigar. 'There's something to be said on both sides, of course, but damn it all, one has to keep abreast of the times!'

Bongrand shook his head and then retorted, in the highest of spirits:

'That's all very well, but nobody these days can splash paint on a canvas without being acclaimed a budding genius. . . . They make me laugh, you know, all these budding geniuses of yours!'

Then, through an association of ideas, he turned to Claude and, in a more serious mood, said:

'What about Fagerolles, by the way? Have you seen his picture?'

Claude simply said that he had; but when his eyes met Bongrand's neither could repress a smile, and Bongrand added:

'There's somebody who's taken a leaf out of your book!'

Suddenly embarrassed, Jory looked down at his feet, wondering whether or not to defend Fagerolles. He must have decided it was to his advantage to do so, for he pronounced in favour of the picture of the actress in her dressing-room, an engraving of which was selling very well, he said. The subject was surely modern enough, wasn't it? It was nicely painted, too, and in the light colour-scale favoured by the new school. Perhaps one might have wished for a little more power of expression, but you'd got to make allowances for people's inclinations, hadn't you, and bear in mind that charm and distinction were not to be picked up at any street-corner?

Bongrand, who usually had nothing but fatherly praise for the young, bent busily over his picture, shaking with rage, though making a visible effort to contain it, but it burst out in spite of him.

'That's all we want to hear about Fagerolles, thank you! . . . What sort of fools do you take us for, eh? . . . Look, if you want to see a great painter, he's here at this moment. Yes, I mean the young man now standing in front of you. What Fagerolles does is simply a stunt; it consists of stealing this young man's originality and serving it up in the insipid guise required by the École des Beaux-Arts. Exactly! You take a modern subject, use light colours, but stick to the correct and commonplace drawing, the pleasant, standardized composition, the formula, in short, guaranteed by the Beaux-Arts to give satisfaction to people with plenty of money and no taste. And you cover up the whole thing with facility, the sort of nimble facility, what's more, that would be just as well employed carving coconuts, the same nice, flowing facility which leads to success and which ought to be punished with hard labour, do you hear!' he shouted, brandishing his brushes and palette in his clenched fists.

'You're very hard,' said Claude, embarrassed. 'Fagerolles has some quite subtle qualities really.'

'I have heard,' Jory ventured, 'that he's just made a very remunerative contract with Naudet.'

The unexpected introduction of Naudet into the conversation made Bongrand relax again and, wagging his head and smiling, he said:

'Oh! Naudet! . . . Naudet!'

He knew Naudet well and kept his young friends very amused by telling them about him. He was a dealer who in the last few years had revolutionized the picture business. Old Malgras, with his subtle taste and shabby morning coat, was out-dated, so were his methods—pouncing on novices' pictures, buying them for ten francs and selling them for fifteen, the connoisseur's little routine, pretending to turn up his nose at the picture he wanted in the hope of getting it cheap, though deep down he was genuinely keen on painting, making a wretched living by the rapid turnover of his limited capital in his cautious deals. Naudet, the famous Naudet, was quite different; he was turned out like a gentleman, perfectly groomed and polished, complete with fancy jacket and jewelled tie-pin and all that goes with them, hired carriage, stall at the Opera, table at Brignon's, and he made a point of being seen in all the right sort of places. In business he was a speculator, a gambler, and heartily indifferent to good painting. He had a flair for spotting success, that was all; he could tell which artist it would pay him to boost, not the one who showed promise of becoming a great and much-discussed painter, but the one whose specious talent, plus a certain amount of superficial daring, was soon going to be at a premium in the collectors' market. And he changed completely the tenor of that market by ceasing to cater for the old type of collector who knew a good picture when he saw one, and dealing only with the wealthier amateur who knew nothing about art, who bought a picture as he might have bought stocks and shares, out of sheer vanity or in the hope that it would increase in value.

Here Bongrand, who had a keen sense of humour and was no mean actor, began to act a conversation between Naudet and Fagerolles—' "You've got genius, my dear fellow, no doubt about it! Ah! You've sold the little thing I saw the other day, I see. What did you get for it?"—"Oh, five hundred francs."—"You're mad, my dear fellow! It was worth twelve hundred. Now what about this one here. How much, eh?"— "Oh, I don't know, really. Shall we say twelve hundred?"— "Twelve hundred! Come, come, my dear fellow, you're not taking me seriously. It's worth two thousand. I'll take it at two thousand, and from now on you work exclusively for me, Naudet! Au revoir, au revoir. And don't waste your energies; your fortune's made, I'll see to that." And out he goes, takes the picture with him and drives round calling on his customers, having previously spread the word that he had discovered an artist who's really out of the ordinary. Eventually one of them bites and asks him the price. "Five thousand."—"What! Five thousand for a painting by an artist no one's ever heard of! What do you take me for?"—"Listen, I'll make you a proposition. I'll let you have it for five thousand and I'll sign an agreement to buy it back from you for six in twelve months' time if you find you don't like it." The customer's tempted; who wouldn't be? He's running no risk. It's a good investment, so he buys. Naudet lets no grass grow under his feet and places nine or ten others in the same way before the year's out. Then vanity and desire for profit combine to send prices up and a fashion is established, so that when he calls on his customer again, instead of coming away with the old picture he sells him a new one, for eight thousand! And in that way prices go up and up, and painting becomes a shady affair, a sort of goldfield on the top of Montmartre launched by bankers and fought over with banknotes!'

Claude was saying it was disgraceful, and Jory that it was rather clever, when there was a knock at the door. Bongrand answered it.

'Why, it's Naudet,' he exclaimed. 'We were just talking about you!'

'I'm very happy to hear it, and very flattered,' said Naudet. He was impeccably dressed and had escaped even the tiniest splash of mud, in spite of the filthy weather. Bowing, he made his entry with the solemn politeness of a man of the world on the point of entering a church.

'You were saying nothing but good of me, I'm sure,' he added.

'On the contrary, Naudet! On the contrary!' Bongrand replied in an even tone. 'We were just saying that your method of exploiting painting is producing a fine generation of young men who are a cross between pictorial clowns and dishonest business men.'

Undaunted, Naudet smiled.

'The verdict is severe, but very charming! Besides, I could never take exception to any judgement passed upon me by your respected self.'

Then, in ecstasy before the picture of the two women sewing:

'Why, bless my soul, what have we here? I hadn't seen this. It's simply wonderful! . . . The light! . . . and the treatment! . . . So firm . . . and so broad! Oh, there's been nothing like this since Rembrandt! . . . Yes, Rembrandt! . . . I was simply calling to pay my respects, but I must have had a guiding star today. . . . Perhaps at last we're going to be able to do business. Let me have this marvel of yours, and I'll give you whatever you ask. There's no limit!'

It was clear from Bongrand's back that every word irritated him more than the last.

'Too late,' he snapped out. 'It's sold.'

'Sold? Dear me, what a pity! Can't you get out of it somehow? Tell me who's bought it and I'll move heaven and earth. I'll give anything. . . . Oh, this is really unbearable! Sold! Are you absolutely sure? . . . Supposing I offered you double?'

'It's sold, Naudet, and there's an end of it!'

But Naudet's lamentations continued. He stayed a few moments longer, rhapsodized over another canvas or two as he went round the studio, his keen eye on the alert, like a gambler stalking his luck. When at last he realized that he had struck a bad moment and that he would get nothing out of Bongrand, he left, bowing his gratitude and still voicing his admiration as he stood on the landing.

No sooner had he gone than Jory, surprised at what he had heard, put a tentative question:

'But I thought you said . . . It isn't really sold, is it?' he asked.

Bongrand did not reply at once, but went back to his painting. Then, in a voice like thunder, full of all his hidden suffering, all the latent strife he was so reluctant to admit, he cried:

'The man's a nuisance! He'll get nothing of mine! . . . If he has money to spend, let him go to Fagerolles!'

When Claude and Jory took their leave a quarter of an hour later, he was hard at work again, making the most of the fading daylight. At the door they separated, but Claude did not make straight for the Rue de Douai, though he had been away from home so long. His head buzzing with the day's encounters, he wanted to go on walking, to give himself up entirely to Paris, so on he went until nightfall, through the cold, muddy streets, under the glimmer of the street-lamps lighting up one by one, like dim stars shining through the fog.

He could hardly wait for Thursday to arrive. That was the day he was to dine with Sandoz who, as ever, still entertained his friends once a week. All were welcome; there was a place set for everyone. He had married, changed his mode of life completely, flung himself wholeheartedly into the battle of literature, but he still kept Thursday free; he had done so ever since he left school and took to smoking a pipe. Nowadays, when he referred to his wife, he said she was 'just another member of the gang'.

'Look here, old fellow, I'm really terribly sorry about this,' he said one day to Claude.

'About what?'

'About your not being married,' was the frank reply. 'If it depended on me, of course, I should be only too pleased to have Christine come too. . . . But I have to be rather careful. You know what fools some people are, always on the look-out for scandal. They might go round spreading all sorts of yarns. . . .'

'Why, of course,' said Claude, 'but Christine herself wouldn't want to come with me. So don't worry. We both understand. I'll come alone, trust me!'

By six o'clock on Thursday Claude was on his way to where Sandoz lived in the Rue Nollet, away up in the Batignolles. But he had the greatest difficulty in hunting out the little cottage his friend had taken. He began by enquiring at the street door of a large house and was directed by the concierge across three courtyards, then along a passage between two other outbuildings and down a few steps where he bumped into a gate opening on a small garden. That was where the cottage was, at the end of one of the paths. But it was so dark, and he had so nearly come to grief on the steps that he did not dare to go any further, especially as his arrival was being announced by the furious barking of an enormous dog. Then, at last, he heard Sandoz coming towards him and calling the dog to heel.

'Ah! It's you!' cried Sandoz. 'What do you think of this? Like being in the country, isn't it? We're going to put up a lantern, to save the guests from breaking their necks. . . . Come in! . . . Quiet, Bertrand! Can't you see it's a friend, silly dog?'

The dog raced along beside them towards the house, wagging his tail and barking a lively fanfare of welcome. A young maid appeared carrying a lantern which she hung on the gate to light up the fearsome steps. In the garden there was a small, central grass plot with a huge plum-tree which withered the turf that grew beneath its shadow. In front of the house, which was very low, with only three windows, a large bower of Virginia creeper was very much in evidence; a bright new garden seat was housed there for the winter, to be brought out when the sunny weather came.

'Come in,' repeated Sandoz, showing Claude into the room on the right of the hall, the drawing-room which he had turned into his study. The dining-room and kitchen were on the other side. Upstairs, his mother, who was now completely bed-ridden, occupied the big bedroom; he and his wife had the smaller one and the dressing-room adjoining. That was all it was, a cardboard box divided into compartments by partitions as thin as paper. A little house, certainly, but a hive of industry, full of hope for the future, vast in comparison with the attics of his boyhood and already bright with the first indications of luxury and comfort.

'There!' cried Sandoz. 'At least we've plenty of room, eh? A damned sight more convenient than the Rue d'Enfer. You see, I have a room all for myself. I've bought myself an oak table to work at, and my wife's given me the palm in that antique Rouen pot. Nice, isn't it?'

At that moment his wife came in. She was tall, with a gentle, cheerful face and fine dark hair. Over her plain black poplin dress she wore a large white apron, for although they had a resident maid she did her own cooking, was very proud of some of her own special dishes and ran her household according to good middle-class standards.

She and Claude were old acquaintances at once.

'Call him Claude, dear,' Sandoz told her, 'and don't forget, her name's Henriette,' he said to Claude. 'No "monsieur" and "madame", if you please, or you'll be fined five sous a time.'

They all laughed and Henriette made her escape to the kitchen where she had been making bouillabaisse, a Provençal delicacy, as a surprise for the friends from Plassans. She had got the recipe from her husband and she had learnt to make it to perfection, he said.

'She's very charming, your wife,' said Claude, 'and I can see she spoils you.'

Sandoz did not reply to his remark, but, seated at the table with his elbows on the pages of his latest book he had written during the morning, he began to talk about the first novel of the series he had planned which had been published in October. His poor book! It was getting a fine old trouncing! Talk about butchery and massacre, he'd got the whole pack of critics at his heels, yelping and cursing him as if he'd committed murder most foul! It made him laugh, it even stimulated him, for he had the quiet determination to pursue the course he had set himself. There was one thing, however, that surprised him more than anything else: the boundless ignorance of these fellows who dashed off their mud-slinging articles, apparently without the faintest notion of what he was trying to do. They consigned everything indiscriminately to the rubbish heap: his novel attitude to physiological man, the importance attributed to environment, nature's process of perpetual creation—in short, life itself, all life from end to end of the animal kingdom, universal life without heights or depths, beauty or ugliness, his bold experiments with language, his conviction that everything may be expressed, that dirty words are occasionally as necessary as red-hot irons, that a language is often the richer for their being brought to the surface and, finally, his attitude towards the sexual act, the origin and everlasting achievement of the world itself, which he had brought out of the shameful darkness in which it is usually hidden and reinstated in its true glory, in the full blaze of the sun. He could understand people taking exception to what he said, but at least he would have preferred them to do him the honour of taking exception to his boldness and not to the ridiculous indecency they themselves read into his work.

'I still think,' he said, 'there are more fools than knaves in the world. . . . It's the writing itself that infuriates them, the type of sentence, the images, the very essence of the style. The root of the trouble,' he concluded sorrowfully, 'is this: the general public loathes literature!'

'Why should you worry?' said Claude, after sharing Sandoz's silence for a moment. 'You're happy, you're working, you're producing something!'

'Oh, yes, I certainly work,' replied Sandoz, rising from his table as if in sudden pain, 'to the very last page of every book I write. But if you only knew, if I could only tell you the torment, the despair . . . and now those idiots of critics have got the notion I'm self-satisfied! I, who am haunted even in my sleep by the imperfections of my work! I, who never read over what I wrote yesterday for fear of finding it so deplorably bad that I shan't have the courage to carry on! I work as I live, because that's what I was born to do, but that doesn't mean I'm any the happier for it, oh no! I'm never satisfied with what I do, and I'm always aware that I might come a cropper in the end!'

He was interrupted by voices at the door. Then Jory appeared, delighted with life, saying he had unearthed an old article for tomorrow's paper and so had managed to have the evening free. Almost immediately Gagnière and Mahoudeau arrived; they had met at the gate and were already deep in conversation. Gagnière, who for the past few months had been taken up with a theory of colour, was explaining his process to Mahoudeau.

'I put it on raw,' he was saying. 'The red in the flag looks paler and yellower because it's next to the blue of the sky, and the complementary colour to blue, orange, combines with the red in the flag.'

Claude was interested at once and was just starting to question him when the maid brought in a telegram.

'It's Dubuche,' Sandoz announced. 'Sorry he'll be late; he's going to look in about eleven.'

At that moment Henriette flung the door wide open and announced that dinner was served. She had taken off her working apron, and, now the lady of the house, was shaking hands with her guests as she ushered them gaily into the dining-room, telling them to lose no time, it was half-past seven and the bouillabaisse would not wait. Jory pointed out that Fagerolles had given his word he would come, but nobody took him seriously. Fagerolles was making himself ridiculous with his posing and pretending to be snowed under with work!

The dining-room they filed into was so small that, in order to fit in a piano, a sort of recess had had to be made out of what had once been a china-cupboard. Still, on special occasions they could seat ten or a dozen guests at the round dining-table, beneath the white porcelain ceiling-lamp, which meant, of course, sitting so close to the sideboard that it was impossible for the maid to get at it when she wanted a plate. It was the mistress who did the serving, however, the master sitting opposite her near the besieged sideboard, ready to reach and hand round anything they might need from it.

Henriette had put Claude on her right and Mahoudeau on her left; Jory and Gagnière sat on either side of Sandoz.

'Françoise!' she called out to the maid. 'Bring in the toast, please. It's on top of the stove.'

When the toast was brought she served it out, two pieces to each plate, and was just pouring the liquid from the bouillabaisse over them when the door opened.

'Fagerolles, at last!' she exclaimed. 'Sit there, will you, next to Claude.'

He made his excuses with a great show of gallantry, pretending he had been detained by a business engagement. He was very elegant these days in his well-fitting clothes, of English cut, so that he looked like a regular clubman, with, in addition, just that rakish artist touch which he was careful to preserve. As he took his seat he shook his neighbour by the hand most heartily, apparently overjoyed to see him again.

'Dear old Claude!' he cried. 'I've been wanting to see you for ages! I intended to come and see you dozens of times when you were out at what's-its-name, but you know what things are like . . . life, and all the rest of it!'

Claude, embarrassed by such fulsome protestations, tried to reply with equal cordiality. It was Henriette, in her desire to finish serving out the bouillabaisse, who saved him.

'Listen, Fagerolles,' she cried. 'What do you take? Is it two pieces of toast?'

'It is indeed, madame. Two pieces, please. I adore bouillabaisse. And you make it so well, it is sheer delight!'

All were loud in its praises, especially Mahoudeau and Jory, who said they had never eaten better in Marseilles. So the young wife, ladle in hand, beaming with pride and still flushed by the heat from the stove, was kept busy filling the empty plates as they were handed up to her. She even had to leave the table and hurry into the kitchen to fetch the rest of the soup, for the maid had completely lost her head.

'Do sit down and get on with your own dinner. . . . And take your time; we'll wait for you,' said Sandoz.

But Henriette insisted on attending to her guests.

'There's really no need,' Sandoz insisted. 'You'd do much better to pass the bread. It's there, behind you on the sideboard. . . . Jory prefers bread to toast in his soup,' he went on, leaving the table himself to help with the service, while the others chaffed Jory about his weakness for 'mash'.

In this atmosphere of cheerful comradeship Claude felt as if he was awakening from a dream as he looked round at them all and asked himself whether it was not as recently as yesterday that he was last with them, or whether four years could possibly have gone by since he last dined with them on a Thursday evening. They were not the same, of course, he felt they had changed; Mahoudeau, soured by poverty, Jory keener than ever on self-advancement, Gagnière more remote and elusive. His neighbour Fagerolles, he thought, seemed to exude coldness, in spite of his exaggerated cordiality. Their faces looked a little older too, a little more worn; but there was something else besides; he felt they were growing apart, he could see they were really strangers to one another, even though they did happen to be packed elbow to elbow round the same table. Besides, the atmosphere was new to him; a woman added to its charm, but her presence also kept a check on their exuberance. Why, then, as a witness of the inevitable sequence of things dying and being renewed, had he a distinct feeling that he had done all this before? Why could he have sworn that he had sat in this very same place last week at the same time? Then, suddenly, at last he thought he understood. It was Sandoz himself who had stayed as he was, just as confirmed in his habits of sentiment as in his habits of work, just as delighted to entertain them as a young husband as he had been to share his simple fare with them as a bachelor. He was immobilized in a dream of eternal friendship, with Thursdays like this one following each other in endless succession to the remotest outposts of time, with all the gang eternally together, having started out together, together attaining their coveted victory.

He must have guessed why Claude was silent, for he called to him across the table, with his frank, boyish laugh:

'Well, here you are back again, old fellow! . . . And we've missed you, by God we have! . . . But nothing's changed, as you can see. We're all just exactly as you left us! Aren't we?' he added, turning to the others, who one and all nodded their assent. Of course they had not changed!

'With the exception of one thing, of course,' he went on, his face beaming with pleasure, 'the cooking, which is rather better than it used to be in the Rue d'Enfer. . . . I daren't think of all the ratatouille I served up to you in those days!'

The bouillabaisse was followed by jugged hare, and the meal was rounded off by a roast fowl with salad. They sat a long time over the dessert, though the talk was far less heated than it used to be. Everyone talked about himself and finally relapsed into silence when he realized that no one was listening. With the cheese, however, when they had all sampled the rather acidic light Burgundy from the cask Sandoz had ventured to acquire, and the conversation turned to the subject of authors' royalties on a first novel, voices were raised and the old animation revived.

'So you've come to an understanding with Naudet, have you?' asked Mahoudeau, whose pinched, starved face looked bonier than ever. 'Is it true he guarantees you fifty thousand francs the first year?'

'That's the figure,' Fagerolles replied, not too convincingly. 'But nothing's settled yet, of course,' he added. 'I'm in no hurry to make up my mind. It's risky to tie yourself up like that. Besides, I'm not exactly bowled over by the offer.'

'You're hard to please, I must say,' remarked the sculptor. 'For twenty francs a day I'd sign anything.'

By this time they were all of them listening to Fagerolles playing the part of the young man overwhelmed by the first fruits of success. He still had the disturbing look of a pretty but thoroughly unscrupulous girl, though with a certain added gravity imparted by the cut of his beard and the arrangement of his hair. He still kept in touch with Sandoz, though his visits were now few and far between, since he was gradually breaking away from the gang and launching himself on the boulevards where he assiduously frequented cafés, newspaper offices, and all the places where he could gain publicity or make useful contacts. It was deliberately and with the firm intention of building up his own personal success that he cultivated the notion that it was preferable to have nothing in common, professionally or socially, with such hot-headed revolutionaries. Rumour had it that he even included a number of society women as pawns in his game, treating them not, as Jory did, with the frank brutality of the male, but with the cold, passionless provocation of the man who has a way with duchesses a little past their prime.

'I say, have you seen what Vernier's written about you?' asked Jory, simply to underline his own importance, as he now claimed to have 'made' Fagerolles as he once claimed to have 'made' Claude. 'Echoing me, of course, like all the rest,' he added.

'He certainly gets into the papers these days,' put in Mahoudeau with a sigh.

Fagerolles answered with a dismissive gesture and smiled to himself, full of scorn for these clumsy fools who persisted in their misguided stubbornness when it was really so easy to conquer the public. Once he had picked their brains it was a simple matter to cut adrift from them. Meanwhile he was the gainer; the public had nothing but praise to bestow on his own carefully subdued painting, while it vented its deadly hatred on the persistently violent canvases produced by the rest of the group.

'Did *you* see Vernier's article?' Jory asked Gagnière. 'He does repeat exactly what I said, doesn't he?'

For the moment Gagnière was absorbed in contemplating his glass and the red shadow cast by the wine on the white tablecloth. Jory's question made him start.

'What did you say? Vernier's article?'

'Why yes, all this stuff that's being written about Fagerolles!'

In his amazement, Gagnière turned towards Fagerolles and said:

'Writing about you? Really? I didn't know, I've never seen anything. . . . Writing about you are they? Whatever for?'

This provoked a general guffaw, while Fagerolles grinned rather sheepishly, suspecting Gagnière of making fun of him. But Gagnière was in deadly earnest. He could not believe that a painter who did not even observe the law of values could possibly be successful. A humbug like that a success? Impossible! Surely somebody had a conscience?

The outburst of merriment which followed these remarks brought the dinner to a lively end. Everybody had stopped eating some time ago, though the hostess insisted on offering them more.

'Look after your guests,' she kept saying to her husband, who was thoroughly enjoying the fun. 'Hand them the biscuits from the sideboard, dear.'

The guests thanked her, however, and all left the table. But as they were going to spend the rest of the evening sitting round it drinking tea, they stood back against the wall and carried on their conversation while the little maid was clearing the remains of the meal, helped by host and hostess, the latter putting away the salt-cellars in a drawer, the former giving a hand with folding the tablecloth.

'You may smoke,' Henriette told them. 'You know I don't mind.'

Fagerolles, who had drawn Claude aside into the window recess, offered him a cigar, which he refused.

'Of course, I'd forgotten. You don't smoke!' said Fagerolles. 'I shall be coming to see the stuff you've brought back from the country. Very interesting, I should think. Besides, you know what I think about *your* work, there's nobody like you. . . .'

He was very humble and genuinely sincere, as he always had been, in his admiration, bearing, as he was bound to do, the stamp of Claude's genius, and having to acknowledge it in spite of all his cleverly calculated attempts to evade the obligation. His humility was coupled, however, with a certain uneasiness, very unusual in him, which sprang from his desire to know why the master of his youth had so far found nothing to say about his picture. At length, with quivering lips, he ventured to ask:

'Have you seen my "Actress" at the Salon? Quite frankly, do you like it?'

of Fagerolles had been closed, there had been long gaps in the conversation and the atmosphere, already heavy with tobacco smoke, seemed to have been made even heavier by a feeling of annoyance and frustration. At one point, even Gagnière left the table and sat at the piano quietly picking out bits of Wagner with the stiff unpractised fingers of someone who had turned thirty before he did his first five-finger exercise.

The arrival of Dubuche about eleven o'clock put the final damper on the proceedings. He had been to a dance and left early in order to pay this, his last duty-call of the day, on his old friends. His evening suit, his white tie and, above it, his pale round face were all expressive of his annoyance at having felt he had to come, of the importance he attached to his sacrifice, and of his dread of compromising in some way or other his recently acquired wealth. He was careful never to mention his wife, so that he would not have to take her with him to the Sandoz's. He shook hands with Claude with as little emotion as if he had met him only yesterday. He refused a cup of tea and, with much puffing out of his cheeks, talked with slow deliberation about the worries of moving into a newly-built house and about the overwhelming amount of work he had to get through since he joined his father-in-law in business; they were putting up a whole street of new houses near the Parc Monceau.

Claude felt plainly now that some link with the past was broken, and he wondered whether they were really gone for ever, those hectic, friendly meetings he used to enjoy before anything had come between them and none had desired to monopolize all the glory. Today, the battle was on, with each man fighting greedily for himself. The rift was there, though barely visible as yet, which had cracked apart the old sworn friendships and which one day would shatter them in a thousand pieces.

Sandoz, on the other hand, who still had faith in eternity, was oblivious to all this and still saw the gang as it had been in the Rue d'Enfer days, shoulder to shoulder, marching to conquest. Why should a good thing ever be altered? Did not happiness consist of the eternal enjoyment of one thing chosen in preference to all others?

When, an hour later, his friends, all suffering from the soporific effect of Dubuche's dreary, self-centred talk about his own affairs, decided to leave, and Gagnière had been aroused from his trance at the piano, Sandoz, followed by his wife, insisted on seeing them all to the gate at the end of the garden, in spite of the cold night.

'See you again Thursday, Claude! . . . See you on Thursday, everybody!' he said as he shook hands with them. 'Don't forget, eh! See you Thursday!'

'See you Thursday!' Henriette repeated as she held up the lamp to light the steps, and Gagnière and Mahoudeau replied gaily, much to everybody's amusement.

'Certainly, young master! . . . Good night, young master! . . . See you Thursday!'

In the Rue Nollet, Dubuche hailed a cab and drove away. The other four walked up to the boulevard, almost without exchanging a word, as if they were weary of each other's company. When they reached the boulevard Jory made off after a girl who caught his eye, pretending he was going back to the office to look over some proofs. Then, when Gagnière automatically came to a standstill with Claude outside the Café Baudequin, where the lights were still burning, Mahoudeau refused to go in and went ahead alone, nursing his gloomy thoughts all the way back to the Rue du Cherche-Midi.

Almost before he realized it, Claude found himself sitting at their old table opposite the silent Gagnière. The café itself had not changed; they still foregathered there on Sundays, and with a certain keenness even, since Sandoz had come to live quite near. But the gang had been rather lost in the flood of newcomers and submerged in the rising tide of banality which characterized the latest recruits to the Open-Air School. At this time of night the café was emptying, anyhow; three young painters, whom Claude did not know, came over and shook hands with him on their way out, and the only other customer left was a local worthy, nodding in front of an empty saucer.

Gagnière settled in and made himself completely at home, paying no attention to the yawns of the last remaining waiter, and sat gazing blankly at Claude.

'By the way,' said the painter, 'what was it you were expounding to Mahoudeau this evening? About the red on the flag turning yellow against the blue of the sky? . . . Do you mean to say you're mugging up the theory of complementary colours?'

Gagnière did not answer. He picked up his glass, put it down again without drinking and murmured with an ecstatic smile:

'Haydn, rhetorical grace, tinkling music for an elderly ancestress with powdered hair. . . . Mozart, the pioneer genius, the first to endow the orchestra with individuality. . . . Between them, they produced Beethoven; that's why *they're* significant. . . . Beethoven! There's power, there's strength through calm, serenity in pain! Michelangelo at the tomb of the Medici! Hero, logician, moulder of human minds, he was all these! The great composers of today all spring direct from the Choral Symphony!'

Tired of lingering, the waiter began to trail around, idly putting out the lights, bringing a strange feeling of gloom down on the deserted café, filthy with cigar-ends and globs of spittle, and reeking of the stale drink spilled on the tables; while the only sound that could be heard from the drowsy boulevard outside was the lonely sobbing of a drunk.

Gagnière, lost to the world, was still viewing his cavalcade of dreams:

'There goes Weber,' he murmured, 'in the setting of a Romantic landscape, leading the Dance of Death among the weeping willows and the gnarlèd limbs of oaks. . . . Next comes Schubert, through the pale beams of the moon along the shores of silvery lakes. . . . And now Rossini, talent in person, gay, unaffected, heedless of expression, snapping his fingers in everybody's face. Not at all my sort of fellow, of course, but amazing nevertheless for his abundant inventiveness and the tremendous effects he gets out of the accumulation of voices and the fuller orchestration of a repeated theme. . . . Out of those three you get Meyerbeer. A smart fellow, Meyerbeer, who knew how to make the most of his chances. After Weber, it was he who put the symphony into opera; it was he, too, who gave dramatic expression to the formula unconsciously produced by Rossini. Oh, there are some magnificent things in Meyerbeer, with his feudal pomp and soldierly mysticism! The thrill he imparts to fantastic legends! He's like a cry of passion echoing through history! On top of that he's a discoverer: the individuality of instruments, dramatic recitative with symphonic accompaniment, characteristic phrase acting as keystone to the entire work. . . . Oh, he's one of the masters, Meyerbeer, one of the really great masters!'

Here the waiter broke in with:

'Monsieur, we're closing.'

But, as Gagnière did not so much as look at him, he went over to rouse the gentleman who was dozing in front of his empty saucer, repeating:

'We are closing, monsieur.'

With a shudder the lingering customer pulled himself together and began to grope about in the semi-darkness for his stick; when the waiter had recovered it for him from under his chair, he departed. But Gagnière went on talking.

'Berlioz brought literature into his music,' he said. 'He is the musical illustrator of Shakespeare and Virgil and Goethe. And what a painter! The Delacroix of music, with his fine conflagration of sounds, the same clashing contrast of colours! Like all the Romantics, he had his mental kink, of course: religion, and a tendency to let himself be swept away into a lot of high-flown ecstasies. No sense of construction in opera, but marvellous in his orchestral work, though he does tend to torture his orchestra by over-emphasizing the separate character of every instrument. He actually thought of them as real people, you know. I always get a delightful thrill out of what he said about clarinets: "Clarinets are women who know they are loved", he said. . . . Then there's Chopin, such a dandy, and so Byronic, the poet of the mind diseased! Mendelssohn, now, is like a faultless engraver, Shakespeare in dancing-pumps, and his "Songs Without Words" are jewels for intelligent women! . . . What comes after can be spoken of only on bended knee. . . . '

There was only one light left burning now, the one immediately above his head, and the waiter was standing behind him in the cold, inhospitable gloom, ready to turn it out. Gagnière's voice now assumed a religious tremor, in preparation for his devotions, for now he had reached the innermost sanctuary, the holy of holies.

'Oh, Schumann! Despair and pleasure in despair. The end of all things, one last, pure, melancholy song, soaring above the ruins of the world! . . . Oh, Wagner! The god, the incarnation of centuries of music! His work, the mighty firmament, where all the arts are blended into one, characters portrayed in all their true humanity, and the orchestra itself lives through every phase of the acted drama. What an onslaught on conventions, what wholesale destruction of ineffectual theories it stands for, the revolution, the breaking-down of barriers to infinity! . . . The overture to *Tannhäuser*, what is it but the mighty hallelujah of the new age! First, the pilgrims' chorus, the calm, slow beat of the profound religious motif, gradually giving place to the Sirens' song, the voluptuous pleasures of Venus, their rapturous delights and fascinating langours imposing themselves more and more, to the point of complete abandon; then, little by little, the sacred theme comes back, takes all the other themes and welds them into one supreme harmony and carries them away on the wings of a great triumphal anthem!'

'We're closing now, monsieur,' the waiter announced again, and Claude who had not been listening, so engrossed was he in his own thoughts, drank up his beer and said in a loud voice:

'Come on old chap! Closing time!'

That brought Gagnière to himself with a start. A look of
pain flashed across his ecstatic features, and he shuddered
as he realized he had returned to earth. He swallowed down
his beer and then, outside on the pavement, he shook his
companion's hand without a word and walked off into the
darkness.

It was nearly two when Claude reached the Rue de Douai.
For a week now he had been doing his round of Paris, and
every night he had come home feverish after the encounters
of the day, but never before had he come back so late, his
brain seething with so much excitement. The lamp had gone
out, and Christine, overcome by fatigue, had dropped to
sleep with her head on the table.

CHAPTER 8

WITH one last flick of Christine's feather duster, their
installation in the Rue de Douai was completed. Besides the
small, inconvenient studio, they had only a tiny bedroom
and a kitchen no bigger than a cupboard, and as the studio
served as both living-room and dining-room, the child was
always in the way. Christine had done her best with their
few sticks of furniture, in her effort to keep down expenses,
but she had had to buy an old bed, second-hand, and she
had even succumbed to the necessary luxury of white muslin
curtains at seven sous a metre. Once they were installed,
the place looked pleasant enough, she thought, in spite of
its drawbacks, and she made a point of keeping up a high
standard of cleanliness, though she had decided to do
without a servant, as living was going to be more costly now
they were in town.

Claude spent the first few months in Paris in a state of
increasing nervous tension. The din and excitement of the
streets, visits to friends, hectic discussions, anger, indignation, and all the newly-fledged ideas he brought home from
the outer world kept him arguing at the top of his voice,

even in his sleep. Paris had got him in its grip again; he could feel it in the very marrow of his bones. It was like going through a furnace and emerging with his youth renewed, full of enthusiasm, ambitious to see everything, do everything, conquer everything. Never had he experienced such an urge to work, never had he known such hope or felt that all he had to do was stretch out his hand and produce masterpieces which would put him in the rank which was his by right, the first rank. As he walked about Paris he discovered pictures everywhere; the whole city, its streets and squares and bridges and its ever-changing skyline opened out before him gigantic frescoes which, in his intoxication with the colossal, he always found too small. He would return home in high spirits, his brain bubbling over with plans which, in the evening, in the lamplight, he would sketch on bits of paper, but without ever being able to make up his mind how or where he would set to work on the series of great works he so often dreamed of.

One serious obstacle was the restricted size of his studio. If only he could have had the old garret on the Quai de Bourbon, or even the huge dining-room at Bennecourt! But what could he do in a long narrow room like this? It was nothing more than a corridor, really, though the landlord had had the impertinence to let it as a studio at four hundred francs a year once he had put in a skylight. What was worse, the skylight, with its northern aspect, was hemmed in between two high walls, so the only light it admitted was of no more value than the dull, greenish light of a basement. He had, consequently, to postpone the realization of his great ambitions and resolved to start on canvases of modest dimensions, consoling himself with the thought that size does not of necessity prove genius.

The moment was most propitious, he thought, for the success of an artist with courage enough to strike a note of sincerity and originality amid the general collapse of the old schools. Even the most recent dogmas were beginning to totter. Delacroix had died without pupils; Courbet was being followed merely by a few clumsy imitators; the masterpieces they left behind in their turn were going to be nothing more than museum pieces, dimmed with age, examples of period art. It seemed a simple matter to forecast the formula which would crystallize out of the work of the younger painters from the burst of blazing sunshine, the limpid dawn that was breaking in so many recent paintings, through the growing influence of the Open-Air School. There was no denying now that the light-coloured pictures which had been the laughing-stock of the 'Salon des Refusés' were now quietly working on a number of artists, lightening a great many palettes. Nobody would admit it yet, but the ball was rolling, and the tendency was becoming more and more obvious at every Salon. What a *coup* it would be if, among all the unconscious copies of the untalented, and the sly or half-hearted efforts of those with the skill, a real master were to declare himself, a painter who presented the new formula boldly and forcefully, refusing all concessions, presenting it as sound and complete as it should be to ensure its establishment as the gospel of the closing century!

With this renewal of hope and vigour, Claude, instead of being assailed by endless doubts, believed in his own genius. The painful crises which used to force him to tramp the streets of Paris day after day in search of his lost courage, ceased and gave place to a fever which steeled him and drove him to work with the blind determination of the artist who tears open his very flesh to bring forth the fruit of his torment. His long rest in the country had given him a remarkable freshness of vision and a renewed delight in execution. He was coming back to his painting, he felt, with an ease and a balance he had never known before, and with them, as he realized the success of his efforts, a sense of accomplishment and a feeling of the deepest content. As he used to say at Bennecourt, he had 'got' his open-air, meaning the painting with the harmonious liveliness of colour which so surprised his friends when they came to see him. They all admired it, and were all convinced that with works so personal in their expression, showing as they did, for the first time, nature bathed in real light, with its interplay of reflections and the continuous decomposition of colours, all he had to do was to show himself to take his place, and a very high place too, in contemporary art.

So for three whole years Claude struggled on, never weakening, clinging firmly to his own ideas, gaining impetus from his failures and marching stoutly ahead in the unshakeable conviction that he was right.

The first year, in December, when the snow was on the ground, he went and stood for four hours a day down behind Montmartre on the corner of a patch of waste land, and painted: in the background, poverty, dismal hovels dominated by great factory chimneys; in the foreground a couple of ragged urchins, a boy and a girl, devouring stolen apples in the snow. His insistence on painting from life complicated his task beyond description, involved him in almost insurmountable difficulties. Nevertheless, he finished his picture out of doors and limited his work in the studio to cleaning up. When he saw it in the cold, dead light of the studio, the picture amazed even Claude by its brutality; it was like a door flung open on the street revealing the blinding snow against which two pitiful figures stood out in dirty grey. He knew at once that a picture like that would never be accepted, but he made no attempt to tone it down and sent it to the Salon as it was. After swearing he would never try to get into the Salon again, he now contended that on principle one should always put something before the Selection Committee, if only to prove it was in the wrong. Besides, he acknowledged the usefulness of the Salon as the only battlefield on which an artist could assert himself at one blow. The Committee rejected his picture.

The second year he tried a contrast. He chose the Square des Batignolles in May: huge horse-chestnuts casting their shadows over a stretch of lawn, six-storey buildings in the background; in the foreground, sitting on a bright green bench, a row of nursemaids and local inhabitants watching three little girls making sand pies. It needed a vast amount of courage, once he had been given permission to do so, to set up his easel and work there among the facetious crowd.

He decided, however, to go at about five o'clock in the morning to work on the background and to be content to make sketches of the figures and finish off the whole in the studio. This time the picture did not look quite so harsh; it seemed to have taken on some of the dreary softness of the light filtered by the glass in the roof. He thought it had been accepted, and all his friends hailed it as a masterpiece and spread the news that it was going to revolutionize the Salon. To their amazement and indignation they heard that the Committee had rejected the picture. This time, without the slightest doubt, there was prejudice, a deliberate attempt to stifle an original artist. Claude himself, after a first outburst of resentment, turned the full force of his anger on the picture itself. It was a dishonest, misleading, disgusting piece of work he said. It had taught him a memorable lesson, and a lesson he deserved. He ought never to have let himself go back to the miserable light of the studio or the revolting trickery of painting figures from memory! When the picture came back he took his knife and ripped it from corner to corner.

The third year he put all his pent-up fury into a work of revolt; he determined to paint blazing sunshine, the blazing sunshine peculiar to Paris, where the pavements on some days are white hot with the dazzling reflection from the fronts of the buildings. No place can be hotter than Paris; it makes even people from tropical countries mop their brows, for it might be some African clime when the heat comes pouring down from a sky like a fiery furnace. His subject was a view of the Place du Carrousel at midday, when the sun beats down without mercy. He showed a cab ambling across in the quivering heat, the driver drowsing on his box, and the horse, head down, perspiring between the shafts, while the passers-by were apparently staggering along on the pavements, all except one young woman who, all fresh and rosy under her parasol, swept with the ease of a queen through the fiery air which was clearly her natural element. But the really startling thing about the picture was its original treatment of light, breaking it down into its components after uncompromising accuracy of observation, but deliberately contradicting all the habits of the eye by stressing blues, yellows, and reds in places where no one expected to see them. In the background, the Tuileries melted away into a golden mist; the pavements were blood-red and the passers-by were merely indicated by a number of darker patches, swallowed up by the overbright sunshine. This time Claude's friends shouted their admiration, as usual, but they were also embarrassed, seriously disturbed even, for they all felt that martyrdom could be the only reward for painting such as this. Claude accepted their words of praise, but he knew that, behind them, a break was in preparation, and when the Committee once again refused to admit him to the Salon, he cried out in a moment of heart-rending intuition:

'Now there's no giving in! . . . I'll die first!'

Gradually, though his valiant determination never seemed to diminish, he began to slip back into his old fits of doubt when his struggle against nature showed any sign of weakening. Every picture rejected he pronounced bad, or rather incomplete, since it failed, he said, to fulfil his intentions. It was this feeling of impotence that exasperated him even more than the Committee's repeated rejections. Of course he could never forgive the Committee for being so obdurate; even the sketchiest of his works was a hundred times better than the rubbish it accepted. What was really unbearable was the inability ever to express himself to the full because his genius refused to give birth to the essential masterpiece! Everything he did had its masterly patches; he acknowledged them and they satisfied him. But why the sudden gaps? Why the worthless patches, unnoticed while the work was in progress, yet an indelible blemish which killed the whole effect of the finished picture? He felt he would never be able to correct himself, as if a great insurmountable wall rose up before him, beyond which he was forbidden to go. Twenty times he would go over the same bit and in the end it would be twenty times as bad as when he started, a meaningless mess of paint on canvas. Then, giving way to his irritation, his vision would become distorted and his power of execution diminish through what was nothing more or less than total paralysis of his will-power. Could there be something wrong with his eyes that made his hands feel as if they were no longer his to control? Could it mean that the lesions, the imagined existence of which had caused him so much worry in the past, were increasing? As his crises recurred more and more frequently, he would spend weeks in unbearable self-torture, hovering between hope and un-certainty, and through all the weary hours he spent wrestling with his rebellious masterpiece one great mainstay was the consoling dream of the picture which he would paint one day, when his hands were freed from their present invisible shackles, and which would satisfy him completely. What happened at present was that the urge to create ran away with his fingers, which meant that whenever he was working on one picture his mind was already at work on the next, so that his one remaining desire was to finish the task in hand as quickly as possible, as he felt his original enthusiasm ebbing away. He persuaded himself that this picture would be worthless, like the rest, that he was going through the stage at which an artist is obliged to ignore his conscience, make the inevitable concessions, and even cheat to a certain extent. But once he had passed that stage, was he not going to produce something which he knew would be superb, heroic, something irreproachable, something indestruct-ible?—Perpetual mirage which, in the world of art, spurs on the courage of the damned! Tender, self-pitying false-hood, without which production would be impossible for all who die of the inability to create a living masterpiece!

Outside this ceaseless struggle with himself, material dif-ficulties were accumulating. Was it not enough, he asked himself, not to be able to bring out what you knew you'd got in you? No, you had to cope with *things* into the bargain! The fact was that, although he refused to admit it, painting from nature, in the open-air, was impossible if the canvas exceeded reasonable dimensions. There were the added difficulties, too, of setting up one's easel in a busy street and of getting people to pose for a sufficient length of time. That meant, obviously, that subjects were limited to country landscapes and a restricted type of urban landscape in which the figures are little more than silhouettes painted in almost as an after-thought. The weather, too, provided endless complications; the wind would blow over the easel, or rain would stop the work altogether. When that happened he would go home in a raging temper, shaking his fist at the heavens, accusing nature of defending itself against being captured and conquered. He complained bitterly of not being rich, for his dream would have been to have mobile studios, one on wheels for use in Paris, one on a boat on the Seine, and live like a gypsy artist. But nothing ever came to his assistance; everything conspired against his work.

Christine suffered as much as he did. She had been very brave, sharing his hopes and, like a good housewife, keeping the studio bright and cheerful; but now, when she saw Claude so weary and helpless, she would slump into a chair, discouraged. Every time he had a picture rejected, she felt it more keenly than ever; it wounded her pride, for, like every woman, she was not indifferent to success. As Claude grew bitter, she grew bitter too; his feelings were hers, so now were his tastes; and she defended his painting, which had become, in a way, a part of her, the one important thing in her life, the one thing she relied upon for her happiness. She sensed that painting was claiming her lover from her a little more every day, and she accepted it for the time being, offering no resistance but letting herself be carried along, determined to be as one with him as long as his effort lasted. But she felt sick at heart at the thought that the moment of abdication might be near; she was afraid of what the future might hold for her and premonitions often chilled her to the very soul. She felt she was growing older and a great pity welled up within her and a desire to weep for no reason at all, a desire which she often satisfied for hours on end when she was alone in the gloom of the studio.

About this time, too, her heart seemed to grow warmer and more expansive as she realized that she could be not only a lover but also a mother to Claude. He was little more than a grown-up child, she felt, and her maternal feelings sprang from the vague but infinite pity which so softened her heart towards him, his perpetual, illogical sense of weakness and the endless calls it made on her sympathy and understanding. He was beginning to make her unhappy now, and his caresses were of the casual, mechanical kind a man bestows on women who have ceased to mean anything to him. How could she love him still when he slipped from her arms and showed every sign of boredom when she enveloped him, as always, in her ardent embrace? How could she love him at all if she could not love him with that same, absorbing affection, the same eternal adoration and sacrifice? Deep down inside her she felt the gnawing of that insatiable desire, for she was still the same passionate, sensual woman with the blood-red lips and determination in her firm, square chin. And so, after the secret sorrows of her nights, she drew a certain bitter-sweet consolation from mothering her man throughout the day and found one last, fleeting pleasure in being kind and trying to make him happy now that their life was no longer what it once had been.

The only one who suffered by this change of affection was little Jacques. Christine neglected him more than ever; he meant nothing to her, since her maternal instinct had been aroused only through physical love. Her real child was the man she adored and desired; Jacques was nothing more than a proof of the great passion that had brought them together. As she had watched him grow up and become less and less dependent on her care, she had made a sacrifice of him, not because she was fundamentally callous, but simply because that was the way she felt about him. At meal-times he was always given second best; the warmest place, near the stove, was not for his little chair. In any moment of imminent danger, her first cry, her first protecting gesture was never for him, the weaker of her men. Whenever she could, she relegated him to the background, or repressed him with 'Jacques, be quiet! Father's tired!' or 'Jacques, be still! Can't you see father's working?'

What was more, Paris did not suit the child. He had been used to roaming at will about the vast countryside; now, boxed up as he was and restricted in his activities, he was stifled. He lost his healthy colouring, did not thrive, but grew up like a puny, serious, wide-eyed little man. He was just five, but by some strange phenomenon his head had grown out of all proportion to his body, which often provoked his father to remark: 'What a head! The youngster'll be a great man one day!' His intelligence, however, seemed to diminish in proportion to the growth of his skull. He was a gentle, timid child, and would spend hours apparently oblivious to his surroundings, without a word for anyone, his thoughts away in the blue; but when he awoke from his daydreams it would be to shout and leap about as madly as any young, playful animal giving way to his instincts. Then 'Be stills' and 'Be quiets' fell thick and fast, for his mother could not understand these sudden bursts of animal spirits and, seeing that Claude, busy at his easel, was about to lose his temper, she was upset and immediately lost hers and rushed the child back into his chair in the corner. There, with a frightened shudder like someone suddenly roused from a dream, he would quickly calm down and doze off to sleep again, his eyes wide open, so uninterested in life that toys, corks, pictures, old paint-tubes, whatever he was playing with, slipped out of his hands to the floor. Several times Christine had tried to teach him his letters; he had always refused to learn and burst into tears, so they had decided to wait another year or two to send him to school, where the teachers were bound to make him learn something.

One thing which scared Christine more than anything else was the threat of poverty. Living in Paris, with a growing child, was dearer than living in the country, and resources were strained to the utmost, at the end of the month particularly, in spite of all kinds of economies. The only income they were certain of was Claude's thousand francs a year; out of that four hundred went on rent, and what could they do on the fifty francs a month that remained? For a time they managed to avoid financial embarrassment by the sale of the occasional picture. Claude had somehow run to earth the amateur collector who used to patronize Gagnière, a hated bourgeois, of course, but one of those with a genuine artist's soul beneath an outward shell of eccentricity. M. Hue, that was his name, was a retired government official and, unfortunately, not sufficiently well-off to be able to buy whenever he wished; all he could do was to deplore the short-sightedness of the public in letting yet another genius starve to death. Convinced of Claude's genius from the very first, he made his choice of the harshest of his canvases and hung them side by side with his Delacroix, swearing they had a similar future before them. Old Malgras, unfortunately for Claude and Christine, had retired, his fortune made—a modest fortune, it is true, a matter of ten thousand francs a year—and, being a careful man, he had decided to enjoy it in a cottage he had bought at Bois-Colombes. It was amusing to hear him talk about the great Naudet and express his contempt for the gambler's millions which, he was convinced, would do him no good in the end. As the result of a chance meeting, Claude managed to sell him one last picture, for his own collection, one of the nudes he had painted at Boutin's studio, that superb study of the abdomen which had always made Malgras's heart beat faster every time he saw it. Poverty, then, was on their doorstep; possible markets were closing instead of opening, and a disturbing legend was beginning to grow up around this painting which was continually being rejected by the Salon, though art such as this, so incomplete, so revolutionary, so provoking by its denial of all accepted conventions, would have been enough in itself to scare prospective buyers. One evening, in a quandary as to how to pay a paint bill, Claude declared he would rather live on his capital than stoop to producing commercial pictures. Christine opposed such an extreme solution to their difficulties with all her might; it was mad, she said; she would cut down expenses even lower, she would prefer anything to letting their capital go; that would send them starving to the gutter in no time!

The year his third picture was rejected, the summer was so perfect that Claude somehow found his powers miraculously restored. There was not a cloud in the sky above the immense activity of Paris, and the days flowed by in limpid serenity. Claude had started his wanderings about the city again, bent on what he called 'spotting somethin worth while', something tremendous, something decisive, he did not know exactly what. September came and he had still discovered nothing; he had put all his energies, for a week or so at a time, into various projects and then decided that it was not what he was looking for. He lived in a perpetual state of tension, always on the alert, always on the point of attaining the realization of his dreams, which always escaped him. At heart, beneath his intransigent, realist's exterior, he was as superstitious as any nervous female; he believed in all kinds of secret and complicated influences; he persuaded himself that success or failure would depend entirely on his choice of a lucky or unlucky subject.

One afternoon, on one of the last fine days of the summer, he took Christine out with him, leaving Jacques, as they usually did when they went out together, in the care of the kindly old concierge. He felt a sudden desire to have her by his side, to revisit with her the places they had once been so fond of, but behind his desire was a vague hope that her presence would bring him luck. So they went down as far as the Pont Louis-Philippe and spent a good quarter of an hour on the Quai des Ormes leaning over the parapet, looking in silence across the Seine to the old Hôtel du Martoy where they first fell in love. Then, still without a word, they started out over the ground they had covered together so often in the old days. They followed the embankment, under the plane-trees, seeing the past rise up at every step as the landscape opened out before them: the bridges, their arches cutting across the satin sheen of the river; the Cité covered with shadow, dominated by the yellowing towers of Notre-Dame; the great sweeping curve of the right bank, bathed in sunshine, leading to the dim silhouette of the Pavillon de Flore; the broad avenues, the buildings on either bank, and between them, the Seine, with all the lively activity of its laundry-boats, its baths, its barges. As in the past, the setting sun seemed to follow them along the riverside, rolling over the roofs of the distant houses, partially eclipsed for a moment by the dome of the Institut. It was a dazzling sunset, finer than they had ever seen, a slow descent through tiny clouds which gradually turned into a trellis of purple with molten gold pouring through every mesh. But out of the past they were calling to mind nothing reached them but an unconquerable melancholy, a feeling that it would always be just beyond their reach, that it would be impossible to live it again. The time-worn stones were cold and the ever-flowing stream beneath the bridges seemed to have carried away something of their selves, the charm of awakening desire, the thrill of hope and expectation. Now they were all in all to each other, they had forgone the simple happiness of feeling the warm pressure of their arms as they strolled quietly along, wrapped, as it were, in the all-enveloping life of the great city.

At the Pont des Saints-Pères, Claude, who could bear it no longer, came to a standstill. He let go Christine's arm and turned back towards the point of the Cité. She felt that the break was more than a physical one, and the thought filled her heart with sorrow; so, seeing him prepared to linger, rapt in thought, she made some attempt to reclaim him.

'It's time to go home, Claude,' she said. 'Jacques will be expecting us back, you know.'

But Claude walked along to the centre of the bridge. Christine had to follow him. There he stopped again, his gaze fixed upon the island riding for ever at anchor in the Seine, cradling the heart of Paris through which its blood has pulsed for centuries as its suburbs have gone on spreading themselves over the surrounding plain. His face lit up, as with an inward flame and his eyes were aglow as, with a broad, sweeping gesture, he said:

'Look! Look at that!'

In the foreground immediately below them lay the Port Saint-Nicolas with the low huts that housed the various shipping offices, the broad sloping wharf, its paving-stones heaped up with sacks and barrels and sand; alongside, a string of loaded barges being swarmed over by a host of dock porters, and, stretched out over it all, the great iron jib of an enormous crane. Against the far bank, an open-air bath, gay with the shouts of the last of the season's bathers, flaunted the strips of grey tenting that served as its roof as bravely as if they were banners. Between the two, the Seine, clear of all traffic, flowed along, greeny-grey, whipped up into little dancing wavelets tipped with white and pink and blue. The middle distance was marked by the Pont des Arts, with the thin line of its roadway, raised aloft on its network of girders, fine as black lace, alive with endless foot-passengers streaming perpetually to and fro like so many ants. Beneath it, the Seine flowed away into the distance to the ancient, rusty stone arches of the Pont-Neuf, away to the left as far as the Ile Saint-Louis in one straight vista, bright and dazzling as a stretch of mirror; to the right, the other arm making a sudden bend, the weir in front of the Monnaie seemed to cut off the view with its bar of foam. Over the Pont-Neuf the great yellow omnibuses and the gaily coloured waggonettes moved with the clockwork regularity of children's toys. Thus the whole background was framed between the perspectives of both banks of the river: on the right bank the houses along the embankment, half-hidden by a clump of tall trees, and beyond them, on the horizon, a corner of the Hôtel de Ville and the square tower of Saint-Gervais stood out against the skyline above the surrounding conglomeration of smaller buildings; on the left bank, one wing of the Institut, then the flat façade of the Monnaie, and beyond that, more trees, stretching into the distance. What occupied the centre of this vast picture, rising from the river-level and towering high into the sky, was the Cité, the prow of the ancient ship, for ever gilded by the setting sun. Below, the poplars on the terrace raised a powerful mass of greenery, completely hiding the statue on the bridge. Above, the sun threw the two shores of the Ile into violent contrast, plunging in shadow the grey stone houses on the Quai de l'Horloge, lighting up so brightly the red-gold houses and the islets of oddly assorted buildings on the Quai des Orfèvres, that all their details, shop-signs, and even window-curtains, were clearly visible to the naked eye. Higher up still, between the ragged lines of chimneys and beyond the tilted chess-board of diminutive roof-tops, the pointed towers of the Palais de Justice and the lofty gables of the Préfecture spread vast expanses of slate, broken by an enormous blue advertisement painted on a wall, its huge letters, visible all over Paris, breaking out like a rash of modernity on the city's fevered brow. Higher again, much higher, higher than the twin towers of Notre-Dame, now the colour of old gold, two spires rose; behind the towers, the cathedral spire, and on the left, the spire of the Sainte-Chapelle, so fine, so graceful that they seemed to sway with the breeze, the lofty rigging of the age-old ship against the full light of the open sky.

'Are you coming, Claude?' asked Christine gently.

Spellbound by the heart of Paris, Claude did not hear her speak. The beauty of the evening intensified the clearness of the view, with sharp lights, clean shadows, a lively precision of detail, and a delightful, transparent quality of the atmosphere, while the life of the river and the activity of the wharves were joined by the stream of humanity flowing down from every side, along the streets and over the bridges into the city's great melting-pot where it steamed and seethed and bubbled in the sun. There was a faint breeze blowing, and a flight of little rosy clouds, high overhead, was drifting across the fading blue of the sky, and from all around there rose the slow pulsation of the city's mighty soul.

Distressed to see Claude so completely absorbed, Christine took him by the arm to lead him away, as if she had sensed evil and felt that he was somehow in danger.

'Come home, Claude,' she murmured. 'You're doing yourself no good. . . . Come, take me home.'

As she touched him, he shuddered like a man aroused from a dream. Then, turning back for one last look, he said: 'Oh God! but it's beautiful!' and let her lead him away. For the rest of the evening, throughout their meal, sitting round the stove afterwards and even up till bedtime, he seemed thoroughly dazed and so preoccupied that he did not make more than a half-dozen remarks, so that Christine, unable to get him to answer, stopped trying to make conversation. She lay looking at him, anxiously, wondering whether he might not be sickening for some serious illness, whether he could possibly have caught a chill as he stood on the bridge that afternoon. Claude meanwhile lay staring blankly into space, his face flushed with mental effort, as if some process of germination were at work within him and something was coming to life, with the accompanying exaltation and nausea familiar to women in pregnancy. At first everything seemed painfully difficult, confused, restrained by endless bonds, then suddenly all was loosened and he ceased his restless tossing and sank into the deep slumber which follows on great fatigue.

Next morning, breakfast over, he left the house at once. It meant a trying day for Christine, who, although she had felt reassured to some extent to hear him whistling Provençal tunes as he was getting up, was worried for another reason which she had kept carefully hidden from him, for fear of depressing him. Today, for the first time, they were faced with want; there was still another week to go before they could draw their meagre interest on Claude's capital, and, as she had spent her last sou that morning, there was nothing left for an evening meal, not even enough to buy a loaf of bread. What was she to do? How was she going to be able to keep on lying to him when he came home hungry? The only solution she could find was to pawn the black silk dress Madame Vanzade had given her all those years ago. But it was not a solution she accepted easily; she trembled with fear and shame at the thought of a pawnshop, the refuge of the down-and-out; she had never set foot in such a place. She was so apprehensive of the future now that out of the ten francs they lent her she only spent enough to make some sorrel soup and some potato stew. A chance meeting just as she was leaving the pledge office had unnerved her completely.

As it happened Claude came home very late, full of life, his eyes sparkling with some secret pleasure. He was famished, of course, and made a scene because the table was not laid. Then, as he sat between Christine and little Jacques, he gulped down the soup and devoured a large helping of potatoes.

'Is this all there is?' he asked. 'You surely might have managed a scrap of meat. . . . Or have you been buying more boots?'

She made some faltering reply, not daring to tell the truth and deeply wounded by his unjust remark. Claude, however, was irrepressible and went on teasing her about the way she made the money go on odds and ends for herself. Then, more and more excited by the keen sensations he seemed disinclined to share, even with Christine, he suddenly turned on Jacques.

'For God's sake be quiet!' he cried.

Jacques, uninterested in his food, was tapping with his spoon on the rim of his plate and looking delighted with the din.

'Jacques! Stop that noise!' added his mother. 'Let father enjoy his meal in peace!'

Scared, and suddenly completely calmed, the child resumed his stolid silence and sat gazing glumly at his potatoes, which he made no attempt to eat.

Claude deliberately ate large quantities of cheese while Christine, mortified, talked about fetching some cooked meat from the charcutier's. But he would not hear of it; he kept her talking, saying things which cut her to the heart. When the table had been cleared and they were all three settled for the evening around the lighted lamp, Christine sewing, Jacques quietly looking at a picture-book, Claude kept drumming on the table with his fingers, his mind far, far away, where he had been during the day. Suddenly he got up, took a sheet of paper and a pencil, and, sitting down at the table in the bright ring of light from the lamp, began to make a rapid sketch. It soon became obvious, however, that the sketch, drawn from memory in the urge to exteriorize the tumult of ideas in his brain, was a far from adequate outlet for his activity. It simply increased his need to express himself until at last the cause of his excitement found its way to his lips and he was able to find relief in a spate of words. He would have talked to the walls had he been alone; as Christine happened to be there he addressed his talk to her:

'Look!' he said. 'It's what we saw yesterday. . . . A superb sight! I spent three hours there today, and now I've got it. Just what I want. Amazing! A knock-out, if ever there was one! . . . Look, this is it. I stand under the bridge, with the Port Saint-Nicolas, the crane and the barges with all the porters busy unloading them, in the foreground, see? That's Paris at work, understand: hefty labourers, with bare arms and chests and plenty of muscle! . . . Now on the other side, there's the swimming-bath, Paris at play this time. There'll be an odd boat or something there, to fill the centre, but I'm not too sure about that. I shall have to work it out a bit first. . . . There'll be the Seine, of course, between the two, a good broad stretch. . . . '

As he talked he lined things in with his pencil, going over some of the more sketchy parts time after time and with so much energy that he cut clean through the paper. To please him Christine leaned across and pretended to be keenly interested in all his explanations, though the sketch, rapidly overloaded with endless summary details, soon became such an inextricable tangle of lines that she could make nothing of it at all.

'You see what I mean?' he asked.

'Why, yes, of course! It's lovely!' she answered.

'Well, in the background, I have the two vistas of river, with the embankments, and in the centre, towering in triumph on the skyline, the Cité. . . . It's a marvel, when

you come to think of it. You see it every day, you don't
even stop to look at it, but it somehow gets into you, your
admiration accumulates and then, all of a sudden, one fine
afternoon, you're aware of it. There's nothing in the world
to touch it! It's Paris in all its glory in a blaze of sunshine!
. . . Wasn't I a fool not to think of it before? The times I've
looked at it and never really seen it! It was sheer luck that
made me stop where I did after our walk along the embankment. . . . And, do you remember, there's a patch of shadow
just here, and there direct sunlight; there are the towers and
there the Sainte-Chapelle with the spire tapering away to a
needle-point in the sky. . . . No, not there; farther to the
right. Wait. I'll show you. . . .'

Never tiring, he went over the entire drawing again,
branching out into endless little characteristic touches his
painter's eye had noted: here, the striking red of a shop-sign
in the distance; here, a little nearer, the river looked green
and there were patches of oil on the surface; the subtle
colouring of some particular tree, the various greys of the
buildings, the particular luminous quality of the sky. And
Christine, meaning well, would always approve and try to
show the necessary enthusiasm.

Jacques meanwhile had begun to assert himself again.
After a long period of silence spent in contemplating the
picture of a black cat in his book, he began to sing quietly
to himself, on and on, to the same dreary tune:

'Oh, nice, nice cat! Oh, naughty, naughty cat! Oh, nice,
nice, naughty, naughty cat!'

To Claude, for a time, it was just a monotonous noise,
and he could not understand why it annoyed him so much
as a background to his talk. Then, suddenly, he grasped the
meaning of the child's tiresome ditty and burst out with a
furious:

'Damn that cat! And stop that row!'

And Christine added:

'Yes, Jacques, do be quiet when father's talking!'

'The kid's an idiot, if you ask me,' Claude went on.
'Look at that head of his; he *looks* an idiot! Oh! It's enough

to. . . . What do you mean, "nice cat, naughty cat"? Which is it?'

To which little Jacques, white with fear and wagging his big head, replied in bewilderment:

'Don't know.'

And as his father and mother said no more, but exchanged despairing glances, he lay one of his cheeks on his open book, his eyes wide open, and neither stirred nor spoke again.

It was getting late and Christine wanted to go to bed, but Claude had launched into further explanations. He would go tomorrow, he said, and make a sketch on the spot, just to fix his ideas. That led him to suggest that he might buy a little portable easel; he had been wanting to buy one for months. From there he went on to talk about money matters, and Christine, now thoroughly upset and at a loss, finally confessed everything, the last sou spent that morning, the dress pawned to pay for their evening meal. Overcome with remorse and pity, Claude took her in his arms and kissed her and asked her forgiveness for complaining about the supper. She'd got to forgive him, he said, for he was capable of anything whenever he felt this damnable need to paint gnawing at his entrails. As for the pawnshop, what a joke! He snapped his fingers at poverty!

'I tell you I've got the very thing this time,' he cried. 'This is the picture that spells success!'

She made no reply; her mind was on her encounter on the steps of the pawnshop; she wanted to say nothing about it, but in her present rather torpid state of mind it was too much for her, and she let it slip out for no very obvious reason, without any kind of transition:

'Madame Vanzade's dead.'

Claude, taken completely by surprise, asked her how she knew.

'I happened to meet her old footman. . . . Quite the gentleman now, and very sprightly, despite his seventy years. I didn't recognize him. It was he who spoke to me. . . . Yes, she died six weeks ago. Her millions have all gone to hospitals, all except a small annuity to the two old servants who have retired to end their days in comfort.'

Claude looked at her, then murmured sadly:

'Poor Christine! You're sorry now, aren't you? She would have provided for you, too, and found you a husband, as I used to say she would. You might have come into her whole fortune instead of starving with a mad fool like me.'

His words awoke her to reality again. She dragged her chair up close to his, flung one arm round him and pressed herself close against him with every particle of her being, crying:

'No, no! Don't say that! . . . I wouldn't have dared to think of getting her money. If I had, I should have said so, and you know I don't lie. I don't really know what was the matter with me; I suddenly felt overcome and sad, somehow, as if I knew the end had come for me, too. . . . It was remorse, I expect, remorse for having left her so thoughtlessly, poor, helpless old woman! She used to call me her little girl. It was an unkind thing to do, and I shall have to pay for it some day. Oh, don't try to deny it! I know, I can feel there's not much left in life now for me.'

She wept bitter tears, for beyond the obsessing thought that her whole existence had been laid waste, life appeared to have nothing in store for her but sorrow.

'Come, dry your eyes,' said Claude, more tenderly now. 'It's not like you to get the jitters and let yourself be worried by all sorts of pointless nightmares! We'll pull through somehow, you know we will! Besides, it was really you who discovered my picture for me! So you see, you can't be cursed since you brought luck to *me*!'

He laughed, and she nodded her head in assent, seeing he wanted her to smile. His picture! That was one of the causes of her sadness, for down at the bridge he had forgotten all about her, as if she meant nothing to him, and since that moment she had felt him moving farther and farther away from her, into a world to which she could never hope to aspire. But she let him console her and they kissed each other as they used to do in the old days, before they left the table and retired to bed.

Little Jacques heard nothing of all this; after lying for a time in a kind of stupor, with one cheek resting on his picture-book, he had gradually dropped off to sleep, his head, the enormous head which marked him as the blemished offspring of genius and was often so heavy he could scarcely lift it, in the full glare of the lamp. When his mother put him to bed, he never even opened his eyes.

It was only about this time that it struck Claude that he might marry Christine. In part he was influenced by the advice of Sandoz who was surprised to see him prolong unnecessarily their irregular relationship, but he was not indifferent to a certain feeling of pity and the need to be kind to her and consequently to deserve her forgiveness for all his misdeeds.

For some time, he noticed, she had been so unhappy, so anxious about the future that he did not know what to do to cheer her up. He for his part had often been surly and given way to his old ungovernable tempers and treated her little better than a servant under notice to leave. Probably, if she were his lawful wife, she might feel that the home was more really hers and be less sensitive to his ill-humour. Christine herself had never brought up the subject of marriage, but had lived somehow detached from the world and fallen in with what she considered his discretion. Still, he knew she felt hurt when she was not asked to go with him to the Sandozes'. Besides, they were no longer either as free or as isolated as they had been in the country; they were in Paris, which meant malicious gossip, certain unavoidable contacts, and a host of other things which can make life unpleasant for a woman who lives with a man. The only objections he had to marriage were the time-worn objections of any artist who desires to retain his freedom. As it was obvious he was never going to leave her, why not give her the satisfaction of being a married woman? And indeed, when he did mention the subject to her, she gave one cry of joy and flung her arms around his neck, surprised herself that she should be so overcome by emotion. For a whole week she was supremely happy. Then, a long time before the actual ceremony, she began to accept the prospect much more calmly.

Claude made no attempt to speed up the various formalities and they had a long time to wait for some of the necessary papers. Meanwhile, he went on making studies for his picture, for Christine appeared to be no more inclined to impatience than himself. What did it matter really? It was certainly not going to bring about any considerable change in their lives. They had decided upon a civil marriage only, not out of any desire to flaunt their contempt for the Church, but solely because it was both quicker and simpler. The question of witnesses caused a certain momentary embarrassment; then, as Christine had no friends at all, Claude said she might have Sandoz and Mahoudeau. He had originally thought of asking Dubuche instead of Mahoudeau, but he saw so little of him nowadays and he was afraid of compromising him. For his own witnesses he would have Jory and Gagnière. In that way it would be entirely a friendly affair and need provide no one with gossip.

Weeks went by, and it was December and bitterly cold before the wedding took place. The night before the ceremony, although they had a bare thirty-five francs between them, they agreed that they could hardly let their friends depart with a simple hand-shake; so, to avoid too great an upset in their studio, they decided to take them to lunch at a little restaurant on the Boulevard de Clichy before they all dispersed.

In the morning, as Christine was busy stitching a collar on to the grey wool dress she had been self-indulgent enough to make for the occasion, Claude, who had already donned his morning coat and was stamping to and fro in the studio for lack of other occupation, suddenly announced he was going to pick up Mahoudeau who, he said, was quite capable of failing to turn up. Since the previous autumn, the sculptor had been living in Montmartre, in a small studio in the Rue des Tilleuls where he had moved after a series of dramatic and shattering events. First, he had been turned out of his ex-fruit-shop in the Rue du Cherche-Midi, for arrears in rent; then he had made a final break with Chaîne, who, despairing of ever making his living with his paint-box, had gone into business, going round suburban fairgrounds, running a stall for a showman's widow; and lastly, there had been the sudden disappearance of Mathilde from the shop next door, which had been sold, lured away in all likelihood to some discreet apartment and kept there to satisfy some gentleman's sinister passions. So now he lived alone, in worse poverty than before, eating only when he was given the job of cleaning up the ornaments on some building or putting the finishing touches to a figure for some more prosperous artist.

'I'm going to fetch him, Christine,' said Claude. 'It's the only way of making sure of him. We've still got a couple of hours to spare. . . . If the others turn up, get 'em to wait. We'll all start out together.'

Outside, Claude hurried along through the biting cold that froze his breath into icicles on his moustache. Mahoudeau's studio was at the far end of a block of tenements, which meant that Claude had to go through a whole row of tiny gardens, all white with frost and as stark and dreary as a graveyard. He recognized Mahoudeau's door from afar off by the huge plaster cast of the 'Grape-Picker' that had once been shown at the Salon, and which it had been impossible to house in the tiny ground-floor room. There it had been left to disintegrate, like a pile of building waste tipped from a dust-cart, a crumbling, distressing spectacle since the rain had hollowed its cheeks with great black tears. As the key was in the lock, Claude let himself in.

'Hello! Come to fetch me?' said Mahoudeau, taken by surprise. 'I've only my hat to put on. . . . But wait just a minute. I was just wondering whether I oughtn't to make a bit of fire. I'm rather anxious about my "Bather".'

The water in one of the tubs was frozen solid, for it was as cold inside the studio as it was out of doors, and, as Mahoudeau had not had a sou in his pocket for over a week, he was eking out the last of his coal by lighting the stove only for an hour or two in the mornings. It was a sinister sort of a place, more like a funeral-vault than a studio, for from its bare walls and cracked ceiling the cold wrapped round one like a winding-sheet. In retrospect, the shop in the Rue du Cherche-Midi appeared a haven of warmth and comfort. Other less cumbersome statues, cast in moments of genuine enthusiasm, exhibited but returned to the artist when they failed to find a buyer, stood shivering in the corners, drawn up, face to the wall like a row of ghastly cripples, for some of them were broken already, exposing their mutilated limbs all thick with dust and spattered with clay. For years these miserable nudes had been dragging out their death-agonies under the eyes of the very artist who had given of his life-blood to create them. At first he had passionately refused to part with them, in spite of the limited space, and had then gradually left them to assume the fantastic horror of all dead things; until one day he would take a hammer and put them out of their misery, ridding himself of an encumbrance at the same time, by smashing them to bits.

'Did you say we'd a couple of hours to kill?' asked Mahoudeau. 'Good! Then I'll make a bit of a blaze, it'll perhaps be wiser.'

As he set about lighting the stove he poured out all his complaints. A dog's life, being a sculptor. Masons' labourers had a better time of it. One piece that the authorities had bought for three thousand francs had cost him nearly two thousand, what with the model, the clay, the marble, the bronze, and what not. All that to see your work stowed away in a government vault because there was supposed to be nowhere else to put it! There were plenty of empty niches on public buildings, if they'd only look for them, and plenty of empty pedestals in the parks too, but officially there was no room! Private commissions were almost out of the question, apart from the odd bust or an occasional bit of statuary done on the cheap for presentation purposes. Oh, yes, it was the noblest, the manliest of the arts, and certainly the one you could rely on for letting you starve!

'How's the latest effort going?' said Claude.

'But for this damned cold it would be finished,' was the answer. 'Have a look.'

He straightened up, once he was sure the stove was drawing properly, and moved over to the middle of the room where, on a table made of a packing-case reinforced with struts, stood a statue swathed in old white dust-sheets frozen so stiff that they clung to it and revealed its lines as if they were a shroud. This was his old dream, the one he had been unable to realize before, through lack of funds: an upright figure, the 'Woman Bathing', a dozen rough models of which had made their appearance in his studios in the last few years. In a fit of impatient revolt he had made his own framework, with broom-handles, not metal, in the hope that wood might be strong enough after all. From time to time he rocked it about to test them, and everything had always held firm.

'Looks as if a breath of warm air'll do it no harm,' he said quietly. 'These things have stuck to it. They're like armour.'

The dust-sheets cracked as he touched them and broke like pieces of ice. He had to wait until the heat had begun to thaw them, and then, with infinite precautions, he began to peel them off, revealing first the head, then the bust, then the thighs, delighted to find it still intact and smiling like a lover contemplating the naked beauty of the woman he adored.

'There! What do you think of that?'

Claude, who had not seen the statue since its early stages, nodded thoughtfully to avoid having to make an immediate reply. There was no doubt about it, Mahoudeau was weakening, being graceful in spite of himself; pretty-prettiness seemed to spring naturally from his stone-dresser's fingers. Since his colossal 'Grape-Picker', his work had become less and less significant, apparently without his realizing it, for he still talked grandly about 'temperament' while his vision was clearly becoming impervious to anything but the merely pleasant. His mighty bosoms

were now simply girlish, his legs long and slim and elegant, revealing his true nature through the gradual defla-
tion of his ambition. There was still a certain exaggeration
about his 'Woman Bathing', but its charm was already
very obvious in the slight shudder suggested by the shoulders and the folded arms tilting her breasts. He had
moulded those breasts with infinite love, spurred by his
desire, keener than ever now that he was too poor to be
anything but chaste, to create forms profoundly disturbing
in their sensuality.

'You don't like it, do you?' he asked in a cross voice.

'Oh, yes, yes, I do. . . . I think you're right to soften
things down a bit if that's the way you feel. Besides, that's
going to be a success. It's going to go down very well, that's
quite certain.'

In the past Mahoudeau would have been horrified by such
a compliment; now he was delighted. He was determined to
make the conquest of the general public, he said, without
abandoning any single one of his convictions.

'It's a hell of a relief to hear you say that!' he cried. 'If
you hadn't liked it and told me to break it up, I'd have
broken it up. Oh, yes I would! . . . Another fortnight's work,
and I shall have to sell myself, body and soul, to pay the
caster. . . . I think it should do pretty well at the Salon,
don't you? Might even get a medal, what?' he went on,
laughing and now very excited, and added: 'As there's no
hurry, you say, why not take a seat? . . . I'd like it to thaw
out completely before we go.'

The stove was getting red now and giving out a tremendous heat, and the statue, which was quite close to it,
seemed to be coming to life as the hot air swept up its back
from its calves to the nape of its neck, while the two friends
sat examining and discussing it in every detail, lingering
over every line and curve of its body. Mahoudeau was in
transports of delight, and as he spoke made round, caressing
gestures. Look at the curve of that belly, now, and that
lovely fold in the flesh at the waist, the way it emphasizes
the curve of the left hip!

Just at the moment Claude saw something which made him think his eyes must be playing him a trick. The statue was moving. A faint quiver ran through the body and the left hip grew taut as if the right leg was going to take a step forward.

'And that smooth gradation down to the small of the back,' Mahoudeau rambled on, not noticing what was happening. 'The care I've taken with that! Just there, old fellow, the skin's like satin!'

Little by little the whole statue was coming to life; the hips were beginning to sway and, as the arms relaxed, the bosom heaved as with a sigh. Suddenly the head dropped forward, the legs crumpled up and the statue began to fall forward in a living mass, with the same fearful anguish and the same rush of pain and despair as a woman flinging herself to her death.

Claude was just realizing what was happening when Mahoudeau gave a heart-rending shout:

'Good God! It's giving way! The bloody thing's collapsing!'

As it thawed the clay had broken the soft wood of the framework and it could be heard splitting and cracking like fractured bones. At the risk of his life, Mahoudeau, with the same loving gesture that had fired his imagination as he caressed it from afar, flung wide his arms to receive it. For one second it quivered, then collapsed, face forward, snapped off at the ankles, leaving its feet fixed to the table.

With an anxious 'Look out! You'll be killed!' Claude tried to hold him back, but, horrified at the thought of seeing it crumble at his feet, Mahoudeau went firmly forward with outstretched arms. It seemed to fall upon his neck, and he folded it in his embrace, hugging it to him as its virgin nudity came to life with the first stirrings of desire. He entered it, the love-filled breasts flattened against his shoulder, its thighs pressing against his own, while the head broke off and rolled along the floor. The impact was so sharp that it sent him toppling against the opposite wall, and there he lay, stunned, still clutching the mutilated body.

'Of all the fools!' muttered the furious Claude, convinced he was killed.

Slowly, painfully, however, Mahoudeau struggled on to his knees and then burst into tears. He had only grazed his face as he fell, and the blood was washed down his cheek by his tears.

'This is where poverty gets you!' he cried. 'This is what happens when you haven't enough in your pocket to buy a couple of rods! Oh! It's enough to drive anybody to the river! Look at her now, just look at her now!' he went on, sobbing as he might have done at a deathbed, and crying aloud like an agonized lover over the mutilated corpse of the creature he adored. With trembling hands he kept touching the shattered members that lay on the floor around him, the head, the body, the splintered arms; but what upset him most was the bosom, now completely flattened, with a great gaping wound, as if it had been operated on for some terrible disease. He could not leave it alone, and his fingers kept on probing the gash through which life had been spilled, while his bloodstained tears splashed red upon the wounds.

'Give us a hand,' he stammered. 'We can't leave her like this.'

There were tears in Claude's eyes, too, for he was not indifferent to a brother-artist's misfortune. He was only too ready to lend a hand, but Mahoudeau, once he had asked for assistance, said he preferred to pick up the bits alone, as though he were afraid another might handle them too roughly. Crawling slowly around on his knees, he picked them up one by one and lay them in position on a board. Soon the figure was made whole again, rather as some wretched woman who has died for love by flinging herself from the top of a building is conscientiously pieced together again before she is taken to the morgue, a sad yet somehow comic sight. His task completed, Mahoudeau, heartbroken, sat on the floor lost in contemplation. Gradually his sobs subsided and, after a time, he sighed:

'Ah, well, I'll have to do her reclining after all. . . . Poor old girl, after I'd gone to all that trouble to make her stand up . . . and a fine girl she was too!'

Claude was worried now about his wedding. Mahoudeau was obliged to change his clothes, and as he had only one frock-coat, the one he had been wearing, he had to make do with an ordinary jacket. Then, once the statue was laid out and covered with a cloth, like a corpse, they rushed away, leaving the stove still roaring and thawing out the studio, bringing trickles of dirty water down its dusty walls.

When they reached the Rue de Douai they found only little Jacques, left in charge of the concierge. Tired of waiting, and thinking there might have been some misunderstanding and that Claude intended to go straight to the Mairie with Mahoudeau, Christine had started out with the three other witnesses. It was only in the Rue Drouot, on the Mairie steps, that Mahoudeau and Claude caught up with them. They all went in together and met with a surly welcome from the clerk on duty because they were so late. The whole ceremony was rushed through in a large, bare room, the Mayor mumbling his part of the service and the bride and bridegroom making short work of the sacramental 'Yes', while the witnesses looked about them and marvelled at the bad taste of the decorations. When they reached the street again, Claude took Christine's arm in his, and that was that.

It was a clear, frosty day and pleasant for walking, so they made their way gently up the Rue des Martyrs to the restaurant on the Boulevard de Clichy, where a little private room had been booked. The lunch was a friendly affair; nobody said a word about the simple formality they had just accomplished, but talked all the time about other things, as if it was just another of their usual informal gatherings.

Thus it was that Christine, who was really deeply moved, in spite of her seeming indifference, had to listen for three whole hours to her husband and his witnesses growing more and more heated in their discussions of Mahoudeau's unfortunate statue. Ever since the others heard what had happened to it they had gone over it again and again in the minutest detail. Sandoz thought it had 'tremendous style'. Jory and Gagnière talked about the strength of the supports, the former worrying about the financial loss involved, the latter using a chair to demonstrate a method which might have kept the figure upright. Mahoudeau, still suffering from shock and beginning to show signs of drowsiness, complained of pains all over his body; he had not noticed it at first, but now he ached in every limb, his muscles were strained, and his skin as bruised as if he had been embraced by a woman of stone. The graze on his cheek had started to bleed again, and as Christine bathed it for him she felt as if his mutilated statue was sitting there at the table with them and that it was the only thing that counted, the only thing in which Claude had any interest, judging by his ceaseless flow of talk about it and the way he had felt when he saw its bosom and its limbs of clay lying smashed to pieces at his feet.

During dessert, however, there was a momentary diversion. Gagnière suddenly said to Jory:

'By the way, I saw you with Mathilde on Sunday. . . . Oh, yes, indeed I did, in the Rue Dauphine.'

Jory, very red in the face, wanted to lie his way out of the difficulty, but first his nose twitched, then his lips, and finally, with a sheepish grin, he said:

'Oh! did you? . . . I'd just met her by chance, like that. . . . Honest, I had. . . . I don't know where she lives. If I did, I'd have told you.'

'What do you mean?' exclaimed Mahoudeau. 'I'd like to bet you're the one who's hiding her! . . . Ah well, you're welcome to her; nobody's going to claim her back.'

The truth was that Jory, contrary to all his usual prudence and avarice, was keeping Mathilde in a little room he had rented for her. She knew his vices, and that gave her a hold over him. Instead of relying for his pleasure on women he picked up in the gutter, because they were cheaper, he was gradually slipping into a regular domestic relationship with the ghoul from the shop in the Rue du Cherche-Midi.

'Why be fussy,' put in Sandoz, philosophical and indulgent. 'You take your pleasure where you find it!'

'Of course you do,' replied Jory casually, lighting a cigar.

They continued to linger on at the end of the meal, and it was growing dusk when they accompanied Mahoudeau back to his studio, as he had decided he would be better if he went to bed. When they reached their own studio after collecting Jacques from the concierge, they found it very cold and so dark that it took them some time to find their bearings and light the lamp. The stove, too, had to be rekindled, and it was striking seven before the place began to feel reasonably cosy. For supper they ate up the remains of a bit of boiled beef, more to encourage the child to eat his soup than because they were hungry. Then, when they had put him to bed, they settled down under the lamplight, as on any other evening. Still, Christine did not bring out any work to do; she was much too upset to settle to any domestic task. She simply sat with her hands folded on the table, watching Claude, who had immediately plunged into his drawing: part of his picture, showing dockers unloading cement at the Port Saint-Nicolas. As she looked on, she could not help letting her thoughts wander regretfully back to the past; she felt herself giving way to deeper and deeper gloom, until her whole being seemed to be numb with pain at the thought of all the indifference, all the boundless solitude she had to face, even when they were together. They were together now, at that very moment he was only on the opposite side of the table, but how very far away she felt he was! He was down at the Ile de la Cité; he was remoter still, in the inaccessible infinity of art; he was so very remote that she knew she would never reach him again. Several times she tried to make conversation, but provoked no reply. Hour after hour went by, and, as she was weary of sitting doing nothing, she took out her purse and began to count her money.

'Do you know how much we've got to start our married life?' she asked.

Claude did not even look up.

'We've got nine sous!' she went on. 'A wonderful start!'

Now he shrugged his shoulders and answered gruffly:

'We'll be rich one day, so don't worry.'

Then there was silence again, and she made no further attempt to break it, but sat contemplating the nine sous laid out on the table. As midnight struck she shuddered, sick at heart now with waiting in the cold.

'Shall we go to bed?' she said timidly. 'I'm all in.'

Claude was so engrossed in his work that he did not even hear her.

'Look,' she said, 'the stove's gone out, we shall both catch our deaths. . . . Do come to bed.'

The note of supplication in her voice made its impression; he gave a sudden start of annoyance and rapped out:

'Oh, go to bed if you want to! Can't you see I have something to finish?'

She lingered another moment or so, taken aback by his sudden flash of anger and on the verge of tears. Then, realizing she was not wanted and that the mere presence of her as a woman sitting there doing nothing annoyed him, she got up from the table and went to bed, leaving the studio door wide open. Half an hour, three-quarters went by; not a sound, not even of breathing, came from the bedroom, though Christine was not asleep; she was lying on her back in the dark, her eyes wide open. After a time, from the depths of her alcove, she risked just one more timid appeal.

'Darling,' she murmured, 'I'm waiting for you. . . . Darling. Do *please* come to bed.'

The only reply was an oath. After that, nothing stirred; maybe she had dropped off to sleep. The studio meanwhile was growing colder and colder and the untrimmed lamp burning with a dull red flame, but Claude, still poring over his drawing, was apparently unconscious of the passage of time.

At two o'clock, however, he got up from the table, furious because the lamp was beginning to burn itself out. He had only just time to take it into the bedroom, as he had no wish to undress in the dark. There, finding Christine lying on her back, still wide awake, he remarked angrily:

'You not asleep yet?'

'No,' she answered. 'I'm not sleepy.'

'Oh, I know,' he retorted, 'it's just another reproach. . . . I've told you dozens of times I hate you to wait up for me.'

Then, as the lamp flickered out, he lay down beside her. She did not move; he, worn out by his labours, yawned a couple of times. They were both wide awake, but still they neither stirred nor spoke; they were both cold too, for his legs were numb and his whole body so thoroughly chilled that it seemed to have taken all the warmth out of the bedclothes. At last, just as his mind was beginning to wander and he was on the point of sleep, he gave a violent start and exclaimed:

'It's a good job she wasn't badly smashed up below the waist, with a belly like that! What a beauty!'

'A good job who wasn't smashed up?' asked the startled Christine.

'Mahoudeau's bather, of course!'

At this unexpected reply she turned quickly away, buried her face in the pillow, and, to Claude's amazement, burst into tears.

'Whatever's the matter?' he asked. But she could not reply, for she was choking with emotion and her sobs shook the whole bed.

'What is it?' he insisted. 'I haven't said anything unkind, have I? . . . My dearest, please don't cry.'

As he talked he gradually realized the cause of her great sorrow, and he admitted to himself that, on that day of all days, he ought to have gone to bed at the same time as Christine. But she couldn't really blame him, he argued, for the notion hadn't even struck him, and besides she knew him well enough now to realize what he was like when he was working on something.

'Come on, darling,' he went on. 'We've been together a long time. Oh, I know; you'd planned it all in your little head. You wanted to play the bride, that's it, isn't it? . . . Come now, don't cry any more. You know I didn't mean to be unkind.'

He claimed her body and she gave it to him, but it was a vain embrace, for the passion that had once been theirs was dead. They knew, as they released their hold upon each other and lay side by side again, that from that moment they were strangers, that there was some obstacle between them, another body whose icy breath had touched them more than once even in the passionate early stages of their love. Never again would they be all-in-all to each other; the rift between them would never be healed. The wife had despoiled the mistress, and marriage seemed to have done away with love.

CHAPTER 9

SINCE Claude was unable to paint his big picture in the little studio in the Rue de Douai, he decided to rent some sort of shed where he would have plenty of space. He found exactly what he wanted on one of his rambles round Montmartre, halfway up the Rue Tourlaque, the street that runs down the hill from the cemetery, and from which you can look out over Clichy and as far as the marshes at Gennevilliers. It was an old dyer's drying-shed, a flimsy lath and plaster construction, fifteen metres by ten, and a meeting-place for all the winds of heaven. The rent was three hundred francs. He took it. Summer was on the way; as soon as he had finished his picture, and that wouldn't take him long, he'd give notice and clear out.

His mind was made up, now that he was determined to work and make a good job of it, to spare no expense. As his ship was bound to come home, why spoil it for a ha'porth of tar? As he now had the right to do so, he broke into the capital that brought him in his thousand francs a year, and soon grew used to indiscriminate spending. He did not tell Christine what he had done for some time, as she had already prevented him from doing it on two occasions. When he finally did tell her, however, after a week or so of worries and reproaches, she too grew accustomed to their altered circumstances, and enjoyed the pleasant feeling that there was always money to be had for the asking. At least, it meant a year or two of ease and comfort.

Claude soon reached the point at which he lived only for his picture. He had furnished his big studio with the odd chair, his old divan from the Quai de Bourbon, and a deal table bought for five francs at a junk-shop; he never craved for luxury as a background to his art. His only extravagance was a travelling ladder with an adjustable platform. His canvas came next; he wanted it eight metres by five and insisted on preparing it himself. He had the frame specially made, and bought seamless canvas which he and a couple of friends had the greatest difficulty in stretching and clamping. Then all he did by way of priming was to lay on with the knife a coat of white lead; he refused to size it, as he wished it to remain absorbent since that, he said, made for light yet solid painting. It was useless, of course, to think of using an easel for a canvas of that unmanageable size, so he rigged up a system of ropes and beams which held it to the wall, just sufficiently tilted to catch the necessary light, and with the ladder running the whole length of the vast white sheet. The whole effect was that of a scaffolding, a cathedral scaffolding, set up around the masterpiece about to be built.

When everything was ready to start he was assailed once more by endless scruples. He let himself be tormented by the thought that, on the site, he had not really chosen the most satisfactory lighting. Wouldn't an early morning light have been best after all? Or perhaps he ought really to have picked a dull, grey day. The result was that he spent another three months viewing the site from the Pont des Saints-Pères.

At all hours of the day, in all kinds of weather, he contemplated the Cité as it rises between the two vistas of river. After a late fall of snow, he saw it draped in ermine, encircled by muddy grey water and backed by a pale slate sky. He saw it in the first spring sunlight, shaking off the

winter, its youth renewed in the fresh green buds of the
trees on the terrace. He saw it on a day of soft mists, vague,
remote, airy as a palace of dreams. Then came the heavy
rains to submerge it and hide it behind the mighty curtain
dropped from the heavens to earth; then storms and the
tawny lightning to give it the air of a sinister cut-throat's
alley, half ruined beneath a crumbling mass of great cop-
per-coloured clouds. After that, it would be swept and
scoured by gales of wind that sharpened all its angles and
stood it up stark naked against a sky of paling blue. At other
times, when the sun filtered like fine gold dust through the
mists of the Seine, it was bathed in diffused light, without
a single shadow, equally lighted from all sides, with all the
delicate charm of a jewel carved in solid gold. He wanted
to see it as the sun was rising, breaking through the morning
mists, with the Quai de l'Horloge burning red on one side
and the Quai des Orfèvres, heavy with shadow, on the other,
and its own towers and spires awakening to life again,
revealed in the rosy morning light as by a mantle slipping
slowly to the ground. He wanted to see it at noon, in the
full force of the midday sun, consumed in the harshness of
its glare, pale and silent as a city of the dead, the only live
thing in it being the heat that quivered on the distant
roof-tops. He wanted to see it as the sun was going down
and night creeping up from the river again, topping all its
buildings with a fringe of glowing light, like sparks on dying
embers, piercing their sombre frontages with bursts of flame
from the raging fires it lighted on every windowpane. But
of all the many aspects of the Cité, familiar now at all hours
of the day and in every kind of weather, he still preferred
the one he admired on that first September afternoon about
four, the Cité standing serene in the flawless atmosphere,
the heart of Paris beating in the gentle breeze, swelling
against the vastness of the sky broken only by a trail of tiny
clouds.

Claude spent all his days now in the shadow of the Pont
des Saints-Pères; it had become his refuge, his roof, his
home, and he had grown used to the ceaseless rumble of

the traffic, like the distant roll of thunder. Installed near the first pier of the bridge, under its great iron girders, he made sketches in both paint and pencil, but he was never completely satisfied that he had captured what he needed and would sketch the same bit of detail over and over again at various times. The employees of the various navigation companies, whose offices were nearby, had come to know him, and the wife of one of the foremen who shared a sort of tarred hut with her husband, two children, and a cat, kept his canvases fresh for him to save him the trouble of carting them through the streets every day. He was de-lighted with his refuge, hearing Paris roaring in the air above, feeling all its life and ardour flowing overhead. First it was the Port Saint-Nicolas that thrilled him with its ceaseless activity like some distant seaport a mere stone's throw from the Institut, with the steam-crane 'Sophie' busy moving great blocks of stone, and carts coming for loads of sand, horses and drivers heaving and panting up the long paved slope leading from the water's edge above the granite wharf, alongside which barges and lighters were moored two deep. For weeks on end he worked on one of his studies: porters unloading plaster, carrying white sacks on their shoulders, leaving a trail of white behind them, covered in white dust themselves, while another boat nearby had been unloading coal and left a great inky blot upon the wharf. Next, he took a side view of the open-air bath on the left bank. Then, on another plane, a laundry with all its glass panels wide open and the washerwomen kneeling in rows at water level, beating away at their linen. For the centre he made a study of a boat with a bargee sculling it, and, in the distance, a steam-tug hauling a train of planks and barrels at the end of its chain. The background he had already worked upon, nevertheless he picked out one or two details for further study: the two vistas of the Seine, and a sky effect showing nothing but towers and spires golden in the sunlight. Working in the shelter of the bridge, as remote as in some hollow in the rocks, he was rarely disturbed by inquisitive passers-by, while the riverside anglers treated him with withering indifference; so his only companion was generally the foreman's cat, which spent its time washing itself, calm and unruffled beneath the tumult of the world above.

At last Claude's preparatory sketches were all complete. In two or three days he worked out a rough sketch of the whole picture and the masterpiece was started. Immediately there began in the studio in the Rue Tourlaque the first battle between Claude and his canvas; it raged throughout the whole summer. He insisted on trying to square up his composition himself, but without success, for he merely piled one mistake upon another, as he was undisciplined to the mathematical accuracy required. In his indignation, he decided to ignore accuracy and to make the necessary adjustments later; such was his feverish urge to create something that he flung all his energies into covering the entire canvas. He practically lived on his ladder, wielding his enormous brushes and expending muscular strength enough to move mountains. At the end of a day he staggered like a drunkard and dropped dead asleep almost before he had finished his meal, so that his wife had to put him to bed like a child. The result of his heroic labours was a masterly sketch, one of those sketches in which genius comes flashing through the otherwise indeterminate mass of colour. Bongrand came to see it and, his eyes brimming with tears, flung both arms round Claude and smothered him with kisses. Sandoz, in his enthusiasm, gave a dinner in its honour, while the others, Jory, Mahoudeau, and Gagnière, went around announcing another masterpiece. As for Fagerolles, he stood for a moment in silent admiration, then burst into congratulations; it was 'too beautiful', he said.

And, indeed, it soon began to look as if Fagerolles's malicious pronouncement had brought Claude bad luck, for from that moment his work on the sketch began to deteriorate. It was the usual story; he worked himself out in one magnificent burst of genius; after that, nothing would come and he was unable to finish what he had started. His impotence returned. He worked on the canvas for two whole years; for those two years it was the sole aim and end of his existence, sometimes sending him soaring to heights of delirious joy, sometimes plunging him into such depths of doubt and despair that poor wretches breathing their last on beds of pain were happy by comparison. Twice he was unable to finish in time for the Salon; for always, at the last moment, when he was hoping to complete his work in a matter of hours, he discovered some blemish or other and felt the whole composition crumble and fall to pieces in his fingers. With the third Salon approaching, he went through another terrible crisis and did not go near the studio in the Rue Tourlaque for a whole fortnight. When at last he did go back, it was like going into a house left uninhabited since the tenant's death. He turned his great canvas face to the wall, pushed his ladder into one corner and would have smashed up the place and set fire to it if he had had strength enough left in his trembling hands. It was the end of everything; in his wrath he wanted to make a clean sweep of the place and talked of tackling little things since he was clearly incapable of handling big ones.

Even then, his first attempt at a smaller picture took him straight back to the Ile de la Cité. Why, after all, shouldn't he do a simple view of the place, on a medium-sized canvas? A wave of modesty, however, strangely tinged with jealousy, kept him from setting up his easel under the Pont des Saints-Pères; he felt the spot was somehow sacred now and that he ought not to deflower the virginity of the greater work, dead though it was. He installed himself, therefore, at the end of the wharf, upstream from the Port Saint-Nicolas. This time, at least, he was working direct from nature, and it pleased him not to have to cheat, as one had inevitably to do when working on an outsize canvas.

Although he finished it off with much more care and in much greater detail than was his custom, the smaller picture met with the same fate as the others when it came before the Selection Committee which was 'scandalized' by painting that looked, according to the expression then current in the studios, as if it had been done 'by a drunk with a broom'.

This was a setback even more serious than its predecessors, as there had been a certain amount of talk about concessions made to the Beaux-Arts to ensure the picture's success.

When it came back, Claude, very embittered and weeping with rage, tore the canvas into little strips and burned them in the stove. It was not enough to stab the thing to death, it had to be destroyed completely.

For another whole year Claude did nothing in particular. He painted by force of habit, but never finished anything, saying, with a pained sort of laugh, that he had lost himself and was trying to find himself again. Even during his long fits of despondency there was no destroying his hopes, for he was never completely unconscious of his genius. He suffered all the torments of the man condemned to roll a rock uphill for ever or be crushed when it rolled back on him; but the future was still before him, and in it the assurance that one day he would be able to pick up his rock with both hands and hurl it away to the stars. In time the light of passion came back to his eyes, and it soon became known that he was beginning to shut himself up again in the Rue Tourlaque. In the past he had always let himself be carried far beyond the present work by his dreams of a greater work in the future. Now he found himself once more at grips with the old subject, the Ile de la Cité; it had become his *idée fixe*, blocking his vision like a brick wall. After a time, in a fresh outburst of enthusiasm, he began to talk about it openly, exclaiming with childish glee that he had found himself again and this time victory was assured.

One morning, after keeping his door bolted for a long time to all his friends, Claude at last allowed Sandoz into the studio. What Sandoz found there was a fine, spirited sketch, done without a model, and admirably coloured. The subject was the same: the Port Saint-Nicolas on the left, the swimming-bath on the right, the Seine and the Cité in the background; but he was amazed to see, in place of the boat sculled by the bargee, another and much bigger boat, filling the whole centre of the composition, and occupied by three women. One of them, wearing a bathing costume, was rowing, another was sitting on the edge with her legs in the water and her bathing dress slipped half-way off one shoulder. The third was standing at the prow, completely naked, her nudity so radiant that it dazzled like a sun.

'I say, what an idea!' said Sandoz quietly. 'What are they supposed to be doing?'

'Bathing, of course,' said Claude calmly. 'They've come from the swimming-bath, you see, and that provides a nude motif. Quite a discovery, don't you think? It doesn't shock you, does it?'

As his oldest friend, Sandoz knew Claude's weakness and, afraid of stirring up the slightest doubt, replied:

'Shock me? Why, of course it doesn't. . . . Only I'm wondering whether the general public is going to misunderstand it again. It could hardly *be* like that, could it? I mean a woman naked like that in the middle of Paris?'

'Do you really think so?' asked Claude in artless surprise. 'Oh, well, it can't matter all that much, can it, so long as she's well painted? I've got to have her in, to feel the thing's worth while.'

In the days that followed Sandoz again brought up the subject of Claude's strange composition and made a gentle plea, since it was in his nature to do so, on behalf of what he thought was outraged logic. How, he asked, could a modern painter, who took pride in painting nothing but reality, jeopardize the originality of his work by introducing such obvious products of the imagination? It was easy enough to find other subjects in which studies of the nude would be natural and essential!

Claude refused to give way, and offered unsatisfactory and violent reasons for his choice, since he did not wish to admit the real reason for it. It was an idea he had had, but an idea so vague that he would have been unable to express it clearly, the outcome of some tormenting secret symbolism, the old streak of romanticism in him that made him think of his nude figure as the incarnation of Paris, the city of passion seen as the resplendent beauty of a naked woman. Into it he poured all his own great passion, his love of beautiful bellies and thighs and fecund breasts, the kind of bodies he was burning to create in boundless profusion that they might bring forth all the numberless offspring of his prolific art.

In face of his old friend's pressing arguments, he pretended at last to give way.

'Very well,' he said. 'I'll see. I'll put some clothes on her later, if that's what shocks you. . . . But I'm still going to keep her in, understand. I like her that way.'

After that, out of sheer obstinacy, he never mentioned her again. He simply hunched his shoulders and gave an embarrassed smile at the faintest allusion to everyone's amazement at seeing Venus rising in triumph from the waters of the Seine, amid the buses on the embankment and the dockers on the Port Saint-Nicolas.

With the return of spring Claude was ready to start work on his big picture again when a decision, made in a moment of prudence, brought about a serious change in his domestic life. Christine had occasionally expressed anxiety about the rate at which they were spending their money and taking great chunks out of their capital, but on the whole they paid little attention to money matters since the source was apparently inexhaustible. Then, after four years, they were horrified to learn, the day they asked for a statement of accounts, that out of their twenty thousand francs three thousand was all they had left. They reacted immediately by practising the most rigid economy, eating less bread and even planning to reduce expenditure on all the necessities of life. Thus it was that, in their first impulsive need for sacrifice, they decided to leave the Rue de Douai. Why pay two rents? There was plenty of room in the old drying-shed in the Rue Tourlaque, still stained all over with splashes of dye, to house three people. Moving in was a simple matter; installation proved more difficult, for the great shed, fifteen metres by ten, meant that they, like regular Bohemians, had only one room for all purposes. In the face of a certain amount of ill-will on the part of the landlord, Claude divided it up. He made a matchwood partition near one end, and behind that rigged up a kitchen and a bedroom. They were delighted with the result, in spite of the draughts that whistled through the cracks in the roof and the rain that came pouring through during bad storms and had to be caught in bowls. It still looked depressingly empty; their few bits of furniture were lost against the big bare walls. They were pleased, however, to be so roomily housed and explained to their friends that at least little Jacques would now have space to run about in. Poor little Jacques was nine now, but still a puny child. The only part of him that seemed to grow was his head. If he went to school for a week, at the end of it he was worn out both mentally and physically with the effort of trying to learn. So now, more often than not, he stayed at home, crawling about the floor or mooning in corners.

It was a long time since Christine had been in close contact with Claude's daily work, but now, once again, she lived with him through every hour of every sitting. She helped him to scrape and pumice his old canvas and gave him hints about attaching it more firmly to the wall. One disaster they discovered was that the damp coming through the roof had made the ladder unsafe, so Claude had to strengthen it with a strip of oak while Christine stood by and handed him the nails, one at a time. That done, everything was ready for a second attempt on the big canvas. She watched him square up his new sketch, standing behind him until her legs gave way beneath her and she dropped to the ground and stayed there, still watching him work.

She would have given anything to win him back from the painting that had won him away from her. That was why she made herself his slave and took delight in doing menial tasks. Ever since she came to play a part in his work again, and the three of them were together, he, she, and the picture, she had been full of hopes. He had managed to escape her, leaving her to cry her eyes out alone in the Rue de Douai, and he had spent his time and his substance in the Rue Tourlaque as if some mistress had held him in thrall, but now maybe she was going to win him back again, now they were with him all the time, she and her passion. Oh that painting! How she loathed it in her jealousy! Yet her attitude towards it had changed. She was no longer the young lady with a fondness for water-colours repelled by its freedom and its superb brutality. No, she had gradually come to understand it, drawn to it first of all by her attachment to the painter and then by the feast of light and by the originality and charm of the touches of white. Now she accepted everything, pale mauve earth and bright blue trees, and she was even beginning to have a certain awe-inspired feeling of respect for works which at one time she thought were abominable. She acknowledged them as powerful and treated them as rivals who must be taken seriously. As her admiration grew, so did her rancour, and she was furious to feel herself belittled in the presence of this other love flaunting itself under her very roof.

Her campaign, though ceaseless, opened quietly. She began by imposing herself, losing no opportunity of letting some part of her body, perhaps only a shoulder or even just a hand, intervene between the painter and his picture. She never left his side but stood as close to him as she could, enveloping him in her breath, reminding him he was hers. Then she revived an old idea; she would paint too; she would go and search him out in the very fever of his art. So for a month or so she wore a smock and worked like a pupil at the side of his master, submissively copying his picture. She stopped, however, when she realized that her attempt had miscarried and that sharing Claude's work simply made him forget she was a woman and treat her on the same friendly footing as a man. There was still one way to get him back; she determined to try it.

Very often, when he was working on his smaller pictures and wanted to fix occasional details of the figures, Claude had asked Christine to model a head, a gesture, or some particular attitude he required. He would throw a cloak over her shoulders, stop her in the middle of a gesture and tell her to hold it. Such small favours as these she was only too happy to render, but she was still loath to undress for him, feeling it was somehow undignified for her to be his model now she was his wife. One day he wanted to work on a thigh-joint; she refused to pose at first and then reluctantly agreed to tuck up her skirts, but only after double-locking the door; she was so afraid that, if anyone discovered that she had sunk to being his model, they might try to identify her nude body in her husband's pictures. She had not forgotten the way Claude's friends, and even Claude himself, jeered and cracked coarse jokes at the expense of a painter whose only model was his own wife and whose nicely turned-out nudes for bourgeois consumption reproduced her now well-known peculiarities: small of the back too long, abdomen rather too high, seen from every possible angle, which meant that all Paris cocked a ribald eye when she appeared encased to the tip of her chin in one of her usual discreetly dark dresses which she always wore particularly high in the neck.

But since she had seen Claude sketch in, with a certain amount of detail, the large central figure of his picture, Christine, as she pondered on it, felt her scruples fall away one by one as she surrendered to an overwhelming obsession; until, when he spoke of engaging a model, she offered to pose herself.

'You!' cried Claude. 'Why you're offended when all I want is the tip of your nose!'

'What do you mean?' she replied with an awkward smile. 'After all, I did sit for your figure in "Open Air", and that was before there was anything between us. . . . Besides, a model's going to cost seven francs a sitting, and we're not exactly well off, so we might as well save what we can.'

The mention of saving made up Claude's mind for him.

'All right,' he said, 'I'm willing. It's really very kind of you to take it on, you know; it's no simple pastime sitting for me. . . . Still, if you want to do it. . . . And anyway, silly, you're afraid of another woman coming here, aren't you? So why not admit it, you're jealous!'

She *was* jealous too, agonizingly jealous, but not of other women. Every model in Paris could come and take off her clothes! She had one rival, and one rival only: painting. That was what was stealing her lover. She was ready to strip herself to the last stitch and give herself to him naked for days or weeks on end; she was ready to live naked if that meant she would win him back and be able to claim him for her own when he sank once again into her arms! What more had she to offer but herself? It was fair enough, surely, for her to risk her own body in this one last struggle, knowing that to lose would be to admit that she was a woman with no more power to charm.

Claude was delighted, and started by making a straightforward study of her in the required pose. They waited till Jacques had gone off to school and then locked themselves in. The sitting lasted several hours. At first Christine found it very painful to stand still for such long periods, but she grew used to it. She was afraid to complain, lest it should make him angry, and when he bullied her she swallowed back her tears. Claude soon began to take her for granted and to treat her merely as a model, making more demands upon her than if he had been paying her and without ever thinking that, since she was his wife, he could ask too much of her. He used her for everything and expected her to be ready to undress for him at any moment, for an arm or a leg or for any odd detail he happened to need. She was reduced to being nothing more nor less than a kind of living dummy which he set in position and copied, as he would have copied a jug or a cooking-pot in a still life.

This time Claude proceeded without any undue haste. For months before he sketched in his central figure he had worn out Christine by scores of attempts to 'steep himself', as he called it, in the true quality of her skin. Then, when at last he did decide to set to work on the sketch, it was on an autumn morning, when there was already a distinct nip in the wind. It was anything but warm in the studio, in spite of the roaring fire in the stove. As Jacques was home from school, suffering from one of his periodic bouts of stupor and fatigue, they decided to shut him in the far end of the studio and tell him to be a good boy. His mother, meanwhile, shivering with cold, undressed and took up the pose near the stove.

For the first hour Claude never spoke a word but, from the top of his ladder, kept glancing down at her with eyes that slashed across her like knives from shoulder to knee. She, overcome meanwhile by a feeling of slow, creeping sadness, kept trying hard not to break down, wondering whether she was suffering more from the cold or from the increasing bitterness of some deep, unaccountable despair. She felt so tired and her legs were so numb that she broke the pose and staggered a few steps forward.

'Already!' cried Claude. 'Why, you haven't been posing much more than a quarter of an hour! Don't you want to earn your seven francs?' he added in a gruff sort of joke.

He was so enthralled by his work that she had hardly regained the use of her limbs and slipped on a dressing-gown before he shouted:

'Come on, now! No slacking! Today's one of the big days. I've either got to show some genius or burst!'

When she had undressed again and resumed the pose in the sickly light, he started to paint again, bringing out an occasional remark, out of the sheer need to make some sort of noise as soon as he felt his work was going well.

'It's extraordinary what a funny skin you've got! It positively absorbs light. . . . You may not believe it, but this morning you're quite grey. The other day you were pink, a sort of pink that didn't look real somehow. . . . It's a bit of a nuisance, really. You never know where you are with it.'

He stopped, half closed his eyes, then ran on:

'Still, you can't beat the nude . . . the way it comes up against the background. . . . It throbs and takes on an incredible life of its own, as if you could see the blood coursing through the muscles. . . . There's nothing finer, nothing better in the whole world than a well-drawn muscle on a firmly painted limb. They're something to worship, like God himself. . . . They're my religion, the only one I've got. I could stay on my knees before them to the end of my days.'

And, as he had to come down to get another tube of paint, he went up to her and, with rising passion, went over every detail of her beauty, touching with his fingers the parts he desired to emphasize. 'There, you see, under the left breast, there's a beautiful bit where those little blue veins bring out the delicacy of the skin. . . . And there, on that curve of the hip, that dimple where the shadow looks golden, a feast for the eye. . . . And there now, under the full round shape of the belly, the pure lines of the groin and the tiniest point of carmine showing through pale gold. . . . That's the part that's always thrilled me more than all the rest, the belly. The very sight of one makes me want to do impossible things. It's so lovely to paint, like a sun!'

Back on his ladder again, he cried, in the fever of creation:

'If I can't turn out a masterpiece with you, then by God I really must be a dud, and no mistake!'

Christine did not answer. Her distress deepened as her situation grew more obvious, and the longer she stood there in that atmosphere of brutal materialism the more painful did she find her nudity. At every point where Claude's finger had touched her it had left an icy impression through which, she now felt, the aching cold was invading her entire body. She knew everything now, so what more was there to hope for? Her body which once he had covered with his lover's kisses, he now viewed and worshipped merely as an artist. Now it was the delicate colouring of her breast that fired his imagination, some line of her belly that brought him to his knees in worship. His desire was blind no longer; he did not crush her whole body against his own, as he used to do, without even looking at her, in an embrace they hoped might fuse them into one.

No! This was the end.

She had ceased to exist, since all he could find to adore in her now was his art, and nature, and life. And she stood there, rigid as marble, staring into the void, holding back the tears she felt welling up in her heart, reduced to the point where she felt too wretched even to cry.

In the next room an impatient voice was suddenly raised accompanied by the beating of small fists on the door.

'Mummy! Mummy! I can't sleep, I'm bored! . . . Open the door, mummy, please!'

It was Jacques. Claude was annoyed and grumbled about never having a minute's peace.

'In a minute or two!' Christine called back. 'Go to sleep! Father has work to do.'

Now she seemed to find yet another cause for anxiety and after casting worried glances towards the door she finally left the pose for a moment and ran and hung her skirt on the key to cover up the keyhole. Then, without a word, she took up her position near the stove, head erect, body thrown back and breasts well forward.

The sitting seemed likely to go on for ever. Hours and hours went by, and still she stood there, offering herself like a diver ready to meet the water, while Claude on his ladder, miles away, burned with passion for the woman he was painting. He even stopped talking to her, and she became merely an object, perfectly coloured. He had been looking at her ever since morning, but she knew it was not her image she would find in his eyes, she was a stranger to him now, an outcast.

At length, out of sheer fatigue, he stopped; seeing her trembling, he said:

'You're not cold, surely?'

'Yes, I am rather.'

'How funny! I'm boiling. . . . Now I can't have you catching cold. That's enough for today.'

When he got down she expected him to kiss her; that was the usual token of husbandly gallantry with which he recompensed her for the strain of a lengthy sitting. Today he was so full of his work that he forgot and immediately started to wash out his brushes, kneeling on the floor and dipping them into a jar of soft soap. Still hopeful, Christine stood where she was, still naked. After a time, surprised to notice her standing there like a shadow, he cast one look of amazement in her direction and then continued vigorously wiping his brushes. And so, with trembling fingers, she hastily put on her clothes in all the painful confusion of a woman disdained. She donned her chemise, struggled with her petticoats, fastened her bodice all awry as if she wanted to escape the shame of her impotent nudity, fit now only to grow old out of sight beneath a covering of garments. Now she was conquered she despised herself for sinking, like the basest of prostitutes, to such depths of carnal vulgarity.

The following morning, however, she had to undress once more in the icy blasts and unforgiving light of the studio. Was it not her job, after all? How could she possibly refuse now that it had become a routine? She would never have done anything to hurt Claude, so every day she took up her position afresh in what, for her burning, humiliated body, was a losing battle. Claude never even mentioned it now; his carnal passion had transferred itself to his work and the painted lovers he created for himself. They were the only women now who could send his blood pulsing through his body, the women whose every limb was the product of his own efforts. Back there in the country, when his passion was at its height, he thought happiness was achieved when he possessed a real woman and held her in his arms. He knew now that that had been nothing more than the old, old illusion, since they were still strangers to each other; so he preferred the illusion he found in his art, the everlasting pursuit of unattainable beauty, the mad desire which could never be satisfied. He wanted all women, but he wanted them created according to his dreams: bosoms of satin, amber-coloured hips, and downy virgin loins. He wanted to love them only for the beauty of their colouring; he wanted to feel them perpetually beyond his grasp! Christine was reality, the aim which the hand could reach, and Claude had wearied of her in a season. He was, as Sandoz often jokingly called him, 'the knight of the uncreated'.

For months posing was torture to her. Life no longer seemed to consist of the two of them living happily together; it was as if a third party had been introduced, a mistress, the woman he was painting with her body for the model.

Between them stood the enormous canvas, like a great unsurmountable wall, and he lived on one side of it with the other woman. She could feel it driving her mad, this jealousy of her own 'double', but, realizing at the same time the futility of her suffering, she did not dare to tell him about it, knowing he would only laugh at her. Yet she was not mistaken; she could feel that he preferred the copy to herself; it was the copy that he adored, that was his sole preoccupation, the object of his affection through every hour of the day. He was killing her with posing while he added to the other's charms; the other alone was the source of his joy or his sorrow, according as she lived or languished under his brush. What was that if not love? And was it not torture to have to make the sacrifice of her own body to help bring the other to life, to make it possible for her nightmare rival to haunt them and be forever between them, more powerful than reality, in the studio, at table, in bed, everywhere? What was she, after all, this other woman? Nothing, really; dust, colour on canvas, an image—and yet she could destroy all their happiness, making him gloomy, indifferent, brutal even, and leaving her tortured by his neglect and despairing of ever being able to drive out the predatory concubine, so terrible in her painted immobility!

Christine knew she was beaten, and from that moment she felt herself oppressed beneath all the weighty sovereignty of art. She had accepted painting unconditionally; now she exalted it—even more, enshrined it in an awful tabernacle before which she lay prostrate as before the mighty gods of wrath to whom homage is paid because of the very hatred and horror they inspire. Her fear was sacred, for now she was certain that it was pointless to resist further, because if she did she would simply be crushed like a straw; the canvases were just like so many boulders, even the smallest ones seemed to triumph over her, and the inferior ones to boast of easy victory. Prone and trembling, she ceased to differentiate between them; to her, all were equally formidable, and she answered all her husband's questions automatically:

'Oh, very good! . . . Oh, superb! . . . Oh, extraordinary, really most extraordinary!'

Yet she bore him no grudge; she still adored him, and wept to see him eating his heart out, since after a few weeks of successful work everything had been spoiled again. He could make no more headway with the main female figure, so he nearly worked his model to death, struggling with all his might for days at a time, then dropping everything for a month. A dozen times the central figure was started, abandoned, completely repainted. One year, two years went by and still the picture was not finished. One day it would be practically completed, the next scraped clean and a fresh start made.

Such is the effort of creation that goes into the work of art! Such was the agonizing effort he had to make, the blood and tears it cost him to create living flesh, to produce the breath of life! Everlastingly struggling with the Real, and being repeatedly conquered, like Jacob fighting with the Angel! He threw himself body and soul into the impossible task of putting all nature on one canvas and exhausted himself in the end by the relentless tension of his aching muscles, without ever bringing forth the expected work of genius. The half-measures and trickery that satisfied other painters filled him with remorse and indignation; they were both weak and cowardly, he said. Consequently, he was always starting afresh, spoiling the good in order to do better, because his painting 'didn't speak to him', finding fault with his women because, as his friends used to say, they didn't step out of the canvas and sleep with him! What was it he lacked, he wondered, to make them really alive? Next to nothing, probably. Some slight adjustment one way or the other. One day, overhearing the expression 'near genius' applied to himself, he was both flattered and horrified. Yes, that must be the explanation, he thought, overshooting or falling short of the mark through some maladjustment of the nerve centres, or through some hereditary flaw which, because of a gram or two of substance too much or too little, instead of making him a great man was going to make him a madman. This was the notion that he could never escape when despair drove him out of the studio, the notion of preordained impotence; he could feel it beating in his head with the persistence of a funeral knell.

It made his existence utterly wretched; never had he been so dogged by self-doubt. He would disappear for whole days at a time; once he stayed out all night and came home the following morning in a daze, unable to give any account of where he had been. Christine thought he had preferred to spend the night tramping the streets rather than face his unsatisfactory painting. Escape was his only relief when his work filled him with such hatred and shame that his courage failed him and he could face it no longer. When he came home again, even Christine did not dare to question him, but considered herself lucky to see him again after all her waiting and anxiety. He scoured all Paris in his furious wanderings, but a desire for self-abasement generally led him to the working-class suburbs to mix with dockers and labourers, for every crisis led him to express his old desire to be a builder's hodman. Happiness, after all, meant having good, strong limbs, limbs made for doing a good job quickly. He had made a mess of his life; he ought to have got himself a job long ago when he used to go for his meals at Gomard's 'Chien de Montargis', where he had made friends with a Limousin, a cheerful young fellow whose fine muscles he envied. Afterwards, when he had returned to the Rue Tourlaque, footsore and light-headed, he would fling himself into his painting, but with the same look of mingled grief and fear that one casts upon a corpse in a death-chamber, until once more the hope that he might yet bring it to life again revived the light in his eyes.

One day Christine was posing and the female figure was practically finished when, gradually, Claude began to turn gloomy and to lose all the childish joy he had manifested at the start of the sitting.

Sensing that all was not well, Christine hardly dared to breathe or move so much as a finger for fear of precipitating the catastrophe. Then, suddenly, there it was; with a groan of pain, flinging his handful of brushes to the ground, Claude roared in a voice like thunder: 'God damn the thing to hell!'

Then, blind with rage, with one despairing gesture he thrust his fist through the canvas.

'Oh, Claude, Claude!' cried Christine, holding out her quivering hands. But by the time she had flung a dressing-gown over her shoulders and moved over towards Claude, she was aware of a pang of joy in her heart at the release of all her pent-up rancour. His fist had smashed clean through her rival's breast, ripped it open and left a great, gaping wound. She was killed at last!

Realizing that his gesture amounted to murder, Claude stood transfixed, glaring at the hole he had made in the painted bosom and out of which the life-blood of his work was draining away. A feeling of tremendous sorrow descended on him as he wondered how he could possibly have slain what he loved best in all the world. His anger gave way now to stupefaction and he began to feel the canvas with his fingers, drawing together the torn edges as if he was trying to close a wound. Choking with sobs, his head swimming with gentle, infinite pain, he stammered:

'Done her in . . . I've done her in. . . .'

This stirred Christine to the very depths of her being, and all her motherly love went out to the childlike artist; she forgave him, as she had always forgiven him. Seeing that his one thought was to mend the torn canvas at once and undo his mischief, she went to his assistance. It was she who held together the strips of canvas while he stuck a patch of material on the back. When she got dressed again the other woman was back again, immortal, with just a faint scar over her heart—enough, however, to revive the artist's passion for her.

With his unbalanced state of mind becoming more and more marked, Claude developed a kind of superstitious devotion to new processes in painting. He condemned the use of oil and spoke of it almost as a personal enemy. Spirit, he decided, made for more solid, matt effects. He had carefully-hidden secret methods too, such as amber solutions, liquid copal and other types of resin which dried quickly and kept the paint from cracking. In consequence, he found himself engaged in a terrible struggle against flat or streaky effects, since his absorbent canvases soaked up the modicum of oil there was in the paint. Brushes were another of his problems; he insisted on a special grip and preferred oven-dried horse-hair to sable. Perhaps the most important thing was the palette knife; like Courbet, he used it for his ground-work and had quite a collection of long, flexible knives, broad, stubby ones, and in particular a specially made triangular one, similar to that used by glaziers and exactly like the knife employed by Delacroix. To use either a scraper or a razor he considered discreditable, though on the other hand he indulged in all kinds of mysterious practices when it came to applying his colours. He concocted his own recipes and changed them at least once a month, believing that he had suddenly discovered the best method of painting when he spurned the old, flowing style allowed by oil and proceeded by a series of strokes of raw colour juxtaposed until he obtained the exact tone-value he desired. It had long been a mania of his to paint from right to left; he never said so, but he was sure it was lucky.

His latest terrible misfortune had been to be led astray by his fast-developing theory of complementary colours. He had heard of it first from Gagnière, who also had a weakness for technical experiments. Then, with characteristic over-indulgence, he had begun to exaggerate the scientific principle which deduces from the three primary colours, yellow, red, and blue, the three secondary colours, orange, green, and violet and from them a whole series of similar complementary colours obtained by mathematical combination. In that way science gained a foothold in painting and a method was created for logical observation. It meant that, by taking the dominant colour of a picture and establishing its complementary or cognate colours, it was possible to establish by experimental means all the other possible variations of colour, red changing to yellow next to blue, for example, or even a whole landscape changing its tone-values through reflection or decomposition of light due to the passing of clouds in the sky. From this true conclusion he argued that things have no fixed colour, but that their colour depends upon ambient circumstances.

When, with all that science buzzing in his brain, Claude came back to direct observation, his eye, now biased, forced the more delicate shades and over-stated the theory by introducing certain garish notes, with the result that the originality of his colouring, once so light and so vibrant with sunshine, gave way to what looked like a stunt, overthrowing all the accepted habits of the eye and producing purple flesh-tints and tricolour skies.

That way, it was obvious, madness lay.

It was poverty, however, that struck the last blow. It had been approaching slowly but surely all the time they had recklessly been drawing on their capital, and when not a sou remained of their twenty thousand francs it pounced on them in all its inevitable horror. Christine felt she ought to take a job, but there was nothing she could do; she could not even sew. Wretched and idle-handed, she vented her frustration on her useless genteel education, which left her with no alternative but to enter domestic service if things continued to get worse. As for Claude, who had made himself the laughing-stock of Paris, he never sold a canvas. An independent exhibition to which he and some of his friends had sent a few canvases had ruined his reputation with collectors; the public had made fun of his pictures, which were nothing but a patchwork of all the colours of the rainbow. Dealers, too, had beaten a retreat. M. Hue was the only one who ventured as far as the Rue Tourlaque and stood in ecstasy in front of Claude's wild productions with all their unexpected fireworks, lamenting the fact that he could not buy them for their weight in gold. It was in vain that Claude begged him to take them for nothing; M. Hue, with his modest means, displayed extraordinary delicacy in the matter and deprived himself even of essentials in order to put aside a sufficient sum to enable him, once in a while, to carry away, with religious solemnity, one of Claude's more hectic canvases to hang alongside the acknowledged masterpieces in his collection. Such windfalls were too few and far between, however, and Claude had to resign himself to doing work on commission, which he loathed, finding himself thrust into a bondage to which he had sworn he would never stoop. Had it not been for the two creatures who shared his sufferings, he would have preferred starvation. He found himself turning out cheap and nasty Stations of the Cross, Saints of both sexes by the hundred, sun-blinds for shops in all the stock designs, and a host of other odd jobs that reduce painting to the lowest level of cheapjack vulgarity. He even had to bear the shame of having some of his twenty-five-franc portraits refused because he failed to produce the 'guaranteed likeness'. He plumbed the lowest depths when he began to work for the sort of obscure little dealers who sold their wares on bridges or provided flashy goods for barter with savages, and who paid him so much a canvas, two francs or three francs a time, according to size.

Such work was not without its physical effects; his health began to fail and he felt physically incapable of carrying through a serious sitting. He would look at his great canvas in despair, with the eyes of a man condemned, unable to touch it for a week at a time, as if he felt his hands were blighted and clogged with filth. Bread was scarce, and, as the winter advanced, the great barracks of a studio grew less and less habitable, though Christine had been so proud of it when they first moved in. Once so industrious in her housework, she now hung about the place without even the heart to sweep the floor. As disaster approached the signs of neglect were more and more in evidence: little Jacques was under-nourished and sickly; their meals were reduced to a crust of bread eaten standing up; their whole existence, in short, devoid of care and organization was allowed to slip into the degradation and filth of the poor who have lost all vestiges of personal pride.

Another year had gone by when, on one of his days of defeat, as he was fleeing his still unfinished picture, Claude met an old acquaintance. He had sworn he would never go back to his studio and had been tramping the streets since noon trying to shake off the pale ghost of his nude figure, still formless after endless recastings and pursuing him now with its aching desire to be born. It was nearly five o'clock and the fog, dispersing in fine, yellowish rain, was leaving the roadway muddy underfoot. As he was crossing the Rue Royale like a man in a dream, in great danger of being run down, his ragged garments now thickly bespattered with mud, a brougham suddenly drew up in front of him and a voice called out:

'Claude, why, Claude! . . . Don't you acknowledge your friends these days?'

It was Irma Bécot, delightfully arrayed in grey silk covered with Chantilly lace, her beaming smile admirably displayed at the open window of her carriage.

'Where are you going?' she asked.

Dumbfounded, he managed to reply that he was going nowhere, at which Irma laughed merrily. As she looked at him there was a glint of vice in her eyes and in her lip that perverse little curl that comes into any fine lady's lip when she is suddenly overcome by the craving to get her teeth into something raw seen on a greengrocer's stall.

'Why don't you get in?' she ran on. 'We haven't seen each other for ages! Come on, get in. You'll get run over,' she added, for they were holding up the traffic and carriages were edging nearer and nearer to hers and the coachmen were beginning to grumble. His head in a whirl, Claude clambered in beside her, bedraggled and unkempt though he was and, sitting half on the lace of her skirt, let himself be carried away in the carriage with the blue satin cushions. The abduction scene raised quite a laugh from the neighbouring carriages as they lined up, ready to move forward now the jam had eased.

Irma Bécot's dream had materialized: she had a house of her own, in the Avenue de Villiers, but it had taken her years to get it. The ground had been bought by one lover, then the five hundred thousand building costs and the three hundred thousand for furnishings had been supplied by others, a little at a time, according to the prevailing passion of the moment. Now its luxury and splendour were worthy of royalty and its subtle refinements of sensual comfort made it one huge boudoir, one enormous bed of pleasure starting at the carpets in the hall and rising and spreading to the quilted walls of the bedrooms. The outlay involved had been tremendous, but now this haven for travellers was more than paying for itself; the privilege of enjoying the regal splendour of its beds and of spending a night under its roof was a costly affair.

Now that she had captured Claude, Irma announced she was at home to nobody; she would rather have set fire to everything she possessed than have failed to satisfy her whim. As they were going into the dining-room together the gentleman who happened to be contributing towards the upkeep of the house at the moment tried to join them, but she ordered him to be sent away, and in a loud voice, without any pretence of discretion. At table, laughing occasionally like an excited child, she ate her share of everything, though usually she had no appetite at all, and between whiles gazed on Claude enraptured, amused at the same time by his unkempt beard and his old working jacket with the buttons missing. Claude, still in a dream, took everything for granted and devoured his food as he always did in his periods of crisis. Neither of them talked during the meal, which was served in haughty dignity by the butler, Louis, who was instructed to serve the coffee and liqueurs in Madame's room.

Though it was only shortly after eight o'clock, Irma insisted on carrying Claude off to her room, where she immediately shot the bolt with a gay: 'Good night. Madame has retired to bed.'

'Make yourself at home,' she said to Claude. 'You're staying with me tonight. . . . We've talked about it long enough, so why not strike while the iron is hot?'

So Claude calmly took off his jacket in Irma's sumptuous bedroom with its mauve silk hangings trimmed with silver lace and its colossal bed draped with antique embroideries like a throne. He was used to being in his shirtsleeves and felt at home at once; besides, it was better sleeping there than spending the night under a bridge, since he had sworn he was never going back home. His life had so fallen to pieces that even this adventure provoked no surprise. Unable to understand anyone sinking quite so low, she simply thought he was 'killingly funny', and, half-naked already, determined to enjoy herself to the full, she began to pinch him, bite him, and engage him in violent horse-play, with all the abandon of a street-urchin.

'You know what *I* call my mug for the mugs, what *they* call my "Titian image"? Well it isn't meant for you. . . . Oh, no! You're different, and you make me different too; true, you do!' she said, and, seizing him with both her hands, she told him how much she had wanted him because he was so unkempt. Laughter came bubbling up, choking the words back in her throat, and she kissed him furiously all over, he was so ugly and so very comical.

About three in the morning, as Irma lay naked between the rumpled and disordered sheets, gorged with physical pleasure and almost inarticulate with lassitude, she murmured:

'What happened to your fancy woman, did you marry her after all?'

Stupid with sleep, Claude opened his eyes for a second and answered: 'Yes.'

'And you still sleep together?'

'Of course.'

Irma had to laugh; her only comment was:

'Poor old Claude! Poor old Claude! What a bore it must be for both of you!'

The following morning she released him. Completely calmed now, fresh and rosy as after a good night's rest, perfectly proper in her dressing-gown with her hair already done, she clasped his hands in hers for a moment, very affectionately, with a look that hovered between laughter and tears, and said to him:

'Poor old Claude! You didn't get much kick out of it, did you? Oh, don't say you did, a woman can always tell, you know. But *I* did, a terrific kick . . . and I want you to know I'm grateful for it, Claude.'

That was the end. Claude would have had to pay very dearly indeed to get her to do it all again.

The shock of his happy adventure sent Claude straight home to the Rue Tourlaque with strangely mixed feelings of vanity and remorse. For the next two days they not only made him totally indifferent to painting, but also made him wonder whether, after all, he might not have made more of a success of his life. He behaved so queerly, being so obsessed by what had happened to him, that when Christine questioned him, though he hesitated a little at first, he confessed everything. There was a scene, of course. Christine wept bitter tears and then forgave him, full of indulgence and even worried lest his night's activities should have over-tired him; while from the depths of her sorrow there sprang a certain unconscious joy compounded of pride in realizing that someone else could love him, amusement at his still being capable of such an escapade, and hope that, since he had been with another woman, he might yet come back to her. He had brought home with him an atmosphere of desire, and that thrilled her to the heart; for she was jealous of one thing, and one thing only, his painting; but that she loathed so much that rather than let him give in to it she would herself have given him to another woman.

About the middle of the winter, however, Claude found the heart to paint again. Tidying up in the studio one day, he discovered, behind a lot of old frames, a piece of an old canvas, the nude reclining figure from his 'Open Air' which he had cut away from the rest and kept when his picture came back from the 'Salon des Refusés'. As he unrolled it he let out a cry of genuine admiration:

'God, but it's beautiful!' He fixed it on the wall at once, with a nail in each corner, and then feasted his eyes upon it for hours. His hands began to tremble and his cheeks grew hotter and hotter as he looked at his work and wondered how he could possibly have shown such mastery. He must have had genius then, he reflected. Could his brain and his eyes and his hands have changed in the meantime? His excitement and the need to express his feelings grew to such a pitch that in the end he called to his wife:

'Come and look at this! . . . There, how's that for painting? . . . Look at those muscles, aren't they delicate? . . . And that thigh there in the full sunlight . . . and this shoulder, and even the curve of the breast there. . . . Why, damn me if she isn't alive! I can feel she's alive, as if I were touching her. I can feel that skin of hers, it's soft and warm; I can even smell it!'

Christine, as she stood by his side, responded in monosyllables. She had begun by being surprised and rather flattered by this sudden resurrection, after all those years, of herself as she had been at eighteen, but the more she felt Claude giving way to his enthusiasm, the more aware she became of her own increasing unhappiness coupled with vague but as yet unspoken irritation.

'Well!' cried Claude. 'Isn't that beauty to bow down to and worship?'

'Oh yes, yes. . . . She's darkened a bit, though, hasn't she?'

'Darkened! What are you talking about?' came Claude's violent retort. 'She would never darken,' he went on. 'She had eternal youth!' He might have been madly in love with her, the way he talked about her as if she were a real person, a person he felt sudden urges to see again from time to time and who made him forget everything else in his haste to keep their rendezvous.

Then, one morning, he got up with a violent thirst for work.

'God in heaven!' he cried. 'I've done it once, I can do it again! . . . And this time I'm a dud if I don't make a go of it!'

Christine had to sit for him there and then, for he was already on his ladder ready to start work again on his big canvas. For a whole month he kept her standing naked eight hours every day, until her feet were quite numb and she herself was exhausted. But he showed her no mercy and stubbornly refused to give way to his own fatigue. He was determined to produce a masterpiece, to make his upright figure as good as the reclining figure, so radiant with life, on his studio wall. He never stopped looking at it, consulting it, comparing it with his model, goaded into despair by the fear that he would never produce its like again. Glancing first at it, then at Christine, then at his canvas, he would fly into a rage and swear violently when he was not satisfied with his work, until at last he turned on Christine.

'No doubt about it, my dear, you're nothing like what you were in those days,' he said. 'There's no comparison. . . . Funny, you know, how well developed you were for one so young. I shall never forget how surprised I was to see you with a breast like a grown woman when the rest of you was as frail as a child. . . . You were supple and fresh in those days, too, like an opening bud, a breath of spring. . . . You can flatter yourself, anyhow, you once had a body worth looking at!'

He spoke with no intention of hurting her feelings, but simply as an observer, with eyes half-closed, considering her body as a specimen that was deteriorating.

'The colouring's still splendid,' he went on, 'but not the line. Not now. . . . The legs, oh, the legs are still all right; they're usually the last thing to go in women. . . . But the belly and the breasts are certainly going to pieces. There, just take a look at yourself in the glass. Near the armpits now, you can see the way the flesh is starting to sag? Not very lovely, is it? Look at *her* body now, there's no sagging there, is there?' he added, with a tender glance in the direction of the recumbent figure. 'It's no fault of yours, of course, but that's obviously the root of the trouble. . . . Pity!'

His every word pained her as she stood listening to him, swaying with fatigue. She had already suffered agonies, posing for him hours on end; now he was turning posing into unbearable torture. What was this latest invention of his, throwing her youth in her face and fanning her jealousy by filling her mind with poisonous regrets for her lost beauty? It was turning her into her own rival, making it impossible for her to look at the picture of herself as she used to be without feeling envy biting into her heart. What a part that picture had played in her life! It had been the source of all her unhappiness from the moment she had unconsciously bared her breast as she slept. Through it, in a gesture of soft-hearted charity, she had bared her whole virgin body for him, and then, after the mocking crowd had ridiculed her nudity, she had given herself to him, and so her whole life had been his to dispose of; through it, she had stooped to becoming his model, and through it she had even forfeited his love. Now it had come to light again, full of life, fuller of life than herself, and ready to kill her outright. Now it was clear to her that there was one work, and one work only; the reclining woman in the old picture was reincarnated in the upright figure in the new one.

With every sitting now Christine felt herself growing older; looking down at herself with tearful eyes, she imagined she could actually see her wrinkles forming and the purity of her figure melting away. She had never examined herself so closely before, and she felt ashamed and disgusted by the sight of her body, which filled her with that infinite despair that comes to all women of her ardent disposition when love slips from their grasp as their beauty fades. Was that why he had ceased to love her, she wondered; was it that made him spend nights with other women or take refuge in his unnatural passion for his painting? Whatever it was, it made her lose all interest in life and fall into the most slipshod ways. She lost all sense of grace and neatness and was quite happy to go about all the time in dirty camisole and skirt, so discouraged was she by the idea that resistance was useless since she was showing such signs of age.

One day, infuriated by an unsuccessful sitting, Claude made a remark so terrible that she never got over it. In one of his fits of uncontrollable rage he nearly put his fist through his canvas, and then vented his wrath on her, crying as he shook his fist in her face:

'It's plain to see I shall never do anything with *that*! . . . When women want to be models, they should never have children!'

She was so taken aback by his outrageous remark that she burst into tears and ran away to dress, but her hands trembled so that she could hardly tell one garment from the other.

Immediately overcome by remorse, Claude came down from his ladder forthwith to console her.

'I'm sorry,' he said. 'I ought not to have said that. I am a miserable wretch. . . . But please hold the pose just a little longer . . . just to show there's no ill-feeling.'

He picked her up in his arms, naked as she was, and stopped her in the act of slipping on her chemise. Once more she forgave him and took up the pose again, but inwardly so quivering with emotion that she felt great waves of pain passing through her limbs and, although she managed to remain motionless as a statue, tears streamed down her cheeks and over her naked breast. Ah, yes, she reflected, it might have been better if that child had never been born! It was he, maybe, who was to blame for everything. She stopped crying, her mind already making excuses for the father as she became aware of her smouldering wrath against the poor little creature who had never aroused her maternal instinct and whom she hated now since she thought it might be he who had destroyed her appeal as a lover.

This time Claude determinedly finished his picture and swore he would send it to the Salon at all costs. He stayed on his ladder from morning till night, tidying up his canvas, until it was too dark for him to carry on. Then, having worn himself out completely, he said he was not going to touch the thing again. That day, when Sandoz went up to see him about four o'clock, he was not at home; Christine said he had just gone up the hill for a breath of air.

The break between Claude and his old friends had slowly widened. His painting they found so disturbing, and were so conscious of the disintegration of their youthful admiration that little by little they had begun to fall away, and now not one of them ever dropped in to see him. Gagnière had even left Paris to go and live in one of his own houses at Melun, where he lived very meagrely on the rent of the other, after amazing all his friends by marrying his music mistress, an old maid who played Wagner to him in the evenings. Mahoudeau said his work kept him away, for now he was beginning to earn a reasonable living touching-up for a manufacturer of art bronzes. Jory's case was rather different; nobody ever saw him now that Mathilde kept him so closely guarded, gorging him with titbits, making him stupid with lovemaking and giving him so much of everything he was fond of that he had stopped scouring the pavements in search of adventure and picking up his pleasures in the gutter because he was too close-fisted to pay for them. Instead he had become as domesticated as a pet dog, given Mathilde control of his purse, and only with her permission did he ever have enough money in his pocket to buy himself a cheap cigar. It was even rumoured that Mathilde, who had at one time been a regular churchgoer, had tightened her hold on him by thrusting religion upon him and talking to him about death, of which he was terribly scared. Fagerolles was the only one who managed to put on some semblance of cordiality whenever he met his old friend, promising to go and see him, though he never actually did so; he had far too many calls upon his time now he was such a great success, boosted, fêted, celebrated, and on the highroad to glory and fortune. The only one of his old friends Claude felt rather sorry to lose was Dubuche, for whom he still felt a certain attachment for old times' sake, in spite of the clashes to which their differences of character had led in recent years. Dubuche, apparently, was not particularly happy either; he was rolling in wealth, of course, but nevertheless wretched; he was in continual disagreement with his father-in-law, who complained that he had been disappointed by his capacity as an architect, and he lived in a perpetual sick-room atmosphere with his invalid wife and his two children, both born prematurely and brought up in cotton-wool.

Sandoz was the only one of the group who still appeared to know the way to the Rue Tourlaque. He used to go there for the sake of little Jacques, his godson, and of poor, wretched Christine, whose passion among so much squalor moved him very deeply, for he saw in her a woman in love he would have liked to portray in his books. He used to go there especially because his sympathy for Claude as a brother-artist had increased since he realized that Claude had somehow lost his foothold and, so far as his art was concerned, was slipping deeper and deeper into madness, heroic madness. At first he had been amazed, for he had had greater faith in his friend than in himself; ever since their schooldays he had considered himself inferior to Claude, whom he looked up to as one of the masters who would revolutionize the art of a whole epoch. Then his heart had been wrung by the spectacle of failing genius, and surprise had given way to bitter compassion for the unspeakable torments of impotence. Was it ever possible, in art, to say where madness lay? he wondered. Failures always moved him to tears and the more a book or a painting inclined towards aberration, the more grotesque and lamentable the artist's effort, the more he tended to radiate charity, the greater was his urge to put the stricken soul respectfully to sleep among all the wild extravagance of its dreams.

The day Sandoz called and found Claude was out, he did not go away at once when he saw that Christine's eyes were red with weeping.

'If you think he'll be back soon,' he said, 'I'll wait for him.'

'Oh, he certainly won't be away for long,' she answered.

'Then I'll stay till he comes in, if I shan't be in your way.'

Never had he felt so sorry for her as he did now; she seemed so despondent and forlorn, so weary of gesture and so slow of speech, so completely uninterested in everything but her own burning passion. For at least a week she had never so much as dusted the furniture or tidied the room, but simply let everything run to dirt and disorder, for she had hardly the strength to drag herself about. It was a heart-rending spectacle: poverty degenerating into squalor, the harsh light from the big window showing up all the filth and untidiness in the great, black shed of a place, that made him shudder with gloom even on that bright February afternoon.

Christine lumbered back to the chair she had been occupying at the side of a bed which Sandoz had not noticed until now.

'What's the matter?' he asked. 'Jacques isn't ill, is he?'

'Yes,' she said, drawing the bedclothes over the child who kept throwing them off again. 'He's been in bed three days now, so we've brought him in here, to be near us. . . . He's never been very strong, you know. He seems to get worse rather than better, too, so we hardly know what to do about him,' she added in a monotonous voice, staring vaguely into space as she answered.

Sandoz was really frightened when he went up and looked at the child, he was so pale and his head seemed larger than ever, and far too heavy for his neck. Had it not been for the heavy breath passing between his bloodless lips, the child might have been taken for dead, he lay so motionless.

'Hello, Jacques,' said Sandoz. 'Don't you know who it is? It's me, your godfather, Sandoz. Aren't you going to say hello?'

The head made a painful but futile effort to raise itself and the eyelids half opened, showing the whites of the eyes, then closed again.

'Haven't you had a doctor?' he asked Christine.

'Oh, doctors! What help can they be?' she replied, with a shrug of the shoulders. 'We've seen one. He said there was nothing we can do. . . . Let's hope it's just another false alarm. It's his age, I think. He's twelve now and growing fast.'

Horrified, Sandoz did not press the point; he had no desire to upset Christine further, since she obviously did not realize the seriousness of the situation. He crossed the room in silence and stopped in front of the picture.

'Aha! This is going well,' he said. 'He's on the right track this time.'

'It's finished.'

'Finished!'

When she added that the canvas was being sent to the Salon the following week, he did not know what to say, but sat down on the divan to contemplate it at leisure and avoid hasty condemnation. The background, the embankment, the Seine, with the prow of the Cité rising triumphantly out of it, were merely sketched in, but sketched in by a masterly hand, as if the painter had been afraid of spoiling his dream Paris by an excess of detail. To the left there was one excellent group, porters unloading sacks of plaster, which was beautifully and powerfully finished. But the boat with the female figures in it simply broke the canvas with a violent burst of flesh tints which were completely out of place. The big nude figure in particular, which had clearly been painted at fever-heat and had the glow and the strange larger-than-life quality of an hallucination, struck a disturbing and discordant note amid all the realism of the rest of the picture.

Sandoz said nothing as his heart filled with despair in the presence of such a splendid failure, until, feeling Christine's eyes fixed expectantly upon him, he managed to murmur:

'Amazing! Really amazing, that central figure.'

He was saved from further comment by the return of Claude, who shouted for joy at the sight of his old friend and wrung his hand with delight before he went across to Christine and kissed little Jacques, who had once more thrown off the bedclothes.

'How is he now?' he asked.

'Still the same.'

'He'll be all right after a rest. Growing too fast, that's what it is. I told you there was nothing to worry about,' he said and then went and sat next to Sandoz on the divan.

There they both lay back and scrutinized the picture, while Christine, sitting by the bed, looked at nothing and apparently thought about nothing in her desolation. Gradually, as night came on, the bright light from the window faded and weakened in the slow, smooth deepening of the twilight.

'So you've made up your mind to submit it, Christine tells me?' said Sandoz.

'Yes, I'm sending it in.'

'You're right. You've been at it quite long enough. There are some fine bits in it; that perspective along the embankment on the left, and that man there lifting a sack. But . . .'

He hesitated a second, then decided to offer his criticism.

'But I still don't see why you've insisted on leaving in those nude figures in the centre. . . . There's no obvious reason for them, is there? And you promised me they shouldn't be just nudes, don't you remember? Are you really determined to leave them as they are?'

'I am,' replied Claude curtly and with that note of obstinacy that goes with an *idée fixe* and indicates that explanations are not worth giving. Reclining with his hands clasped at the back of his head, he started to talk about something else, though gazing all the while at his picture, over which the twilight was beginning to cast a fine veil of shadow.

'Do you know where I've been?' he asked. 'I've been calling on Courajod. . . . You know Courajod, the landscape painter, his 'Pool at Gagny' is in the Luxembourg. Don't you remember, I thought he was dead, and then we discovered he lived quite near here, just on the other side of the hill, in the Rue de l'Abreuvoir? Well, Courajod had got me puzzled. I'd discovered where he lives once when I was walking round that way to get some fresh air, and I'd never been able to pass it since without wanting to go in. Who wouldn't, knowing that a great master lived there, the fellow who made landscape painting what it is, living there ignored, played out, buried away like a mole? . . . And as for the street and the place itself, well, you can't imagine. The street might as well be in a country village; it has grassy banks on either side and poultry all over the roadway, and the cottage is more like a doll's house than anything else, with its tiny windows, tiny doors, and tiny garden—hardly a garden, really, just a steep strip of land with four peartrees, cluttered up with a hen-run made of mouldering lath and plaster and rusty iron railings tied together with string.'

His speech slowed as he lay back with his eyes half closed, succumbing to the irresistible preoccupation with his picture until it became a distinct impediment to his expression.

'Today,' he went on, 'I spotted Courajod himself on his doorstep, a wizened old codger, well over eighty, shrunk to the size of a small boy. Incredible! He had to be seen to be believed, with his clogs and his peasant's jersey and his old woman's headscarf! Anyhow, I walked straight up to him and said: "Monsieur Courajod, I know who you are. You have a masterpiece hanging in the Luxembourg. May I shake hands with you, as an artist, in acknowledgement?"—Oh, if you could have seen the way he took fright immediately and stammered and backed away as if I'd been going to attack him! He would have run away if he could. But I followed him, and he soon calmed down and showed me his hens and his ducks and rabbits and dogs, a full-blown menagerie, in short, including a raven! That's all he lives for now, his pets. And the view he has to look out on! The whole plain of Saint-Denis, stretching away to the horizon, full of rivers and towns, smoking factories and steaming trains. A real hermit's retreat, you know, up on the hilltop, looking away from Paris out over the limitless countryside. . . . Of course, I took up the subject of painting again and told him how much we all admire his genius. "You're one of our glories," I said. "You'll be remembered as the father of us all!" At that his lips began to quiver again and he looked simply stupefied with horror; he couldn't have turned me away with a more beseeching gesture if I'd actually unearthed some skeleton from his long-lost youth! What he said was impossible to understand, really; just a series of disjointed expressions chewed over by his toothless gums, the vague ramblings of an old man returned to second childhood: "Didn't know . . . long way off . . . too old . . . what does it matter?" was all I could catch. The long and the short of it is, he turned me out, and I heard him give a mighty turn to his key as he barricaded himself and his pets against all attempted admiration from passers-by. Imagine a man of his calibre ending his days like a retired grocer, deliberately reducing himself to a cipher, in his own lifetime! What price glory, then, the thing *we*'d die for?'

His voice had grown quieter and quieter as he spoke, and tailed off in a long-drawn-out sigh. Night had begun to fill the room like a rising tide, welling up first in the corners, then rising slowly, inexorably upwards, submerging the legs of the chairs and the table and all the untidy litter on the studio floor. Now the lower half of the picture was covered, and Claude peered despairingly at it through the mounting gloom, passing a last judgment upon it in the fading light of day. Meanwhile the deep silence was broken only by the heavy breathing of the sick child, at whose side Christine still sat like a motionless black shadow.

At last Sandoz spoke. Like Claude, he was lying back on a cushion, his hands clasped behind his head.

'I wonder,' he said, 'whether it might not be better to live, and die, unknown? What a cheat for us all if this glory we talk about existed no more than the paradise promised in the Catechism and which even children don't believe in nowadays! We've stopped believing in God, but not in our own immortality! We're a sad lot, really!'

Then, giving way to the sadness of the falling twilight, he made his own confession and lay bare all the torments aroused in him by his sensitiveness to human suffering.

'Take my own case,' he said. 'Maybe you envy me because I'm beginning to do good business, as the bourgeois say, publishing my books, making some money. Well, between you and me, it's getting me down. I've told you that already more than once, but you never believe me because for you, who find production so difficult and can make no headway with the public, happiness naturally means abundant production and being in the public eye, favourably or otherwise even. . . . Get yourself accepted at the next Salon, go into the fray, paint more and more pictures, and then tell me whether you're as happy as you hoped to be! . . . The thing is, work has simply swamped my whole existence. Slowly but surely it's robbed me of my mother, my wife, and everything that meant anything to me. It's like a germ planted in the skull that devours the brain, spreads to the trunk and the limbs, and destroys the entire body in time. No sooner am I out of bed in the morning than work clamps down on me and pins me to my desk before I've even had a breath of fresh air. It follows me to lunch and I find myself chewing over sentences as I'm chewing my food. It goes with me when I go out, eats out of my plate at dinner and shares my pillow in bed at night. It's so completely merciless that once the process of creation is started, it's impossible for me to stop it, and it goes on growing and working even when I'm asleep. . . . Outside that, nothing, nobody exists. I go up to see my mother, but I'm so absorbed that ten minutes afterwards I'm asking myself whether I've been up to her or not. As for my wife, she has no husband, poor thing; we're never really together any more, even when we're hand-in-hand! Sometimes I feel so acutely aware that I'm making them both unhappy that I'm overcome with remorse, for happiness in a home depends so much on kindness and frankness and gaiety. But do what I will, I can't escape entirely from the monster's clutches, and I'm soon back in the semiconscious state that goes with creation and just as sullen and indifferent as I always am when I'm working. If the morning's writing's gone smoothly, all well and good; if it hasn't, all's *not* so good; and so the whole household laughs or cries to the whim of almighty Work! . . . That's the situation. I've nothing now I can call my own. In the bad old days I used to dream about foreign travel or restful holidays in the country. Now that I could have both, here I am hemmed in by work, with no hope of so much as a brisk walk in the morning, a free moment to visit an old friend, or a moment's self-indulgence! I haven't even a will of my own; it's become a habit now to lock my door on the world outside and throw my key out of the window. . . . So there we are, cribbed and confined together, my work and me. And in the end it'll devour me, and that will be the end of that!'

There was a moment's silence in the deepening shadow before he took up his complaint again.

'If only one felt some satisfaction,' he said. 'If only one got some semblance of pleasure out of leading such a dog's life! . . . I don't know how they do it, the people who smoke cigarettes and sit blissfully stroking their beards while they work. There are people, apparently, to whom production comes easily and even pleasantly, and who can work or not work as the spirit moves them, without any more ado. And they think it's wonderful, that everything they write is perfect, distinguished, and of unmatchable beauty! . . . But when I bring forth I need forceps, and even then the child always looks to me like a monster. Is it possible for anyone to be so devoid of doubt as to have absolute faith in himself? It amazes me to see these fellows who can't find a good word to say for anybody else cast all criticism and common sense to the winds when it comes to admiring their own bastard offspring! There's always something repulsive, in my opinion, about a book. I don't see how you can possibly like it once you've gone through the messy business of producing it. . . . Then there are all the brickbats you get hurled at you. Fortunately, I find them stimulating rather than discouraging, but I know some people they upset terribly, the sort of people who don't mind admitting that they need to feel the public sympathetic. Some women, I know, would die rather than fail to please. Perhaps it's only natural. Still, there's something healthy in a bit of honest invective, and unpopularity's a very sound training-school; there's nothing better for keeping you in trim than the insults of the common herd. So long as you can say to yourself that you've put your whole life into your work, that you expect neither immediate justice nor even serious appreciation, that you're working without hope of any kind, simply because the urge to work beats in your body like your heart, because you can't help it, you can let yourself die happy and console yourself with the illusion that you'll be appreciated one day. . . . People would be surprised if they knew how lightly I take their fury. But there's still myself to reckon with, and I am so completely merciless that I never allow myself a moment's happiness. From the moment I start a new novel, life's just one endless torture. The first few chapters may go fairly well and I may feel there's still a chance to prove my worth, but that feeling soon disappears and every day I feel less and less satisfied. I begin to say the book's no good, far inferior to my earlier ones, until I've wrung torture out of every page, every sentence, every word, and the very commas begin to look excruciatingly ugly. Then, when it's finished, *when* it's finished, what a relief! Not the blissful delight of the gentleman who goes into ecstasies over his own production, but the resentful relief of a porter dropping a burden that's nearly broken his back. . . . Then it starts all over again, and it'll go on starting all over again till it grinds the life out of me, and I shall end my days furious with myself for lacking talent, for not leaving behind a more finished work, a bigger pile of books, and lie on my death-bed filled with awful doubts about the task I've done, wondering whether it was as it ought to have been, whether I ought not to have done this or that, expressing with my last dying breath the wish that I might do it all over again!'

Choking with emotion, he had to struggle a moment for breath before he could give voice to the passionate outburst of all his impenitent lyricism:

'Oh, for another life! Who'll give me a second life, a life for work to steal! A chance to die a second death in harness!'

It was quite dark now, and the stiff black shadow of Christine was no longer visible, while the child's painful breathing seemed to come from the darkness itself, like some mighty, remote sorrow rising from the city streets. In the prevailing gloom of the studio the only object over which a faint pale light still hovered was the big canvas on which the naked figure of the woman was still discernible, though vague, like a fading vision, incomplete, the legs lost in shadow already, one arm gone and only the curve of the loins still clear, the colour of moonlight.

After a long silence, Sandoz asked:

'Would you like me to go with you when you take in your picture?'

Claude made no answer, and Sandoz thought he heard him weeping.—Was it the same infinite, despairing sorrow he had just experienced himself?—He waited a moment, then repeated his question; this time, swallowing back his tears, Claude managed to answer:

'No, old fellow. Thanks all the same. The picture's not going in.'

'Not going in? But I thought you'd decided it was!'

'So I had. . . . But I hadn't really seen it then. I've seen it now, though, in the fading daylight. . . . And it's another failure! Oh yes, it is! It struck me clean between the eyes, like a blow from a fist, a staggering blow.'

Hidden in the darkness, he let his hot tears stream slowly down his cheeks. He had held them back as long as he could, shattered by the silent drama being played out in his heart, but now he could restrain them no longer.

'My poor Claude,' said Sandoz gently, himself very upset. 'It's a hard thing to have to admit to oneself, but perhaps after all you're right to keep it back and go over parts of it again. . . . What's making me angry now is the thought that I've discouraged you by my everlasting dissatisfaction with everything.'

'*You* discourage me?' said Claude simply. 'Of all the ideas! Why, I wasn't even listening. . . . I was too busy watching everything going to pieces on that damned canvas. As the light was fading it reached one particular point, a very fine, grey half-light, at which I suddenly realized what was wrong. I saw how inconsistent it all was, apart from the background, which is bearable. But the nude figure in the centre clashes violently with all the rest and isn't even properly balanced; the legs aren't right somehow. . . . It was enough to strike a man dead on the spot; I could actually feel the life beginning to break away from my body. . . . Then, as darkness went on pouring into the room, I felt my head in a whirl again, as if everything was being swallowed up, the earth dropping into the void, the whole world coming to an end. Soon the only thing I could see was the curve of her belly, shrinking away like a waning moon. And look at her now, look! Nothing left at all now, not even a glimmer. She's dead now, and black, nothing but black!'

The picture had, indeed, completely disappeared. Claude got up from the divan, and Sandoz heard him mumbling in the darkness.

'Dead, black . . . but what the hell does that matter? . . . I'm going to start afresh! . . . I'm going to . . .'

He was interrupted by Christine, who had also left her chair and with whom he collided in the darkness.

'Be careful,' she said, 'I'm lighting the lamp.'

She lit it, and her pale face emerged once more from the darkness, as she shot a look of fear and hatred at the painting. What was this? It wasn't leaving, then, the old torture was to start all over again?

'I'm going to start afresh!' Claude repeated. 'It can kill me, it can kill my wife, it can kill my child, it can kill the lot of us, but this time it'll be a masterpiece, by God it will!'

Christine went back to her chair and the two men went over to look at Jacques, whose restless little hands had worked off the bedclothes again. Still breathing heavily, he lay quite inert, his head buried in the pillow, like a weight too heavy for the bed. As he took his leave Sandoz told them he was worried about the child, but Christine seemed utterly dazed, and Claude was already hovering in front of his canvas, his future masterpiece, torn between its passionate illusion and the painful reality of his suffering child, the flesh of his flesh.

The following morning, as he was finishing dressing, he heard Christine's terror-stricken voice call out to him:

'Claude! Claude!'

She had fallen into a deep sleep on the uncomfortable chair near the child's bed, and woken with a start.

'Look!' she cried. 'He's dead!'

Claude stumbled across to her in a moment, aghast, not quite understanding.

'He's dead?' he repeated, as they both stood gazing down at the bed where the poor little creature lay on his back, his enormous head that marked him as the child of genius looking deformed and swollen like a cretin's. He did not appear to have stirred all night; his mouth had dropped open and the colour gone from his lips; there were no signs of breathing, while his vacant eyes had not remained closed. His father touched him; he was icy cold.

'It's true,' he murmured. 'He *is* dead.'

Their stupefaction was such that for a moment no tears came to their eyes; they were so struck by the brutality of the situation that they could hardly believe what had happened.

Then suddenly Christine dropped to her knees at the bedside, shaking with sobs, her head on her folded arms on the edge of the mattress. In the first terrible moment her despair was deepened by a sharp pang of remorse for not having loved the child enough. As the past flashed before her eyes, every day gave her reason for regrets—sharp words, grudging caresses and sometimes even blows. Now it was too late, now she would never be able to make up for having deprived him of all her mother-love. He had so often been disobedient; this time he had obeyed only too well. She had told him so often to 'be quiet and let father get on with his work' that now he was going to be quiet for a long, long time. The thought was more than she could bear, and her every sob was a muffled cry of remorse.

Claude had begun to walk to and fro across the studio out of the sheer nervous desire to keep moving. His face was convulsed with grief, but his tears came slowly and he wiped them away mechanically with the back of his hand. Every time he passed the child's dead body he felt obliged to look at it, as if the glassy, staring eyes were exercising some kind of power over him. He tried to resist it at first, but the attraction grew stronger and stronger to the point of obsession, until at last he gave way, fetched out a small canvas and set to work on a study of the dead child. For the first few moments his vision was fogged by tears, but he kept on wiping them away and persisted in plying his wavering brush. Work soon dried his eyes and steadied his hand, and the dead body of his son became simply a model, a strange, absorbing subject for the artist. The exaggerated shape of the head, the waxlike texture of the skin, the eyes like holes wide open on the void, everything about it excited him, filled him with ardour and enthusiasm. He stood back to see the effect; he was pleased, and a vague smile appeared on his lips as he worked.

When Christine looked up she found him completely absorbed and, as she burst into tears again, all she could find to say was:

'Oh, you can paint him now. He'll keep still enough this time!'

For five whole hours Claude worked solidly away, and two days later, when Sandoz came back with him after the funeral, the little picture filled him with pity and admiration. It was a picture worthy of the past, a masterpiece of lighting, power-fully handled, with the addition of a certain overwhelming sadness, a feeling that everything was ended, that with the death of the child life itself had been extinguished for ever.

Sandoz could not praise it too highly, but he was rather taken aback to hear Claude say:

'You really like it? . . . Then that settles it. As the other thing isn't ready, I'm sending this to the Salon!'

CHAPTER 10

THE morning after Claude had taken his 'Dead Child' to the Palais de l'Industrie, he was out strolling near the Parc Monceau when he met Fagerolles, who greeted him most cordially.

'Well, if it isn't old Claude!' he cried. 'What's been happening to you lately? What are you doing? Nobody ever sees you these days!'

Then, when Claude, full of his latest production, told him he had just sent his little picture to the Salon, he added:

'Fine! Fine! I must see to it they accept it. You know I'm a candidate for the Committee this year.'

And indeed he was, for as a result of the everlasting grumbling and dissatisfaction among the artists, and after endless futile attempts at reform, it had been officially decided that exhibitors should have the right to appoint their own Selection Committee. The result had been a furore in the world of sculpture and painting and a violent outbreak of election fever complete with all the ambition, cliques, intrigues, and chicanery that have brought politics into such disrepute.

'Come along home with me,' Fagerolles went on, 'and have a look at this little place I've got. You've not seen it yet though you've promised often enough to drop in. It's not far . . . just on the corner of the Avenue de Villiers.'

Since he had gaily taken Claude by the arm Claude had to go with him, torn between shame and desire as he found himself thinking that his old school-friend might be able to get his picture accepted. When they reached the small mansion in the Avenue de Villiers he stopped to take in the façade, a dainty, rather precious bit of architecture, the exact reproduction of a Renaissance house at Bourges, with mullioned windows, turret, and fancy lead roofing. It was a gem, just flashy enough for a kept woman, he thought; but he was rather surprised when he turned round and noticed straight across the road the palatial residence of Irma Bécot, where he had once spent a night, the memory of which still haunted him like a dream. It looked vast, substantial, almost severe in its regal splendour and made its neighbour opposite look like a bit of fancy jewellery.

'What about Irma over there?' said Fagerolles, with a note of respect in his voice. '*She*'s got herself a cathedral. . . . But then *I*'ve got nothing to sell but pictures! . . . Come inside.'

The interior was both magnificent and bizarre in its luxury, starting in the hall with antique tapestries, old weapons, and an amazing collection of antique furniture and Oriental curios. In the dining-room, on the left of the hall, the walls were panelled with lacquer and the ceiling hung with a red-dragon tapestry, while the carved monumental staircase streamed with banners and bristled with exotic plants. The greatest marvel of all was the studio upstairs. Not too big, without a picture on the walls which were entirely hung with Oriental draperies, one end of it was occupied by an enormous fireplace with chimeras supporting the mantelpiece, while the other was filled by a kind of tent composed of sumptuous hangings stretched on lances, under which, on a profusion of magnificent carpets, was a huge divan, very low, but heaped high with furs and cushions.

As Claude was taking everything in a question came into his mind which he refrained, however, from asking. Was all this paid for? Since Fagerolles had been officially decorated a year ago he was said to have been asking ten thousand francs a portrait. Naudet, once he had launched him, exploited him openly and never let one of his canvases go for less than twenty, thirty, or even forty thousand francs. Orders would have come in thick and fast if Fagerolles had not affected the indifference and the overstrain of the artist whose tiniest sketches are always eagerly sought after. And yet all this show of luxury reeked of debts and part-payments, and all the money it represented, money made as easily as by gambling on the Stock Exchange, simply ran to waste through the artist's fingers and that was the end of it. Still enjoying the full blaze of his new fortune, so suddenly acquired, Fagerolles never worried about expenditure. Confident that he would always be able to sell, and at higher and higher prices, he revelled in the glory of the fine position he was securing for himself in the world of modern art.

After a time Claude noticed a small canvas on a blackwood easel draped with red plush. It represented the artist's tools just as he had put them down, including a rosewood paint-box and a box of pastels.

'Neat bit of work,' said Claude to please Fagerolles. 'What about your "Salon"? Has it gone in?'

'Oh, yes, it's gone in, thank goodness! You should have seen the callers I've had. One endless procession, day in, day out; kept me on the run for over a week. . . . I didn't want to send anything; it's looked on as rather *infra dig.*, you know. Naudet was against it, too. But you know how it is. I've been solicited from every side, and all the young-sters want to get me on the Committee so that I can stand up for them. . . . The thing I've sent in is quite simple: "A Lunch Party"—that's what I've called it—two men and three women, house-party guests, taking an *al fresco* lunch in a forest clearing. . . . It's rather original, I think you'll agree when you see it.'

His voice wavered as his eyes met Claude's gaze fixed on him, but he turned aside his obvious uneasiness by a light-hearted reference to the little canvas on the easel.

'This is a bit of rubbish Naudet asked me to do. Oh, I'm very much aware what I'm short of, my friend: a bit of what you've got too much of. . . . And I'm still on your side, you know; why, I was defending you only yesterday, believe it or not,' he added, slapping Claude on the shoulder.

He had sensed his old master's silent contempt and wanted to win him over again by applying his usual wiles and flattery, like a common woman admitting she *is* common in the hope of being loved all the more. But it was very sincerely and with a kind of anxious deference that he promised yet again that he would do everything in his power to get Claude's picture accepted.

At that moment callers began to arrive, and within the next hour fifteen or twenty people passed through the studio: fathers introducing young pupils, exhibitors recom-mending their pictures for the Salon, colleagues to compare notes on persons with influence, and even women wielding their charm in the hope of winning a little protection for their talent. It was an eye-opener to Claude to see Fagerolles playing the part of the election candidate, shaking hands with all comers, saying to one: 'Very nice, the picture you've sent in this year, very nice indeed. I like it'; feigning amazement as he said to someone else: 'What! You still haven't had a medal!'; saying to all and sundry: 'If I'd anything to do with it, I'd show them when a picture's worth looking at!' The result was that he sent his callers away delighted, closing the door behind every one of them with an air of extreme amiability, behind which there was just the faintest suggestion of a snigger he had retained from his raffish past.

'Now you can see for yourself,' he said to Claude in one of the rare moments when they were alone, 'the time I have to waste on all these brainless idiots!'

Moving over to the bay window he suddenly flung it open, revealing on one of the balconies of the mansion opposite a white figure, a woman in a lace *négligée*, waving her handkerchief. In reply, Fagerolles raised his hand three times, then both windows closed.

Claude had recognized Irma and, after a moment's awkward silence, Fagerolles quietly explained the situation.

'Very handy, as you observe. We can communicate direct; we even have a complete telegraphic code. She wants me, so I'll have to go across. . . . There's a girl who could teach you and me a thing or two!'

'What, for example?'

'Why, everything, if it comes to that. Vice, art, intelligence, she has it all . . . including a flair for success. Oh, yes, an extraordinary flair. It's she who tells me what to paint! It is, seriously. . . . And in spite of it all, she doesn't change. She's just the same cheeky urchin she always was, always ready for a bit of fun, and once she's taken a fancy to you there's no holding her!'

As he spoke two red patches came up on his cheeks, like flames, and his eyes clouded for a moment, like troubled water. He had taken up with Irma again since they both came to live in the same street, and rumour had it that he, the smart, hardened Parisian adventurer, was letting her bleed him white, perpetually sending her maid to claim considerable sums—for a tradesman, for a passing fancy, for nothing at all, very often, except the sheer pleasure of emptying his pockets. That explained, in part, his being in such straitened circumstances, his ever-increasing debt in spite of the regular upward trend of the price of his pictures. He knew, too, that to her he was just a useless luxury, a distraction for a woman fond of painting, enjoyed behind the backs of the serious gentlemen who footed her bills as if they were her husbands. She thought it a great joke, and, as their perversity had forged just sufficient of a link between them and given just that extra flavour of dishonesty to their relationship, Fagerolles thought it funny too, and gloated over being her secret lover without a thought for all the money it was costing him.

Claude put his hat on, ready to go, as Fagerolles also was clearly anxious to go and kept casting anxious looks at the house across the road.

'I don't want to hurry you away,' he said, 'but you see she's expecting me. Well, anyhow, it's all settled, your picture's in . . . unless, of course, I'm not elected. . . . Why not come down to the Palais de l'Industrie the night they count the votes. There'll be a hell of a crush, of course, but then you'd know at once whether I can be any use to you.'

At first Claude swore to himself he would do no such thing. Protection by Fagerolles was almost more than he could bear, until he realized that there was only one thing he was afraid of: that the villain might not keep his promise if he thought there was any chance of failure. And so, when voting day arrived, it was more than he could do to stay at home and wait; he went out and wandered about the Champs-Élysées, pretending he was going for a good long walk. The Champs-Élysées was as good as any other place, after all, for he had stopped working—though he would not admit that it was because the Salon was approaching—and resumed his lengthy rambles around the city. He had no vote himself, as he had not yet had a picture accepted, but he kept walking past the Palais de l'Industrie, fascinated by the noise and activity near the entrance: voters passing in and out, pounced upon by men in dirty smocks shouting lists of candidates. There were at least thirty different lists, he noticed, representing all possible cliques and opinions: Beaux-Arts lists, liberal, die-hard, coalition lists, 'young-school' lists, and ladies' lists. It was exactly like the rush at the polling-booths the day after a riot.

At four o'clock in the afternoon, when voting finished, Claude could not resist his curiosity and went up to see what was happening. The staircase was clear, and anyone could go in who pleased. At the top of the steps he found himself in the huge Committee Room, overlooking the Champs-Élysées. A table twelve metres long stood in the middle and in a monumental fireplace at one end whole trees were burning, while the talk and laughter of some four or five hundred voters, their friends and a sprinkling of sightseers who all wanted to watch the counting, rose to the lofty ceiling with a roar like thunder. Around the table tellers were preparing, or had already started, to work. They worked in threes, two to count, one to check, and there were to be about fifteen such groups in all. Three or four more were still required to make up the number, but there were no more volunteers; everybody was fighting shy of a laborious task which would keep them hard at it through most of the night.

It so happened that Fagerolles, who had been on the go ever since morning, was doing his best to make himself heard, and shouting:

'Come along, gentlemen, one volunteer wanted! One volunteer, gentlemen!'

Then, catching sight of Claude, he pounced on him and brought him to the table by brute force.

'Just the man we want. Now do us a favour; sit down here and give us a hand. It's all in a good cause, so you can't refuse!'

On the spot, Claude found himself made a 'checker', a function he carried out with great solemnity, being naturally shy, and not without a certain subdued excitement, for he seemed to think that the acceptance of his picture depended in some way on his conscientious application to the task in hand. It was he who had to call out the names on the lists prepared and handed to him by his tellers, with the most frightful din going on all round him, twenty or thirty different voices shouting twenty or thirty different names pelting like hailstones against the never-ceasing rumble of the crowd. As he could do nothing in cold blood, he grew more and more excited as the lists kept coming in, downcast when Fagerolles's name did not appear, elated when he had to call it out again. This last sensation, be it said, he experienced fairly frequently, for the young man in question had made himself popular, having been seen everywhere, frequenting cafés favoured by the powers that be, risking even certain professions of faith, taking up the cudgels on behalf of the younger painters, but not forgetting to kowtow to Members of the Institut. The tide of support was rising, and Fagerolles was obviously a general favourite.

Night fell, on this wet March day, about six o'clock. Attendants brought in lamps and round them gathered the dark, silent shapes of wary artists keeping a weather eye on the counting. Others, in a more carefree mood, began cat-calling, and there was even an attempt at yodelling. But it was at eight o'clock, when a collation of cold meats and wine was served, that the fun really started. Bottles were emptied in a twinkling, everybody stuffed himself at random with whatever he could lay his hands on, and soon the huge room, lighted like a forge by the huge logs burning in the fireplace, was like a village fair in full swing. When everyone started to smoke the atmosphere grew so dense that it dimmed the yellow light of the lamps. The floor was ankle-deep in rubbish, a thick carpet of scrap paper and discarded voting forms, corks, crusts of bread, and even a few broken plates. People let themselves go. One pale-faced little sculptor stood up on a stool to harangue the crowd, while a painter with a waxed moustache and a beaky nose sat astride a chair and galloped round the table, saluting like the Emperor.

As time went by, however, a certain number tired of the jollifications and went home, and by eleven o'clock only about two hundred were left. But after midnight the crowd was swelled again by the arrival of late-comers in evening dress on their way home from theatres or parties, keen on getting the results of the voting before the rest of Paris. There were some reporters among them, too, and they could be seen dashing out of the room as soon as any partial results were announced.

Claude, now thoroughly hoarse, was still busy calling out names. The smoke and the heat were getting unbearable and the stench of a stable was rising from the filth on the floor. One o'clock struck, then two o'clock, but Claude was still busy counting so conscientiously that all the other tellers had finished long ago while he was still firmly entangled in columns of figures. At last, when all the partial lists had been pooled, the final results were announced. Fagerolles came out fifteenth out of forty, five places above Bongrand, who was on the same list but whose name must often have been crossed out. Day was breaking when Claude reached home in the Rue Tourlaque, worn out but delighted.

Then for a fortnight he lived on his nerves. A dozen times he thought of going to ask Fagerolles what was happening, but shame always prevented him. Besides, as the Committee discussed exhibits in alphabetical order, it was impossible for them to have reached a decision already. Then, one evening, on the Boulevard de Clichy, his heart leapt when he recognized a broad-shouldered figure with a rolling gait coming towards him.

It was Bongrand, who seemed embarrassed by the meeting. It was he who spoke first.

'Things are not going too smoothly down at the Palais,' he said. 'But there's still hope; Fagerolles and I are keeping an eye on things. Rely on Fagerolles, my lad, for I'm scared to death I might say something to spoil your chances.'

The truth was that Bongrand was continually at loggerheads with Mazel, a famous teacher from the Beaux-Arts and one of the die-hards of the elegant, glossy school, who had been appointed chairman of the Selection Committee. Although they called each other 'dear colleague' and exchanged many cordial handshakes, their hostility had been manifest from the very first day; one had only got to propose the acceptance of a picture for the other to vote for its rejection. Fagerolles, on the other hand, who had been elected secretary, had constituted himself official jester to Mazel and fawned so successfully on him that the master very readily forgave his renegade pupil. But the pupil, now a master, had already a reputation for ruthlessness and was known to be far harder on novices or over-adventurous painters than any Member of the Institut. But he could suddenly become human when he wanted to get a picture accepted; then, with his endless flow of witticisms and his clever handling of intrigue, he would carry the vote with all the coolness and ease of a conjuror.

Being on the Committee was no light task; it used to tire out even the sturdy Bongrand. Every day its work was prepared by the attendants, who set out an endless display of canvases, laid out flat on the ground, propped up around the walls, running through all the first-floor rooms of the entire Palais de l'Industrie. Every afternoon, starting at one o'clock, the forty members of the Committee, led by their Chairman armed with a little bell, started out on their round, which they repeated until they had gone through every letter in the alphabet. Verdicts were pronounced on the spot, and they made as short work of it as they could, casting out the obvious failures without even taking a vote. Occasionally a discussion would hold them up; they would squabble for ten minutes or so and then have the picture put on one side for the evening's second viewing. Meanwhile a couple of men with some ten metres of rope would stretch it tight about four paces from the row of pictures, to keep the judges from getting too close, as they tended to do in the heat of their discussion. Even then an occasional paunch would bend the rope considerably out of the straight. Behind the Committee came seventy white-coated attendants, working to the orders of a foreman. It was their job, after the decisions had been announced by the secretaries, to sort out the rejected pictures and lay them aside, like corpses after a battle. It took two good hours to do the whole round, without a rest or a chance to sit down, in an exhausting tramp through a suite of cold, draughty rooms which made even the least susceptible among them wrap themselves up in heavy fur coats. No wonder, then, that the three o'clock collation was so welcome! It meant half an hour's rest at a buffet where claret and chocolate and sandwiches were served and where all the bargaining for mutual concessions and the bartering of influence and votes were indulged in. Most of the Committee were so heavily bombarded with recommendations that they carried little notebooks to make sure they were forgetting no one, and freely consulted them when agreeing to vote for a colleague's protégé if he would vote for one of theirs. Others, on the contrary, either on principle or through lack of interest, remained aloof from all the intrigues and stood about, gazing into space, smoking their cigarettes.

After the break the task was resumed, but in a more leisurely manner, in one room, where there were chairs to sit on and even tables provided with pens, ink, and paper. There, all pictures measuring under one and a half metres were judged 'on the easel', lined up ten or twelve at a time along a sort of platform covered with green baize. Many of the Committee sat there happily ignoring the proceedings, some settled down to deal with their correspondence, and the chairman had to assert himself at frequent intervals to ensure a decent majority. Occasionally there would be a wave of enthusiasm, everybody would jostle everybody else, and the vote by a show of hands would mean a violent agitation of hats and sticks above a seething mass of heads.

It was there, 'on the easel', that the 'Dead Child' eventually appeared. For a whole week Fagerolles, his notebook overflowing, had been engaged in all kinds of complicated bargaining to ensure votes in favour of Claude. But it was uphill work; it clashed with other promises he had made and he met with nothing but refusals whenever he mentioned his friend's name. He complained, too, of getting no assistance from Bongrand, who did not keep a notebook and who was so tactless that he ruined even the best of causes by his ill-timed outbursts of frankness. Fagerolles would already have dropped Claude a score of times if he had not firmly

made up his mind to test his strength in obtaining an
acceptance which was generally considered impossible. He
wanted to prove that, if need be, he could force the Committee's hand. Perhaps, too, deep down in his conscience,
he had heard a call for justice and was aware of a certain
lurking respect for the man whose talent he was plundering.

On that particular day Mazel was not in the best of
tempers. To begin with, the foreman had come running up
with the announcement that:

'Something went wrong yesterday, Monsieur Mazel. An
hors concours was turned down. Number 2530; you know the
one, sir, a naked lady under a tree.'

He was right; the picture in question had been unanim-
ously consigned to the scrap-heap without anybody noticing
it was by an old classical painter, highly esteemed by the
Institut. The idea of such a summary execution and the look
of horror and amazement on the foreman's face produced
some irritating sniggers among the younger members of the
Committee, who looked upon the matter as a priceless joke.
Mazel, on the other hand, strongly resented such incidents,
considering them detrimental to the authority of the École
des Beaux-Arts. With an angry gesture he replied sharply:

'Fish it out again and put it with the accepted ones,'
adding 'There was an unbearable row going on yesterday,
anyhow. How anyone can judge like this, at the gallop, I
really don't know, if I can't even guarantee silence!'

And he rang the bell furiously.

'We are ready to start, gentlemen!' he called. 'Your kind
attention, if you please!'

Unfortunately, no sooner had the first group of pictures
been set up than something else went wrong. One of the
pictures struck him as being particularly bad and so harsh
in its colouring that it set his teeth on edge. As his sight
was failing he bent down to look at the signature, muttering
as he did so:

'Who the devil produced this monstrosity?'

He was so shattered to read the signature of one of his
own friends, another bastion of the holy doctrines, that he

straightened up at once and, hoping that no one had heard his previous remark, exclaimed:

'Beautiful! . . . A number one for this, gentlemen. Do you agree?'

So the picture was granted a 'number one', giving it the right to be hung on the line. Mazel was pained, however, and his temper did not improve when he saw his colleagues laughing and nudging each other as they voted.

They were all in the same position, really; many of them said exactly what they thought at their first glimpse of a picture and then had to eat their words when they deciphered the signature; so that after a time they learnt to be tactful and craned forward to cast a wary eye on the signature before expressing an opinion. Now, whenever a friend's canvas or some doubtful effort by a member of the Committee was under review, they took the precaution of making signs behind the back of the artist in question, meaning 'Be careful! Mind your step! It's his!'

In spite of the tense atmosphere, Fagerolles won a first victory over an abominable portrait by one of his very wealthy pupils whose family had entertained him on several occasions. It had meant taking Mazel on one side and trying to soften his heart by a touching story about a wretched father of three little girls starving to death; but the chairman was not easily moved. If you're starving to death, you give up painting, he argued. You don't drag three young girls down with you like this. Nevertheless, he and Fagerolles were the only ones who raised their hands in favour of the portrait. There were protests, and feelings ran high; even two Members of the Institut were up in arms about it, until Fagerolles whispered to them that he had done it for Mazel's sake.

'He begged me to vote for it,' he said. 'It's by a relative, I believe. Anyhow, he wants it accepted.'

Immediately the two Academicians put up their hands and were followed by a large majority.

Jeers, laughter, cries of indignation greeted the next picture placed on the easel. It was the 'Dead Child'. What would they send in next, the Morgue? The younger members made jokes about the size of the head; it looked like a monkey that had choked on a pumpkin, they said. The older members simply recoiled in horror.

Fagerolles felt at once there was no hope. He started by trying to be smart and to jolly them into voting for it.

'Come along now, gentlemen. An old stalwart, you know. . . .'

He was interrupted by a burst of angry exclamations. No! Not that fellow! They knew him of old. He was a crank; he'd been pestering them for the last fifteen years, fancied himself a genius, talked about making a clean sweep of the Salon, but had never been able to submit an acceptable picture! There was all the hatred of unbridled originality, of the potentially successful rival, of invincible strength triumphant even in defeat, behind their shouts and exclamtions, all meaning 'Out with him! We don't want him!'

Then Fagerolles made the mistake of becoming cross himself, giving way to anger at the realization of how little real influence he had.

'You're not being fair!' cried Fagerolles. 'You might at least try to be fair!'

That brought the matter to a climax. He was surrounded, jostled, threatened, a target for a volley of pointed remarks.

'You're a disgrace to the Committee!'

'You're only defending *that* to get your name in the papers!'

'You're not competent to judge!'

Fagerolles was so angry that his powers of repartee deserted him. The only reply he could muster was: 'I'm just as competent as you!'

'Not you!' came the quick retort from one little painter with a scathing tongue and a head of yellow hair. 'So don't think you can palm your duds off on us!'

'Hear, hear!' was heard on all sides. So was the word 'dud', repeated with great conviction, though it was usually applied only to the lowest dregs of their rejects and the flat, insipid daubs produced by the most obvious amateurs.

'Very well,' said Fagerolles, clenching his teeth, 'I call for a vote.'

Ever since the argument had taken a more violent turn Mazel had been ringing his little bell for all he was worth, and his face had flushed with anger at seeing his authority so flouted.

'Come, come, gentlemen!' he kept saying. 'There should be no need for me to have to shout! Gentlemen, I ask you. . . .'

At last he managed to obtain a moment's silence. Fundamentally he was not an unkind man. Why shouldn't he accept this little picture, he asked himself, even though he *did* think it was unspeakably bad? Plenty of others got accepted, so why not this one?

'Gentlemen, a vote has been called for,' he announced, and was just wondering whether to raise his hand when Bongrand, who so far had not said a word, though he was very red in the face through trying to contain himself, suddenly and unexpectedly gave way to his outraged conscience and cried:

'Why, for God's sake, there are scarcely four men in this room who are capable of turning out a piece like this!'

The only response was a sort of general snarl; the blow had been struck home so smartly that no one could find a reply.

Mazel, much paler now, repeated curtly: 'Gentlemen, a vote has been called for.'

But the tone of his voice was enough to indicate the latent hatred and the merciless rivalry that could lie behind jovial handshakes. It was rare for quarrels to reach such violence as this one. Generally they were quickly patched up, though beneath the surface outraged vanity was often left with wounds that never healed and creeping death was often hidden by a smile.

Bongrand's and Fagerolles's were the only hands raised in favour, so the 'Dead Child' was rejected, and its only remaining chance of being accepted was the final revision.

The final revision was a wearisome task. Although, after meeting daily for three weeks, the Committee granted themselves two days' rest to enable the attendants to put the pictures in order, they always shuddered the afternoon they found themselves dropped in the midst of three thousand rejected pictures out of which they had to pick sufficient to bring up the total number of accepted works to the regulation two thousand five hundred. Three thousand pictures set out side by side all around the exhibition rooms and even in the outer gallery—everywhere, in fact, even on the floor, where they lay in stagnant pools separated by tiny pathways running between their frames. They were like a flood rising higher and higher till it filled the Palais de l'Industrie and finally submerged it beneath the dirty waters of all the madness and mediocrity that painting ever produced! And they had one single session, six desperate hours, from one to seven, in which to tear through this baffling maze of canvas. For a time they managed to keep fatigue at bay and their vision clear, but the forced march soon took the strength out of their legs and the flicker of colours irritated their eyes. Still they had to go on, walking, looking, judging till they were ready to drop. From four o'clock onwards they were a disorderly rabble, a conquered army in retreat, with some of the stragglers left breathless far away in the rear, while individuals here and there found themselves marooned on the little pathways between the frames on the ground and wandered helplessly about without any possible hope of ever finding their way out.

In such circumstances how could they expect to be fair? What could they possibly salvage from such a heap of horrors? All they could do was to pick out at random a portrait or a landscape—did it matter which?—until they had made up the requisite number. Two hundred. Two hundred and forty. Still eight short. Eight more wanted. Which? This one? No, that. Whichever you like. Seven, eight, and that's the lot! They had finished at last, and now they could hobble away in safety, free men!

Another scene had held them up for a time in one of the rooms, around the 'Dead Child' which was lying on the floor with all the other jetsam. This time they treated it as a joke. One of them pretended to stumble over the frame and put his foot through the canvas, others walked all round it pretending to see which was the right side up and then swore it looked better upside-down. Fagerolles, too, joined in the fun.

'Don't be shy, gentlemen, don't be shy! What am I bid now? . . . Take a look at it, gentlemen, handle it, examine it, and you'll see you're getting your money's worth. . . . Now, please, my kind gentlemen, think again! Do your good deed for the day and take it off my hands!'

Everybody laughed at the joke, but there was a harsh note of cruelty in their laughter that made it plain their answer was 'Never!'

'Why don't you take it yourself for your "charity"?' somebody asked.

It was a custom that each member of the Committee should have a 'charity', that is, the right to pick any canvas, however bad, which was then accepted without question. Usually this was done as a kind of gesture towards artists who were known to be poor, and the forty pictures thus picked out at the last moment were like the starving beggars who were allowed to slip in and pick up the crumbs of the banquet.

'For my "charity"?' Fagerolles repeated blankly in embarrassment. 'But I've already got a "charity" . . . a flower-piece . . . by a lady I . . .'

Hecklers broke in at once with 'Really! Is she pretty?' and facetious remarks, which were anything but gentlemanly, were made about the lady's painting. Fagerolles did not know what to do, for the lady in question was one of Irma's protégées, and he was already trembling at the thought of the scene there would be if he failed to keep his promise. Then he suddenly thought of a way out.

'What about you, Bongrand?' he said. 'Can't you take that funny little dead child for *your* "charity"?'

Heartbroken and disgusted by the shameless trafficking, Bongrand flung both arms in the air and cried:

'I, insult a genuine artist! What do you take me for? . . . No! Let him learn a bit more self-respect, for God's sake, and never send another blasted thing to the Salon!'

So, since the others were still sniggering, Fagerolles, determined to have the last word, put on his boldest front and shouted, as if the last thing he was afraid of was being compromised:

'That settles it! I'll take it!'

He was greeted with cheers, sarcastic applause, mocking salutes, and handshakes of congratulation. Hail to the hero who had the courage of his convictions! Meanwhile an attendant picked up the canvas that had been the object of so many jeers, so much manhandling, so much mud-slinging, and carried it away. Thus was the picture by the painter of 'Open Air' accepted by the Salon Selection Committee.

The following morning a couple of lines from Fagerolles broke the news to Claude that he had managed to get the 'Dead Child' accepted, though not without a certain difficulty. Claude's delight on receiving the good tidings was not, however, entirely unalloyed. There was something about the curtness of the note, its tone of condescension, even of pity, that made the whole affair sound unbearably humiliating. For a moment he was so unhappy about his victory that he would willingly have withdrawn his picture and hidden it away. Then gradually his sensitiveness wore off and he felt his artist's pride grow weaker and weaker with his growing yearning for the success which had been so long in coming. Now, after all, it was practically here, so what else mattered? And as the last vestige of his pride fell away he began to look forward to the opening of the Salon with all the feverish impatience of a novice, living in a dream-world where wave after wave of seething humanity hailed his picture as a masterpiece.

With the passage of years it had become established in Paris that 'varnishing day', originally reserved for artists to put the last finishing touches to their pictures, was an important date in the social calendar. Now it was one of those acknowledged 'events' for which the whole town turned out in full force. For a whole week beforehand artists monopolized both the press and the public. They fascinated Paris and Paris focused all its interest on them, their pictures, their sayings and doings and everything else about them, in one of those sudden, violent, irrepressible crazes that sent swarms of trippers and soldiers and nursemaids elbowing their way through the place on 'free' days, and accounted for the startling figure of fifty thousand visitors on certain fine Sundays when the main army of sightseers was followed by an ignorant goggle-eyed rabble filing through what was, for it, just a glorified print-shop.

At first Claude felt rather afraid of the famous 'varnishing day'. He did not like the idea of the fashionable crowd he had heard so much about and thought he would wait for the more democratic opening-day proper. He even turned down Sandoz's offer to go with him. Then, when the day came, his excitement reached such a pitch that he suddenly changed his mind and was ready to go by eight o'clock in the morning, almost before he had given himself time to gulp down a bit of bread and cheese. As he was leaving, Christine, who felt she had not the courage to go with him, called him back to give him one more kiss and say to him anxiously:

'Darling, whatever happens, don't be downhearted.'

Claude was quite out of breath when he reached the central hall of the exhibition, and his heart was pounding in his breast as he hurried up the grand staircase. Outside the sky was cloudless; here the May sunshine was filtered through the awning stretched beneath the glass roof into smooth, white daylight, while through the doorways that opened on to the garden balcony came refreshing wafts of cool, damp air, for the atmosphere indoors was already beginning to feel heavy, and the faint odour of varnish was still discernible through the discreet musk worn by the ladies.

As he stood still for a moment to get his breath Claude cast an eye round the pictures on the walls. Straight in front of him was an immense massacre scene, streaming with red, flanked on the left by some colossal but insipid saint or other, and on the right a commonplace illustration of some official ceremony commissioned by the State; then, round the rest of the walls, portraits, landscapes, interiors, all looking violently acid in the gilt of their brand-new frames. But his persistent fear of the notoriously select public for this great social occasion drew his attention back to the crowd, now growing visibly every minute. The circular seat with the greenery in the middle that stood in the centre of the room was entirely occupied by three female monsters, all abominably dressed, already settled in for a good day's scandal-mongering. Behind him a husky voice grinding out a sequence of harsh noises turned out to be an Englishman in a check jacket explaining the massacre scene to a jaundiced-looking wife swathed in an enormous dust-coat. The room was not yet too crowded to allow small groups to form, break up and then re-form again a little farther away. Everybody was looking up; the men carrying walking-sticks and overcoats, the women moving gently along and turning half round when they stopped to look at the pictures. As a painter Claude was struck by the flowers on their hats which looked particularly garish against the surrounding waves of shiny black toppers. He noticed three priests and, most unexpectedly, a couple of private soldiers among the endless files of gentlemen wearing decoration ribbons and the processions of mothers and daughters which kept holding up the traffic. Many of the visitors knew each other, so there were many exchanges of smiles and nods and hasty handshakes as they met and passed on. Tones were hushed, however, and the voices were drowned by the ceaseless tramp of feet.

When Claude started out in search of his picture he tried to locate it by taking the rooms in alphabetical order, but he made a mistake and began with the rooms on the left. As all the doorways opened ahead of each other he was faced with a long vista of antique tapestry hangings broken only by a corner of an occasional picture. He went all the way down it as far as the great West room and returned by the rooms on the other side without even finding the one that corresponded to his own initial letter. By the time he had reached his starting-point again the crowd had grown and circulation was already noticeably restricted. This gave him time to look about him again and now he recognized a number of painters, all of them doing the honours of the house, for today, after all, was *their* day.

One young man, an old acquaintance from the Boutin days, obviously eaten up with a desire for publicity and determined to get himself a medal, was very busy roping in visitors who were likely to have any influence and almost dragging them to look at his pictures. Then there was the wealthy celebrity, a smile of triumph on his lips, holding a reception against a background of his own works, and being ostentatiously gracious to the ladies who flocked to pay court in an endless procession. He noticed rivals who he knew hated each other exchanging loud-voiced compliments; diffident ones hanging round the doorways watching their friends being congratulated; shy ones who would not for the world have gone into the room where their pictures were hung; others cracking a joke to hide their great disappointment; earnest ones completely absorbed, going round trying to make sense of everything and forecasting which would be the medallists. Artists' families were there in force too; a charming young mother with her baby, all dainty and beribboned; a sour-faced, ultra-respectable mamma, flanked by a pair of ugly daughters wearing black; a big blousy body resting on a bench with a tribe of snotty-nosed youngsters clambering over her; a middle-aged lady, with still some claim to beauty, her grown-up daughter by her side, smiling calmly at each other as they passed a lady of the town, the father's mistress. The models were there, too, dragging each other round to look at pictures of themselves in the nude, talking at the tops of their voices and all deplorably dressed, distorting their magnificent figures in dresses that made them look like hunchbacks compared with the well-turned-out Parisian dolls who would have had nothing to show once their clothes were removed.

When at last Claude managed to force his way through the crowd he made for the rooms on the right of the central hall. His letter was on that side, but he went round all the sections marked 'L' and found nothing. Perhaps, he thought, his picture had been misplaced, or used to fill up some small gap in another room. So, as he had now reached the great East room, he ventured into the suite of little rooms which runs behind the bigger and busier ones, where pictures seem to darken out of sheer boredom, and which all painters regard as one of the terrors of the Salon. There again his search was unrewarded. Bewildered, on the point of despair, he wandered out on to the garden balcony and continued his quest there, where the overflow from the inside rooms was accommodated and looked very pale and chilly in the broad light of day.

In the end his peregrinations brought him back a third time to the central hall. This time he found it packed with a swaying mass composed of all that was famous, rich, or fashionable in Paris, including everyone with any claim to being a 'big noise'—talent, millions or good looks, being a leading novelist, playwright, or journalist, or being well-known in clubland, on the turf or on the Stock Exchange—the whole freely sprinkled with women of all ranks, prostitutes, actresses, and society matrons. His temper frayed by his fruitless wanderings, Claude was surprised by the general vulgarity of faces seen like this, in the mass, by the uneven standard of the fashions which ran more to dowdiness than elegance, and by the complete absence of any form of dignity, with the result that his fear of high society gave way to contempt. Were these the people, he asked himself, who were going to scoff at his picture, if ever they found it? Nearby two little flaxen-haired reporters were busy compiling lists of celebrities present; a critic was pretending to make notes in the margin of his catalogue; another was airing his views in the middle of a group of amateurs; a third, his hands clasped behind his back, stood completely detached in front of each picture, majestically refusing to let himself be in any way impressed.

What struck Claude most was the general herd-like movement of the crowd, its mass curiosity devoid of all youth and enthusiasm, its harsh voices and drawn faces, the universal air of pained malevolence. Envy was clearly at work already—in the gentleman making skittish remarks to the ladies, in the man who, without saying a word, gave a terrific shrug of the shoulders and turned away, in the two people who spent a quarter of an hour huddled together over one little picture, whispering like a couple of grim conspirators.

Fagerolles had just arrived. Immediately he became the centre of interest first of one group then another, shaking hands all round, apparently being everywhere at once, putting his whole heart and soul into playing the double rôle of budding celebrity and influential Committee-man. Bombarded with congratulations, thanks, requests, he responded to them all with perfect composure, though ever since early morning he had been hounded by all the minor painters of his connection who thought their pictures badly placed. It was the usual opening-day rout, with everybody looking for his own picture and running round to see everyone else's, bursting with resentment, and with voices raised in furious and apparently unending complaints—they were hung too high, the light was bad, their effect was killed by the pictures on either side, they had a good mind to remove their pictures altogether. One lanky young man was specially persistent and followed Fagerolles wherever he went, in spite of the latter's vain endeavour to explain that what had happened was not his fault and that he could do nothing about it. The pictures were hung, he explained, according to a numbered list; the exhibition panels were laid out on the floor and the pictures arranged on them before they were attached to the wall, and nobody's was given preference. He even went so far as to promise to lodge a complaint when the rooms were reorganized after the medals were awarded, but did not satisfy the lanky young man, to whose badgering powers there seemed to be no limit.

Claude was just on the point of breaking his way through the crowd to ask Fagerolles what had happened to his picture when a flash of pride stopped him. Fagerolles was so much in demand, and besides it was both foolish and humiliating to be perpetually dependent on somebody else. It struck him, too, at that moment that he must have missed one whole series of rooms on the right of the hall, as indeed he had, for when he went into them he discovered a host of other pictures. He ended up in a room filled with people milling in front of a huge canvas that filled the place of honour in the centre. It was impossible at first to see the picture itself over the heaving mass of shoulders, the mighty wall of heads and the battlement of hats, for it had caused a stampede of panting admirers. By standing well on the tips of his toes, however, he did at last manage to get a glimpse of the wonderful work; he recognized the subject at once remembering what he had already heard about it.

It was Fagerolles's picture 'The Lunch Party', on which Claude saw at once the stamp of his own 'Open Air'. The light effect was the same, the theory behind it was the same, but toned down, faked, warped to produce a skin-deep elegance, cleverly arranged to satisfy the taste of an untutored public. Fagerolles had not made the mistake of posing his three women naked, but he had none the less managed to make them look undressed in their daring, fashionable clothes. The bosom of one of them was perfectly visible through the fine lace of her bodice; another one was showing her right leg up to the knee as she stretched backward to pick up a plate, and the third, while she did not reveal even a square inch of bare flesh, was encased in a gown so clinging that there was something alarmingly indecent about the way it made her hindquarters reminiscent of a fine, sleek mare. Their two gentlemen companions were the very acme of distinction in their smart sports jackets. In the background a manservant was lifting another hamper from the carriage drawn up under the trees. Everything—figures, materials, the still-life study of the food—stood out in the full sunlight against the darker background of trees and greenery; but the supreme touch of smartness lay in the artist's brazen assumption of originality, the false pretences on which he bullied his public just enough to send it into ecstasies. It was like a storm in a jug of cream.

As he could get no closer to the picture, Claude listened to what was being said about it. Here at last was somebody who could make reality look real! He didn't pile it on like those heavy-handed moderns; he could get everything out of nothing. There were nuances for you! . . . the fine art of suggestion . . . respect for the public . . . and such delicacy, such charm, such wit! He's not the kind to let himself go in for a lot of incongruous, high-flown bravura pieces, or to let his creative power run away with him. No, if he noted three points from nature, he produced three points, no more, no less. One columnist who happened to be there went off into raptures and then found just the words for the occasion: 'truly Parisian painting'. The expression caught on and after that nobody thought of looking at the picture without saying that it was 'truly Parisian'.

The thought of all the admiration rising from the sea of rounded shoulders and craning necks so exasperated Claude that he felt he must see what sort of faces go to make a triumph. So he worked his way round the fringes of the crowd until he was able to stand with his back to the picture. There he had the public in front of him, in the greyish light that filtered through the sun-blind, leaving the centre of the room dim, while the bright daylight that escaped round the edges of the blind fell sheer on the pictures on the walls, putting the warmth of sunshine into the gilt of the frames. As soon as he saw the faces, Claude recognized the people who had once laughed his own picture to scorn; at least, if it was not the very same people, it must have been their brothers, now in serious mood, enraptured, graced by their air of respectful attention. The malignant looks, the marks of overstrain and envy, drawn features, and bilious colouring he had noted earlier were all softened and relaxed in the communal enjoyment of a piece of amiable deception. Two very stout ladies he saw simply gaping in beatitude, and several old gentlemen narrowing their eyes and trying to look wise. There was a husband quietly explaining the subject to his young wife, who kept tilting her chin with a very graceful movement of the neck. There was admiration on every face, though the expression varied; some looked blissful, others surprised or thoughtful or gay or even austere; many faces wore an unconscious smile, many heads were plainly swimming in ecstasy. The shiny black toppers were all tipped backwards, and the flowers on the women's hats all drooped well down towards their shoulders, while all the faces, after a momentary halt, were pushed along and replaced by others in a never-ending stream, and all exactly the same.

Bemused by the passing of the triumphal rout, Claude forgot his own quest for a time. The room meanwhile was getting too small for the crowds of visitors who still kept piling in in greater and greater numbers. There were no little isolated groups now, as there had been earlier in the day, no breath of cool air from the garden, no lingering odour of varnish; the air was hot and the atmosphere soured by perfume which soon gave way to a predominating smell of wet dog. It was evidently raining outside, a sudden spring shower it seemed, for the latest arrivals were very wet, and their heavy garments soon began to steam in the heat of the room. Patches of darkness had been crossing the sun-blind overhead for some time, and as Claude looked up he imagined great rain-clouds scudding across the windswept sky and deluges of rain beating on the skylights in the roof. The walls, too, were mottled with floating shadows and the pictures grew more and more dim, while the crowd itself was lost in darkness until the cloud had passed. Then Claude saw all the faces emerge from the dusk, all round-eyed and open-mouthed with the same idiotic rapture.

There was yet another bitter shock in store for him. On the left-hand panel, paired with Fagerolles's picture, was Bongrand's painting. But in front of it there was no crush, merely a passing stream of indifferent visitors; and yet it was Bongrand's mightiest effort, the blow he had been longing to strike for years, one last great work conceived in his desire to prove that his virility was still unimpaired. His pent-up hatred for the 'Village Wedding', his first master-piece, which had been allowed to overshadow all the rest of his career, had at last impelled him to produce a directly contrasting subject, a 'Village Funeral', showing a young girl's funeral procession straggling through fields of oats and rye. It was to be his reaction against himself, his proof that he was not played out and that his experience at sixty was as good as the happy vigour of his early years. But experience had lost the day and his work was proving a dreary failure, one of those quiet, old man's failures, which do not even catch the visitors' eye. It was not without its masterly touches, however, such as the little chorister with the Cross, the Children of Mary carrying the bier, their white frocks and ruddy countenances making a lively contrast with the stodgy Sunday black of the rest of the procession against the background of green fields. But the priest in his surplice, the girl carrying the banner, the dead girl's family, the entire canvas, really, were lifeless creations, rendered ugly by an excess of technique and stiff with the painter's own obstinacy. It was an unconscious but inevitable return to the tormented romanticism from which the artist's early work had developed, and therefore the saddest part of the whole story; for the cause of the public's indifference lay in the painting itself. It belonged to an older generation, it was too static, too dull in colouring to catch the eye now that dazzling sunlight had come into fashion.

At that moment Bongrand himself came into the room, as shy and hesitant as any unfledged novice, and Claude's heart ached to see the way he glanced first at his own neglected picture, then at Fagerolles's, the centre of a riot. At that moment he must have been acutely aware that, as a painter, he was finished. Hitherto the gnawing fear of slow decay had been nothing more than a doubt; now, all at once, it had become a certitude; he knew he had outlived himself, his genius was dead, he would never beget another living work. He turned very pale and was just turning to make his escape when Chambouvard the sculptor, with his usual train of disciples, came in at the opposite door and called across to him in his thick, booming voice, ignoring the roomful of people:

'Aha, you old rascal! Caught you red-handed this time, admiring your own work!'

His own contribution that year was an abominable 'Harvester', one of those stupid, unconvincing female figures that his powerful hands managed to turn out so unexpectedly. He was nevertheless beaming with satisfaction, convinced he had produced another master work, and so eagerly parading his godlike infallibility in front of the crowd that he did not hear the laughter he provoked.

Bongrand made no reply; he simply looked at him, his eyes burning with emotion.

'What do you think of my effort downstairs?' Chambouvard ran on. 'You've seen it, I expect. . . . These young things have a lot to learn yet! We're still the only ones who count, you know, the Old School!' he added, as he moved on, still followed by his train and bowing to the crowd as he went.

'Swine!' Bongrand muttered to himself, choking with grief and as revolted as if he had witnessed some thoughtless boor bursting in on the peaceful sanctity of a death-chamber.

On noticing Claude he went over to him. It was cowardly, after all, to retreat, so he decided to show his courage and to prove that his mind, as always, was above envy.

'Friend Fagerolles appears to be a success!' he said. 'I should be lying if I went into ecstasies over his picture, because I don't think much of it, but Fagerolles is a nice fellow. . . . By the way, he was damned decent about you. . . . Did his absolute utmost for you.'

Claude made a point of saying something complimentary about the 'Funeral'.

'The little graveyard in the background is beautifully done,' he said. 'How people can possibly . . .'

Bongrand stopped him.

'No condolences, please, my lad,' he said in a harsh voice. 'I'm not blind.'

As he spoke someone acknowledged the pair of them with a familiar gesture, and Claude at once recognized Naudet, looking bigger and showier than ever now that he was making a success of handling big business. Ambition had gone to his head and he talked glibly of sweeping every other art-dealer out of the market. He had built himself a palace where he had set up as king of the art world, running a vast clearing-house for painting and opening a number of great modern galleries. That there were millions in the offing was obvious the moment one crossed his threshold. He organized exhibitions under his own roof as well as in galleries in town, and annually, in May, he awaited the arrival of American collectors to whom he sold for fifty thousand what he himself had bought for ten. He lived like a prince, complete with wife, children, mistress, horses, estates in Picardy, and hunting-lodge. He had begun to make his money when works by dead masters such as Courbet, Millet and Rousseau, who had been neglected during their lifetime, began to fetch high prices, with the result that he now despised all works signed by artists who were still in the thick of the fight. But already there were a number of ugly rumours abroad. The number of known canvases was limited, as was also in some degree the number of possible collectors, so the time was not far off when business would not be so easy. There was even talk of a syndicate and an agreement with certain bankers to keep up the high prices. At the Salle Drouot they were having to resort to faked sales, the dealer buying back his own stock at very high prices. Bankruptcy seemed to be the inevitable conclusion to all this speculation and outrageous jobbery.

'Ah, good morning,' said Naudet to Bongrand. 'So you've come, like everyone else, to admire my Fagerolles.'

His attitude to Bongrand had changed; he was no longer respectful, humble, ingratiating as he had been in the past. He talked of Fagerolles, too, as if he owned him, as if he were simply a hired labourer who needed perpetual chivvying. It was he who had installed Fagerolles in the Avenue de Villiers, forced him to have an expensive establishment flashily furnished, and run him into debt buying carpets and *objets d'art*, in order to have him at his mercy ever afterwards. Now he was beginning to accuse him of being heedless and of compromising himself. This picture now—a serious artist would never have sent it to the Salon. Oh, of course, it caused its bit of a stir, and there was some talk of giving it the *médaille d'honneur*; but nothing could be worse for keeping up prices. When you wanted the American market you had to learn to stay quietly at home, like a god in his holy of holies.

'Believe me, my dear Bongrand,' Naudet continued, 'I would rather have given twenty thousand francs out of my own pocket than have those idiotic newspapers make such a to-do about this year's Fagerolles.'

Bongrand, listening bravely, in spite of his suffering, smiled.

'Perhaps they *have* been rather too indiscreet,' he said. 'Why only yesterday I read somewhere that Fagerolles eats two boiled eggs every morning!'

He was poking fun at the sudden outburst of publicity which, for the past week, as a result of an article published before his picture had been exhibited, had been giving Paris its fill of the youthful celebrity. Every available reporter had been pressed into the campaign, and they had practically stripped him naked, telling everything there was to tell about his childhood, his father the art zinc manufacturer, his schooling, where he lived, how he lived, the colour of his socks, and his trick of pinching the tip of his nose. He was the rage of the moment, the very painter the public wanted, since he had been lucky enough just to miss the Prix de Rome and to break with the Beaux-Arts while retaining its methods. His good fortune would be a short-lived affair, brought by the wind, the passing whim of a nerve-racked city; and his success, hinged on half-measures and false courage, the accident which staggers the public in the morning but by evening is recounted with indifference.

Naudet had noticed the 'Village Funeral'.

'So this is your picture, is it?' he said. 'You've been wanting to match the "Wedding", I see. . . . If you'd asked me, I'd have advised you against it. . . . Ah, the "Wedding", that was a picture!'

Still listening, still smiling, though with a painful twist about his trembling lips, Bongrand forgot all his own masterpieces and his own assured claim to immortality, thinking only of the immediate, effortless success coming to this young whipper-snapper, who was not even worthy of cleaning his palette, and pushing him, Bongrand, into oblivion, he who had had to struggle for ten years to gain recognition! If they only knew, these younger generations, when they make up their minds to bury you, what tears of blood they make you shed in death!

As he was slow in answering, he was afraid he might have given some hint of his suffering. He was surely not going to give way to jealousy; he had not yet sunk so low? The way to die was standing on one's own feet, he reminded himself angrily, so he pulled himself together and instead of the violent answer he had ready on the tip of his tongue, he said quietly:

'You're quite right, Naudet. It's a pity I had nothing better to do the day I thought of painting that picture.'

'Ah, there he is! Excuse me!' cried Naudet, and turned tail.

'He' was Fagerolles, who had just appeared in the doorway. He did not come into the room, but stopped discreetly on the threshold, smiling, bearing his good fortune with characteristic ease. He was looking for someone and eventually motioned to a young man to whom he wished to speak. The news he had to impart was evidently good, for the young man positively overflowed with gratitude. Two other young men rushed up to Fagerolles to congratulate him; a woman detained him for a moment, to point out, with a martyred expression, a still life hanging in a particularly dark corner. Then he disappeared after casting one solitary glance at the crowd in ecstasies in front of his picture.

Claude, who had been taking everything in, felt sorrow welling up in his heart. The throng was increasing every minute and there he was gazing into a lot of staring faces, all damp with perspiration in the now unbearable heat. Between him and the door stood a rising mass of heads and shoulders, and in the doorway itself all the people who could not see the picture eagerly pointed to where it hung with their umbrellas still streaming with rain from the storm outside. Bongrand never stirred; he was too proud to go but stood firm, taking his defeat as an old soldier should, looking thankless Paris squarely in the face, determined that his end should be worthy of his courage and his all-embracing human kindness. Claude, as he received no answer when he spoke to him, realized at once that from behind the calm, cheerful face the soul had fled, stricken with grief, tortured with unspeakable pain; so, filled with awe and respect, he said no more but slipped away without Bongrand even noticing he had gone.

Claude had yielded, too, to the impulse of another idea that had come to him as he watched the crowd go by. He had been unable to understand why he had not found his own picture, but surely the answer was a simple one. There must be one room in the place where people were laughing and joking and jostling each other to scoff at some particular picture. If there was, that picture was sure to be his. He could still hear the laughter at the 'Salon des Refusés', after all those years. So now he began to listen at every doorway for jeers as an indication of his picture's whereabouts.

Back again in the great East room, the death-chamber of art on a grand scale, where they dump all the outsize canvases of clammy, gloomy, historical, and religious subjects, a sudden shock brought him to a standstill. He had been through this room twice already, but wasn't that his picture up there? It was; but it was hung so very high up that he could barely recognize it, it looked so tiny, clinging like a swallow to the corner of a frame, the huge ornamental frame of a tremendous canvas ten metres long representing the Flood, a seething mass of yellow people struggling in a dark red sea. On the left hung yet another depressing full-length portrait of yet another pale-grey general, and on the right a nymph of colossal proportions in a moonlit landscape, like the bloodless corpse of a murder victim lying putrefying on the grass, while all around, above, below and on every side, were pink effects, mauve effects, a variety of sorry visions, even a comic scene of monks getting drunk in their monastery, and an 'Opening of the Chamber of Deputies' with a long screed on a gilded scroll and a line reproduction of the Deputies' heads, each one carefully labelled. And there, high up among all its sickly-looking neighbours, the little canvas, so much bolder in treatment than all the rest, stood out in violent contrast, like a monster grinning in pain.

So that was the 'Dead Child', poor little thing! Hanging where it did it was just a confused mass, like the carcass of some shapeless creature cast up by the tide, while the abnormally large head might have been any white, swollen object, a skull or even a bloated belly, and the wizened hands on the shroud looked like the curled-up claws of a bird that has died of cold. The bed, too, was a sorry mass of white upon white, pale limbs on pale sheets, one cancelling out the other, the bitter end! In time, however, it was possible to distinguish the light, glassy eyes and to recognize a child's head, a pitiful case of some dread disease of the brain.

Claude moved first in one direction, then the other, to get a better view, for the light was so bad that the canvas was one mass of reflections. Poor little Jacques! They'd placed him very badly, probably out of contempt, but more likely out of shame and the desire to be rid of his baleful ugliness. But Claude saw him differently; he remembered him away in the country, all fresh and rosy, rolling on the grass, then in the Rue de Douai, pale-faced and rather dull-witted, and then in the Rue Tourlaque, unable to lift his head, dying one night all alone, while his mother slept on at his side. Claude thought of her, too, the mother of his child, who had stayed at home with her sorrow, to weep most likely, for now she would often weep the whole day through. Perhaps she had been wise, after all, not to come; it might have been more than she could bear to see their poor little Jacques, already cold in his bed, cast aside like a pariah and so harshly treated by the light that his face looked contorted in a horrible grimacing laugh.

Claude suffered even more deeply to see his work ignored. Surprised and disappointed, he looked about him for the crowd, the throng he had expected, and wondered why there was no one there to scoff. The jeers, the insults, the indignation he had had to hear in the past, though painful at the time, had given him a zest for life. Where were they now? This time there was nobody even to spit and pass on. It was death. Obviously bored, visitors tended to file hastily through the great room, where the only picture that tempted them to linger was the 'Opening of the Chamber of Deputies', which was never without its small group reading the inscription and picking out the various Deputies. Hearing someone laughing behind him Claude turned to look, only to discover that the cause of the merriment was the picture of the monks on the spree, the humorous picture of the year which some gentlemen were describing to their fair companions as 'brilliantly witty'. But everybody passed beneath little Jacques without even looking up, for not a single person realized he was there!

Claude's only hope seemed to be two gentlemen, one fat, one thin, both wearing decorations, sitting well back on the upholstered seat in the middle of the room, looking up at the pictures and talking very earnestly. He went and stood near them to listen.

'Well, I followed them,' the fat one was saying, 'down the Rue Saint-Honoré, along the Rue Saint-Roch and the Rue de la Chaussée d'Antin, then up the Rue Lafayette. . . . '

'You spoke to them, I suppose,' said the thin one, deeply interested.

'No, I didn't. I was so afraid of losing my temper.'

Claude moved away again, but on three occasions he listened with bated breath when the odd visitor stopped and looked up towards the ceiling; for he had a morbid desire to hear some remark about his picture, however brief. Without criticism, what was the use of exhibiting? How was one to know what people thought? He would have preferred anything to this terrible torture of silence. He was beginning to find it utterly unbearable when he saw a young couple approaching, a pleasant-looking husband with a small blond moustache and a ravishing wife as frail and delicate as a Dresden china shepherdess. It was she who saw the picture and, finding she could make no sense of it, asked her husband for the title. When the husband had gone through the catalogue and discovered it was entitled 'Dead Child', she was horrified, and seizing him by the arm dragged him away, exclaiming:

'How dreadful! The police ought to forbid that sort of thing!'

So Claude was left staring transfixed, oblivious of the milling herd around him which ignored the one sacred object he alone could see. It was there, with everybody elbowing their way round him, that he was discovered by Sandoz.

Sandoz, too, was alone; his wife had stayed at home with his mother, who was unwell. He had just stopped to look at the little picture, which he had only discovered by accident, and his heart had been wrung as he thought how disgustingly pointless life can seem to be. In a flash he lived through all their youth again, the school at Plassans, the long escapades on the banks of the Viorne, their carefree rambles in the blazing sun, and all the burning enthusiasm of their earliest ambitions. He recalled, too, how they had all worked together in later life, their certainty of victory, their insatiable hunger for success and the feeling that they could swallow Paris in one mouthful. How often, in those days, had he seen Claude as the great man, the man whose unbridled genius would leave the talents of all the rest of them far, far behind! He remembered the studio on the Quai de Bourbon, the mighty canvases they dreamed of, the projects that were going to 'shatter the Louvre', their untiring struggles, working ten hours a day, giving themselves body and soul to their art. And all to what purpose? After twenty years of passionate striving, this; this mean, sinister little object, universally ignored, isolated like a leper, a melancholy, heart-breaking sight! All the hopes, all the sufferings of a whole lifetime spent on the arduous task of bringing into the world what? This, this, this! Oh God!

Finding Claude standing quite close to him, Sandoz spoke, and there was a quiver of brotherly emotion in his voice.

'So you came after all,' he said. 'What made you refuse to call for me?'

Claude offered no excuse. He seemed very tired and incapable of any strong reaction, as if he were ready to drop gently off to sleep.

'Come now,' Sandoz continued. 'Don't stay here. It's after twelve, so come and lunch with me. I'm expected at Ledoyen's, but we'll forget about that. Come along down to the buffet and see if that'll rejuvenate us a bit!'

Linking his arm warmly through Claude's, Sandoz led him away, doing his utmost to draw him out of his gloomy silence.

'Look here, old friend,' he said, 'what the hell is the good of being down in the mouth? Maybe they have hung your picture too high, but that doesn't prevent it from being a damned fine bit of painting! . . . Oh, I know, you'd expected something different, but you're not dead yet, and where there's life there's hope. Besides, you've every reason to be proud, come to that. The Salon's *your* victory this year. Fagerolles isn't the only one to plagiarize you, far from it! They're all doing it. They all got a good laugh out of "Open Air", but it nevertheless caused a revolution! Look around you. Look, there's another "Open Air", and there's another and another, the whole Salon's "Open Air"!' he cried, pointing first to one picture, then another, as they walked through the exhibition.

He was right; broad daylight, after gradually filtering into contemporary painting, had at last come into its own. The old Salon with its grim, dark-coloured pictures had given place to a Salon full of bright spring sunshine. The dawn of this new day had first begun to break all those years ago at the 'Salon des Refusés'; now it was spreading rapidly, putting new life into painting, filling it with light subtly diffused and decomposed into nuances without number. On every side the famous blue tone was manifest, even in portraits and in the historical scenes which are really glorified genre pictures. The old-style academic subjects had disappeared with the dreary academic colouring, as if the rejected doctrine had taken with it all its ghostly personifications, imaginary beings and events, the cadaverous nudes of pagan and Catholic mythology, the legends not founded on faith, the anecdotes not founded on fact—in short, all the Beaux-Arts bric-à-brac worn threadbare by generations of painters, brainless and unscrupulous alike, was gradually disappearing, and even among the die-hards, both young and old, the influence was obvious: the light of day had dawned. Even from a distance it was plain to see. On every side there were pictures that were like holes in the wall, open windows on the world outside. It would not be long before the walls themselves crumbled and made way for nature itself; the breach was already wide, routine had gone down before the lively onslaught made by youth and daring.

'You'll come into your own yet, old fellow,' Sandoz went on. 'You're bound to. The art of the future is going to be your art. These chaps are where they are now because you've *made* them.'

Claude opened his mouth at last and muttered dourly:

'What the hell's the use of having "made" them, if I haven't "made" myself? . . . You know as well as I do it was too much for me, and that's just what I can't stomach.'

A despairing gesture was enough to indicate his train of thought—his inability to be the genius of his own artistic creed, his frustration at being the forerunner who sows the idea but cannot reap the glory, his despair at seeing himself robbed and despoiled by a gang of slapdash painters, a swarm of facile daubers without any conception of concerted action, who were simply cheapening the new art before he or anybody else had had the strength to produce the masterpiece that would be a landmark in contemporary painting.

Sandoz did not agree. The future was still before them, he said. Then, to distract him, he stopped him as they were crossing the central hall.

'Look at that woman in blue standing in front of that portrait,' he said. 'That's a fine slap in the face for painting!

. . . Do you remember how we used to watch the Salon public in the old days, the clothes they wore, the way they behaved? There wasn't a picture in the place that would bear the comparison. The pictures today stand up to it better. In one landscape I just noticed over there, there was much more life in the yellow tone-values than there was in the women who were going up to look at it.'

Claude winced; his suffering was beyond words.

'Let's go,' he said. 'Take me out, Pierre, will you? I can't stand any more.'

Down in the buffet they had the greatest difficulty in finding a table. The place was stifling, packed with people, like a great gloomy cave made of brown serge hung between the girders that supported the metal floor above. At the far end, half-hidden in the darkness, three sideboards were set out with dishes of fruit, all symmetrically arranged, while to right and left were two counters, each presided over by a lady, one dark, the other fair, who kept an eagle eye on the jostling crowd beyond. Out of the murky depths of the great dark cavern there rose a stream of little marble tables and a boiling tide of chairs, all tightly packed and hopelessly entangled, which filled the cave itself and flooded into the garden and the daylight provided by the thick glass roof.

Noticing some people preparing to leave, Sandoz pounced upon their table and took it by force.

'Got it, thank God!' he said, gasping. 'Now, what are you going to eat?'

Claude indicated that he had no preference, and it was perhaps fortunate, for the lunch was anything but good; the trout was soggy, the roast beef over-cooked, the asparagus tasted of wet rag. They had to fight for service, too, as the waiters, over-worked and flustered, kept finding themselves held up and unable to reach their tables because chairs were being pushed farther and farther back until the gangways, which were too narrow in any circumstances, were completely blocked. From behind the draperies on the left came a deafening clatter of pots, pans, and crockery, for that was where the kitchens had been rigged up, on sand, like the open-air kitchens on a fairground.

Sandoz and Claude had to sit sideways to eat, squashed between two parties of people whose elbows practically met over their plates, while every time a waiter came by he gave their chairs a violent jerk with his hip. But everyone took the discomfort and the abominable food as part of a huge joke, and a free and easy atmosphere was soon established among the company as it made an otherwise unhappy situation into a pleasure party. Strangers rapidly struck up acquaintance; people carried on loud conversations with friends three tables away, talking over their shoulders, and making gestures over their neighbours' heads. The women were specially animated. The throng had intimidated them at first, but now they were taking off their gloves and turning up their veils and laughing gaily after their first glass of wine. It was this promiscuity, this rubbing of shoulders between people of all classes, good women, bad women, great artists, and obvious failures that gave 'varnishing day' an added spice, a chance assembly, a mixing-together of people that was at once unpredictable and faintly improper, and which brought a glint even to the most respectable eye.

Sandoz, meanwhile, had decided he could not finish his meat, so he shouted to Claude through the general hubbub:

'Like a bit of cheese? . . . And how about some coffee?'

But Claude did not hear. He was gazing dreamily down the garden. From where he was sitting he could see the central group of tall palms against a background of brown draperies, surrounded by a wide circle of statues. He could see the back and shapely rump of a female faun; the dainty profile of a young girl, the curve of her cheek, the tip of her firm little breast; a full-face view of a Gallic warrior in bronze, a colossal piece of sentimentality and mindless patriotism; the milk-white body of a woman suspended by her wrists, some Andromeda or other from the Place Pigalle; and beyond all those, statues and still more statues, rows and rows of shoulders and hips lining every pathway, flights of white forms among the luscious greenery, heads and bosoms, legs and arms all irrevocably mingled in the receding perspective. To the left, stretching far away into the distance, was a row of bosoms, a ravishing sight; while nothing could have been more amusing than one extraordinary series of noses, starting with a priest's enormous pointed nose and followed by a maidservant with a little turned-up nose, a Quattrocento Italian lady with a magnificent Roman nose, a sailor with a nose that was sheer fantasy, and a host of other noses, the judge's nose, the magnate's nose, the gentleman-with-a-decoration's nose, an endless row of noses, not one of them moving.

But all Claude really saw was just a series of light grey patches in a vague green light, for his stupor persisted. He was aware of one thing, however, and that was the richness of the dresses. He had misjudged them in the rush and bustle of the picture galleries. Here in the garden they could be seen to as great advantage as if they were in some spacious conservatory. All the elegance in Paris was there, the women had come to show off their clothes and the clothes had been carefully chosen with one eye on tomorrow's newspaper reports. One well-known actress attracted a great deal of attention as she swept round the garden like a queen, on the arm of a gentleman friend whose obliging air made him the perfect prince consort, while Society women, got up like ladies of the town, deliberately undressed each other with a look, totting up the cost of the silks, measuring up the lace, taking stock of everything from the toes of each other's dainty boots to the tips of the feathers in their hats. Some of them had drawn their chairs together and settled down as if they were in the Tuileries watching the fashion parade. Two friends went hurrying by, talking and laughing, while one woman kept walking to and fro in silent, solitary gloom. Others, who had been separated in the crowd, were overjoyed to find each other again. The less vividly clad masculine element moved around in a succession of stops and starts, congregating around a marble statue, dispersing in front of a bronze; and, although there was a faint sprinkling of nonentities, the crowd was made up largely of men with some claim to Parisian celebrity. Famous names were on everyone's lips; a particularly illustrious one heralded the approach of a large, badly-dressed gentleman, and the name of a fashionable poet marked the passage through the crowd of a man with a face as pale and expressionless as a door-keeper's.

Lively though it was, there was a certain sameness about this stream of fashion and celebrity imparted by the carefully filtered daylight. But suddenly, as the sun came out from behind the clouds, flamed on the skylights, lighted up the splendour of the stained-glass and filled the air with a shower of golden light, everything seemed warmer, the snow-white statues, the bright green of the freshly-cut lawns, the yellow-sanded pathways, the dresses with their highlights of satin and pearls, and even the voices seemed to change from a vast self-conscious murmur to the brisk, spontaneous crackle of burning twigs. The gardeners, who were finishing laying out the flower-beds, turned on the sprinklers and busied themselves with watering-cans, and a faint steam rose from the turf as they passed. Meanwhile one solitary sparrow, bolder than the rest, came down from the forest of girders in the roof, in spite of the crowd, to forage in the sand around the buffet, and kept one young lady amused for a long time by picking up the crumbs she scattered for it.

All that reached Claude's ear was still the roar like an ocean overhead made by the public milling through the picture-galleries, and he remembered a similar occasion, and the gusts of laughter, like a mighty hurricane, that swept round a picture of his. This time, however, there was no laughter, but all Paris breathing aloud its approval of a picture by Fagerolles.

Sandoz, who had been looking round at the latest arrivals, suddenly turned to Claude and announced: 'There's Fagerolles.'

Fagerolles and Jory, without noticing the other two, had just settled down at a nearby table. Jory was just saying in his usual loud voice:

'Yes, I've seen that dead kid of his. The poor bugger. What a way to end up!'

Fagerolles replied with a violent dig in the ribs, whereupon Jory, as soon as he saw the others, carried straight on with:

'Well, if it isn't old Claude! . . . How's things? . . . I haven't seen that picture of yours yet, but they tell me it's a marvel.'

'An absolute marvel!' put in Fagerolles, before expressing his surprise at finding them at the buffet.

'You haven't really lunched here, have you?' he said. 'It's so notoriously bad. We've just been to Ledoyen's . . . a bit of a crush, but very good fun! . . . Why not push up your table and let's get together.'

So the two tables were pushed together, though Fagerolles in his triumph was already besieged by flatterers and petitioners. Three young men several tables away stood up and gave him a noisy reception. A woman stopped and gazed at him in smiling contemplation after her husband had whispered his name in her ear, while the long lanky artist who was badly placed and had been dogging his footsteps ever since he arrived, left his table to come over and continue his request to be put 'on the line' immediately.

'Oh, for God's sake leave me alone!' snapped Fagerolles, who by this time had come to the end of both amiability and patience. Then, when his tormentor had retreated muttering veiled threats, he added:

'It's hopeless trying to be kind-hearted all the time; they'd drive you crazy in the end. . . . They all want to be "on the line", as if the whole place could be "line". . . . It's a thankless job being on the Committee, you can take my word for that. You can't please everybody, so all you get out of it is a lot of enemies!'

Claude stared at him blankly, then, though apparently still half asleep, he mumbled:

'I did write to you, and I intended to call and thank you. . . . Bongrand told me what a hard time you'd had. . . . It was good of you, and I'm grateful. . . . '

'Grateful! Don't mention it,' Fagerolles broke in. 'It was for old times' sake. *I*'m the one who ought to be grateful for the pleasure of doing something for *you*.'

His old embarrassment returned, as it always did now in the presence of the unacknowledged master of his youth, and he was overcome by an irrepressible feeling of humility as he talked to the one man whose silent disdain at this particular moment was enough to take the pleasure out of his success.

'First-rate, that picture of yours,' added Claude slowly, determined to let himself be neither jealous nor discouraged.

That simple word of praise released in the heart of Fagerolles an emotion so keen and so inexplicable in one so hardened and self-centred that his voice trembled as he answered:

'Thanks, old chap. It's nice of you to say that, it really is.'

Sandoz by this time had acquired two cups of coffee, but as the waiter had forgotten the sugar he had to be satisfied with the odd lumps left by a party on a neighbouring table. There were fewer people now, but the atmosphere was all the more relaxed in consequence. One woman laughed out so loud that everybody turned to look at her. Most of the men were smoking and a fine blue haze hung over the crumpled, wine-stained tablecloths cluttered with dirty crockery. After Fagerolles had managed to obtain a couple of Chartreuses, he settled down to talk with Sandoz, whom he regarded as a person to be reckoned with and handled carefully in consequence. Jory meanwhile turned to Claude, who had sunk back into his gloomy silence.

'By the way, I never wrote to tell you I was married, did I?' he said. 'We kept it very quiet—just the two of us—on account of circumstances. . . . Still, I *did* intend to let you know. . . . Forgive me for not doing it.'

Jory proved very expansive and gave a detailed account of his doings largely because it satisfied his egoism to feel himself well fed and successful in front of a wretched failure. He had given up his newspaper work when he realized it was time to take life seriously and had raised himself to the status of editor of a big art review, a post which, it was said, brought him in some thirty thousand francs a year, plus what he made by some obscure traffic in connection with the sale of art collections. The middle-class acquisitiveness, inherited from his father, which had urged him to speculate in secret and on a very modest scale as soon as he was earning his own living, he now indulged to the full, with the result that he was becoming notorious for bleeding white any artist or collector who fell into his hands.

Seeing his financial position fully assured, the all-powerful Mathilde, after proudly refusing him for six whole months, had now brought him to the point of begging her, with tears in his eyes, to be his wife.

'When you've got to live together,' he went on, 'it's best to regularize the situation, isn't it? You ought to know, since you've gone through it yourself. . . . And, do you know, she didn't want to do it, really! She was scared people might misinterpret her motives and that she might in some way injure my career. . . . Oh, she's a fine, sensible woman, Mathilde! . . . You've no idea what a splendid woman she is; very devoted to me she is, a wonderful housekeeper, very canny, and her advice is always worth listening to. Oh, I was a lucky man the day I met Mathilde! I never do a thing now without asking her advice; she has a completely free hand, and, believe me, she makes good use of it!'

The truth was that Mathilde had reduced him to the state of a small boy who is too afraid to be disobedient and is kept on his best behaviour simply by the threat to deprive him of jam. A domineering, grasping, ambitious wife, deter-mined to command respect at all costs, had evolved from the lascivious ghoul of the old days. She was even faithful to him and, apart from some of the old practices which she now reserved for him alone and through which she had firmly established her power in the household, as sour and straight-laced as any genuinely virtuous woman. They were even said to have been seen at Communion together at Notre-Dame de Lorette. They kissed each other in public and called each other all kinds of pet names, but every evening he had to account for both his time and his money. If one single hour looked dubious or if he did not produce the last centime of the day's takings, she took care that he spent such an appalling night, threatening him with all kinds of dread diseases, religiously repelling all his advances, that he paid for her forgiveness more dearly every time he transgressed.

'So we waited till my father died,' said Jory, thoroughly enjoying his own story, 'and then I married her.'

All the time Jory had been talking Claude's mind had been far away, though he had kept nodding assent as if he was listening. The only words he really heard were the last ones.

'What!' he said. 'You've married her? . . . Mathilde?'

His last exclamation was full, not only of amazement, but of memories of Mahoudeau's studio. He recalled the revolting epithets Jory used to apply to Mathilde and the things he had told him one morning, in the street somewhere, about the disgusting orgies in the room behind the little shop that reeked of herbs and spices. The whole gang had had her at some time or other, and Jory had always referred to her in fouler language than any of the others. Now he'd married her! Obviously, thought Claude, a man must be a fool to speak ill of any mistress, however much she deserved it, for he never knew whether he might not marry her one day after all.

'Yes, Mathilde,' Jory answered with a smile. 'Nobody makes a better wife than an old mistress, they say. I think they're right, don't you?'

His mind was clearly at peace, his memory stone dead, for he showed not the slightest sign of embarrassment in front of his friends. She might have been a total stranger he was introducing to them for the first time, and not a woman they had all known as intimately as he. When the

conversation dropped, Sandoz, who had been following it
with one ear, since he was particularly interested in their
remarkable case, exclaimed:

'What about a move? . . . I'm stiff with sitting.'

As he was speaking Irma Bécot appeared. She was looking
radiantly beautiful, with her hair freshly tinted to make the
most of the tawny-haired Renaissance courtesan effect she
always cultivated. Her dress was a tunic of pale blue brocade
over a satin skirt covered with Alençon lace of such priceless
beauty that she was escorted by a kind of bodyguard of
admirers.

When she caught sight of Claude she hesitated, feeling
ashamed and even rather afraid to claim acquaintance
with such an ill-clad, ugly, dejected-looking wretch. Then,
with the courage of her old caprice, she went up and, to the
round-eyed amazement of her punctilious escort, shook hands
with him first. Laughing, though not unkindly, but with just
a hint of friendly mockery tightening the corners of her mouth,
she said to him gaily: 'No ill feelings,' then laughed again to
think that he and she were the only ones who understood the
full import of her words. It was their whole history in brief,
the story of the young man she had had to take by force and
who had not liked it!

Fagerolles was already paying for the two Chartreuses and
preparing to join forces with Irma when Jory decided to do
the same, so Claude was left watching the three of them—
Irma with a man on either side—move away through the
crowd, admired and greeted like royalty.

'Mathilde's restraining influence seems to have slipped,'
said Sandoz quietly. 'But think of the clip on the ear he'll
find waiting for him when he gets home!'

He asked for the bill, for by this time all the tables were
being cleared and there was little left on them but the
littered remains of bones and bread-crusts. Two waiters
were already washing down the marble table-tops, while a
third, armed with a rake, was engaged in scratching up the
surface of the sand into which scraps of food and globs of
spittle had been trodden. From behind the brown serge

draperies where the staff were now at lunch came sounds as of hearty chewing, laughter from mouths stuffed with food, and appreciative smacking of lips, all suggestive of a camp of gypsies mopping up the remains of a feast.

As Claude and Sandoz were on their way round the garden they came across a statue by Mahoudeau, very badly placed, in a corner near the East vestibule. It was his upright figure of a woman bathing, but scaled down to the proportions of a girl of ten or so: a charming, elegant little thing with slender thighs and tiny breasts and a gesture of hesitation which gave her all the exquisite delicacy of a ripening bud. It had atmosphere and that peculiar hardy and tenacious grace which is not acquired, but which springs up and flourishes where it will, in this case in the clumsy fingers of a workman so ignorant of his capabilities that for years he had remained unaware of its existence.

Sandoz could not repress a smile.

'To think,' he said, 'that a chap like that has done so much to spoil his own talent. . . . If his work weren't so badly placed, he'd be a roaring success.'

'He certainly would,' said Claude. 'That's a lovely bit of work.'

As they were talking they saw Mahoudeau himself, just inside the entrance hall, making for the staircase. They called out and hurried to meet him, and the three of them stood talking for several minutes. Standing in the long, empty ground-floor gallery, newly sanded, lighted by great round windows, was rather like standing under a railway bridge. It was built of steel girders supported by heavy metal pillars, and there was a perpetual icy blast from above which helped to make the ground damp and soggy underfoot. At the far end, behind an old, ragged curtain, were rows of statues, the rejects from the sculpture section, plaster casts which some of the poorer artists did not trouble to fetch away; the whole effect was of a sadly neglected, dirty-white morgue. The most surprising thing, however, was the ceaseless din overhead made by the public tramping through the galleries upstairs. At times it was deafening; it went on and on as if endless trains running at full speed were rattling over the network of girders.

When the others had congratulated him, Mahoudeau told Claude he had looked in vain for his picture and asked him where the devil they had stuck it. Then he began to enquire after Gagnière and Dubuche and to sentimentalize about the old days: the way they used to invade the Salon in a body, stalking provocatively through the rooms as if they were enemy territory, scorning everything, then talking their heads off in violent discussions afterwards! Nobody ever saw Dubuche these days. Two or three times a month Gagnière rushed in from Melun for a concert, but he had so lost interest in painting that he had not even come in for the Salon, although, as he had done for the last fifteen years, he had sent in his customary landscape: the banks of the Seine, very pleasantly grey and conscientious and so very discreet that no one had even noticed it.

'I was just going upstairs,' said Mahoudeau. 'Do you feel like coming with me?'

Claude, deathly pale, kept looking up towards the terrible roar of tramping feet, the passing of the monstrous, all-devouring mob, for he could feel it beating in his very bones. He said nothing, but held out his hand.

'You're not leaving us?' cried Sandoz. 'Come round with us again, then we'll all leave together.'

Then, seeing him so weary, he felt sorry for him, realizing that his courage had run out and that all he wanted now was to be alone, to hide his wounds in solitude; so he said:

'Goodbye, then, old chap. . . . I'll be round to see you tomorrow.'

Claude staggered away, pursued by the thunder from above, and was soon lost to sight in the garden.

Two hours later, after losing Mahoudeau and finding him again in the company of Jory and Fagerolles, Sandoz discovered Claude in the East room standing gazing at his own picture, exactly as he had found him the first time. The poor wretch, instead of going home, had been unable to help himself and had wandered back to the place, obsessed.

The sweltering five o'clock crush was at its height, for by this time the mob was worn out and dizzy with doing the round of the galleries and beginning to panic and jostle like cattle making futile attempts to find the way out of a pen. The early morning chill had gone, and the heat of human bodies and the smell of human breath had made the atmosphere thick with a brownish-yellow vapour, while fine dust kept rising up from the floor like mist to join the exhalations from the human stable. Occasional visitors would still stop to look at the pictures, though only for the sake of the subjects now; but in general people were either simply wandering aimlessly about or marking time where they stood. The women, in particular, were proving obstinate, refusing to budge until the last moment when the attendants would usher them out on the stroke of six. A number of the stouter ladies had been driven to find seats, while others, having failed in their quest for somewhere to sit down, bravely propped themselves up on their sunshades, exhausted but undaunted, and keeping a keen or suppliant eye on the closely packed benches. Not a head in all those thousands but was throbbing with the last symptoms of fatigue: legs turned to water, features drawn, forehead splitting with headache, that brand of headache peculiar to Salons, brought on by perpetually staring upwards at a blinding conglomeration of colours.

The only persons who were apparently unaffected were the two gentlemen wearing decorations who were still on the same seat where they had been in earnest converse since midday, and still leagues removed from their immediate surroundings. They might have moved in the meantime and returned, but they might just as easily never have stirred.

'So you went straight in,' the fat one was saying, 'as if you noticed nothing amiss?'

'Exactly,' the thin one answered. 'I looked straight at them and raised my hat. . . . What else could I do?'

'Amazing! Absolutely amazing!'

All Claude could hear was the gentle beat of his own heart; all he could see was his own picture away up near the ceiling. He stood there fascinated, unable to take his eyes off it, as if he were nailed to the spot and without the will-power to tear himself away. The jaded crowd swept round him unheeded, trod on his toes, jostled him, carried him along. Like some inanimate thing, he offered no resist- ance, but let himself float and always found himself back in the same place, still with his head in the air, unaware of what was going on down below, living only away up there with his work and his child, his poor, bloated little Jacques. Two great tears hovered on his eyelids, blurring his vision, but he still stared on, as if he could never see too much of him.

His heart wrung with pity, Sandoz pretended not to see his old friend, as if he thought it wiser to leave him in solitude, lamenting at the tomb of his fruitless life. As in the old days, the gang was going around again, this time together, Fagerolles and Jory leading; but when Mahoudeau asked him where Claude's picture was Sandoz lied, drew his attention to something else and so got him out of the room.

That evening all Christine could get out of Claude was a few brief remarks; everything was all right, the public had taken it very well, the picture made a good show, hung a little on the high side, perhaps. But in spite of his deliber- ately cool, collected manner, he seemed strange, and she was afraid.

After dinner, coming back from taking some plates into the kitchen, she found he had left the table. One of the windows looked out on to a piece of waste land; he had opened it and was leaning so far out that at first she did not see him. Then, terrified, she rushed up and dragged him in by his coat tail.

'Claude!' she cried. 'Claude! What are you doing?'

He turned to face her, white as a sheet, his eyes blazing like a madman's.

'Just looking,' he answered.

With trembling hands she closed the window, but the shock had been so great that she lay awake the whole night long.

CHAPTER 11

THE following day Claude was back at work again. The days flowed by and the whole summer passed in sluggish tranquillity. He found himself a job, doing small flower paintings for the English market, which brought in enough to keep the two of them; but all his spare time he devoted to his big canvas. His fits of anger and frustration now seemed to be a thing of the past, and he appeared calmly resigned to his endless task, to which he applied himself with great determination though with little hope of success. There was still a strange, mad look in his eyes, though the light in them seemed to die out whenever he contemplated his abortive master work.

About this time, too, a great sorrow overshadowed Sandoz's life. His mother died, and his whole mode of life was disturbed. He had grown so used to the three of them sharing their happy intimacy with a few chosen friends. He came to hate their house in the Rue Nollet. But as success suddenly came his way and, after a rather difficult start, his books began to sell, he put his newly acquired wealth to good use and rented a huge apartment in the Rue de Londres, the installation of which kept him occupied for several months. His bereavement and his consequent disgust with things in general brought him and Claude together again. After what he had seen at the Salon, Sandoz had been very anxious about his old friend, for he realized then that his being had split irreparably apart and there was an open wound through which Claude's life was ebbing slowly and imperceptibly away. Then, seeing him so calm and diligent, he began to feel more reassured, though he still paid frequent visits to the Rue Tourlaque, and whenever he happened to find Christine alone he questioned her, for he could see that she, too, was living in dread of something she never dared to put into words. She had that nervous, tortured look of a mother nursing her sick child and trembling lest the slightest sound should mean that death was close at hand.

One July morning when he called, he said to her:

'You must feel much happier now, Christine, now that Claude's really settled down to work again?'

'Oh, yes, he's working again,' she answered, with a glance at the picture, her usual glance, sidelong and full of hatred and dread. 'He wants to get everything else finished before he starts on the woman.'

She still refrained from putting her obsessive fear into words, but she added in a quieter voice:

'His eyes, have you noticed his eyes lately? He's still got that look in them. Oh, he can't take *me* in! I know he's shamming, pretending to be calm and collected. . . . He wants taking out of himself, Pierre, that's what he needs. . . . So please come and fetch him out whenever you can. You're all he has now, so please, please help me.'

After that, Sandoz invented endless reasons for long walks. He would call on Claude early in the morning and drag him away from his work, for he practically always found him firmly settled on his ladder, sitting on it when he was not actually painting. Fits of lassitude often rendered him inactive and sometimes a strange feeling of numbness would so befog his brain that for minutes on end he was quite incapable of wielding his brush. In those moments of silent contemplation there was even a certain religious fervour in his glance as it kept reverting to the female figure which he still left untouched. Aware that his desire was hovering on the brink of blissful death, he deliberately withheld himself from a love so infinitely tender and yet so awe-inspiring, which was bound to cost him his life. Then he would go back to the other figures and the backgrounds, still aware of her presence, his eye so unsteady when it lighted on her that he knew he would avoid losing his head only so long as he never touched her body and she did not take him in her arms.

One evening at Sandoz's, Christine, who was welcomed there now and who never missed a Thursday, hoping it might help to cheer up her ailing grown-up child, took her host on one side and begged him to 'drop in' on them the following morning. So the next day, as he had to go out beyond Montmartre to make some notes for a novel, Sandoz descended on Claude, dragged him away from his work and kept him out the whole day.

They went down to the Porte de Clignancourt, where there was a fairground with roundabouts, shooting galleries, and cafés open all the year round, and suddenly, to their amazement, they found themselves face to face with Chaîne lording it over a large and prosperous-looking booth. It was like a very ornate sort of chapel enshrining a row of four turntables loaded with glass and china ware and all kinds of knick-knacks which flashed like lightning and tinkled like musical glasses when a customer set them spinning and rattling against the pointed feather. There was even a white rabbit, the first prize, on one of them, all decked out with pink ribbons and quivering with fear as it whirled round and round with the crockery. All this wealth was framed in red curtains and draperies, in the midst of which, at the back of the booth, in a kind of holy of holies, hung Chaîne's three masterpieces of painting which followed him round from fair to fair, from one end of Paris to the other: the 'Woman taken in Adultery' in the centre, the copy from Mantegna on the left, and on the right Mahoudeau's stove. At night, when the naphtha flares were lit and the wheels were whirling and sparkling like stars, nothing looked more beautiful than those three paintings against the rich blood red of the draperies; they never failed to draw a crowd.

It was the sight of them in all their splendour that made Claude exclaim:

'Good God, but they're wonderful . . . and perfect for that job!'

The Mantegna especially, with its gaunt simplicity, was rather like a faded print nailed up for the enjoyment of simple folks, while the meticulous, lop-sided rendering of the stove, balanced by the ginger-bread Christ, looked un-expectedly funny.

As soon as he saw his two friends Chaîne greeted them as if they had parted only a matter of hours ago, quite calmly and without any indication that he was either proud or ashamed of his present circumstances. He looked no older but just as leathery as ever; his nose was still lost between his two cheeks, and his uncommunicative mouth hidden in the scrub of his beard.

'Well, well, it's a small world!' said Sandoz cheerfully, ' . . . and those pictures of yours look wonderful up there.'

'Yes, and what do you think about him setting up a Salon of his own like this? Very clever, I call it,' Claude added.

Chaîne's face beamed with delight and he managed to answer:

'Isn't it?'

Then, as his artist's pride was aroused, he forgot his usual grunting monosyllables and even spoke a whole sentence:

'Oh, if I'd had money behind me like you two, I should have made my mark like you have.'

He was convinced of that fact. He had never doubted his own talent; he had simply given up because he could not make a living by it. To produce masterpieces like those in the Louvre, he was positive, was only a matter of time.

'Why worry, anyhow?' said Claude, now serious again. 'You've no cause for regrets, you're the one who's made a success of things. . . . Business is good enough, isn't it?'

There was an undertone of bitterness in Chaîne's mumbled reply. Not a bit of it; nothing was doing well, not even the lucky wheel business. The working-classes had stopped spending their money on that sort of thing so as to have more to spend on drink. You could buy third-rate junk for prizes and work for all you were worth the old trick of slapping the table to prevent the feather stopping at the big ones, but there was only the bare bones of a living in it these days, he said. Then, as there were a number of people in front of the booth, he broke off and startled his friends by suddenly shouting in a voice which they would never otherwise have associated with him:

'Try your luck, ladies and gentlemen, try your luck! Every number guaranteed a winner!'

A man carrying a sickly-looking little girl with big, greedy eyes paid for two goes. The table whirled and rattled, the ornaments flashed as they spun, and the live rabbit, its ears well back, went round and round at such a rate that it lost all semblance of a rabbit and became just a blurred white circle. There was a moment of hideous tension; the little girl nearly won it.

Then, after shaking Chaîne's still trembling hand, the two friends resumed their walk. It was Claude who broke the silence.

'*He*'s happy, anyhow!' he said.

'Happy!' exclaimed Sandoz. 'He thinks he might have got into the Institut, and it's killing him!'

Some time after their encounter with Chaîne, about the middle of August, Sandoz thought it might be amusing to go and spend a whole day in the country. He had met Dubuche not long before and found him very depressed and feeling rather sorry for himself, but very eager to talk about the old days; so, as he was going to be out at 'La Richaudière' for another fortnight with his two children, he had invited his two old friends to go out there to lunch one day. Sandoz therefore suggested that, since Dubuche was so keen to see them both again, they should pay him a surprise visit. But although he insisted that he had sworn not to go without Claude, Claude obstinately refused to go with him. It was as though he were afraid at the thought of seeing Bennecourt again and the Seine and the islands and all the countryside where his years of happiness had died and been buried. It was only after Christine had intervened that he gave way, though very reluctantly. He was going through one of his periods of feverish activity and had worked very late the previous night and was still eager to paint again that morning, which was a Sunday, so he found it almost physically painful to tear himself away. What was the use of going back to the past? he argued. What was dead was dead and didn't exist any more. The only thing that existed now was

Paris, and in Paris only one prospect: the Ile de la Cité, the vision that haunted him always and in all places, the one bit of Paris to which he had lost his heart.

In the train he was still so obviously agitated and stared so ruefully out of the window, as if he were leaving the city for years, watching it gradually recede into the distant haze, that Sandoz, to distract him, started to tell him all he knew about Dubuche's affairs. Delighted to have a medallist for a son-in-law, old Margaillan had begun by taking him everywhere and introducing him as his partner and prospective successor, a young fellow who knew how a business ought to be run and all about cheaper and better building, who had burnt the midnight oil, damn it all, and got his diplomas! Unfortunately, Dubuche's first idea had been a miserable failure. He had invented a brick-kiln and had it built on some of his father-in-law's land in Burgundy, but on such disastrous terms and to such unsatisfactory plans that the whole affair was written off for two hundred thousand francs. After that he turned to building with the idea of trying out some personal theories which would revolutionize the whole art of construction. They were the old theories he had picked up from the revolutionary friends of his youth; they stood for everything he had promised himself he would do when he was free to act upon his own initiative, but they were badly digested and applied with the typical well-intentioned clumsiness of the plodder without a spark of creative faculty. He went in for tiling and terra-cotta decorations, vast constructions of glass and iron, especially iron—iron beams, iron staircases, iron roofs—and since all these materials increase costs, he had ended once more in disaster, and all the more rapidly because he was a hopeless administrator and wealth and advancement had gone to his head and robbed him of all aptitude for work. This time old Margaillan lost all patience, as well he might, since for thirty years he had been buying land, building, re-selling, estimating at a glance for blocks of flats—so many metres at so much a metre, making so many flats at a rent of so much—and there he was saddled with a duffer who underestimated for lime and bricks and grit, put in oak where pine would have done and treated floor space as if it was sacred, afraid of cutting it up into a maximum number of rooms! No wonder he said he was sick of the whole thing and refused to have anything more to do with Art, though up to then he had always had a lurking ambition, being an uneducated man, to introduce what he called 'a touch of Art' into his otherwise routine jobs! From that point relations between the old man and his son-in-law began to deteriorate. They quarrelled violently, one haughtily entrenched behind his superior knowledge, the other crying aloud that a common labourer knew more about building than any new-fangled architect. In the end his millions were in jeopardy, so one fine day Margaillan threw Dubuche out of his office and forbade him ever to set foot there again, telling him he hadn't gumption enough even to manage a couple of men and a boy. That meant the end of Dubuche and a serious come-down for the Beaux-Arts, discredited like that by a glorified mason!

'So what is he doing now?' asked Claude, who had gradually begun to listen to Sandoz's story.

'I don't know; very likely nothing,' Sandoz replied. 'He said he had been very worried about his children's health and that they take up a good deal of his time.'

Pale, scraggy Madame Margaillan had died of consumption; it ran in the family. Since her marriage her daughter Régine had developed a significant cough, and at the moment was taking the waters at Le Mont-Dore. She had not dared to take the children with her, however, for the previous year they had been seriously ill after a season in air that was too strong for their frail constitutions. That explained why the family was so broken up: the mother in Auvergne with just a lady's maid; the grandfather in Paris, back on his big building schemes, keeping his four hundred workmen well in hand and proclaiming his contempt for laziness and incompetence; the father in exile, looking after his boy and girl at 'La Richaudière', interned like an invalid incapacitated in his first engagement in the battle of life. In a burst of confidence, Dubuche had even given Sandoz to understand that, as his wife had nearly died in giving birth to their second child and now fainted at the slightest physical shock, he had decided it was his duty to refrain from all conjugal relations. So even that consolation was denied him.

'A happy marriage,' was Sandoz's quiet summing-up.

It was ten o'clock when the two friends rang the bell at the gate of 'La Richaudière'. They were amazed, when they got inside, for this was their first visit, to see how the grounds were laid out; first, beautifully wooded parkland, then a formal terraced garden worthy of a royal palace, three enormous greenhouses and, most striking of all, a tremendous waterfall, a weird combination of rockery, cement, and water-pipes rigged up at the cost of a small fortune to flatter the pride of the ex-mason's labourer whose property it was. They were even more amazed at the deserted, melancholy aspect of the place, the freshly raked but untrodden paths, the lawns and avenues unfrequented, except by an occasional gardener, the house itself apparently dead, with shutters closed at every window but two and barely open even there.

A footman did condescend to come to the door, however, and ask them their business, but when he discovered they were calling on the master he told them insolently that Monsieur was round the back of the house, at the gymnasium, and then withdrew.

They followed the path indicated and when they came out at one end of a lawn the sight they encountered made them suddenly stop dead. There was Dubuche standing in front of a trapeze holding up his son Gaston, a puny child whose limbs, at ten years old, were still those of a young baby. Near them, in a push-chair waiting her turn, was the little girl, Alice. Alice had been born prematurely, and nature had made such an incomplete job of her that at six she was still unable to walk. Completely absorbed, the father was engaged in exercising the boy's spindly limbs; he swung him to and fro for a moment, then tried to make him pull himself up by his wrists, but in vain. The effort, faint though it was, made the child perspire so much that his father took him away and rolled him in a blanket. The whole scene was enacted in solitary silence beneath a huge sky, a pitiful, heartrending spectacle in such a magnificent setting. Looking up from his task, Dubuche discovered his two friends.

'You here!' he cried, and added, with a disconsolate gesture:

'On a Sunday, and you never let me know!'

He hastened to explain that on Sundays the housemaid always went to Paris, and as she was the only person to whose care he dared entrust his children, Alice and Gaston, it was impossible for him to leave them for a minute.

'I'll bet you were coming to lunch!' he said.

At a beseeching look from Claude, Sandoz quietly answered:

'Oh no! We're just on a flying visit. . . . Claude had to come out this way on business. He used to live at Bennecourt, you remember. As I was with him, we thought we'd include you in our round. Somebody's expecting us, so don't let us put you out.'

After that, much relieved, Dubuche made a show of not hurrying them away. . . . Surely they could spare him an hour or so, for goodness sake! . . . So the three of them stood about and talked. Claude looked at him again and again, surprised to see how he had aged. His round, chubby face had wrinkled and turned a bilious yellow broken by tiny red veins. His hair and moustache were going grey. His whole body seemed to have grown sluggish, and there was bitter weariness in his every gesture. . . . So financial failures were as hard to bear as artistic ones? . . . Voice, eyes, everything about him in his defeat gave away the humiliating state of dependence in which he was having to live: his ruined future perpetually flung in his face; the endless accusations of having contracted for a genius that had never been his and consequently of swindling his wife's family; food, clothing, pocket-money, everything doled out to him as though he were a poor relation they could not decently shake off.

'Don't go yet,' said Dubuche. 'Let me just have another five minutes or so with one of my poor darlings here, then we'll be finished.'

With infinite precaution and as gently as any mother, he took little Alice out of her chair and held her up to the trapeze, laughing and talking baby-talk to give her confidence. For two minutes or so he let her hang on to the bar, to exercise her muscles, but he followed every movement she made with open arms in order to save her from hurting herself if her frail waxen fingers lost their grip and she fell. She had big, pale eyes, and never spoke, but always did as she was told, though the exercise obviously terrified her; she was so pitifully light that she did not even tighten the ropes, like those poor, half-starved little birds that drop off their twigs without even bending them.

When he turned for a second to look at Gaston, Dubuche was horrified to see that the blanket had slipped, leaving the child's legs uncovered.

'Good heavens!' he cried, distractedly. 'He'll catch cold on the grass! What can I do? I can't leave Alice. . . . Gaston, my little one! He always does the same thing, waits till I'm busy with his sister, then . . . Sandoz, please cover him up. . . . That's it! Thanks! Thanks very much! And don't be afraid of folding the blanket well over!'

This was what his fine marriage had done with the flesh of his flesh: produced a pair of helpless half-finished creatures ready to perish like flies at the least puff of wind. He had married a fortune, but all he had got out of it was this: the everlasting grief of seeing his own flesh and blood, embodied in his two pitiable children, fall into decay, and his hopes for the future of his race decline, wither away and rot in the last stages of scrofula and consumption. From a self-centred young man he had become an admirable father, with one great passion burning in his heart, with only one desire: to make his children's life worth living; and for that he struggled every hour of every day, rescuing them every morning, living in fear and dread of losing them by evening.

Now that his own life, through the bitter taunts and insults of his father-in-law and the cheerless days and still more cheerless nights he shared with his unhappy wife, had lost its meaning, his children alone counted, and he was determined, by a miracle of untiring affection, to nurse them into life.

'There, darling, that's enough, isn't it? Oh, you'll be a fine strong girl one day, if we keep it up!' he said to Alice as he carried her back to her chair. Then, refusing all offers of assistance from his friends, he picked up Gaston, still wrapped in his blanket, with one hand, and pushed Alice's chair with the other.

'Thanks,' he said to Claude and Sandoz, 'but I'm quite used to it. Poor little things, they're not very heavy. . . . And you can never really trust servants.'

At the house, Claude and Sandoz saw the insolent footman again and noticed that Dubuche himself trembled in his presence, which made it clear that the servants' hall reflected the contempt shown by the father-in-law who paid their wages for the man who married his daughter and whom he treated as a beggar to be tolerated out of charity only. Every time they laid out a clean shirt for him or offered him, when he dared to ask for it, more bread, the servants went out of their way to make him feel they were doing him a favour.

Sandoz found the atmosphere unbearable.

'We must be going,' he said. 'Goodbye, Dubuche.'

'Oh, don't go yet . . . The children are just going to have lunch, then we'll all three come along the road with you. . . . They've got to have their little walk, you see.'

Every day was mapped out, hour by hour, beginning with the morning bath, then physical exercises, followed by lunch, which was quite a complicated affair, as they had to have special food, all carefully chosen and scrupulously weighed. Even the water with a faint dash of wine which they drank with their meal was slightly warmed, lest they should catch a chill if it happened to be too cold. On this particular day they had yolk of eggs beaten up in beef-tea and the eye of a chop cut up by their father into tiny pieces. Lunch was followed by a walk, the walk by afternoon rest.

When the children were ready Dubuche started out with his friends down the broad avenues leading back to the gate; Alice was in her chair again, but Gaston was allowed to walk. It seemed natural, as they walked along, to talk about the grounds, but all the time Dubuche looked as worried and scared as if he were trespassing. He appeared to know nothing about the property or to take any active interest in it. His mind seemed to have become so warped and atrophied through his enforced leisure that he actually had forgotten what he was accused of never having learned: his job as an architect.

'How are your parents keeping?' Sandoz asked, and immediately the light came back into Dubuche's eyes.

'Oh, they're very well and happy,' he answered. 'I bought them a little house, and they're living on the income from some money I settled on them. . . . After all, mother had laid out a lot on my education, so I'd got to pay her back as I'd promised I would. . . . So far as that's concerned, at least, I've given my parents no grounds for complaint.'

At the gate they stood and talked a few moments longer, before Dubuche, looking thoroughly dispirited, took leave of his two visitors. When he shook hands with Claude he said, without any trace of resentment, as if he were stating a simple fact:

'Goodbye. Try to make a go of it. . . . I've made a mess of *my* life.'

And they watched him trudging back towards the house, pushing Alice's chair, supporting Gaston who was already showing signs of fatigue, and looking himself like a weary, round-shouldered old man.

It struck one as Claude and Sandoz, depressed and hungry, hurried down into Bennecourt. There, too, a melancholy reception awaited them, for death had passed that way since their last visit. The Faucheurs, husband and wife, were both in their graves, so was old Poirette, and the inn had fallen into the hands of the feather-brained Mélie.

Everything in it was disgustingly filthy and the lunch they were served was practically inedible; there were hairs in the omelette, the chops were greasy, while the dining-room itself, which opened straight on to the dunghill, was so full of flies that the tables were black with them. The smell, on that blazing August afternoon, was more than they could bear. They did not have it in them to wait for coffee and beat a hasty retreat.

'To think you used to sing the praises of Mother Faucheur's omelettes!' said Sandoz. 'They're a thing of the past now, and no mistake! . . . How about a walk round?'

Claude nearly said no. Ever since they had arrived his one desire had been to get the whole thing over by walking as quickly as possible, as if every step were one step nearer Paris, where he had left his mind and his heart and his soul. He looked neither to right nor left, but forged straight ahead, ignoring the beauty of the trees and the fields, with one idea fixed so firmly in his head that at times he would have sworn he saw the Ile de la Cité rise up and beckon to him across the cornfields. Still, Sandoz's proposal did not fail to arouse certain other memories, so in a moment of weakness he answered:

'Good idea! Let's take a look round.'

But as they walked along beside the Seine he realized, to his sorrow, that he ought to have refused. The place had been altered almost beyond recognition. A bridge had been built to link Bonnières with Bennecourt . . . a bridge, if you please, instead of the old ferry-boat creaking on its chain that used to put just that necessary touch of black on the surface of the stream! To make things worse, there was now a barrage downstream at Port-Villez; the water-level was now so high that most of the islands were submerged and the little backwaters flooded. All the beauty-spots, all the shady retreats swept clean away! It was enough to make one want to murder every engineer on the face of the earth!

'That clump of willows sticking up there on the left, see it? That used to be Le Barreux, the island where we used to go and lie out on the grass and talk, remember? . . . Oh, the vandals!' Claude cried.

Sandoz, too, who could not bear to see a tree cut down without shaking his fist at the woodcutter, was just as livid with fury at the thought of anyone being allowed to treat nature in so ruthless a fashion.

As they drew near his old cottage Claude clenched his teeth and relapsed into silence. It had been sold to some townspeople, who had put up railings and a gate against which he now pressed his face. The rosebushes were dead, so were the apricot trees, but the garden was very neatly and tidily laid out, with little paths and little flower and vegetable beds bordered with box, all reflected in a huge ball of silvered glass set up in their midst on a pedestal. The cottage itself had been freshly distempered, and the corners and the door and window surrounds painted to imitate stonework, giving it a blatant, ostentatious, over-dressed look which irritated Claude beyond words. Everything about it that could have reminded him of Christine, their great love, and their happy early years had gone. To make absolutely sure, he went up behind the cottage to look for the little oak wood and the shady spot that had known the thrill of their first embrace. Like the rest, the little wood was dead, cut down, sold, burnt as firewood. When Claude saw this, restraint gave way to emotion. Cursing the whole world with a gesture, he poured out his sorrow to the lovely countryside he had found so changed, swept clear of every vestige of their former happiness. So a few years were enough to blot out the places where a man had worked and loved and suffered! Why, then, all this fuss about life if, as a man goes through it, the wind behind him sweeps away all traces of his footsteps? He knew that he should never have gone back. The past was but the cemetery of our illusions: one simply stubbed one's toes on the gravestones.

'Let's get away from here!' he cried. 'Come on! Let's get away! It's enough to break anybody's heart, and it isn't worth it!'

When they came to the new bridge Sandoz tried to calm him down by drawing his attention to a motif which had not been there in the old days: the stately sweep of the Seine, now that it was broader and filled its bed to the brim. But Claude refused to be interested. For him the only appeal it had lay in the fact that it was the same water which had streamed past the old wharves of the Cité, and as he leaned over the bridge to look at it he imagined he saw the reflections of the towers of Notre-Dame and the spire of the Sainte-Chapelle in all their glory being carried down the river to the sea.

The two friends missed the three o'clock train and found the two hours' wait a painful burden to bear. They had, fortunately, warned their families that they might return by an evening train if Dubuche kept them after lunch; therefore, as they were not expected at home they decided to dine together at a restaurant in the Place du Havre, hoping to put themselves in a better frame of mind by lingering over their dessert, chatting as they used to do in their bachelor days. It was nearly eight o'clock when they sat down to their meal.

No sooner was Claude outside the station, with his feet on the Paris pavements again, than his nervous agitation disappeared; he felt he was back on his own ground. But he remained cold and aloof in his now customary manner, in spite of Sandoz's attempts to cheer him up by treating him to a flow of lively conversation, rich, savoury food, and heady wines worthy of a lover trying to win round a mistress. Cheerfulness, however, refused to be coaxed, and in the end Sandoz's own gaiety abated. That thankless countryside, the Bennecourt they remembered but which had forgotten them, where they had not found so much as a stone to recall the days they had spent there! It shattered all the hopes of immortality he had ever held. If things, which are everlasting, forget so quickly, how can men be expected to remember even for an hour?

'That's the sort of thing that brings me out in a cold sweat,' he went on. 'Has it ever struck *you* that posterity may not be the fair, impartial judge we like to think it is? We console ourselves for being spurned and rejected by relying on getting a fair deal from the future, just as the faithful put up with abomination on this earth because they firmly believe in another life where everyone shall have his deserts. Suppose the artist's paradise turned out to be as non-existent as the Catholic's, and future generations proved just as misguided as the present one and persisted in liking pretty-pretty dabbling better than honest-to-goodness painting! . . . What a cheat for us all, to have lived like slaves, noses to the grindstone all to no purpose! . . . And it isn't impossible, after all. There are some accepted masterpieces for which I myself wouldn't give a twopenny damn. Classical training has given us a wrong view of everything and forces us to acclaim as geniuses a lot of fellows who are no more than just competent, facile painters, while what we might really prefer is the work of more emancipated but less even artists known only to the initiated few. Immortality at present depends entirely on the average, middle-class mind and is reserved only for the names that have been most forcefully impressed upon us while we were still unable to defend ourselves. . . . Perhaps that's the sort of thing that's best left unsaid. It's certainly the sort of thing that gives me the shudders! How could I possibly have the courage to carry on and stand up to all the mud-slinging if I couldn't console myself with the illusion that one day I shall be accepted and understood?'

Claude, after listening despondently, answered with a gesture of bitter indifference.

'What the hell does it matter, anyway?' he asked. 'The future's as empty as the present, and we're bigger fools than the ones who kill each other for a woman. When the earth falls to dust in space like a withered walnut, our works won't even be a speck among the rest!'

'True enough,' replied Sandoz, now deathly pale. 'So what is the good of trying to fill the void? We *know* there's nothing beyond it, yet we're all too proud to admit it!'

On leaving the restaurant they strolled about the streets and fetched up after a time at a café. There they sat philosophizing and plumbing the depths of sentimental misery in reminiscences of their childhood. It was one o'clock in the morning when they decided it was time to go home.

Then Sandoz talked about going with Claude as far as the Rue Tourlaque. It was a magnificent August night, warm, with a sky thick with stars, and as they were making a detour and going up through the European quarter, they had to pass the old Café Baudequin on the Boulevard des Batignolles. It had changed hands three times since the old days, and the inside had been completely reorganized and redecorated and now sported two billiard tables. As time went by new layers of customers had come and heaped up on top of each other till the old originals were buried beneath them like so many lost tribes. Curiosity, however, mingled with the sentimental attachment for things of the past which they had been reviving all day, sent the pair of them across the boulevard to cast an eye over the café through the wide-open door. They both wanted to see their old table at the far end on the left.

'I say, look there!' said Sandoz in a startled voice.

'Gagnière!' murmured Claude.

And Gagnière it was, sitting all alone at the same table at the far end of the empty café. He must have come in from Melun for one of the Sunday concerts he was so fond of, and then, to kill time afterwards, have wandered up to the Café Baudequin out of sheer force of habit. Not a single one of his old friends ever went there now, but he had gone and sat there, as of old, the solitary witness of an earlier age. He still had not touched his glass of beer, but sat staring at it, so lost in thought that he did not even stir when the waiters began to pile the chairs on the tables all around him ready for the cleaners the following morning.

The two friends hurried away, disturbed by the sight of the vague figure from the past, like children afraid of a ghost. At the Rue Tourlaque they separated.

'Ah, that miserable Dubuche!' said Sandoz as he shook Claude's hand. 'He certainly spoilt the day for us!'

As soon as November came round and all his old friends were back in Paris again, Sandoz planned to get them all together at one of his regular Thursday evening dinner-parties. He had never dropped his 'Thursdays', and they still gave him more pleasure than anything else. His books were selling, he was making money, his flat in the Rue de Londres was nothing short of luxurious in comparison with the little place in the Batignolles; but he himself was still the same.

This time, in his usual kind-hearted way, he meant to take Claude completely out of himself by giving him an evening like the ones he so used to enjoy in his carefree younger days, so he paid particular attention to the invitations. There would be Claude and Christine, of course; Jory and his wife, for now they were married she could hardly be left out; Dubuche, who always came alone, Fagerolles, Mahoudeau, and Gagnière. That would make ten, all belonging to the old gang; not a single outsider, so everyone would feel at home with the rest and enjoy himself.

Henriette, however, was not so certain and hesitated over their list of guests.

'Fagerolles?' she said. 'Do you really think he'll fit in with the others now? They're not quite as fond of him as they used to be, are they? . . . Nor of Claude, what's more. I've noticed a certain coldness . . .'

'A certain coldness!' Sandoz broke in, determined not to agree. 'Women are funny! They never know when a thing's serious and when it isn't! Men can rag each other mercilessly and still remain good friends.'

For this particular Thursday Henriette prepared her menu with the greatest care. She had a small staff now: a cook and butler, and although she no longer did her own cooking she kept an excellent table, out of consideration for her husband, whose only vice was a liking for good food. She accompanied the cook to the markets and went in person to deal with her suppliers. They were both fond of exotic dishes, and on this occasion they decided on oxtail soup, grilled red mullet, fillet of beef with mushrooms, ravioli *à l'italienne*, hazel-hens from Russia and a truffle salad, as well as caviar and kilkis for hors d'œuvre, a praline ice-cream, a little Hungarian cheese, green as an emerald, some fruit and pastries. To drink, simply some decanters of vintage claret, Chambertin with the roast and sparkling Moselle as a change from the same old champagne with the dessert. By seven o'clock they were ready to receive their guests, Sandoz in ordinary morning clothes, Henriette very elegant in a plain black satin dress, for their parties were never formal affairs.

Their drawing-room, which they had been furnishing by slow degrees, was now an amazing array of antiques; furniture, tapestries, ornaments, and bric-à-brac of all periods from all over the world poured into it in an uncontrollable stream which sprang originally from the piece of old Rouen pottery Henriette gave to her husband for one of his birthdays when they lived up in the Batignolles. Now they used to scour the antique-shops together and derived endless pleasure from their purchases. To Sandoz it meant satisfying the desires of his youth, realizing all the romantic ambitions he had gleaned from his early reading. The result was that this notoriously modern writer lived in the now old-fashioned medieval setting which had been his ideal when he was fifteen. He excused himself by saying that fine modern furniture was too expensive, and that you could so easily give a room both colour and character with old things, even though not of the best. He was no collector; all he was interested in was a setting, a striking general effect. And there was no denying that his drawing-room, lit by two old Delft lamps, produced a remarkable over-all effect of soft, warm colouring, compounded of the dull gold of the dalmatics used to upholster the chairs, the yellowing inlays of the Dutch and Italian cabinets, the delicately blended tints in the Oriental hangings, and the hundred and one touches of colour from the ivories, china, and enamels, all softened by the passage of time, contrasting with the neutral, deep red paper on the walls.

Claude and Christine were the first to arrive, Christine wearing her only black silk dress, a poor, threadbare garment she carefully kept in good repair for such special occasions. Henriette immediately took both her hands and drew her over to a settee. She had taken a great liking to Christine and was surprised to see her looking unusually pale, with a restless, anxious look in her eyes; but Christine assured her, when she asked what was the matter, whether she was not feeling well, that she was perfectly happy and very glad she had been able to come. And yet she kept on glancing at Claude as if she wanted to be sure what was going on in his mind. Claude himself appeared very excited, and was much more lively and talkative than he had been for months. Once in a while, however, he would be suddenly calm, would stop talking and gaze wide-eyed into space, as if he was aware of something calling to him from a long way off.

'I finished your book last night, Pierre,' he said to Sandoz, as they stood in front of the great log fire. 'A damned fine piece of work, old fellow! You've shut the critics up this time.'

Sandoz's latest novel had just come out, and although the critics had not yet laid down their arms, it had been one of those resounding successes which make any man proof against the attacks of his adversaries, however persistent. Besides, Sandoz knew perfectly well that even when he had won his battle fighting would break out again every time he published a new book. His *magnum opus*, the series of novels he had planned, was now well advanced, and he was bringing out volume after volume with steady determination, making straight for the goal he had set himself, refusing to let anything, obstacles, calumny, or fatigue stand in his way.

'So you really think they're weakening, do you?' replied Sandoz gaily. 'Well, one of them has certainly committed himself so far as to acknowledge my good intentions, so it does look as if degeneration's set in! . . . But don't worry, they'll make up for it. Some of them I know are too far removed from my way of thinking ever to be able to accept

my literary concepts, my outspoken language, my "physiological men", and the influence of environment . . . and I'm
speaking now of fellow-writers I respect, not of the vulgar
herd of fools and blackguards. There's only one way of
working and being happy at the same time, and that is never
to rely on either good faith or justice. If you want to prove
you're right, you've got to die first.'

Claude's eyes suddenly turned towards one corner of the
room and apparently looked through the wall into space to
where something had beckoned to him. They clouded for a
moment, then they turned back to Sandoz, to whom Claude
replied:

'That's only your way of looking at it. If *I* were to kick
the bucket, I should still be in the wrong. . . . Still, that
book of yours certainly gave me something to think about.
I've been trying to paint all day, but couldn't do a stroke.
It's a good job I can't be jealous of an author; if I could,
you'd lead me a hell of a dance!'

At this point the door was opened and in sailed Mathilde,
followed by Jory. She was handsomely dressed, in a tunic
of nasturtium-coloured velvet over a straw-coloured satin
skirt, diamond ear-rings, and a large spray of roses on her
bosom. Claude, who remembered her as scraggy and wizened, was so surprised that he hardly recognized her, she
had turned into such a fine, buxom blonde. Her disturbingly
vulgar ugliness had blossomed out into a sort of middle-class
comeliness and her mouth, once full of great black gaps,
when she deigned to smile or rather curl up her lip, now
revealed a set of teeth of unexpected whiteness. Obviously,
she had scaled the topmost heights of respectability and her
forty-five years gave her a certain air of authority, since her
husband was so many years her junior that he might have
been her nephew. The only thing she had not lost was her
liking for violent perfumes. She drenched herself with the
most overpowering essences, as if she wanted to drive out
all the aromatic odours that had impregnated her skin when
she lived at the herb-shop. But do what she would, the
bitter tang of rhubarb, the sharp smell of elder, and the

fiery breath of peppermint persisted; and no sooner had she walked across the drawing-room than it was filled with the indefinable odour of a drug-store, corrected by a dash of musk.

Henriette, who had risen to greet her, offered her a chair facing Christine.

'You know each other, of course,' she said. 'You've met here before.'

Mathilde acknowledged Christine by a cold, distant glance at her modest finery, and that was all. Christine had lived in sin for a long time before she was married, so Mathilde had heard, and on that point she had very firm ideas, especially since the broad-mindedness of the artistic and literary world had opened the door of one or two drawing-rooms to her. Henriette thought her unbearable, and resumed her conversation with Christine after a minimum of formalities.

After shaking hands with Sandoz and Claude, Jory joined them in front of the fire and at once began offering apologies to his host for an article that had appeared in his review that morning, severely criticizing Sandoz's novel.

'You know what it's like,' he said. 'Nobody's master in his own house. . . . I ought really to do everything myself, but I haven't got the time! Do you know, I hadn't actually read that article; I printed it on trust, so you can imagine my fury when I read it through just now. . . . I can't say how sorry I am. . . .'

'Don't worry about that,' said Sandoz quietly. 'It's the sort of thing that was bound to happen. Since my enemies are beginning to sing my praises, there are only my friends left to run me down!'

The door half opened again, and this time Gagnière stepped in very unobtrusively, like some vague, colourless wraith. He had come straight in from Melun, alone, for he kept his wife strictly to himself. When he came in to dinner like this he always brought the dust of the provinces in on his boots and carried it away again when he went to catch the night train. Otherwise he was practically unchanged; he seemed to grow younger and blonder as the years went by.

'Ah! Here's Gagnière!' cried Sandoz, and while Gagnière was busy greeting the ladies Mahoudeau made his entry. His hair was quite white now, and his shy-looking face was heavily lined, though there was still something childlike in his flickering eyes. He still wore his trousers too short and his jacket too tight across the back, in spite of all the money he was making; for the dealer he worked for had put on the market some charming statuettes of his which were now a familiar sight on drawing-room mantelpieces and side-tables.

Sandoz and Claude turned away from the fire, eager to witness the meeting of Mahoudeau and Mathilde and Jory. But everything went off very simply. Mahoudeau was just on the point of making a respectful bow when Jory, with his typical blissful ignorance, decided it was his duty to introduce them, which he did, for what was probably the twentieth time.

'My wife, old fellow! Shake hands now, the pair of you!'

And with all the gravity of two well-bred people who find themselves hustled into rather rapid familiarity, Mathilde and Mahoudeau shook hands. But as soon as the latter had gone through all the motions that were expected of him, he went over to join Gagnière in one corner of the room, and the pair of them were soon smirking quietly together as they recalled, in no uncertain terms, the orgies of the herb-shop days. She'd got some new teeth now, eh? It was a good job she couldn't bite in the old days!

The party was still waiting for Dubuche, who had faith-fully promised he would come.

'There are only going to be nine of us, not ten,' Henriette explained. 'We had a note from Fagerolles this morning, saying he was sorry, but he had an official banquet to attend at very short notice. . . . He's going to try to get away and look in about eleven.'

At that moment a telegram was brought in. It was from Dubuche: 'Sorry impossible come. Worried Alice's cough.'

'Ah well, that makes us eight,' said Henriette, with the vexed resignation of a hostess who sees her guests falling away one by one.

So when the manservant opened the dining-room door and announced that dinner was served, she added:

'Well, we're all here. . . . Claude, may I take your arm?' and led in her guests.

Sandoz took in Mathilde and Jory Christine, while Mahoudeau and Gagnière brought up the rear, still making crude jokes about what they called '*la belle* Mathilde's upholstery'.

After the discreetly shaded drawing-room, they found the big dining-room ablaze with lights. The old-fashioned plates hanging all round the walls were as gay and cheerful as brightly coloured prints, while the two dressers, one for glass, the other for silver, sparkled like jewellers' show-cases. Under the huge chandelier in the middle of the room the table, too, was one flickering mass of light and colour, all thrown into high relief by the spotless whiteness of the cloth—the cutlery, in orderly array between the hand-painted plates, the cut glass, the red and white decanters, the hors d'œuvre symmetrically arranged around the centrepiece, a basket of purple roses.

Henriette sat between Claude and Mahoudeau; Sandoz had Christine on one side, Mathilde on the other, while Jory and Gagnière sat at the ends of the table. The butler had hardly finished serving the soup before Madame Jory let drop a few unfortunate words. With the best of intentions, not having heard her husband's excuses, she said to her host:

'Well, were you pleased with this morning's article? Edouard read the proofs himself, *so* carefully!'

Jory, terribly embarrassed, immediately corrected her.

'Indeed I did not! It's a dreadful article! It went through the other night when I was away; you know it did.'

By the awkward silence that followed she knew that she had said something wrong, but she made the situation even more awkward by giving him a withering look and saying in a loud voice, intending to crush him with her disapproval:

'I see. Another of your lies! . . . I was only repeating what you'd told me, so why do you try to make me look a fool? I don't like that sort of thing.'

That cast a blight over the meal from the start. Henriette did her best to rouse an interest in the kilkis, but in vain. Christine was the only one who liked them. Sandoz, tickled by Jory's embarrassment, gaily reminded him, when the grilled mullet were brought in, of a lunch they had once had in Marseilles. Marseilles! The only place where people know how to eat!

Without any transition, Claude, who had been lost in thought, suddenly asked, as though wakening from a dream:

'Have they decided yet who's going to do the new decoration at the Hôtel de Ville?'

To which Mahoudeau replied:

'Not yet, but they will soon. . . . I shan't be doing anything, as I've got no connections. . . . Even Fagerolles isn't too sure. He's quite worried, really. Things are not going too smoothly, so I suppose that's why he's not here tonight. . . . Ah, the days of plenty are over for him. It's all turning to dust, them and their paintings at fancy prices.'

He laughed, and there was a note of satisfaction in his laugh which was echoed at the other end of the table by a similar snigger from Gagnière. Then the pair of them began to grow gleeful over the impending disaster which was causing consternation among the younger artists. It was bound to happen, they pointed out; it had all been foreseen; the inflated prices pictures had been fetching were bound to lead to a crash. As soon as private collectors, following the lead given by the Stock Exchange, panicked at the prospect of a falling market, prices had started to go down with a wallop and were dropping every day, so nobody was selling a thing. And what a sight the famous Naudet had been in the midst of the rout! At first he had managed to hold his own. He had invented the 'American' trick: the single canvas hanging in sacred isolation in a gallery and for which he would not even take the trouble to name a price, he was so sure he could never find the man rich enough to pay it, but which he sold in the end for two or three hundred thousand francs to a New York pig-breeder who was only too proud to have been able to treat himself to the most expensive picture of the year. But that sort of thing could not be done indefinitely, and Naudet, whose expenditure had increased with his income, had let himself be swept off his feet by the movement for which he was himself responsible. Now he was faced with the prospect of seeing his house and his fortune vanish before the onslaught of his creditors.

'Mahoudeau, won't you have some more mushrooms,' Henriette broke in, doing her duty as hostess.

The butler was handing round the roast, everyone was eating, the wine was flowing freely, but the talk had grown so sour that the delicacies were passing unnoticed, much to the hostess's sorrow and her husband's.

'What?' said Mahoudeau, 'Mushrooms? No thanks,' and went on with his story.

'The joke is that Naudet is suing Fagerolles. Yes! What do you think of that? Going to have him sold up! Damned funny, I think, the whole business! Oh, there's going to be a fine clean-up in the Avenue de Villiers among the artist-princes! Mansions will be going cheap next spring, you'll see! . . . Well, it was Naudet who forced Fagerolles to build his little place, and it was he who furnished it like a high-class brothel, so now he's claiming back his belongings, curios, and what not. . . . But Fagerolles's borrowed money on them, apparently. . . . You see the situation! . . . Naudet accuses Fagerolles of having ruined his market by indiscriminate exhibiting to satisfy his personal vanity; Fagerolles retorts that he's had enough of being exploited; so it looks like a fight to the death. I hope it is!'

From the far end of the table came Gagnière's inexorable, day-dreamer's voice:

'Done for, Fagerolles. . . . Never been a real success anyhow.'

The others protested. What about his hundred thousand a year from sales? What about his medals and his decoration? But Gagnière remained unshaken and sat smiling and looking mysterious, as if facts could make no difference to his inspired belief.

'Don't try to argue with me,' he said. 'Fagerolles never had the faintest notion of values.'

Jory was just going to defend Fagerolles, whom he regarded as one of his own creations, when Henriette called for a truce in honour of the ravioli. So there was a short lull, broken only by the tinkle of glasses and the subdued clatter of forks, while the table, its admirable symmetry already seriously impaired, seemed brighter than ever, as if it had borrowed some light from the flare-up of opinions.

Sandoz was worried and surprised. What was it that made them go for him like that? he wondered. Hadn't they all started life together? Weren't they all going to have their share in the final victory? For the first time his dream of eternity had been disturbed, that long succession of precious Thursdays, every one the same, every one perfectly happy, which he had always imagined stretching away to the far end of time. It was not a pleasant feeling, but for the time being at least it was easily thrown off.

'Look out, Claude!' he said with a laugh. 'Save some room for the birds! . . . Eh! Claude! Where are you?'

Since the conversation had dropped Claude had floated back into his dream, and without looking, without even knowing what he was doing, was helping himself to more ravioli. Christine, looking very serious and very charming, said nothing, but never took her eyes off him. He started, and chose himself a leg when the hazel-hens were brought round, their strong sauce filling the room with the smell of resin.

'There!' cried Sandoz. 'Can you smell *that*? If that doesn't make you think you're eating all the forests in Russia, nothing will!'

But Claude had already reverted to his original topic.

'So Fagerolles is going to do the Council Chamber, is that right?' he said.

That was enough. Mahoudeau and Gagnière were off again at once. A nice mess he'd make of it if he got the Council Chamber! And he was ready to stoop to anything to get it. Ever since the bottom had dropped out of his market he'd never stopped pestering the authorities. . . . And he was the man who used to pretend to turn up his nose at commissions, as if he were a great master with more patrons than he could satisfy! Could anybody imagine anything less dignified than an artist trying to get round a government official? The kowtowing, the concessions, the downright prostitution! It was a disgrace; art reduced to such a state of servility, art having to depend on the likes and dislikes of some fool of a minister! No shadow of doubt that Fagerolles at his official banquet was conscientiously licking the boots of some half-witted Under-Secretary or other!

'And why not?' cried Jory. 'Why shouldn't he look after Number One? He can't rely on such as you to pay his debts!'

'Indeed he can't!' retorted Mahoudeau. 'Why should he? *I* don't have debts. I know what it is to be poor. I don't build palaces. I don't have a mistress like Irma to ruin me!'

Once more Gagnière broke in with his strange, cracked voice, like some distant oracle.

'But Irma doesn't ruin him. She's the one who pays!'

There were more sharp words, interspersed with jokes in which Irma's name was frequently mentioned; and now Mathilde, who, to show her good breeding, had so far remained silent and aloof, suddenly vented her indignation with the expression of a pious prude undergoing physical assault.

'Gentlemen! Please!' she exclaimed with a horrified gesture. 'That dreadful woman! In our presence! How could you!'

From that point, much to their dismay, Henriette and Sandoz witnessed the final collapse of their dinner-party. The truffle salad, the ice, the dessert, gave no one any pleasure, feelings ran so high; while the Chambertin and the sparkling Moselle were no more appreciated than drinking-water. Henriette kept a smiling face, though to little effect, and Sandoz, making allowance for human weaknesses, did what he could to make peace. But not one of them would give way, and everyone went on attacking everyone else on the slightest provocation. In the old days their parties had often ended rather drearily in a mixture of vague boredom and sleepy repletion. This time everybody was in fighting trim and bent on destroying his adversary. The candles in the chandelier were burning with longer, pointed flames; on the wall, the flowers on the china plates bloomed with unusual vividness, and even the table, its orderly array now in utter confusion, seemed to reflect something of the heat and violence of the talk and activity to which it had been submitted in the past two hours.

As everybody was talking at once, Henriette rose from the table, hoping that the change might quieten them. Just as she did so Claude was heard saying:

'The very thing for me, the Hôtel de Ville job ... if I could get it! ... It's always been my dream to paint the walls of Paris!'

In the drawing-room, where the small chandelier and the wall-brackets had been lit and it felt almost cold after the Turkish bath atmosphere they had just left, coffee calmed the ruffled tempers for a time. Apart from Fagerolles, no other guests were expected, for it was a very exclusive household. Sandoz and Henriette did not make use of their drawing-room either for recruiting a favourable public or muzzling the Press by a flow of invitations. Henriette heartily disliked social functions, and her husband used to say, with a laugh, that it took him ten years to get to like somebody and be sure it was for good. Happiness, surely, which some people said was unattainable, meant a few well-tried friendships and a haven of homely affection! So in the Sandozes' drawing-room there were never any musical soirées and no one had ever stood up within its four walls to read a line of either verse or prose.

Time seemed to pass very slowly on this particular Thursday evening, for the general irritation, though subdued, persisted. The ladies gathered round the fire, which had now burnt low, and when the butler had cleared the table and reopened the dining-room doors they were soon left alone with their conversation while the men retired to smoke and drink beer.

Sandoz and Claude, as they did not smoke, soon returned to the drawing-room and sat on a sofa near the door. Delighted to see his old friend happy and talkative, Sandoz had begun to revive old memories. Yesterday he had had some news from Plassans. Yes, about Pouillaud, who used to be the life and soul of the dormitory and then ended up as a staid, respectable solicitor. Well, he'd got into trouble. He'd been caught in compromising circumstances with some twelve-year-old girls! Oh, he always was a bit of a lad, Pouillaud, wasn't he? But Claude made no response; his interest was elsewhere. He had heard his name mentioned in the dining-room and was trying to catch the rest of the conversation.

It was Jory, Mahoudeau, and Gagnière who had returned ravening and insatiable to the slaughter. Their voices had risen from a discreet whisper to what was now almost a shout.

'Oh, as a man, you can take him and keep him,' Jory was saying, speaking of Fagerolles. 'He was never up to much in my opinion. And he's certainly got the better of you two, make no mistake about that, breaking with you as he did and using you as stepping-stones to his own success! Oh, you weren't very smart, or you'd have seen his game!'

'How could we help it?' retorted Mahoudeau furiously. 'We'd only got to be known as friends of Claude's for every door to be slammed in our faces!'

'Yes, he's been the death of us two!' said Gagnière firmly.

And so they went on; after criticizing Fagerolles for going over to the enemy, for grovelling to the Press, for making up to elderly duchesses, they left him alone to vent their fury on Claude, the source of all their troubles. What was Fagerolles, after all? Just an artist like a lot of others, with an eye to the main chance, determined to be a 'draw' at all costs, even if it meant breaking with his friends and tearing them to pieces behind their backs. But Claude, the great painter who had missed the mark, who, in spite of his high opinion of himself couldn't paint a decent figure if he tried, what had he done for them? Nothing, except put them in an awkward position and shown them no way of getting out of it. Their only hope of success lay in breaking with him, that was clear. Another time they wouldn't be such damned fools as to sacrifice themselves for what was obviously a hopeless cause! They accused Claude of having paralysed them and exploited, yes, exploited them, but so heavy-handedly that he had got nothing out of it for himself.

'Take me, for example,' said Mahoudeau. 'Why, at one time he practically turned my brain. When I think of it now I wonder how ever I came to join his gang at all? I'm not like him, am I? Could we have had anything in common? . . . I really don't know. . . . And it's maddening to wake up to things so late in the day!'

'What about me?' put in Gagnière. 'All he did for me was pinch my originality. Do you think I've enjoyed it, these last fifteen years, hearing *my* pictures described as "perfect Claudes"? . . . No! I've had as much as I can stand of that sort of thing. I'd rather never paint another picture. . . . I ought never to have had anything to do with him. I can see that now.'

Panic-stricken to discover that, having been like brothers since their early youth, they were now suddenly become strangers and enemies, they were deliberately breaking the last bonds that had held them together. Life had scattered them as the years went by, and serious differences had sprung up between them; now all that was left of their old enthusiasms and their hopes for a victory in which each one would have played his part was a bitter taste in the mouth and a feeling of vindictiveness.

'Still, you've got to admit,' said Jory with a grin, 'Fager-olles wasn't such an idiot as to let someone else pinch his ideas.'

This annoyed Mahoudeau, who retorted:

'I don't see what you've got to laugh at; you didn't exactly play the game yourself. . . . Always saying you'd give us a hand up when you had a paper of your own, and . . .'

'Ah, yes, but remember . . .'

Jory's reply was cut short by Gagnière joining in on Mahoudeau's side.

'He's right, you did,' he said, 'and you can't tell us now that your stuff's subbed beyond recognition, because now you're the boss. But have you ever said a good word for either of us? Not you! In your last Salon report you never even mentioned our names.'

At a loss for an answer, Jory covered his embarrassment by giving vent to his own candid opinion.

'If there's anyone to blame for that,' he cried, 'it's that god-forsaken Claude! . . . Why should I lose my subscribers to please you two? You're both impossible, though you may not realize it. You, Mahoudeau, can work till you drop turning out nice little statues, and you, Gagnière, needn't ever handle a paint-brush again, but you've both got the sort of labels on your backs that it'll take ten years to get off . . . if you ever do get 'em off, and there are plenty of men who don't. So far as the public's concerned you're just a couple of fools . . . the only men who still believe in the genius of a tomfool crank who'll probably end up in the madhouse.'

Jory's outburst so stimulated the others that in the end all three were talking at once, vying with each other in the ferocity of their attacks, their jaws working with such violence that they looked as if they were biting.

Sitting on the sofa near the door, Sandoz at length found himself obliged to interrupt his flow of amusing reminis-cences to listen to the tumult in the dining-room.

'Hear 'em?' whispered Claude, a faint smile of pain on his lips. 'They seem to have got me sorted out! . . . No, no!

Don't go in to them. I deserve it for making a mess of things.'

Pale with indignation, Sandoz sat still and listened to all the vehemence and rancour poured out by personalities in conflict in the struggle for existence, sweeping away his cherished dream of eternal friendship.

Fortunately, Henriette heard the angry voices too and, wondering what they signified, got up and went to the dining-room where she upbraided the smokers for neglecting the ladies to spend their time quarrelling. Thereupon they all went back to the drawing-room, still sweating and panting from the violence of their onslaught, and when Henriette looked up at the clock and remarked that Fagerolles could not possibly be coming so late in the evening they all looked at each other and grinned. Fagerolles had a flair. He knew better than to butt in on old friends for whom he had no more use and who couldn't stand him anyhow!

Fagerolles did not come, and the evening drew to an uncomfortable close. Back in the dining-room the candles were lighted again and tea was served on a Russian cloth with a stag-hunt embroidered upon it in red. There was a large brioche, plates of cakes and sweetmeats and an exotic array of drinks: whisky, gin, kummel, Scio raki, joined later by punch, brought in by the butler, who then attended to the guests' requirements while the hostess was filling the teapot from the steaming samovar. But all the comfort, the delicacies and the subtle aroma of freshly-made tea did nothing to ease the tension. The conversation had somehow reverted to the subject of success and failure. Was there anything more disgraceful than the way they awarded medals and decorations for one sort and another? What could be more degrading for artists? Why should they be expected to remain schoolboys all their lives? That was the reason for all the platitudes: docility and sucking up to the masters, to make sure of a good mark!

In the drawing-room again, as Sandoz was quickly reaching the point when he would be relieved to see the last of

his guests, he noticed Mathilde and Gagnière sitting side
by side blissfully talking music, while everybody else had
apparently talked themselves dry. Gagnière was going
off into rapturous flights of poetry and philosophy, while
Mathilde, like the flabby, middle-aged trollop she was,
showed the whites of her eyes, swooning under the caress
of invisible wings, surrounded as always by her unsavoury
odour of herb-shop. They had noticed each other at a
concert the previous Sunday and now, in a give-and-take
of high-flown, far-fetched eulogies, were comparing their
impressions.

'Ah, monsieur, the Meyerbeer, the *Struensée* overture,
that death motif and then the peasants' dance, so wonder-
fully fiery and colourful, and then the death tune again,
and that C on the 'cellos! Ah, the 'cellos, monsieur, the
'cellos! . . .'

'And the Berlioz, madame, the feast theme in *Roméo*! Oh,
the passage where the clarinets—"women beloved", I call
them—take up the melody alone, with harp accompaniment!
Sheer ecstasy, don't you think? A sort of floating whiteness.
. . . Then the feast itself, a magnificent outburst, like a
Veronese—his "Marriage at Cana", for example—for tumul-
tuous activity! And the way the love theme is picked up
again, *very* softly at first, then swelling up and up and up.
. . . Oh, magnificent!'

'Oh, and monsieur, don't you feel that that slow, funeral-
knell passage in Beethoven's Seventh is like something
knocking on your own heart? . . . Oh, I can see you feel
exactly as I do, that music is really a sort of communion! . . .
Beethoven, don't you know, I think there's something *so*
wonderful, and at the same time *sad* somehow, in sharing
your appreciation of him with someone else and knowing
that you're both simply dying. . . .'

'And what about Schumann, madame, and Wagner! . . .
Oh, that *Reverie* of Schumann's. The unaccompanied
strings, you know; it's just like soft, warm rain on acacia
leaves brushed away by a sunbeam; just a faint, faint
suggestion of a tear. . . . Then Wagner, madame, the over-

ture to the *Dutchman*. You *do* like it, don't you? Oh, say you do! I find it really overwhelming, shattering, madame. It simply takes my breath away.'

And their voices dwindled into enraptured silence as they sat there, elbow to elbow, not even looking at each other, but gazing far away into realms beyond the bounds of space.

Sandoz, taken completely by surprise, wondered where Mathilde had picked up all her jargon. From one of Jory's articles, perhaps, though he had often noticed that women could talk music quite convincingly without knowing the first thing about it. Grieved already by the acrimonious bickering of his other guests, he found Mathilde's affected languishing more than he could endure. If the others liked tearing each other to pieces, all well and good, but this middle-aged harlot gushing and working herself up over Beethoven and Schumann, no! It needed only that to put a preposterous end to such an evening.

Gagnière, fortunately, suddenly sprang to his feet; even in ecstasy he was aware of the time and realized he would have to hurry now to catch his train. So after flabby handshakes and silent leave-takings, away he went to his bed at Melun.

'There's a dud for you,' said Mahoudeau when he had gone. 'His music's killed his painting, and now he'll never be any good at either.'

When it was his turn to leave, the door had hardly closed behind him before Jory remarked:

'And there's another dud. Have you seen his latest paper-weight? He'll end up modelling cuff-links, and he had the makings of something really powerful.'

Now Mathilde was on her feet; after taking a curt leave of Christine and treating Henriette with what she considered well-bred familiarity, she bundled her husband into the hall where he humbly helped her into her cloak, terrified by the look in her eyes which indicated trouble in store.

Sandoz could not prevent himself, when they had gone, from exclaiming:

'We might have expected that. It would be the journalist, the scribbler who battens on the stupidity of the public, who describes everybody else as "duds"! Still, we must always remember that Mathilde's motto is "Vengeance is mine!" '

Christine and Claude still lingered. Since the drawing-room had begun to empty Claude had subsided into an armchair in another of his trances, saying nothing, but just gazing stiffly into the remote distance, far beyond the walls of the room. From the tense expression on his face and the way he kept craning his neck, it was clear he could see the invisible and hear the silence calling to him.

When Christine got up to go, full of apologies for being the last to leave, Henriette took both her hands in hers and begged her to come again often and to treat her as a sister, while poor Christine, looking very touching in her black dress, nodded her gratitude and smiled.

'Listen, Christine,' Sandoz said to her quietly, after a glance in Claude's direction. 'You must try not to worry so much. . . . He's talked quite a lot and been much more cheerful this evening. Everything's all right, really.'

'It isn't, Pierre,' Christine answered in a terrified voice. 'Look at his eyes. As long as he has that look in his eyes I shall be afraid. . . . You've been very helpful; you've done your best. Thank you. What you can't do, nobody else can. If you only knew how it hurts to feel you don't count any more, to feel as helpless as I do!'

Then, turning to Claude, she added: 'Are you coming, Claude?'

She had to repeat her question, for he heard nothing the first time. Then, with a shudder, he stood up and said: 'Yes, I'm coming, I'm coming,' just as if he were answering some distant call from far away beyond the horizon.

When they had gone and Sandoz and his wife were left alone in their drawing-room, stifling now with the heat from the lamps and heavy with melancholy silence after the recent clamour of furious voices, they looked at each other and let their arms drop to their sides in dismay at their evening's failure. Henriette did her best to make light of it, and said quietly:

'I did warn you; I felt it might happen. . . .'

Her husband interrupted her with a gesture of despair. Why should she feel like that about it? Did she mean this was the end of his illusions, the end of the eternity he had always dreamed of, believing that happiness was made of a few friendships chosen in one's youth and cherished into old age? A lamentable choice his had been if this was all it added up to—liquidation, failure, bankruptcy, you might call it! A heart-breaking prospect. He could not understand how he could have left so many of his friends behind and broken so many strong attachments; why the affections of others seemed to be perpetually changing while he noticed no change in his own. The thought of his poor Thursday evenings moved him almost to tears. What had they been but the protracted death of something he had loved, leaving him only with a host of memories to mourn? Did it mean that now his wife and he must resign themselves to living in the wilderness, cut off by the hatred of the world around them? Or did it mean they would now open their doors to a flock of indifferent strangers? Slowly, in the depths of his grief, he began to realize one thing: in life everything comes to an end, but nothing is ever repeated. Accepting the apparently inevitable, he sighed and said to Henriette:

'You were right. . . . We'll never invite them all together again. They'd devour each other.'

No sooner had Claude and Christine reached the Place de la Trinité than Claude let go of Christine's arm, mumbled something about having some business to attend to and begged her to go home without him. She had felt a violent shudder run through his body and, in surprise and apprehension, asked him what business at this time of night, after twelve o'clock; where was he going, and why? But he had already turned and left her. She ran after him and, pretending she was frightened, begged him not to let her make her way back to Montmartre alone, so late. That was the only argument he seemed prepared to listen to. He took her arm again and they climbed up the Rue Blanche and the Rue Lepic together. On their doorstep in the Rue Tourlaque, he rang the bell for the concierge, then turned and left her again.

'There, you're home. Now I'll attend to my business,' he said, and started off down the street at a tremendous pace, gesticulating like a madman. The door had been opened, and Christine made no attempt to close it again, but started in pursuit. In the Rue Lepic she could have overtaken him, but as she was afraid of upsetting him even more she thought it better not to let him know she was there but simply to follow him and not let him out of her sight. When he left the Rue Lepic he turned down the Rue Blanche again, then went along the Rue de la Chaussée d'Antin and the Rue du Quatre Septembre till he came to the Rue Richelieu. When she saw him turn down there her blood ran cold; he was making for the river, the very thing she was afraid of, the haunting dread that kept her awake at night. What should she do, she wondered—go with him, cling to him to the bitter end, or try to hold him back? She staggered on in his wake, feeling the life ebbing out of her limbs as every step brought them nearer the river; for that was where he was going, past the Théâtre Français, across the Place du Carrousel to the Pont des Saints-Pères. He walked a few paces along the bridge, then went up to the parapet and looked down into the water. She was sure he was going to throw himself over and would have cried out to him, but her strength failed her, her throat was paralysed.

She was mistaken. He had stopped and was now looking straight up the river. She knew then what he had had in his mind. It was the Cité haunting him, the heart of Paris that filled his thoughts incessantly, the place he could see when he gazed through walls into space, the place he alone could hear calling to him wherever he happened to be. Still she did not dare to hope, and hung back watching him closely, though her head was in a whirl, for she imagined that even now he might fling himself into the water, yet she had to resist the urge to go up to him lest her appearance on the scene should precipitate disaster. Her womanly passion outraged, her motherly heart bleeding for him, there was nothing for her to do but watch, without even being able to lift a finger to stop him.

He, meanwhile stood, a tall, motionless figure, gazing into the night.

It was a wintry night, pitch dark, with a cloudy sky above and an icy west wind blowing. Paris was asleep, and the only signs of life were the street lamps, discs of scintillating light shrinking away in the distance to a dusting of fixed stars. Along the embankments they were like double strings of luminous pearls lighting with their glow the fronts of the nearby buildings: on the left the houses on the Quai du Louvre, on the right the two wings of the Institut, then, beyond that, a confused mass of bricks and mortar lost in deeper shadow, dotted with distant sparks. Between the two retreating strings of lamps ran lines of lights on the bridges, each tinier than its predecessor, each like a cluster of spangles hanging in the air. Down below, the Seine was ablaze with the nocturnal splendour known only to the waters of cities, reflecting every lighted lamp as a comet with a streaming tail. The nearest ones, overlapping, lit up the water in regular, symmetrical fans, while those in the far distance were tiny points of stationary fire. The great, flaming tails, however, were never still, but lashed about the water, the quivering of their black and gold scales revealing the ceaseless flowing of the stream. Along the whole of its length the Seine was ablaze, its depths mysteriously illumined beneath its glassy surface, as by some brilliant celebration or sumptuous transformation scene. Over this conflagration and the embankments bespangled with lights, a red haze hovered in the starless sky: the hot, phosphorescent vapour that nightly rises out of the sleeping city as from a dormant volcano.

The wind began to blow colder. Her teeth chattering, her sight blurred with tears, Christine felt as though the bridge was swaying beneath her and everything was being swept away in some tremendous débâcle. Claude had moved. He was climbing over the parapet! No! Everything was still again suddenly, and there he was still at the same spot, obstinate as ever, peering through the darkness towards the point of the invisible Cité.

He had answered its call, though it was too dark now for him to see; all he could distinguish at this hour was the bridges, their framework delicately etched against the glowing stream. Beyond that, all was lost; the island itself was sunk in darkness, and he would not even have been able to say where it lay but for an occasional belated cab trundling its lights across the Pont-Neuf, like sparks running over dying embers. Down on the weir near the Monnaie, a red lantern shed a trail of blood upon the water, while some enormous, sinister object, a corpse perhaps, or, more likely, a drifting boat, floated slowly down through the reflected lights, visible for a moment, then swallowed up again by the shadows. What had become of his proud and stately island? Where had it sunk? Into the blazing depths of the Seine? As he peered in vain into the shadows, he gradually became aware of the rippling of the river as it flowed through the night, and he began to lean over towards the great, chill, apparently unfathomable moat with the dancing mystery of its lights, drawn by the melancholy sound of its waters, ready—so deep was his despair—to respond to their call.

This time Christine knew, by the way her heart throbbed, that the terrible thought had flashed into his mind, and she held out her quivering hands towards him through the stinging wind. But Claude made no move, drawn up now to his full height, struggling against the proffered sweetness of death. For another full hour he stood, oblivious of time, gazing towards the Cité as if, by some miracle, his eyes might of their own accord create the light by which to see it.

When at last he staggered back off the bridge, Christine had to pass him and run on ahead, to be home in the Rue Tourlaque before him.

CHAPTER 12

IT was three o'clock before they went to bed that morning
in their icy room off the studio swept by the sharp November wind. Still breathless from hurrying, Christine had
slipped hastily under the blankets so that Claude should
not know she had been following him; and Claude, when
he came in, exhausted, had quickly undressed without
saying a word. For many months now theirs had been a
cold, loveless couch on which they lay down like two
strangers since they had gradually sundered all carnal
bonds through the self-imposed chastity which, in theory,
was to enable him to put all his virility into his painting
and which, in spite of her torturing passion, she had
accepted with proud, unspoken grief. But never, until
this particular night, had she been aware of such an obstacle, such coldness between them, as if nothing could
ever make them warm to each other again and fall into
each other's arms.

For a good quarter of an hour she struggled to ward off
sleep, though she was very weary and her mind was already
numb; but she refused to let herself give way so long as
Claude was still awake. As on every other night she knew
she could never settle to rest without being sure that he was
asleep first. Still he did not blow out the candle, but lay
with eyes wide open, letting himself be blinded by the flame.
What could he be thinking about now? Was he still down
there in the darkness, in the cold, damp breath of the river,
looking at Paris riddled with stars like a frosty sky? What
inner debate, what resolution to be taken so convulsed his
face? The question still in her mind, she succumbed at last
to her weariness and fell fast asleep.

An hour later, a sudden, anguished sensation, a feeling of
loneliness, awakened her with a violent start. Immediately
she reached out with her hand and felt the place beside her
already cold; Claude had gone, and in her sleep she had

been aware of it. Half awake, her head heavy and throbbing with sleep, she was just beginning to panic when she noticed a thin shaft of light shining through the open doorway from the studio. That reassured her; she thought he had gone to fetch a book to read himself to sleep. Then, as he did not come back, she got up very quietly to see what he was doing. The sight that met her eyes so startled her that she stopped dead, too scared to show herself.

Cold though it was, Claude, clad only in shirt and trousers, his feet in slippers, was standing on his big ladder in front of his picture. With his palette at his feet, he was holding the candle in one hand and painting with the other. His eyes were wide open, like a sleepwalker's, and his stiff, precise gestures as he bent down to fill his brush, then straightened up again, cast on the wall a big, fantastic shadow with staccato movements like a mechanical doll. Not a sound, not a breath even broke the awful silence of the huge, dark room.

As she stood shivering in the doorway Christine realized what had happened. It was his obsession, the hour he had spent down on the Pont des Saints-Pères that had made it impossible for him to sleep and driven him back to his picture, determined to see it again in spite of the dark. Perhaps when he climbed up on to his ladder it was simply to get a closer view; then, irritated by some slight defect that so preyed upon his mind that he was unable to wait to remedy it until it was daylight, he had picked up a brush, intending only to touch it up in that one place; and, as one correction had led to another, he had ended up by painting like a madman, candle in hand, in the pale, inadequate light made fearful by his gestures. In the throes of his impotent urge to create, oblivious both of time and place, he was wearing out body and soul to give his work the breath of life.

Her heart wrung with pity, her eyes streaming with tears, Christine stood and watched him. For a moment she thought she would leave him to his ill-timed task, as one humours a maniac in his madness. One thing was certain now: his picture would never be finished. The harder he worked on it the more incoherent it was becoming, deteriorating into an inextricable mass of dull, drab colours, devoid of all sense of drawing. Even the background, the group of dock porters especially, which had once been so well drawn, was beginning to lose its original firmness. But his mind was made up; he was determined to finish off everything else before he would touch the central figure, the naked Woman, now as always the desire and torment of his working hours, the flesh that would turn his brain and encompass his destruction the day he tried to bring it to life. For months he had not touched it, and the knowledge of that fact was a comfort to Christine and made her much more tolerant and sympathetic in her gnawing jealousy. So long as he kept away from that desired but dreaded mistress, she did not feel quite so forlorn.

Her bare feet numb with cold, she was turning to go back to bed when she noticed something which instantly changed her mind. She had not realized at first what was happening; now she suddenly saw, and understood. His brush filled with flesh colour, Claude was painting madly away with rounded, caressing gestures. There was a fixed smile on his lips and he was not even aware of the hot wax from the candle trickling over his fingers as the great, black shadow of his impassioned movement was cast on to the canvas, grappling with the painted limbs and coupling with the painted body in a violent embrace. He had gone back to the naked Woman.

Pushing the studio door wide open, Christine walked in, impelled by the irrepressible fury of a wife affronted under her own roof, deceived while she lay asleep in the next room. Yes, there he was with the other woman, painting her legs and body like some infatuated visionary driven by the torments of the real to the exaltation of the unreal, making her legs the gilded columns of a temple and her body a blaze of red and yellow, a star, magnificent, unearthly. Nudity thus enshrined and set in precious stones, demanding to be worshipped, was more than Christine could tolerate. She had gone through too much already; she would put an end to this betrayal.

Yet when she spoke her words were words of despair and supplication, the words of a mother admonishing her headstrong child.

'Claude, what are you doing?' she said. 'You're not being very reasonable, are you, Claude, behaving like this? . . . Please come back to bed. Don't stay up there on that ladder, you're bound to catch cold.'

He did not answer, but bent down again to fill his brush; then, with two firm strokes, brought out the lines of the groin with two streaks of flaming vermilion.

'Claude, *do* listen! Come back, Claude, please,' she went on. 'I love you, Claude, you know that, so why do you do things to upset me so? . . . Please come back, unless you want me to catch my death as well, through waiting for you.'

In his frenzy he did not even look at her, but rapped out, in a voice choking with fury, as he marked in the navel with a flourish of carmine:

'For God's sake leave me alone, can't you! I'm busy!'

For a moment Christine said nothing, but a dark flame kindled in her eyes and her whole gentle being flared up in revolt. She braced herself, then burst out, with all the pent-up hatred of a slave goaded beyond endurance.

'No! I can't leave you alone, and I won't leave you alone! . . . I can stand it no longer! I'm going to tell you now what it is that's been choking the life out of me ever since I met you. . . . It's this painting, *your* painting! It's killing me, poisoning my whole life. And I knew it would happen from the very first. It's like a monster; I was afraid of it as soon as I saw it; I thought it was horrible, loathsome. But I was a coward; I was in love with you, so I couldn't afford not to like it, and I made myself get used to it, though I knew it would kill me in the end, it tortured me so! I can't remember a single day in the last ten years when it hasn't reduced me to tears. . . . No, don't stop me now! It's a relief to talk, now I've the strength to do it. . . . Ten whole years of neglect and repression; ten years of meaning nothing to you, of being cast further and further aside and reduced to being nothing but a servant; seeing this other creature stealing you from me, thrusting herself between us and flaunting her triumph in my face! . . . For you daren't deny she's taken possession of every inch of your body, brain and heart and all! She's like a vice; you can't shake her off, and now you're hers to devour. . . . But she's your wife now, isn't she, not me? She's the one who sleeps with you now, not me, the hateful bitch!'

Her outburst, her cry of suffering had surprised Claude into listening to her, although, since half his mind was still engrossed by the task of creation, he did not really understand why she was talking as she did. His blank amazement and slight tremor of impatience that made him look like a man surprised and disturbed in an act of debauchery made her angrier than ever. She climbed up the ladder, wrenched the candle from his fist and used it, as he had done, to light the picture.

'Look at this,' she cried, 'and see what you've come to! It's lamentable, it's hideous, it's grotesque, and it's time you knew it! There! Isn't it ugly? Isn't it mad? . . . You can see for yourself you're finished, so why go on struggling? . . . It's so pointless, isn't it? And that's what's so revolting about it. . . . If you can't be a good painter, we still have life! Ah, life, life!'

She put down the candle on the platform at the top of the ladder, and since he had clambered down she jumped down to join him. Kneeling at his feet as he sat down on the bottom rung, she took his helpless hands and held them tight between her own.

'Remember that, Claude; we have our lives to live,' she went on, 'so let's go and live them together, and forget about your nightmares. . . . It's silly, don't you think, for us to grow old before our time, torturing each other and forgetting we could be happy? We shall be dead and buried soon enough, so let's be warm as long as we can. Let's live, Claude, and love each other, as we used to do at Bennecourt, remember? . . . Listen. I'll tell you my dream. It's to take you away from here first thing in the morning, right away from this loathsome Paris to somewhere quiet and peaceful, and show you what I could do to make life worth living. It would be so wonderful, to forget everything else and just be in each other's arms! We should sleep in our big double bed, spend our mornings lounging in the sun enjoying the smell of lunch cooking; then, after a lazy afternoon, we'd spend the evening quietly in the lamplight, and there would be no more worries and torments, nothing but life for the pleasure of living! . . . What more could you ask? I love you. I adore you. I'll be your slave, I'll exist only for your pleasure. . . . Do you hear? I love you, I love you, I love you! Isn't that enough?'

He released his hands from hers, and with a gesture of refusal, answered glumly:

'No, it isn't enough. . . . I don't want to go away with you. I don't even want to be happy; all I want is to paint.'

'And to kill me as well as yourself, and make us end our days in blood and tears! . . . Art alone exists, Art is all-powerful, Art is the jealous god who strikes us both down, the god you worship! Art is your master; it can destroy us both, and you'll offer up a prayer of gratitude!'

'Yes. Art *is* the master, *my* master, to dispose of me as it pleases. If I stopped painting it would kill me just the same, so I prefer to die painting. . . . My own will doesn't really enter into it. That is the way things are; nothing else matters, and the world can go to blazes!'

She leapt to her feet at once as her anger flared up again.

'But what about me?' she cried, in a voice now hard again with fury. 'I'm alive, but the women you're in love with are dead! . . . Oh, don't try to deny it, they're your mistresses, I know they are, every one of your painted ladies. I've known it from the start, before you and I were lovers; I'd only got to see the way you caressed their naked bodies, the way you sat mooning over them afterwards for hours on end. It was a morbid, stupid thing for any man to do, falling in love with a lot of pictures, trying to embrace an illusion. What's more, you know it was, and that's why you were always on the defensive, because you didn't dare to admit it. . . . Then you fell in love with me, or thought you did, and told me a lot of nonsense about your love-affairs with the women in your paintings and tried to pass it off as a joke. Do you remember the way you used to pretend to be sorry for them when you were making love to me? . . . And you *were* sorry for them, or you wouldn't have gone back to them as quickly as you did, like a maniac to his mania! I was real, but I didn't matter any more. They, the dream women, were the only real things in your life. . . . What I've suffered on their account you'll never know, because you know nothing about real women. I've lived with you all these years, but that doesn't mean you understand me. I was jealous of them, did you know that? And when I posed for you, on this very spot, stark naked, I found courage to do it because I'd only one thing in mind. I wanted to beat them at their own game; I wanted to win you back; but what did it bring me? Nothing. Not even a kiss on the shoulder before I put on my clothes again. Oh, the shame I've had to hide, the bitterness I've had to swallow, when you not only ignored me but despised me as well! . . . And since then you've despised me more and more; so that now we go to bed together, night after night, lie down side by side and never lay a finger on each other. That's how it's been for eight months and seven days. I've counted them. Eight months and seven days since we last made love to each other!'

Sensual though she was, Christine was also modest, and, though ardent in the act of love, her lips swelling with cries of pleasure, she was discreet and disliked to talk about these things afterwards, turning away her head in smiling confusion. But now, impassioned by her own desire, outraged by her husband's abstinence, she spoke her mind frankly and boldly. Her jealousy had not deceived her in her accusations against Claude, for the virility he withheld from her he expended on her rival, the woman he preferred. She knew, too, exactly how he had come to forsake her. It had begun by his refusing her when she nestled close to him in bed the night before he had important work to do; he said it tired him. Later he pretended that when they made love it took his brain three days to clear sufficiently for him to produce anything worth while. That was how they had gradually drifted apart; a week would go by while he was finishing off a picture, then a month while he was preparing and starting work on another, and so, with postponements and neglected opportunities, abstinence had grown to be a habit and ended in complete estrangement. Now she found herself at grips with the theory she had heard expounded hundreds of times before: genius must be chaste, its only love must be work.

'You push me away,' she cried, 'at night when I want to be near you, or else you edge away from me as if I were loathsome to you, and you turn to something else for your love. And to what? To something and nothing, a bit of oil and colour on a canvas! . . . Now look at her, look at her, I say, up there, the woman you love, and see what a monster you've made of her in your madness! Was any woman ever that shape? Did any woman have bright gold thighs and flowers growing out of her loins? Wake up! Open your eyes and come down to earth again! You're lost!'

Automatically obeying her commanding gesture, Claude stood up to look at his picture. The candle, which had been left on the top of the ladder, lighted up the female figure like an image on an altar, while the rest of the vast studio remained in total darkness. He was beginning now to awaken from his dream, and as he looked at his painted Woman from where he was standing, below and at a certain distance away from her, he was dumbfounded. Who could have painted what looked like an idol belonging to some unknown religion? Who could have made her of marble and gold and precious stones and shown the mystic rose of her sex blooming between the precious columns that were her thighs, beneath the sacred canopy that was her belly? Could he himself have unconsciously produced this symbol of insatiable desire, this extrahuman image of the flesh turned to gold and jewels in his hands as he strove in vain to bring his work to life? It frightened him, as he stood there gaping in amazement and trembling to realize how he had plunged into something beyond reality, and how completely reality itself had evaded him despite his fruitless efforts to master it and improve it with the aid of ordinary human hands.

'Now do you see?' said Christine in triumph.

And he murmured quietly in reply:

'What have I done? . . . Is creation impossible? Are human hands powerless to make things come to life?'

His courage was flagging and, realizing it, Christine took him warmly in her arms.

'Why worry about such foolish things,' she said, 'so long as you have me? . . . You've made me pose for you; you wanted to make copies of my body, but why? Surely I'm worth more than all the copies you could ever make! At best they're ugly, besides being as cold and stiff as so many corpses. . . . But I love you. I want you. Don't you understand? Why do I have to tell you all the time? Can't you feel it when I'm always near you, when I offer to pose for you, when I'm always wanting to touch you? Do you understand now? I love you. I'm alive and I want you,' she ended desperately, twining her naked limbs about him as she spoke.

Her nightgown torn half off, she pressed her naked bosom against him as if she would have ground her flesh into his. Now her passion was aroused for its last determined onslaught. She was passion itself as she fought; passion unbridled and devastating, freed from all the chaste reserve she had used to show; passion burning to say everything and do everything, intent on conquest. Her whole face flushed and her gentle eyes and limpid brow were hidden by her loosened hair, giving full prominence to her square jaw, her resolute chin and her blood-red lips.

'Don't! Let me go!' Claude murmured. 'I'm too wretched.'

'Maybe you think I'm old,' she went on heatedly. 'You do. You've told me I wasn't what I once was, and I thought you were right, and I used to look myself over as I was posing, looking for wrinkles. . . . But there weren't any. It wasn't true! I can feel I haven't aged. I'm still young, and strong. . . . '

Then, as he was still struggling to free himself from her embrace, she cried:

'There! Look for yourself!'

She stood away from him, and with one gesture ripped off her nightgown and stood before him naked in the pose she had held for so many lengthy sittings. With a tilt of her chin she drew his attention to the figure in the picture.

'Now you can compare, and you'll find I'm still younger than she is. You can cover her all over with jewels, she'll still be as wizened as a dead leaf. . . . I'm still as I was at eighteen, and the reason is: *I* love you.'

And indeed, as she stood in the pale candlelight, she looked radiant with youth. As her love welled up within her, her legs looked longer and finer as they swept up to the broader, silky curve of her hips, and her breasts stood out firm and erect, as they throbbed with the pulse of her desire.

She took him at once in her arms again, clinging to him, unhampered now even by her flimsy nightgown, caressing him without restraint, his thighs, his shoulders, as if she were searching out his heart in her determination to possess him entirely and make him her own, kissing him ravenously with hungry, insatiable lips, on his skin, his beard, his sleeves, and even on the air around him. Her voice faded to less than a whisper; her speech was just a series of excited gasps punctuated by sighs.

'Come with me,' she murmured, 'and love me. . . . Aren't you human? Is that what makes you be satisfied with pictures? Come with me, and you'll see life's still worth living. . . . It is, you know, if we live it in each other's arms, if we spend all our nights wrapped up in each other, like this, for ever and ever. . . . '

She felt a thrill run through his body and some slight response to her embrace, for the other woman, the idol, had frightened him. Sure now that his resistance was wavering, she continued her blandishments, knowing she was bound to conquer in the end.

'I know the dreadful thought you've got in the back of your mind,' she whispered. 'I've never dared to speak of it because it doesn't do to provoke bad luck, but it keeps me awake at night, I'm so terrified. . . . Tonight I followed you all the way down to that terrible bridge. Oh, how I hate it! And I trembled with fear because I thought it was the end. I thought I was losing you. . . . Oh, God! What should I do without you? I need you so badly, it's killing me, killing me, do you hear? . . . Love me again, Claude, and let me love you, as we used to do!'

Such boundless passion was too much for him; he broke down completely, feeling himself and the whole world swept away as by some tremendous sorrow, and clung distractedly to her, sobbing and stammering:

'It's quite true; that dreadful thought was in my mind. . . . I should have done it, too, if the thought of this picture unfinished hadn't helped me to resist. . . . But how can I go on living if there's no point in going on working? How can I go on living after what I did just now, after spoiling my greatest effort?'

'You can go on living because I love you.'

'Ah, but you'll never love me enough! . . . I know that because I know myself. The only thing that could make life worth living would be something that doesn't exist, the sort of joy that would make me forget everything else. . . . You've already proved you couldn't give me that, and I know you never will.'

'Oh, yes, I will! I will, and I'll prove it. . . . This is what I'll do. I'll take you in my arms like this and I'll kiss you on your eyes and your lips and on every part of your body. I'll warm you at my breast; I'll twine my legs round yours and clasp my arms around you and I'll be you; I'll be your breath, I'll be your flesh, I'll be your blood. . . .'

This time he was conquered; filled with the warmth of her desire, he gave himself up to her entirely, burying his head in her bosom, covering her body with his kisses.

'Save me then, take me,' he murmured, 'if you don't want me to do away with myself. . . . Produce your happiness, if you can; see what you can devise to make me think life's worth while after all. . . . Coax my mind into submission, reduce me to insignificance, make me your slave, your thing, to be worn and trodden on like the sole of your slipper! Oh, the marvel of being able to live by the scent of your body, obey you like a faithful dog, eat, love you and sleep, nothing more! If only I could! If only I could!'

Her reply was a shout of victory:

'You're mine at last! Now I know I'm the only one! *She*'s dead, now and for ever!'

She tore him away from the sight of the hated picture, and with one inarticulate cry of triumph drew him towards the adjoining room and her bed. On the ladder the guttering candle flickered for an instant behind them and died out. The cuckoo clock struck five. There was not the faintest sign of dawn in the misty November sky, so the studio was left to the darkness and the cold.

Christine and Claude groped their way back to their room and flung themselves across the bed. Never, even in their earliest days, had they been swept away by such raging passion. The whole of their past pulsed back through their hearts, but renewed and so intensified that their senses floated away in delirious ecstasy. The darkness around them glowed as they were carried aloft on wings of flame, far away, far above this earth, in smooth and rhythmic flight. Even Claude could not refrain from crying aloud as he felt himself leaving his sorrow behind and rising to a new and happier existence. It was then that Christine provoked him, forced him even, to blaspheme.

'Say that painting's a fool's game,' she said, with a laugh full of sensual pride.

'Painting's a fool's game,' he repeated.

'Say you'll never paint again; say you despise it; say you'll burn all your pictures to please me.'

'I'll burn all my pictures. I'll never paint again.'

'And say there's nobody else but me, and that holding me as you're holding me now is the one and only happiness; and say you spit on the other one, the bitch you painted on canvas. Spit then! Go on, spit; let me hear you!'

'There. I spit on her. There's nobody else but you.'

She gripped him so tightly in her arms, he could hardly breathe; he was hers; she took him and they started out together again on their vertiginous ride through the stars. Their raptures renewed, three times they felt they were soaring to the utmost heights of heaven. Here indeed was happiness! Why had he never thought before that happiness so certain could be the remedy of his ills? She was his for the taking; so now that he had discovered ecstasy he was saved, wasn't he, and bound to be happy for the rest of his days?

It was almost daybreak when Christine dropped blissfully to sleep in Claude's arms, still holding him close to her with one thigh across his legs, as if she wanted to be sure he would never escape her again. And, with her head comfortably pillowed on his chest, she breathed softly away and smiled as she slept. At first Claude, too, had closed his eyes, but heavy with fatigue though he was he soon opened them again and lay staring into the shadows. Sleep was passing him by and, though every muscle in his body felt shattered by his efforts, as he cooled down and his mind began to recover from its voluptuous intoxication he was aware, lying there dozing, of a subtle influx of strange, confused thoughts. When the first light of dawn showed like a dirty yellow smear, a trickle of liquid mud, on the window-panes, he shuddered, for he thought he heard a voice calling to him from the studio. That brought his thoughts flooding back to his mind, torturing thoughts that printed on his face such a bitter, hollow-cheeked expression of disgust that he looked like a careworn old man. The woman's thigh across his own weighed down on him like lead; he felt as if, for his sins, his knees were being crushed by a millstone. Her head, too, weighed on his chest, slowing down his heart-beats, stifling him. For a long time, however, he hesitated to disturb her, though his whole body was being slowly exasperated and an irresistible feeling of repugnance and hatred was goading it into revolt. What irritated him more than anything else was the powerful yet natural smell of her streaming hair. Suddenly the voice from the studio called out again, louder this time and more imperative. Now his mind was made up; this was the end. He could bear no more; life itself was not worth living since everything in it was a worthless, hollow sham. Very gently he let Christine's head, still vaguely smiling, slip off his chest; then, with infinite precaution, he began to release his legs from her thigh, easing it off very, very slowly, making it move as naturally as if she had moved it away herself. The chain was broken at last; he was free. At a third call from the studio he hastened into the adjoining room, saying: 'Here I am! I'm coming!'

Dawn was slow in breaking and the day began in typical wintry gloom. After about an hour Christine awoke, shivering with cold. Why, she did not know. She did not know, either, why she was alone. Then she remembered going to sleep with her head on his breast, her limbs entwined in his. How, then, had he got away? Where could he be? All at once, numb though she was with cold, she leapt from the bed and rushed to the studio. Could he possibly have gone back to *her*? Could *she* have lured him away again? And she thought she had made him her own for ever!

At the first glimpse, she saw nothing; the studio looked empty in the cold, grey light. Then, feeling reassured, finding nobody there, she looked up at the picture, and a heartrending cry rose at once to her gaping lips:

'Claude! Oh, Claude!'

Claude had hanged himself from the big ladder in front of his unfinished, unfinishable masterpiece. He had simply taken one of the ropes he used to attach the frame to the wall, climbed up the ladder to attach it to the big oak beam he had fitted up one day to strengthen the uprights, and then jumped off. And there he hung, in his shirt, barefooted, an agonizing sight, his tongue blackened and his eyes bloodshot and starting from their sockets, stiff, motionless, looking taller than ever. His face was turned towards the picture and quite close to the Woman whose sex blossomed as a mystic rose, as if his soul had passed into her with his last dying breath and he was still gazing on her with his fixed and lifeless eyes.

Christine stood terror-stricken, as grief and fear and wrath surged up within her, filling her whole body and finding expression in one long, uninterrupted howl. Turning to the picture, she lifted both her arms and cried as she shook her fists:

'Oh, Claude! Oh, Claude! . . . She took you back! She killed you, the bitch! She killed you, killed you, killed you!'

Her legs gave way beneath her and, as she turned away, she crashed to the ground. Excess of suffering had drawn all the blood from her heart, and she lay in a dead faint, white and limp, pitiful to look on, a woman defeated, crushed by the tyrannical sovereignty of Art. Above her, in triumph, radiant with all the symbolic splendour of an idol, stood the painted Woman. Painting had won in the end, deathless and defiant even in its madness.

The following Monday morning—for suicide had meant formalities and delay—when Sandoz arrived for the funeral at nine o'clock, he found only about twenty people outside the house in the Rue Tourlaque. He had not been left unoccupied in his grief; for the last three days he had had no rest, he had had so many things to attend to. First he had had Christine, whom they had found lying half dead where she had fallen, taken to the Lariboisière Hospital; then he had done the usual round: registry, undertaker, Church, paying out right and left, making all the customary arrangements in complete indifference, since the clergy had deigned not to refuse their good offices to the corpse with a black ring round its neck. The group on the pavement, he discovered, consisted of a few neighbours and the usual onlookers; there were, too, some spectators craning out of windows and discussing the tragedy in excited undertones. Friends would be turning up any moment, he supposed. He

had not been able to write to the family, as he had no
addresses; but he stood aside when he saw two relatives
arrive, drawn most likely by the curt announcement in the
papers from the oblivion to which Claude himself had long
ago consigned them. There was an elderly female cousin
who looked like a rather shady second-hand dealer, and a
second cousin, a man, obviously rich, wearing a decoration.*
He was the owner of one of the big Paris department stores
and very open-handed when he thought he had a chance to
prove his enlightened taste for the arts. The woman went
straight upstairs to the studio, took one glance at its stark
poverty, sniffed and came down again, tight-lipped and
annoyed at the thought of her thankless mission. The man,
on the contrary, threw back his shoulders and took the head
of the funeral procession, walking immediately behind the
hearse, a proud, dignified, and even charming figure.

Just as the cortège was moving off, Bongrand joined it
and walked with Sandoz after shaking his hand. He was in
a gloomy frame of mind and, after casting an eye on the
handful of mourners, he muttered:

'Poor devil! . . . You don't mean to say we're the only
two?'

Dubuche was at Cannes with his children. Jory and
Fagerolles were not coming; one said he couldn't stand
deaths, the other was too busy. Of the rest, Mahoudeau fell
into the procession as it was going up the Rue Lepic.
Gagnière, he said, had almost certainly missed his train.

Slowly the hearse made its way up the steep, winding
slope that leads to the top of Montmartre, cutting across
streets that drop straight down the hill, revealing the vast,
deep tract of Paris spreading like an ocean at its feet. When
it reached the church of Saint-Pierre and the coffin was
lifted out, for one short moment it dominated the mighty
city. Under a grey, wintry sky, with great swathes of mist
floating on an icy wind, Paris looked vaster than ever, its
utmost limits lost in the mist that filled the horizon with
its waves like an encroaching tide; while the poor dead
wretch who had set out to conquer it and had broken his

neck in the attempt, passed before it, nailed down beneath
an oaken lid, returning to the dust, like the mud of the
Paris streets.

When they came out of the church, the female cousin
disappeared; so did Mahoudeau. The second cousin resumed
his place behind the hearse; seven others, all strangers,
decided they, too, would go on; and the cortège moved off
again for the new cemetery at Saint-Ouen, vulgarly known
by the sinister, disturbing name of 'Cayenne'.* There were
ten of them in all.

'Well, it certainly looks as if we're going to be the only
two,' Bongrand repeated as he moved along at Sandoz's side.

Preceded now by the mourning-coach in which the priest
and his acolyte had been accommodated, the cortège moved
slowly down the other side of the hill of Montmartre where
the streets are as steep and tortuous as paths on a mountain
side. The horses drawing the hearse kept slipping and the
wheels bumped clumsily over the muddy roadway, while the
ten mourners following behind found the descent so difficult
and were so preoccupied with picking their way through the
puddles that they had not yet found time to talk. When
they reached the bottom of the Rue du Ruisseau, however,
and found themselves at the Porte de Clignancourt, on
the broad, flat stretch that carries the outer boulevard, the
suburban railway and the moats and embankments of the
fortifications, there were sighs of relief; a few words were
exchanged, and the little procession began to spread itself.

Sandoz and Bongrand soon found themselves at the tail
end, as if to cut themselves off from all these people they
did not know. Just as the hearse was going past the city
barrier Bongrand said:

'The wife. What's going to become of her?'

'It's a sad case,' Sandoz replied. 'I went to see her at the
hospital yesterday. She has brain-fever. The doctor says
she'll pull through, but it'll take all her strength and put
ten years on her age. . . . Her mind was a complete blank,
you know. She couldn't remember a thing, not even her
A B C. It's terrible to see anybody brought so low, so

completely crushed as she's been; a nice girl like that
reduced to the mentality of a kitchen wench! Oh, if we don't
take very great care of her and treat her properly as an
invalid, she'll end up as a drudge in somebody's scullery.'

'Penniless, of course.'

'Penniless. I hoped I should be able to find some of the
studies he'd made from nature for his big picture; they were
wonderful things, but he made such bad use of them. But
I never found a thing; I looked everywhere. He used to give
them away, and what he didn't give people stole. No, there
was nothing to sell; not a single decent canvas, nothing but
that huge thing and that I destroyed and burnt with my
own hands—and very glad I was to do it. It was like taking
vengeance!'

They were silent for a moment or two as they trudged
along the long, wide road to Saint-Ouen which seemed to
run straight to infinity. It was a pitiful sight, the tiny funeral
procession straggling across the open country along that
dreary highway streaming with mud. Fences on either side
separated it from vast stretches of waste land, with only
here and there a factory chimney rising in the distance and
a few tall, white houses built well away from the road. At
Clignancourt they had to go through the fairground; past
all the deserted booths and circuses and roundabouts, their
canvas quivering in the cold; past empty refreshment stalls
and rusty swing-boats and a stagey-looking farm, now dreary
and desolate with its trellis-work torn off and smashed.

'Ah, those early canvases of his, the ones he had at the
Quai de Bourbon, remember? Extraordinary pieces, every
one of them, weren't they? Provençal landscapes, nudes done
at Boutin's, a little girl's legs, I remember, and a woman's
belly, particularly. A marvel! . . . Old Malgras must have it
somewhere. A study by a master hand that not one of the
so-called "masters" of today could hope to equal. . . . Oh,
there's no doubt about it, the lad was no fool! He was a
great painter, quite simply!'

'And to think,' added Sandoz, 'that all the dabblers and
scribblers at the Beaux-Arts and in the Press accused him

of being lazy and ignorant, all repeating one after the other
that he'd always refused to learn his job. Lazy! Why, good
God, I've seen him faint away with fatigue after sittings
lasting ten hours! Lazy, a man who put his whole life into
his work, who was so mad on it that he killed himself for
it! As for not knowing his job, of all the brainless accusations! Will people never understand that anyone who produces something new, and that's an honour that doesn't
come to everybody, anyone who produces something new is
bound to depart from received wisdom. Delacroix didn't
know *his* job because he couldn't stick to exact lines. Oh,
the fools, like a lot of good little schoolboys, scared to death
of anything they've been taught is wrong!'

He walked on a little in silence, then added:

'He'd a hero's capacity for work; he was a brilliant
observer with a brain packed with knowledge and the temperament of a great and gifted artist . . . and yet he has
nothing to show.'

'Nothing at all,' Bongrand affirmed. 'Not a single canvas;
nothing, so far as I know, but a few notes and sketches that
every artist turns out and are not meant for the public. No
doubt about it, the man we're burying today is a dead man;
dead in the fullest sense of the word!'

As they talked the hearse had left them behind, and now
they had to hurry to catch it up. After a slow progress
between rows of alternating wine-shops and displays by
monumental masons, it was now turning to the right, along
the short avenue leading into the cemetery. They caught up
with it just as it was going through the gateway and tacked
themselves on to the little procession led now by the priest
in his surplice and the acolyte carrying the holy water.

It was a vast, flat cemetery, still quite new, mathematically
laid out on a stretch of suburban common and divided up
like a draught-board by broad, symmetrical walks. An occasional tombstone had been erected here and there on the
main pathways, but for the most part the graves, already
far too closely packed, were simply low mounds of earth
casually arranged and not intended to be permanent. The

maximum grant obtainable was only for five years, so families hesitated to go in for expensive installations; stones gradually sank into the ground for lack of foundations; young trees never had the chance to mature, so there was a 'here-today-and-gone-tomorrow' feeling about the place, a sense of poverty, a cold, clean, bare look that made it as melancholy as a barracks or a charity ward. Not a scrap of poetry, no weeping willow, no solitary path beneath the boughs, no quiver of mystery, not a single family vault to speak of pride or life everlasting! This was the new cemetery, all carefully plotted and numbered; the cemetery provided by democracy, where the dead seem to sleep in official pigeon-holes, today's batch taking the place of yesterday's with clockwork regularity; everyone kept 'on the move', by order, like the crowd at a fair, to prevent a hold-up.

'Hell!' muttered Bongrand. 'This is a cheerful sort of place!'

'What's wrong with it?' Sandoz asked. 'It's convenient, it's airy . . . and even though there's no sun, it's not without colour. Look at it.'

And indeed, beneath the grey November sky, swept by the keen winter wind, the low-lying graves covered with flowers and beaded wreaths provided a subtle picture full of delicacy and charm. Some were all white; others, according to the beads, all black, a contrast quietly framed in the pale green of the surrounding shrubs. As their grants were for five years only, families honoured their dead while the opportunity lasted and, as All Souls' Day had just gone by, graves had been lavishly heaped with fresh tokens of family affection. The natural flowers, in their pots with paper frills, had already faded; a few wreaths of yellow immortelles shone out like freshly beaten gold; but most in evidence were the beads. The place was streaming with them; they hid the inscriptions, covered stones and graves, and overflowed on to the pathways. There were beads worked into hearts, festoons, medallions; beads framing a host of things in glass cases—bunches of pansies, pairs of hands affectionately clasped, bows of satin ribbon and even photo-graphs, cheap, yellowing photographs of women, poor, graceless faces, all with awkward smiles.

As the hearse moved on towards the Rond-Point, Sandoz, reminded of Claude as he viewed the cemetery with his painter's eye, said:

'This is the sort of cemetery he would have understood, he was so keen on everything modern. . . . He must certainly have suffered a great deal from that kink in his genius, those three grammes more or less that would have made all the difference, as he used to say when he accused his parents of making such an unsatisfactory job of him. But his trouble was not all personal by any means; he was the victim of his period. The generation we belong to was brought up on Romanticism; it soaked into us and we can do nothing about it. It's all very well our plunging head first into violent reality, the stain remains and all the scrubbing in the world will never remove it.'

Bongrand smiled.

'What about me?' he said. 'I was head over ears in it. My whole art grew from it, and I'm not ashamed to admit it. If that's the reason for my ultimate failure, what does it matter? I can't deny my religion at this stage! . . . But what you say about yourselves is very true; you are the younger generation in revolt. He, for example, with his great nude woman in the middle of the Cité, the wild, fantastic sym-bolism. . . .'

'Oh, that Woman!' Sandoz broke in. 'It was she who strangled him. If you only knew what she meant to him, and how impossible it was to get him away from her! How could he be expected to take a clear, sane, balanced view of anything when his brain was never free of such weird and wonderful notions? . . . Even with your generation between us and the Romantics, ours is still too clogged up with lyricism to produce anything really sound. It'll take another generation, probably two, before painters and writers work logically in the pure and lofty simplicity of truth. Truth and nature are the only possible bases, the essential controlling factors in art. Without them everything verges on madness, and no one need be afraid his work's going to be insipid in consequence; temperament is always there, and temperament will out. Who would ever dream of denying personality? Why, it's just that that puts the last instinctive touch on a man's work and marks his production as his!'

Turning away suddenly he added:

'What's that burning smell? . . . Surely they're not lighting bonfires in this place?'

The cortège had changed its direction, having reached the Rond-Point, in the middle of which, surrounded by lawn, stood the ossuary, the common vault in which the remains dug up from the graves were deposited and which was itself almost buried under the heaps of wreaths laid upon it by pious relatives who no longer had any dead to call their own. As the hearse was moving gently along Avenue No. 2, a loud, crackling noise had made itself heard and a dense cloud of smoke had begun to rise behind the young plane-trees that lined the side-walk. Gradually, as the cortège moved slowly towards it, a great smouldering heap of earthy-looking objects came into view. What was happening was now obvious. The burning heap was on the edge of a huge square patch of ground, dug very deep in broad parallel trenches to enable the coffins to be removed before the soil was prepared to receive a fresh consignment, just as a farmer ploughs up a stubble-field before he sows it again. Alongside the long, yawning trenches, mounds of soggy earth lay sweetening in the open air. The burning objects in one corner of the plot were rotten coffin-boards, piled up into an enormous bonfire of split and broken wood, reduced by the soil to the consistency of dull red mould. They refused to burn briskly, for they were damp with human clay; instead, they made dull, cracking noises and gave out vast clouds of smoke which rose, thicker and thicker, into the grey-white sky and were blown back by the November wind, torn into rusty-looking wisps and sent flying over all the flat and formless graves in one half of the cemetery.

Sandoz and Bongrand looked at the fire without a word; then, when they had passed it, Sandoz picked up the thread of conversation.

'His trouble was that he was not the man for his own artistic formula. By that I mean he hadn't quite the genius necessary to establish it on a firm foundation and impose it on the world in the form of some definitive work. . . . And now what is there to see for all he's done? Nothing; nothing but effort being frittered away on all sides; nobody producing anything more than sketches or hasty impressions; nobody capable of being the master everyone's looking for. Could anything be more frustrating than seeing his new notation of light, his passion for reality pushed to the point of scientific analysis, the evolution he started with such originality, delayed, trifled with by a lot of smart nobodies, leading to nothing, simply because the man for the situation has yet to be born? . . . But he will be, one day! Nothing's ever completely wasted, and there's simply *got* to be light!'

'Don't be too sure!' replied Bongrand. 'Life, too, miscarries occasionally, you know. . . . I listen to all you say, Sandoz, but I haven't got a great deal of faith. I'm dying of depression, and I feel everything else is dying too. . . . We're living in a bad season, in a vitiated atmosphere, with the century coming to an end and everything in process of demolition; buildings torn down wholesale; every plot of land being dug and redug and every mortal thing stinking of death. How can anybody expect to be healthy? The nerves go to pieces, general neurosis sets in, and art begins to totter, faced with a free-for-all, with anarchy to follow, and personality fighting tooth and nail for self-assertion. . . . I've never seen so much squabbling or heard so much nebulous talk as I have since people claimed to know everything.'

Sandoz had turned pale and, as he watched the clouds of rusty smoke swirling in the wind, he said, half aloud, half to himself:

'It was inevitable. All our activity, our boastfulness about our knowledge was bound to lead us back again to doubt. The present century has cast so much light on so many things, but it was bound to end under the threat of another wave of darkness. . . . And that is the root of our troubles. We have been promised too much and led to expect too much, including the conquest and the explanation of every-thing; and now we've grown impatient. We're surprised things don't move more quickly. We're resentful because, in a matter of a hundred years, science hasn't given us absolute certitude and perfect happiness. Why then con-tinue, we ask, since we shall never know everything and our bread will always be bitter? The century has been a failure. Hearts are tortured with pessimism and brains clouded with mysticism for, try as we may to put imagination to flight with the cold light of science, we have the supernatural once more in arms against us and the whole world of legend in revolt, bent on enslaving us again in our moment of fatigue and uncertainty. . . . I'm no more sure of things than anyone else; my mind, too, is divided. But I do think that this last shattering upheaval of our old religious fears was only to be expected. We are not an end; we are a transition, the beginning only of something new. . . . And it's that sets my mind at rest, and somehow encourages me: to know we are moving towards rationality and the firm foundations that only science can give. . . .'

Then he added, his voice breaking with the depth of his emotion:

'Unless of course madness makes us come a cropper in the dark and we all end up like our old friend sleeping there in his coffin, strangled by our own ideals.'

The hearse was now leaving Avenue No. 2 and turning to the right into Avenue No. 3, where Bongrand drew Sandoz's attention to a plot full of graves they were passing.

It was a children's cemetery full of tiny graves, all set out in perfect order, separated by narrow little pathways. It was a children's city of the dead, built of tiny white crosses and tiny white edge-stones almost entirely covered by a mass of white and blue wreaths, making the whole quiet plot of milky blue appear to be blossoming with all the childhood buried in its soil. The crosses told the ages of the children:

two years, sixteen months, five months. One poor little cross on a grave without an edge-stone and dug a little out of line, announced simply: EUGÉNIE, AGED THREE DAYS. So young, and already sleeping there alone, like children who, at family gatherings, are given their own little table!

The hearse stopped at last, halfway down the avenue. When Sandoz saw the open grave on the corner of the next plot, across from the children's graves, he murmured tenderly:

'Dear old Claude! You'd a heart like a child's; you'll be in good company here.'

The undertakers lowered the coffin into the grave; the priest stood waiting, glum and cold, and the grave-diggers were ready with their spades. Three neighbours had dropped out on the way, so the ten were now only seven. The second cousin who, in spite of the bitter weather, had held his hat in his hand ever since they left the church, moved up to the graveside. All the others removed their hats and the prayers were about to begin when a piercing whistle made everyone look up.

At the far end of Avenue No. 3 a train was going by on the suburban line which ran on a high embankment overlooking the cemetery. At the top of a grassy slope the telegraph posts and wires made a geometrical pattern in black on the pale grey sky; beneath them stood a signalman's cabin and the signal itself, its quivering plate providing the only splash of red. As the train thundered by, the coaches, and even the shapes of the people sitting near the windows, stood out like transparencies in a shadow show. When it had passed, the track itself was just a clean black line on the horizon. Then, in the distance, a series of other whistles started up, calling each other in agonized tones, some shrill with fury, others hoarse with suffering or choking with distress. They were followed by one sinister blast on a horn.

'*Revertitur in terram suam unde erat . . .*' intoned the priest, who had opened a book and was racing through the service.

But his voice was soon drowned by the arrival of a huge, puffing locomotive engaged in shunting on the line immediately above him. This one had a big, thick voice and a throaty, tremendously melancholy whistle. Up and down it went, panting like some ungainly monster; then suddenly it let off steam in one furious, tempestuous hiss.

'*Requiescat in pace*,' said the priest.

'*Amen*,' came the response from the boy.

And the proceedings were rushed to a close to the ear-splitting accompaniment of violent clanks and crashes in prolonged succession like endless gunfire.

Furious, Bongrand looked up at the engine, and was relieved when it stopped and there was silence again. Sandoz had tears in his eyes, moved now by the things he had let himself say as he followed his old friend's coffin, feeling as if they had been having one of the enthralling talks they used to have in the old days. He felt he was burying his own youth, that it was part of himself, and the best part, the illusions and enthusiasms, which the men were lowering into the grave.

At that terrible moment an accident occurred to add to his grief. It had rained so heavily during the past few days, and the earth was so very soft, that one side of the grave suddenly fell in and one of the grave-diggers had to jump down and clear it with his spade; which he did with slow, rhythmic gestures that seemed likely to go on for ever, greatly to the annoyance of the priest but to the excitement of the four neighbours who, though nobody knew why, had stayed with the funeral party to the end. Up on the embankment the railway engine was in action again, backing and blasting out showers of red-hot cinders into the dull grey sky.

At last the grave was cleared and the coffin lowered into it, the holy water was passed round and all was over. Standing at the graveside, correct and charming as ever, the second cousin shook hands with all these people he had never seen before, in memory of the relative whose name he had forgotten till yesterday.

'Decent fellow, that draper,' said Bongrand, swallowing back his tears.

'Very decent,' answered Sandoz through his own.

The mourners dispersed; the surplices of priest and acolyte disappeared among the green trees, the neighbours scattered and meandered away, looking at the inscriptions on the graves, and Sandoz, deciding at last to turn away from the grave which was already half filled-in, said quietly:

'We shall be the only ones who really knew him. . . . And this is the end; not even a name.'

'He's lucky where he is,' said Bongrand, 'with not even a half-finished picture to worry about . . . lucky to be away from it all, instead of wearing himself out, as we do, producing offspring who are either headless or limbless and never really alive.'

'Yes, you've got to swallow your pride and cheat and make do with half-measures in this life. . . . My books, for example; I can polish and revise them as much as I like, but in the end I always despise myself for their being, in spite of my efforts, so incomplete, so untrue to life.'

Pale with emotion, the two men moved away side by side past the white graves of the children, the novelist in the full vigour of his work, at the height of his fame, the artist on the decline but covered with glory.

'There's one, at least, who was both logical and brave,' Sandoz continued. 'He admitted his impotence and did away with himself.'

'True enough,' said Bongrand. 'If we weren't all so keen on preserving our own miserable skins, we should all do the same, don't you think?'

'I believe we should. Since we can't really create anything, since we're nothing more than a lot of feeble reproducers, we might just as well blow our brains out at once.'

They were back again near the heap of smouldering coffins which, now that they were properly alight, were steaming and crackling, though still showing no signs of flames. The thick, pungent smoke alone had increased and was being blown in great swirling clouds across the cemetery, covering it as with a funeral pall.

'Good Lord! Eleven o'clock!' said Bongrand, looking at his watch. 'Time I was home.'

Sandoz, too, expressed his surprise:

'Eleven o'clock already!' he cried.

Half blinded still with tears, he took one last, despairing look at the vast expanse of graves as they lay, all prim and proper, covered in the blossom of their beads, and added:

'And now, back to work!'

EXPLANATORY NOTES

11 *the young 'open air' painters*: see Introduction, p. xiii.

30 *his mother, a decent, hardworking laundress . . . local school*: a reference to the story of Gervaise, Lantier, and Coupeau in *L'Assommoir*.

31 *from their earliest years . . . 'the three inseparables'*: the following account is based on Zola's own childhood friendships with Paul Cézanne and Baptistin Baille. See Introduction, p. x.

40 *you know the one I did . . . scrapped it*: a reference to an incident from Claude's days as a young art student in *The Belly of Paris*.

42 *Ingres*: Dominique Ingres (1780–1867), whose paintings are noted for their classical technique and purity of line.

Delacroix and Courbet: Eugène Delacroix (1798–1863), leader of the Romantic school of painting, noted for the originality of his technique, in particular his bold use of colour; and Gustave Courbet (1819–77), famous for his choice of everyday subjects (as opposed to those taken from mythology or the Bible).

59 *'to hell with Rome': signed, Godemard*: a reference to the prestigious Prix de Rome awarded annually on the basis of a competition held at the École des Beaux-Arts and enabling the winner to study at the French Academy in Rome (the Villa Medici) for three years at state expense.

68 *to draw for conscription*: those eligible by age for military service drew lots to see who would serve and who were exempt.

76 *who was Jules Favre . . . Rouher?*: Jules Favre (1809–80), Republican politician and member of the French Academy, who proposed the resignation of the Emperor Louis-Napoleon in 1870, was a member of the ensuing government of National Defence, and negotiated the Treaty of Frankfurt in May 1871 following French defeat in the Franco-Prussian War: and Eugène Rouher (1814–84), Minister of State and

later President of the Senate under Louis–Napoleon, sometimes known as the 'vice-emperor' and a key model for Zola's
Eugène Rougon.

81 *Musée du Luxembourg*: works of art by living artists were
purchased by the state and displayed in this museum before
being transferred to the Louvre (or elsewhere) when the artist
died.

126 *the opening of the 'Salon des Refusés'... was being hung*: see
Introduction, p. xii.

414 *there was an elderly female cousin... wearing a decoration*:
respectively, Sidonie Rougon who features in *The Kill* and
Octave Mouret, the unscrupulous tycoon, from *Pot-bouille*
and *Au Bonheur des Dames*.

415 *'Cayenne'*: Cayenne, the capital of French Guiana, to which
criminals were deported and from which they seldom returned. The prison on Devil's Island off the coast of French
Guiana became especially notorious when Alfred Dreyfus was
sent there after being falsely condemned for espionage in
1894.

FANNY BURNEY: Cecilia
or Memoirs of an Heiress
Edited by Peter Sabor and Margaret Anne Doody

THOMAS CARLYLE: The French Revolution
Edited by K. J. Fielding and David Sorensen

LEWIS CARROLL: Alice's Adventures in Wonderland
and Through the Looking Glass
Edited by Roger Lancelyn Green
Illustrated by John Tenniel

GEOFFREY CHAUCER: The Canterbury Tales
Translated by David Wright

ANTON CHEKHOV: The Russian Master and Other Stories
Translated by Ronald Hingley

JOHN CLELAND:
Memoirs of a Woman of Pleasure (Fanny Hill)
Edited by Peter Sabor

WILKIE COLLINS: Armadale
Edited by Catherine Peters

JOSEPH CONRAD: Chance
Edited by Martin Ray

Victory
Edited by John Batchelor
Introduction by Tony Tanner

NORMAN DAVIS (Ed.): The Paston Letters

DANIEL DEFOE: Colonel Jack
Edited by Samuel Holt Monk and David Roberts

CHARLES DICKENS: Christmas Books
Edited by Ruth Glancy

Sikes and Nancy and Other Public Readings
Edited by Philip Collins

FËDOR DOSTOEVSKY: Crime and Punishment
Translated by Jessie Coulson
Introduction by John Jones

The Two Drovers and Other Stories
Edited by Graham Tulloch
Introduction by Lord David Cecil

SIR PHILIP SIDNEY:
The Countess of Pembroke's Arcadia (The Old Arcadia)
Edited by Katherine Duncan-Jones

TOBIAS SMOLLETT: The Expedition of Humphry Clinker
Edited by Lewis M. Knapp
Revised by Paul-Gabriel Boucé

ROBERT LOUIS STEVENSON: Treasure Island
Edited by Emma Letley

ANTHONY TROLLOPE: The American Senator
Edited by John Halperin

A complete list of Oxford Paperbacks, including The World's Classics, OPUS, Past Masters, Oxford Authors, Oxford Shakespeare, and Oxford Paperback Reference, is available in the UK from the Arts and Reference Publicity Department (RS), Oxford University Press, Walton Street, Oxford OX2 6DP.

In the USA, complete lists are available from the Paperbacks Marketing Manager, Oxford University Press, 200 Madison Avenue, New York, NY 10016.

Oxford Paperbacks are available from all good bookshops. In case of difficulty, customers in the UK can order direct from Oxford University Press Bookshop, Freepost, 116 High Street, Oxford, OX1 4BR, enclosing full payment. Please add 10 per cent of published price for postage and packing.